The
Longest
Interview

The Longest Interview

SAMUEL C CRAWFORD

PRIMIX
PUBLISHING
THE WRITE CHOICE

Primix Publishing
11620 Wilshire Blvd
Suite 900, West Wilshire Center, Los Angeles, CA, 90025
www.primixpublishing.com
Phone: 1-800-538-5788

This is a book of fiction, an imaginary tale, and completely fabricated for your reading enjoyment and amusement.

Published by Primix Publishing: 11/03/2023

ISBN: 979-8-89194-028-4(sc)
ISBN: 979-8-89194-029-1(e)

Library of Congress Control Number: 2023919785

CONTENTS

I wish to give special thanks and appreciation to Suzanne Dawson and Joyce Kerlin for their support and honest feedback. To my wife Pat, I love you all day, everyday, now and forever.

To our daughter Stephanie, your life was a blessing, your memory a treasure. We hold you in our hearts, until we can hold you in our arms again in heaven.

INTRODUCTORY EVENT

THE EMPLOYMENT SECTION IN THE local Delaware newspaper had one ad that was four columns wide, centered in the page, a real eye-catcher in a page where the other ads were only one column wide. Additionally, it was in color, not the norm for an employment section for this particular newspaper. This ad for R.E.A. International went on and explained that there were a number of immediate openings with many positions at all levels, in their Middletown, Delaware location.

There were no other details given. Not even a hint of the type of company that it was, and not clear if this was a factory, office center, or a farm. Even with, 'International' in the name, still, there were no clues that this was an American or foreign company. There were no explanations on what positions were available or even how many openings there were. Only that they were hiring and that anyone interested in gainful employment should call the number listed to arrange an appointment. 'For more information, call 1-800-REA-INTL.'

This particular newspaper, the Summit Post, reached all of central Delaware.

Located to the West of Middletown, was the lovely, but the very flat, Eastern Shore of Maryland. Employment there was mostly related to farming, chickens, and fishing. If one of your parents farmed the land, raised chickens, and had or was working on the Chesapeake Bay, you did the same. Therefore, from Maryland, there would be no one interested in working in lower, slower, Delaware.

The Summit Post was a weekly newspaper, printed only on Wednesdays. Most newspapers would supply the number of copies printed each time, listing the current number of home deliveries, promotions, waste, and over the counter sales. The Summit Post, only stated that it printed thousands and thousands, in the same way that McDonald's would say, 'Billions and Billions served.'

CHAPTER 1

IN THE BEGINNING, THE MEN

V AN CAMP, AN OLD GUY who should have retired years ago, was once more out of work because of yet another layoff. Van Camp had held a number of positions near the top of many companies. He had been a VP for several and a senior VP for a few others. What he did not realize was that he was canned from each one. He had been hired for those jobs and positions based on how well he had interviewed.

His references were always excellent, because previous employers did not have the balls to say anything negative about his performance, or to furnish truthful grounds for his release. Apparently, Van Camp could talk a good game, but when he came up to bat, he always went down, 'swinging.' And if he was going down, 'swinging,' and he swings like a sissy.

Van Camp scanned the Want Ads for his next career target that he believed he would, and should, eventually take control, as in working his way up and into the most senior spot. It crossed his mind that, with his experiences and impressive resume, that there were companies looking for him.

He felt strongly, that only common people spent time looking at Want Ads, or kids, fresh out of school. With this attitude, he was pleased with himself to find the ad for R.E.A. International so quickly. With little effort, Van Camp made the call, even as he thought that he should have hired someone below him, in authority, to actually dial the phone and make the appointment for him. It was a little difficult as he dialed the phone with his eyes down, all the while, trying to keep his nose pointed up.

With no one to talk down too, or big corporate decisions to make, the phone call was simple and, the appointment was set for 9:30, the next morning. He felt good with this, and strongly believed that they must have known about his availability, which was why they were in such a hurry to bring him in the next day. Moreover, 9:30 had to be the first unqualified and unequaled in performance, appointment of the day, giving them time to cancel out his competitors that had a later time.

Ben, AKA, Benny Ala-King, Ben Ben-Laid, and Benny Beencool, sat in the holding area, waiting for his release papers from Gander Hill Prison, after serving five years of a four-year sentence. He impatiently thumbed through the newspaper that was scattered all over five or six chairs with some pages trashed on the floor. Even with the newspaper being several days old, it was the first time he had the opportunity to read a newspaper in five years. Ben knew full well, that there was nothing that he could reference from his previous line of work. He searched the Want Ads hoping for a break.

He had skill sets that were not in much demand. He had a combination of home invasions, grand larceny, assault and battery, and selling drugs to school age children, along with two DUI's with many moving violations. With nothing to acknowledge or reference about his work history, this ad from R.E.A. International, stood out like an unlocked car with the keys inside and the motor running in front of a 7/11. Ben liked this ad as it did not explain the,'what fors,' 'how tos,' or even the 'whens and wheres,' or 'there or abouts.'

He then figured, 'what the hell,' that he could do that job. Besides, whatever questions the employer could throw at him, Ben thought with great confidence, 'I will con my way out of, and or, into what ever was needed.'

Applying there, in Middletown Delaware, if not for anything else, it was convenient. Convenient that the plant was just a few miles from where he was, a short walking distance. No big deal, however, if a similar job opening had been available, and, if it were more than a few miles away, he could, and would, easily steal a car for transportation.

With little effort, Ben made his way over to a bank of pay phones, used mostly for those arrested and needing to make that one phone call, and he dropped a quarter down the slot. After two clicks and a ding, a dial tone was generated.

The number was keyed in and the phone was answered before the first ring. Ben assumed that this was because the location that he was calling was close by, or that his call was being taped. Then, before he could ask any questions, or even be asked anything, his appointment was set for tomorrow morning at 9:30.

Ben, after he placed the phone back in the cradle, suddenly realized that he was just in a position where he had no control. As in, he had zero input to manipulation of this simple phone call conversation. No questions asked and none answered. He did not like the fact that he, an above average conman, was just conned into a meeting time and place where he had no say. His first choice would have been an afternoon meeting so he could have slept in late for the first time in years. In addition, he was going to a meeting where he was not prepared. Without doing any homework on this company, how could he even consider conning a better deal for himself?

Before Ben could lose any sleep over this phone call, he was asked to step up to the checkout counter for his discharge process. His complete focus now was on what forms he needed to sign. His next tasks would be to gather up his personal belongings, after they were again searched, and find a hotel for the night. He hoped that the hotel, that was close by, would be staffed with hookers in the lobby. He had missed more than reading a newspaper in the last few years and wanted to make up the lost time.

Billy Bob Brown and Bob Billy Brown, twins from birth, sat in the personnel office at, 'The Cold Spot', a cold storage warehouse in

Rising Sun, Maryland. Their names really were Billy Bob and Bob Billy. The names, William and Robert, were not associated with their names and Billy Bob and Bob Billy are listed that way on their birth certificates, Social Security Cards, and their driver's licenses.

These two were there for their exit interview. Reason or reasons for their termination were not very clear to them. Their understanding about their job descriptions, as noted in their employee handbook, was clear on how to keep unwanted personnel out, with no reference on how to respond, should someone make it inside.

The company rules for everything else were well written in their employee's handbook. Only that it had references to holidays, vacations, and sick time, along with instructions on how to complete their weekly time sheet accurately.

The brother's assumption, from their point of view, was that once someone had broken in, that it would be a poor reflection of their ability to do their job. That was how they saw it, therefore, the part of getting an intruder out of the building was in part, needed to repair or correct the inability of them to do their job correctly. They had to get even.

The employee handbook had no rules or examples on how to achieve this, or better yet, how this was not to be accomplished. As a result, it was understood that they would make the call themselves and take whatever actions, seemed needed.

Well, an intruder was killed after breaking into the Cold Spot. There was no remorse from Billy Bob or Bob Billy; they were simply doing their job to the best of their ability. Besides, a dead man generated less paperwork. Time and manpower would not be spent keeping a guard on him until the police arrive, no need to take time off from work to verify the bad guy at a police lineup, and no need to attend a trial.

Naturally, 'The Cold Spot' management, and lawyers, were not impressed with the results of their actions. According to the videotape of the incident, it was impossible to tell if it was Billy Bob, or Bob Billy that had beaten too death the trespasser. At first, both brothers admitted to have been the hero. Each brother wanted to take advantage of any credit, bonus money, or promotion that should have accompanied his actions for this heroic deed. However, as soon as criminal charges were mentioned, each brother pointed to the other as the cohort in this horrible crime. Lawyers of 'The Cold Spot' quickly realized that based on the videotape and the brothers, on-again and off-again accounts of what really happened, no charges were deemed to be in the best interest of the company. Besides, the dead man apparently had no family, and after two weeks, no one had reported him missing. This was a, 'nobody' that required, no action. And this was soon to be placed under the rug, and then down into a grave, a grave with, no marker.

The only unfinished item was the employment of the two brothers. 'The Cold Spot,' management wanting to put a positive spin on this, had already placed a call to R.E.A. International, and had an interview set up for the two of them tomorrow, at 9:30am. The Cold Spot' lawyers claimed, and convinced the twins, that their exit paycheck was a combination of severance and reward pay. It was also announced that once word got out that anyone that broke into this warehouse, would end up dead, that there would be no need for security guards.

With no lost time from work, a pat on the back for a job welldone, walking away with an extra chunk of change, no charges being filed against them, and a job interview set for the next day, they felt that they had won the lottery.

For 'The Cold Spot' Company, it was simply; 'good bye, forever,' and it only cost them a little cash with a little due-diligence on their part to update their employee handbook.

The twins had always worked in security together. They had a knack of giving the impression that there was only one of them on duty at a time. You never saw them working sideby-side, even on the same shift. This way, they felt that if you planned on breaking and entering, as long as you could see the location of one guard, then you would break into another area of the warehouse, and still are caught. All of there lives; they had been treated as one, not as two people that happened to be identical twins.

This type of situation started back when they were born and even their names came to be based on confusion at the hospital at the time of their births. Their parents, Beverly and Brent were not aware that they were going to have twins. As it happened, at the birth of the first child, the nurse approached Brent with the newborn boy in her arms and asked him for a name. He shouted, "Billy Bob," and off they went to wipe clean this new arrival. He decided not to name his son after his father, Butch.

Beverly had no knowledge about the first birth. It happened that she had pushed and pushed so hard and for such a long time, that she passed out and missed the first delivery totally. For her second delivery, it was smooth, like a Barry White song. It was a good thing that she had not pushed very hard because the baby would have just shot across the room.

When asked by the second nurse about a name for her new son, without hesitation, she shouted out, "Bob Billy." She had agreed with her husband to name the boy, if it was a boy, Billy Bob, but in the excitement, she transposed the name, thus naming him, Bob Billy. In addition, like her husband, she did not want to name her son after her father, Brian.

If their newborn(s) would have been a little girl(s), Barbara Bee was their agreed upon name. With both baby boys spending their time with the nurses, the happy couple were together again going over and over this exciting event in their lives, still with no knowledge that there were two boys. Even during feeding time, the boys were brought in at different times. Beverly assumed that Bob Billy was just one hungry, healthy baby boy that needed seconds.

Later that day, when Beverly and Brent took a walk, they passed by the viewing area where all the newborns were lined up in neat rows behind the glass window. The two of them spent time looking, with great pride, at their newborn son(s). In that they were lined up side by side, it appeared to each of them, that they were both looking at the same baby boy. It was not until the next day, at her discharge from the hospital, that they realized that they had twins.

Billy Bob and Bob Billy Brown looked at each other at the end of their exit interview. Then it was all smiles followed by a highfive, two low-fives, and some knuckle knocking. Next was a trip to the bank just down the street to cash in their reward. With cash in hand, a quick bite to eat at the burger place was next in line, before a few drinks at the strip club. They figured they might as well celebrate their good fortune before starting a new career tomorrow, at 9:30am.

On a side note, Billy Bob had beaten the man to death. Bob Billy would have never done something like that. Bob Billy probably would have asked the intruder nicely to simply head out the way he came in. With that, everything would have been cool, as long as no company items were taken out of the building. Only if there were trouble, would Bob Billy have called Billy Bob to step in and take care of the situation.

Jerry was having a cup of coffee with his Dad at the kitchen table. Jerry had completed high school a number of months ago and had yet to find a job. He did not care, his rent was free, and he was able to get an allowance from his mother that his father did not know about. Not having a car was not an issue, as he would simply drive his parent's car around.

He does not date, gamble, drink, or smoke, items that usually take up most of your income. He would get a few videos from the video store and watch the same ones repeatedly until his parents came home from work. Then he would head out to see friends that were just getting home from their jobs or school.

For the most part, he did much of nothing. He was not worth much, he did not spend much, and much was not asked of him. However, today, his Dad had enough of his laziness and the non-productive attitude he had towards life. The Dad's theory was simple, get a job, or get out. Let someone else pay your way. His Dad, with some compassion, said, "Here are the Want Ads.

There must be something that you can do in the 21 pages of open, job listings. Check it out, take some notes, and make some calls." Jerry realized that his life, as he knew it, was about the change.

His Dad had always told him that laziness paid off now, but hard work will pay off in the future and that right now, he had no future.

He would tell his Dad at times that no one cared about him, except for his parents. His Dad would respond with, 'Buy something on credit, miss a few payments and you will see who cares about you.'

His Dad was a good Dad, he was fair and balanced, like FOX News, but at times, he would give news that Jerry did not want to hear. For example, today, 'look for a job.'

His Dad took one last sip of his coffee and headed out the door for work. Jerry figured, 'let me fine just one job, set up time for just one interview, and then just blow it.' His assumption was that as long as he was looking and going on interviews, he could still milk his way through life.

Jerry, wanting to spend as little time as possible looking over the Want Ads, so he could see the movie, Howard the Duck, for the fifth time, then he would scan through the ads as quickly as possible.

Settling down with a fresh Diet Coke, with crushed ice, and a Payday candy bar at the kitchen table, Jerry was ready to attack the Want Ads. With this being his first time actually paying attention to what he was reading, he found the Want Ads were very educational and entertaining.

One ad in particular, was looking for a Bouncer at a Gentlemen's Club. Requirements were that he be able to throw a 200-pound bag of potatoes 12 feet. Police record for assault and battery a plus. Apply in person or via your parole officer. 1-888-KICK-ASS.

Under the medical heading, came Prostate Examiner, Level II. Must have short fingernails and long index fingers. Job requires lots of bending over. Call 1-800-BUTHOLE (1-800-288-4653). Below that one came, Dental Hygienist Wanted. Job requires good teeth and fresh breath. Must enjoy close face to face with customers. 1-800-IN-U-FACE.

For some unknown reason, Large Dog Dingle-Berry Hairstylist, was under the Medical Heading with RN's and dental techs. The ad went on to require that anyone applying must have a real love for dogs and a gentle hand. Sheep farmers need not apply.

Jerry would cycle in red the ads that he felt would score points with his Dad. There was one ad that he read repeatedly, but did not circle it, PORN STAR TRYOUTS. Sat morning 1am4am. Rear parking lot, Walmart, Elkton, MD. Bring your own sunglasses with fake nose and mustache. Clean socks and underwear are optional.

That particular ad just cannot be real, but it would be worth driving by, just to check it out.

For those that can type, COBOL programmers needed. If good with numbers and with a zero personality, e-mail your resume to COBOL @ NO PERSONALAITY.COM.

For those that cannot type, Speil cheeker wantted. Rite two: K-Mart Publishing, Ltd. 1600 Pennsilvina Avenue New Yok, New Yok. 08960.

Realizing that he was getting a late start to watch his show, Jerry looked for that one ad, that he could call. Sure enough, the big colored ad for R.E.A. International did catch his attention. Without looking at any other ads, Jerry dialed the number, and without asking anything, he was set for an interview first thing tomorrow morning, at 9:30am.

Feeling proud of how things just went with such little effort, he left his father a note of his accomplishments, and then he hopped, skipped, and bounced right back into his room to watch the movie, Howard the Duck, again.

At the Naval Air Test Center at Patuxent River, in Southern Maryland, Eddie, a marine, along with, Steven, a Coast Guardsman, were just outside of the base personnel office. They were sitting in the lobby waiting their turn as both men had opted to leave the military life behind them. They were both in the process of being discharged.

Eddie, a tough looking Marine, but in reality, he was a sissy. His thoughts were when entering the Marines, that it would make a man out of him in more ways than one. It did not work, even after eight years of active duty; he was still a sissy boy.

Well, after eight years as a US Marine, he was now a sissy man. Eddie never wanted to get into a bar fight and he was able to do so successfully because of his looks and built. He had a chiseled face and at 6 foot 6, and 235 pounds, and in uniform, no one wanted to mess with him. That was just fine in that he would rather give a man a hug, than to fight with him. He was not queer or gay; he was just a sissy, a big sissy, a big sissy in a Marine uniform.

Eddie had never had an issue with following orders as he did that rather well. When it came to issuing orders, well, that was difficult for him. He felt that it would be polite to ask to have a task completed rather than to order it done. The Marine Core was disappointed that he had decided to leave the Core. It needed good men that gave, and those that followed orders.

Sitting next to Eddie, was a US. Coast Guard sailor waiting his turn to be processed out of the service. Steven was no sissy, even for a Coast Guards sailor, he was a little man with the Napoleon attitude. Steven always wanted to get into a fight, whether it was verbal or physical. It did not matter how the fight started, he just loved anything that involved, altercations. If he was unable to get into a fight, then put him in charge of whatever it was, that should be taken under his charge. He liked barking orders and liked it even better when they were not obeyed or carried out to his exact specifications. After four years of duty, the Coast Guard was glad that he decided not to make it a career.

The Second Class Yeoman behind the desk announced, "Who was next?"

Both men got up at the same time, and as expected, Eddie looked as if he wanted someone to let him in on who was really next. As for Steven, he knew that it was his turn, no matter what, even if they both arrived at the same time. He marched over to the desk and just before he placed his orders in front of the Petty Officer, he looked back at Eddie and was disappointed that he had made no effort to butt in front of him.

Eddie, before he sat back down, and knowing that he had some additional time to kill, walked over to the magazine rack and collected the local newspaper to look over.

As Steven was being processed out, Eddie took his seat and glanced at the headlines. Then it hit him, it had never occurred to him that after today, that he did not have a job. The thoughts of what to do next, just never came up. With some fear, he raced to find the Want Ads. Afraid that he had no time to waste, he used his cell phone and called on the first ad that caught his attention. The R.E.A. International was that ad, and in no time at all, he had an interview set up for tomorrow, at 0930.

What a relief that was to him. It was not so much that he had an interview set up, but that he had completed this task by himself. He had made that decision on his own, and not followed an order. Well done, he thought. "I am going to enjoy civilian life," he mumbled softly to himself.

As for Steven, he returned to his seat after about thirty minutes. He ordered Eddie to report to the Petty Officer behind the desk. No way was this an order, it was simply just a request that Steven was asked to pass along when he returned to his seat. Anything coming out of Steven's mouth always sounded like an order, never a request or suggestion.

It did not faze Eddie the way Steven talked to him, Steven placed his newspaper down and made his way to the Petty Officer for his turn at the discharge process.

Steven had some papers to fill out for the Petty Officer. After they were completed, and with Eddie still at the desk, he picked up the newspaper left behind to kill some time until he was called back. It was opened to the Want Ads and Steven, who was not going to search for a job for a few weeks, figured that he would 'check it out,' to see what was out there in the civilian world.

Naturally, the ad for R.E.A. International was front and center. Steven figured that he would call and order up an appointment for two weeks from now. Only, it did not happen that way. It was suggested that he should interview tomorrow at 0930, and if they came to an agreement, that he could start in two weeks.

Steven accepted this arrangement without creating an argument. He wanted it one way, with the interview set for two weeks from now, and here he was with an interview set for tomorrow. He was unable to change the order of things, as he had no authority to order anything or anyone around now.

"I am not going to enjoy civilian life," he spoke aloud to himself.

Later that afternoon, both men were process out and they headed in different directions only to team up again, tomorrow at 0930.

Burt was sitting in the waiting area at the Department of Motor Vehicles in New Castle, Delaware. He had been sitting there for almost an hour waiting for his number to be called. His number was 57 and they had just called up number 11. He had thought that by getting to the DMV early, that he would get out before noon. Nope, not today, as it appeared that everyone in Delaware was ahead of him.

Burt was there to renew his driver's licenses. He was authorized to drive almost anything on the road from motorcycles, 18-wheeler, charter buses, and limos and a taxi. As a teenager, he had spent a number of summers working construction and had easily picked up the skills to operate equipment from front-end loaders to a number of different types of cranes. What he could not pick up or move around, he could dig it into a hole and cover it up.

The only thing that he was unable to drive was wide loads and hazardous materials. The only thing that he had not driven, that he wanted to drive, was a tank. It just seemed to him like a cool way of getting around. If something was in his way, he could run it over, and if it were too big, he would blow it away.

With lots of time to kill, Burt drove his fingers across the newspaper that was in the empty seat beside him. Almost out of habit, he would review the classifieds. Large, over the road, truck companies were always hiring. He would spend the extra time looking over each ad to see which ones had any type of hiring bonus. He found one that happened to be next to the ad for R.E.A. International.

With his cell phone, he dialed the incorrect number for the trucking company. By mistake, he keyed R.E.A. International. They had no questions for him, and, as he assumed that he had dialed the number correctly, he accepted the appointment that was set for tomorrow, at 9:30am.

After the call, Burt realized his error, but figured that this just might not be that big of a deal, and that maybe it was time for a career change. If this did not work out, he could always enlist in the military so he could drive a tank.

Jeff Harden, was a nice guy to work with when it comes to writing computer programs. Not the computer programs for games, but the programs that are used by big businesses working with massive numbers to crunch. Because he was so one-sided, it was difficult for an employer to give him more responsibilities outside of writing programs. He was not a good candidate to be a team leader and that normally kept him stagnant with his positions. In his career, he was never considered for promotions. It was this reason that Jeff was always looking at the Want Ads for something better. A position where he could excel and earn decent increases every year, even with his shortcomings. The business world did not need an Einstein for a computer programmer, nor could they afford one. Jeff was one-dimensional and he knew it.

As he viewed the Want Ads, at his desk, at work, making no effort to hide the fact of what he was doing, he came across the ad for R.E.A. International. He surmised that a company that big, solely based on the size of the ad, must have a department full of computer programmers.

With little delay, he placed the call, and without lowering his voice, made an appointment for an interview for tomorrow morning, at 9:30. After he completed the call, he walked over to the next cubical to visit his manager. He requested to take tomorrow morning off and to use a ½ day of his personal time. His reasoning was that he had to take his ailing mother to the doctors.

His manager, thinking to himself, after over hearing the phone call, 'you idiot,' granted Jeff the time off. It was too much effort to confront him about this; it was just easier to let him take the time off.

Sitting in front of his 42" HDTV screen that was sandwiched between two VHS VCR's, one Bata VCR, one CD player/recorder, one DVD player/recorder, one disk player, an 8-track deck, two cassette players, two reel-to-reel recorders, one turntable, eight speakers of various sizes and types, two receivers, and a mixer was Joe-Joe.

His eyes were always wide open because he parked himself so close to his TV. He sat so close that if two people were on the screen at the same time having a conversation; he needed to turn his head in the direction of the one that was doing the talking. Sitting next to him was sort of like sitting next to someone on the 50-yard line during a tennis match.

The wiring required in connecting each of the components made it necessary for his system to have its own fuse box, along with three circuit breakers. Without exaggeration, if everything were turned on at the same time, this most certainly will cause a brownout for a six-block area surrounding his apartment.

On the wall behind him, were shelves and shelves and more shelves of every type of recording mediums known to man. VHS and Bata video tapes, CD and DVD disks, 8-tracks, cassettes, and reel-to-reel tapes, 33 1/3, 45's, and 78 speed records, along with a 100 yard spool of speaker wire, two heads sets and three pairs of 3-D glasses.

Joe-Joe always wanted a computer, but there was no room for one, nor was there a place to plug it in for power. Besides, whatever he wanted to know about, or had a question on, he had a video for it. He had a collection of tapes from National Geographic, World at War DVD's, both WWI and WWII. His Time Life collections covered hit songs from the 50's through the 90's, twelve volumes of home repair, and another 12 volumes of medical stuff from health, first aid, and childbirth. A set of six DVDs on famous crimes, auto repair made easy VHS tapes.

Two shelves were set aside for TV series. Everything from the lost episodes of I Love Lucy, the first season of CSI New York, behind the scenes of Gilligan's Island, seasons two, Survivors, and MacGyver, seasons one and two. If it was on TV and a DVD or videotape was available, either Joe-Joe had it on one of these shelves or it had been ordered and will be in soon.

On the top shelve; he kept a few items that were not exactly in plain view. Joe-Joe had tapes from the Girls Gone Wild collection, Playboy exercise tapes, and a few tapes on sensual massages. If it were not for his day job, he would never get up from his imitation leather, with two-cup holders, theater chair. If he could figure how to run a hose from his seat to the bathroom toilet, hell, he would never need to get up, to go. He also had a fresh supply of batteries for his remotes.

Speaking about day jobs, Joe-Joe needed one now. He had just lost his last job based on bad habits. He had one bad habit of getting to work late because he would not leave his house until his shows were over. It did not matter what the show was, it would always be his show, which he was watching at the time. Another bad habit was leaving work early to get home in time to see another of his shows. Same thing, it did not matter what the show was, but if he wanted to see it, it was his show, and he wanted to watch it from the beginning.

The real kicker from this bad habit of his, finally cost him his job. This was the one where he would leave work at lunchtime, and rush home to see another show. It was all right if this was a thirty-minute show, as that allowed him time to get to and from work within his allowed lunchtime of one hour. It was when he started to try to make the hour-long shows during lunchtime that he gotten into more trouble. He tried to explain to his manager that the few minutes before and after lunch where he would leave early and return late could be taken from his two break times that he never took advantage.

Well, that story did not fly with his company, and Joe-Joe was released from work. He would have taken more time off before looking for a job, but he needed the income to keep the electric company happy with electric bills that were paid on time. He could manage with cutting down on food and any other expenses, but no way did he want to lose power.

Forcing himself to view the Want Ads in the Summit Post, Joe-Joe made a quick look-see each time commercials interrupted his shows. He felt that he had struck it rich with the ad for R.E.A. International, as this ad was effortless to find, an easy number to dial, and after the phone call, an easy appointment to set up for 9:30, the next day.

Joe-Joe was not concerned about what the job duties would be or what the pay was. As long as they had a TV in the break area, he would accept any position. In addition, R.E.A. International was closer to his apartment than his last job. With some creative thinking and timing, he might be able to make the onehour shows at lunchtime and not lose this job. Assuming that he even was hired.

CHAPTER 2

THE LADIES

Rose Marie was right at this moment, walking out on her job, as in, she had just quit. No notice and no warning, just, "I am out of here. Good-bye everyone. See ya." Not that she could afford to do so easily, but because she had about enough of, the '101 Things to do with a Dead Cat,' jokes from her co-workers.

Rose Marie has a few cats at home, and they are like her children. Recently, one had died of old age and a cat dying from any reason, was covered in the '101 Things to do with a Dead Cat,' book that came out recently. Her co-workers, thinking that they were being funny, but were in fact, really being down right mean with their taunting, had caused her to break into tears on more than one occasion.

Normal people, she thought, would have stopped at the first sign of tears, but in her workplace, filled with nasty women, even a hint of tears, had turned them into a frenzy bunch of evil bitches. Rose Marie wanted very much to scratch their eyes out, or at the very least, place a few hairballs in their coffee. Instead, she announced that she was quitting as she packed up the few things from her desk. Including the five pictures of her cats along with a cat wall calendar. She even packed up her mouse pad, which had a cat on it.

Those things, she threw into her moving box, but her cat clock, the one where the eyes move one way and the tail moves the other, was neatly packed after being wrapped with green bar, computer printout paper. One co-worker joked, "What, no farewell lunch? We won't get to do Chinese."

'You ladies are nasty, nasty people. I would much rather eat at the soup kitchen with hobos than to endure a, 'good-bye' lunch with any of you. If you were my neighbor, I would donate my house to the ASPCA. I hope very much that each of you gets rabies and a bad case of worms. The type of worms that crawl out of your ass and then bite you on the ass.' Those were a few of the things that Rose Marie wanted to say, but did not want to lower herself to their level. It was just easier for her to move on with life. It was bad enough that she had just buried her cat JR, Joshua Ryan, but it was made worse by her co-workers' nastiness.

Returning a dirty look, she ignored their comments and headed out.

Walking to her car with her things piled in her box, she was a little disappointed that her manager, or any of the managers, did not catch up with her, to see if they could work something out. It was just as well, she thought to herself, I wanted to leave this job anyway, and now I have a good reason. To continue working with nasty people, well, she believed that there would be no happy future with this job.

Now that she was in her car, heading out, she needed to decide where to go. It was too early to head home, not enough time to go shopping or to get, again, the DVD, Cat Woman from Blockbusters, but with some thought, she talked herself into grabbing a good cup of coffee to help her relax. With no traffic backup and in quick fashion, she had made it to Starbucks in Glasgow, Delaware.

After getting her coffee, with two cookies, she headed to find a place to drink her expensive hot coffee. Not that she is in the habit of drinking pricey coffee, but when you don't have a job, getting a cup of coffee at Starbucks is costly. On second thought, she should have only gotten one cookie.

On her way to a seat, she almost ran into a young girl who was heading out and she had to step aside to avoid a collision with her.

Initially, she was going to say something, but decided not to after she noticed that she had left her newspaper behind, and not only that, it was opened to the Want Ads. Besides, that girl should have apologized for almost knocking her down. Whatever, she was a blond and she apparently just learned to walk.

After taking her seat, Rose Marie did take a quick look-see to tell if this girl would return to claim her newspaper, but she was too busy looking at herself each time she passed a mirror on the way out to be thinking about returning to her seat and her cold cup of coffee that she left behind. That was just fine with Rose Marie, as she started to glance at the newspaper, with the Want Ads right on top, and take a few sips from her coffee.

It was not hard to notice the large ad for R.E.A. International, as with everyone else that had seen this ad, she noticed that the ad was very appealing and had caught her interest. Not much in substance on what the job openings were, but the ad did its job well, causing her to read it.

After a few more sips from her coffee and making a general review of other ads, she made the call using her cell phone. Because the ad had caught her attention so quickly, she felt this to be a positive omen and now was as good a time as any to apply for a job. Besides, no need to wait a few weeks to find work, just to end up not being paid for that lost time. She had to pay her bills, buy cat food, cat medication, pay her rent, buy more cat treats, pay the electric and phone bills, and then to buy more cat treats and litter box stuff along with keeping a supply of lint rollers to cat hair from her clothes.

To her surprise, the call went right through and no time was spent hitting the options. You know, option four, then option three, then option two, Et cetera, Et cetera, Et cetera, after hitting option one for English. Her appointment was set for 9:30am.

Another good omen she believed because this happened quickly and without much effort.

With a new lease on life, Rose Marie headed home and looked forward to greeting her cats, as the three of them would race to be the first to welcome her home. Gracie, a beautiful blue-eyed Himalayan was the oldest, and the slowest. The only times that she was first to welcome Rose Marie home, was when she was sleeping by the door. She would wake up, stretch, then purr as Rose Marie rubbed her head with much affection.

Her other two, Dulcinea, Dahlia, also very beautiful, and they both had blue-eyes. They were always together whether playing or sleeping and would consistently; arrive at the same time to greet Rose Marie with much competition and affection. Whatever Rose Marie had in her hands, was set aside, so she could rub both of them at the same time. Rubbing one at a time, was not a wise move, as the odd one out would always get pissed with her purring turning into hissing.

With her arrival rituals out of the way, Rose Marie was off to find her interview suit and spend a little time cleaning off the cat hair.

Alice, one real old woman whose birthstone was lava, was looking at the Want Ads once again. She only receives a small amount from Social Security and with no 401K to draw from or pension to collect, she needed additional income just to survive. She had spent most of her working career babysitting her grand children while her children were off working, adding too their Social Security, 401K, and pension funds. Other than free meals and a place to stay, her children never gave her anything else. As one of her grandchildren grew up and started school, another grandchild was in need of a, stay-at-home-nanny. With four children of her own, and eight grandchildren spaced out over thirty-five years, there was never time for Alice to do anything else. Other than graduating from high school, and raising twelve children, she had nothing to offer up as work experience. Her husband had died so long ago that her life seemed to her as if he was never around. Only her grandchildren were important to her now, more so than her own children. She knew that her children always took advantage of her, but they would never admit it. With no more grand kids in the pipeline as the youngest was now in school for the entire day, her four children could not agree on who would take care of her, now that there was no longer a need for a babysitter.

Alice felt that if her children were to draw straws, she would end up living with the loser. Being unneeded was far worse than being unwanted. Then again, being unwanted by her children, was an unwanted and uncalled for reality after raising their kids. Alice wanted a job away from her children, but close to her grand kids.

With some free time to read the newspaper, she came across the ad for R.E.A. International. To her, this ad was not asking for any particular skill sets. With her having no skills to offer, this might be the job for her. With apprehension, she dialed the number and was a little surprised that an interview was set up without the asking about her skills.

It did not matter, she had an interview, and once she displayed them the pictures of her grandchildren, they would certainly hire her on the spot. Therefore, tomorrow morning at 9:30, she would be there with her Social Security card, a state issued photo ID, and with two or more pictures of each of her eight grandchildren. Kitty, a tall, well built, real knockout of a beauty, and not presently employed as a model or successful movie actress, was sipping down the very last drop of her $4.25 espresso coffee at the little Starbucks store in Glasgow, Delaware. Unless she finds a job very soon, this will be her last cup of Starbucks coffee she could afford.

Being unemployed at this time happened to be something that she had trouble dealing with. She had always assumed that anyone as good looking as she was, should be hired on sight and placed in plain view of everyone to see, to be jealous of, and to bring beauty to the working place.

She had a strong belief that a pretty smile from a pretty woman could and should disarm anyone that had a reason or cause to be upset with her or the company that she was representing. A pretty person, a woman in particular, had an easy life as long as her makeup was fresh and that her hair was kept in place.

Yet, here she was, unemployed. Kitty was laid off from her last job at the bank as the result of minor cutbacks, or so she was told. She never believed that to be the real reason behind her termination because just before she was let go, a good-looking, gay guy, was hired to work along side with her. As in, for him to work with her all the while picking up her job duties and responsibilities. She always believed that her manager was gay and that these two might have been an item.

Kitty knew that her gay guy replacement had a pretty smile that would disarm anyone that had a reason to be upset with him or the company that he was representing. A pretty person, this gay guy in particular, had an easy life as long as his face was clean-shaven and his hair was in place. Not fair, not fair at all she thought aloud to herself that a person should keep their job based solely on looks. Good looks or not, this was just not very rational. She felt that the word 'pretty,' should only be associated with pretty women, and not pretty men.

The man sitting next to her at Starbucks, finished off his cup of coffee and simply got up and left. She did not take this to be anything unusual, that he would leave his newspaper behind, just that it was odd that he did not take the time to look her way. He did not even bother to smile at her, strike up a conversation, or anything else that most all men do when they were in eyesight of her.

He must be gay she thought, as only gay men would not look at her with interest. Well some gay men did, but they were interested only in what she was wearing. Interested in, did her shoes match her outfit properly and was her purse in good taste. On a positive note, leaving his newspaper behind gave her the opportunity to review the employment section.

Finding the Want Ads did take some time, as she had to complete the comics first. Dagwood was unhappy with his job and his boss, as always, but he did have a job and he would never quit. Hagar The Horrible wanted to make a career change to please his wife, but there was nothing for him, sort of like the Vikings on the Capital One commercials. For Dilbert, well, nothing ever went right at his job, or for anyone else at his company. There were too many people in-charge with not enough knowledge about the things to be in-charge-of. The Wizard of ID was trying to create a resume for himself, but the paper he was using kept bursting into flames. Then, there was Charlie Brown, in the Classic Peanuts comics. He wanted to get a job for Snoopy to help pay for his room and board. Naturally, the only job Snoopy wanted was one where he could nap all day.

The ad for R.E.A. International did as it was expected; it caught her attention right away. Not troubling with any other ads, she dialed the number from her cell phone, half-hoping that no one would answer, or that the line would be busy. As long as she made the effort to find a job today, that would be fine. Well, someone did answer and after thirty seconds or so, a time for her interview was set for tomorrow morning at 9:30am.

The ad was very vague about what openings were available, but she easily imagined that she could be interviewing along side with Dagwood, Hagar The Horrible, Dilbert and half of his office staff, The Wizard of ID, and with Snoopy.

With nothing else to do, as her job search had resulted in an appointment, along with her coffee being cold, it was time to go. She was in such a hurry to leave, and to take a quick glance in the mirror to ensure that her hair was in place, that she almost bumped into a lady coming in to find a seat. It was a narrow escape and Kitty should have apologized, but she didn't.

Lisa walked out of the Weight Watchers meeting all ticked off at the facilitator. Just because she, the facilitator, was in charge, had lost weight and kept it off for a few years, along with being a sympathetic, compassionate person, those things did not give her the right to tell her how and what to eat. A low-carb diet was the way to go and that was what she was going to do, this time.

This low-carb diet for Lisa will be the fifth, weight loss program, that she will try this year. She had a hard time comprehending on how anyone could gain a few pounds overnight and yet, with all the previously tried programs, it would always take a few weeks to lose, those same few pounds.

Everyone and every program was just plain wrong. Not only wrong for her, but wrong for anyone that desired to lose weight. She even hated those charts that showed the ideal height and weight as goals. Hell, she had the perfect weight if she could only grow another 6 inches in height. She was almost as wide as she was tall.

Lisa headed home to graze on a bag of chips and finish off a 2-liter bottle of Jolt. Her only concern was that she had enough onion dip to allow her to dip three of four chips at a time. No need to waste arm movements from the bag, to the dip, then to her mouth, as that would always tire her out.

Sitting there at the kitchen table with plenty of dip, Lisa, after opening her second 2-liter bottle of Jolt, scanned the newspaper that she had difficulty in picking up off the sidewalk outside by her front door. Bending down was easy; it was the getting back up that was difficult. Nothing she read in the newspaper ever amused her, but this was something that she could do while feeding.

She did not like being over weight, she did not like trying to lose weight, she did not like-not losing weight, and worst of all, she did not like her job. At her job, she was the biggest person there. She had small legs and a not so big torso. However, it was that big ass, set of hips that she had. It looked as if she had a hula-hoop under her skirt. The chairs at work were too small and when she got up, she had to hold it down by the arms to keep the chair from sticking to her ass.

Even the toilet seats were too small for her. She always had to use the handicap stall and getting in was not easy. Lisa had to back in to the stall, as there was not enough room for her to turn around once she was inside. She also had to remember to collect toilet paper before she backed in. Once she sat down, her hips covered up the toilet paper dispenser and made it impossible to reach.

With the amount of heavy burden that she carried around, this made for one mean, nasty, fat girl. In addition, to top this all off, she was ugly. So ugly that if she were to pass out, and or fall down, and needed mouth-to-mouth, she was going to die. No one wanted to touch anything that ugly. She was so ugly that even a blind person could tell.

Looking at her, and with the way she carried herself, both physically and emotionally, she would make a great ad for birth control. If not birth control, then ethnic cleansing should be an option. She flipped the pages, all the while using her greasy fingers to smear smudges on the ads that displayed thin women.

Lisa always visited the Want Ads hoping to find an ad looking for fat people that had nothing to do with zoos or the circus. Today, one ad did catch her attention, R.E.A. International. She figured, what the hell, that she would try this one, and if she made it to the interview process, that she would make it a point to check out the toilets for size, width, and the location of the toilet paper.

It took her several attempts to dial the correct number as her greasy fingers would slide across the keypad and she would key in the wrong numbers. Once connected, an appointment was set for the next day at 9:30am. Her immediate concern was not what she would be doing or how much she would be paid, only that they had a big, sturdy, toilet seat and a nice break area or lunch room. There was no reason to skip a meal just because you had a job.

With the date and time set, she needed to put aside some time, to iron her interview dress. She always had to iron it herself, as she hated taking her clothes to the cleaners. She would lay her dress on the counter and they would always quote her a price to have drapes cleaned.

CHAPTER 3

R.E.A INTERNATIONAL

In the parking lot of R.E.A. International, around 7:15am, employees started to pull in. The early ones normally were able to find the same spots everyday. The drivers with the nice cars, or the ones who thought they had nice cars, would always park close to the curb at the end of a row in belief that as other cars parked next to them, that they would only get dings from careless and inconsiderate parkers on just the one side. It was generally understood that those careless and inconsiderate parkers, drove crappy cars anyway, and that they did not care if they got door dings, or gave them away. It was not until little after 9am that the interviewees started to arrive.

Van Camp drove up and out of habit, looked for an assigned parking space for VP's and other senior managers. When he did not find any, he thought that as his first duty as VP, that he would set aside parking spaces for the management team. It was just the natural thing to do, if not for the company, at least for him.

One thing Van Camp did not like to do was to park next to low-level employees, as in anyone that was not in upper management. Everyday, run of the mill employees were just beneath him and parking side by side, would put them on equal footing. However, he would not say anything until he had his one-on-one interviews with upper management. Nothing could or would be said to secretaries, receptionist, and or to the HR people just yet about his new rules and regulations for parking.

Kitty pulled up with just enough gas in her car to get there. She did not have the cash for gas, but she still could afford her morning cup of the $4.25 espresso from Starbucks. Before getting out of her car, she touched up her makeup, made a few corrections to her hair, and practiced her conceited smile that would unquestionably guarantee her this job.

After telling each of her cats, 'good-bye,' handing them all a treat, then telling them to be, 'good cats,' followed again with, 'good-byes,' Rose Marie was off to her interview with R.E.A. International wearing her interview suit that was wiped clean of all cat hair. Wiped clean yes, but she had forgotten to take out some old cat treats from her inside jacket pocket.

Inside her car with the windows rolled up, the smells of the cat treats/catnip were very strong and Rose Marie knew that she had to do something. Throwing the treats out of the car, and leaving all the windows opened, with the AC blowing full force, she hoped that the wind would blow away any smells that the treats/catnip had left behind.

Then again, leaving the windows opened and with the wind blowing in her face, that would mess up her hair. What a crappy decision she must make right now, either to smell like catnip, or to look like an old alley cat. Then after some thought, Rose Marie decided to keep her windows down for only the first half of the drive to R.E.A. International. After about a twenty-minute drive, Rose Marie pulled into the parking lot and noticed that she had a few minutes to kill before it was time to go inside.

Ben arrived by cab as he did not want to be seen walking along the road leading up to the parking lot. However, he did have the cab driver drop him off at the back of the lot. The driver thought that this was odd, but it was quickly dismissed as he knew that he was only hired to pick up and deliver passengers, and not to be concerned about where they were coming from prior to getting into his cab, or where they were headed once they got out.

Ben paid the fair without leaving a tip. His thoughts on tipping a cab driver were clear to him. Unless the cabbie did something in addition to driving from point A to point B, like handling luggage, that he did not deserve a tip. His fare would be sufficient. The reason Ben wanted to be dropped off where he was, was elementary. It gave him a chance to look over the cars that were in the lot. Based on the year, make, and models of the majority of the cars, he would estimate the income of the employees. Each car he passed was given the, once over, checking if they were locked, had an alarm or those that left packages on the car seats, and or on the front or back seat floors. Older cars with the windows down or cracked a little, he would ignore. Assuming that the drivers of those vehicles did not care if anyone broke inside, as there was nothing of value in their car.

Ben also took notice that there were no spaces set aside for senior managers, and he approved. By having the higher paid employees vehicles mixed in with everyone else, he could easily park next to one of them for future break-ins. It was in his plans that as he would break into cars, that at least one of his break-ins would be claimed to have taken place in his own car. It was easier to see how an investigation was proceeding, as you could inquire often, if you were one of the victims. He likes it here already.

Billy Bob and Bob Billy Brown drove up and parked at the back of the lot. Backing into a parking space was something they always did. They always liked walking to work from the most distance parking spot from the building. This way, they would survey the lot before their shift, looking for anything out of the ordinary. They noticed and commented about the lighting, fencing, and that there were no parking spots set-aside for senior managers.

It was better for them if the senior managers parked together. It was easier to keep them under observation and less lightly, that they would be targeted for by thieves. Besides, when a manager's car was violated, it created additional paper work and they had to answer more questions than if an employee's car had been broken into. Having assigned parking for senior managers will be one of their first requests to place before upper management. Naturally, assuming that they were hired, that they were hired as security, and that they were hired as security and had a voice on what to request.

Billy Bob did a low-handed point, and said in a soft voice, "Check out that guy over there." He was pointing towards Ben.

Bob Billy acknowledged with a little nod that he had noticed the same thing. He responded with, "Yeah, I see him checking out the cars. See how he ignores the older models and does a double take on the newer cars."

It was at this time that Ben noticed that he was noticed. He knew the look of security people and he acted accordingly by maintaining the same speed and direction of his walk. He made it an effort not to look at them, or into any other cars. At this time, Ben assumed them to be employees of R.E.A. International. A minute later, all three men were inside the lobby.

Jerry parked his Mom's car and repeatedly reviewed in his head on what to say in the interview that would ruin his chances for employment.

The more negative he could start out, the quicker the interview would end. He could then get home early, collect his allowance from his Mom, leave his Dad a note that he gave it a shot, and watch a movie or two before his friends got home from school or work. Overall, if this plan worked, he would call it a successful day.

Eddie spent most of his morning deciding if he should wear his dress blues or civilian clothes. He opted not to wear his uniform, because he figured that now, that he was a civilian that he might as well get on with the program. The suit that he had was a few years out of style, but was clean and fitted him well. If anything, he would make a good first impression.

He decided not to, 'sir' everyone, as loud and as often as he had done by habit over the past eight years, as there was no need to scare the interviewer. Thought was even given on how he would walk, stand, or sit. He wanted to get the military mannerism out of his walking, standing, talking, and how he sat. He believed that it would be hardest for him not to sit at attention, but knew he could do it. He would just consider it an order, from himself, not to sit at attention.

Steven, after parking his car smartly between the lines, and marched right up to the front door as if he was there to take control. His plan was to, 'sir' everything and everyone with direct eye contact and with a stern voice. He believed that they would be impressed with his mannerism, and his take-control attitude. He would even sit at attention.

Lisa dragged her fat ass out of her car and if you were near by, you would swear that you heard the springs and shocks of her car moan a sigh of relief. In addition, for the first time since she got in the car, it sat level.

Everything in her life made her a nasty bitch. Even bitchy people could learn from her. One example of her bitching was the way she had learned to cross a parking lot. She tried to avoid walking between two parked cars as she would wipe the sides of them clean, and all the dirt would then end up on her dress.

If she had to walk between two parked cars, she would only do so if both cars were facing the same direction. Then she would approach from the front and proceed to the rear of the vehicle. This way, as she would bang into the side mirrors, they simply would flip back-in, towards the car. If she walked from the rear towards the front, they would either brake off or leave large bruises on her hips. Not to mention that on several occasions, she had set off car alarms. Even the good ones that do not go off with a single bump, but only if one end of the car was raised as if on a tow truck, or a big enough hit that will register on the Richter scale.

For parking, she would make it a point to park at an end space. With the room needed to get in and out of her car, it was a lot easier when her door was able to open all the way. Once outside her car, and after catching her breath, she would make her way to wherever, walking in the main driveway instead of between parked cars. The longer the walk, the nastier she became and the more she would bitch to herself. Lisa had always wanted a handicap tag for her car, but never got around to having one issued. This was just another item to add to her bitchy mood list. So already, Lisa was in a nasty bitchy mood.

Alice, after driving into the parking lot, looked for a handicap spot and found one. Her walk to the lobby would be a short trip. It just happened that Lisa was walking by; she gave Alice a dirty look. Alice did not know why and only responded with a smile, and thinking, 'you bitch.'

Alice got in behind Lisa and as they approached the door to the lobby, Alice was about to say, 'Let me go first. That way, if you get stuck in the doorway, I won't be late and miss my interview because I can't get in the building.'

She did not say anything and Lisa did make it inside without difficulty. Not that Lisa had it easy; she still rubbed some on both sides of the doorway. Once inside the lobby, and after they had registered, Alice looked for a chair and Lisa looked for a love seat. For Lisa today, she had good fortune; in the lobby was one of those fat chairs. The ones that are out now that are a little bigger than a chair, but smaller than a love seat and even that was a tight fit for her massive butt.

Once Lisa slid snugly into her seat, fear overwhelmed her, as she was in need to fart. For most people, you could hold it in, only letting out a little at a time, but not for Lisa, it was all or nothing.

The last time she farted at home, it had killed her pet parakeet and caused her neighbor's dog to run away. It also changed the channel on the TV and raised the volume all by itself.

Without making a face, she was able to hold it in, not as easy as you would think because she was unable to cross her legs. With luck, she could hold it in until she was walking back to her car, and most importantly, before she started to drive away. She had, 'cut lose' once before, as she was driving and it caused her to change lanes unexpectedly.

Alice, after she settled in her chair, took out some photos of her grandchildren. She spoke to them softly. Each one got a, 'you are a good child. Remember that your grandmother loves you,' and, 'Pray for me that I get this job.'

Burt drove into the parking lot in a rental car. He was driving a silver, 4-door, mid-size Chevy Malibu. He believed that when applying for a job, that you should not drive up in a piece of crap. It would give the impression that you had been out of work for a long time. It also gave the notion that you were willing to work for less than normal.

If your car was too nice, then it gave the impression that you had it made in the past and will require a large salary.

If you had a van, then you are married with children still at home. If you drove a sports car, then you might be married but have no children at home. By driving in a silver car, the most common color for a car, you are not trying to stand out.

Burt found a spot and backed in, dead center, into a parking space. He had a style of getting into and out of cars. For the most part, each move was an imitation of how Jackie Chan did it. With his rental car locked, Burt could set out to find the loading docks. He would not go in that way, he just wanted to do a little homework on the trucks that the company might own. This way, he would strike up a conversation with the recruiter based around the equipment that they had.

Jeff arrived at 9:15. After parking and while he was on his way walking to the lobby, he looked around. He did not know why he was looking around; it just seemed to him to be something to do. His time now was spent on what story he would tell his manager about his ailing mothers doctor's visit, instead of reviewing his skill sets in his head for the technical interview process.

After he signed in and took his seat, he just daydreamed about nothing. With luck, the interviewer would only want to see if he was a good guy and someone that could follow instructions.

Before getting out of his car, Joe-Joe placed some eye drops in his eyes. Not only were his eyes red, but also they were tired. He knew that the interview time was 9:30, but he never referenced, time by time. He would make his time based, on what was on TV. For example, he knew that World News on ABC, CBS, and NBC came on at 6:30 in the evening. Instead of saying 6:30, it was World News time. The news came on at 10pm for Fox News at 10. For him, it was Fox News time, not 10pm. For 9:30am, weekdays, it was I Love Lucy time, channel 54.

This system would always work as long as he was home. Once outside and or out of view of a TV, he was lost. He knew to leave his apartment at the conclusion of 'Leave it to Beaver,' to be at R.E.A. International by I Love Lucy time, channel 54.

After Joe-Joe signed in, he took a seat right below the TV that was showing a cable news station. There was no volume, only some woman talking. Above her head going across the screen, was the current stock quotes. Below her, going across the screen was text messages of what she was saying. For Joe-Joe, this was more than he could handle. It was just a little too difficult for him to comprehend. There were the stock quotes up top, her talking in the middle of the screen, and what she was saying was on the bottom. Even for a TV connoisseur, this was too much for him to handle. He sat a goal that if he were hired, that he would find a way to modify the TV viewing habits at this location.

CHAPTER 4

THE LOBBY

J ERRY WALKED INTO THE LOBBY chewing his gum in an exaggerated manner. Plenty of chewing and smacking noises seemed to be the proper thing to do. Might as well start out making a negative impression.

He signed in and headed towards a seat next to the magazine rack and in view of the TV. It did not matter to him what was on TV, he just wanted to be entertained until his name was called.

Van Camp walked in the lobby and found it disappointing that the lady behind the counter treated him like the job applicant before him. Jerry got there just before he did, and other than being told to sign in and have a seat, nothing else was said differently. Van Camp thought that it was a mistake on R.E.A. International's part to treat him like a common worker. He was 'VP material.'

He wanted the seat that Jerry took. His magazine of choice was Business Week or Time, not Auto World that Jerry had in his lap. Were Jerry was bored with the TV news and stock quotes, Van Camp stared at it in anticipation that any news of importance would benefit him. Also, it would give the impression that he would be someone that could make the news. First impressions were good, even if it was from across the room.

Kitty walked in, signed in, and headed straight for the ladies room before taking her seat. She did not need to go, but had to make a pit stop to insure that her hair and makeup were still in prime condition after her short walk from the car.

She made it a point to sit near the receptionist and the doorway. Kitty was in anticipation that should someone be walking down the hall, that each one of them would take notice of her.

It worked, of course. Men would be walking by and she would make a point to smile back at them, not a sexy smile, just the kind you would get from an older person just trying to be nice. She was not sure who these people were and it did not matter.

Ben signed in and out of habit; he signed his name in a different way. No two signatures by him were ever the same. This was done on purpose in the event that his handwriting was to come under investigation.

Bob Billy and Billy Bob signed in right behind Ben. As Ben headed to a chair on the far end of the room, the brothers kept an eye on him. They did not like this guy, did not like him at all. Ben sat down at the far wall and looked back at the brothers.

He did not like them either, he did not like them either all. These guys might be trouble for him, he surmised. He figured, let them stare, as he caught up with a little shuteye, until his name was called.

Steven marched into the lobby and something seemed out of place. It took a second or two, but he realized that there were no flags in the lobby. In any military office or lobby, there would always be the American flag, the Coast Guard or Navy flag, and a flag designating the unit or military base. In addition to that, there would be a picture of the current President of the United States, the Commander In Chief, framed on the wall above the photos of the base commander and other dignitaries assigned to the base.

Steven was not very thrilled with this set up as he felt that there should be at least an American flag or the presidents' photo on the wall. Civilian life sucks already Steven thought.

Eddie walked into the lobby and as he stood behind Steven, who was signing his name, Eddie liked the idea that the lobby was not filled with flags and pictures of everyone on base that had an important position. Civilian life was cool and there would be no standing guard duty at night anymore.

After he signed in, he made it a point not to sit at attention. He was not slouched or sitting sloppy, he was just not at attention. Lisa was now making faces, as it was too difficult to conceal the way she was feeling. She was about to cut loose and she knew that this was not going to be funny. She was alone on this side of the room and when she sounded the alarm, everyone would look her way. This was just another reminder, of another reason, why she hated her life so much.

Rose Marie made it to the front desk and signed in without being told why, when, or where. Same with finding a seat, she knew that once she was signed in, taking a seat was the next item in line of things to do when applying for a job.

Once seated in the middle of the room, the next item on her list was to make a check for any cat hair that she might have missed on her interview suit. Once she was happy that she was presentable, it was time to review the next stage on her pre-interview steps. They consisted on the answers she would give on her best guess estimated questions to be asked. She knew these to be canned answers to canned questions, but she worked hard on acting if she had never been asked these questions before. No need at this point to portray yourself as someone that was smarter than the one giving the interview, or someone that had been on many interviews.

Burt, just before he signed in, looked at his hands. He wanted to make sure that there was no grease or dirt under his nails. They were clean and looked like they were well manicured. Burt never did bite his nails and kept them cut short and neat.

Burt took a seat near the magazine rack, and noticed that Jerry had the one, and only, copy of Auto World. He would just there sit and wait, as he had no desire to read Jet Magazine, Red Book, or Green Peace. For some unknown reason, he was not into anything black, red, or green unless he was looking at colors on new cars or trucks.

Jeff took the last seat near the magazine rack and looked for something medical. He did find one magazine that had medical terms on the front cover. It happened to be an older copy of Readers Digest. With the time that he had available, he would find something that he could turn into his Mom's situation. Jeff might as well get the terminology correct with the proper ailment. Not to mention some knowledge on cause, treatment and in some cases, the cost. He might as well work up something that might allow him, to take another personal day, and not be suspected of job-hunting, if he were to be called back for a second interview.

At the receptionists' desk, Joe-Joe needed to ask where it was that he had to sign in. Even with a huge clipboard on the counter, he felt he needed to ask to make sure. Not only that, he had to ask the receptionist where it was that he should sit.

She pointed a finger directing him towards the back of the waiting room. No need to have him sitting close to her desk, only to be asked more stupid questions, she thought to herself. Joe-Joe did as suggested and looked at the magazine rack before he took his seat. He looked for a copy of TV Guide, no luck.

CHAPTER 5

THE INTERVIEW ROOM

THE CLOCK ON THE WALL behind Sandy, the receptionist, would click at each minute hand change. This type of wall clock would not simply swing around, minute to minute, it would snap from one minute to the next making a clicking sound. It was not a very loud click, but you could hear it.

Sandy was already out from behind her desk when the clock clicked at 9:30. She was a pleasant lady with a warm smile that would disarm even the nastiest of person. She announced for everyone to form a single line and be prepared to follow her.

"Be sure to bring all of your things with you as you will not be returning to this room," she added.

Van Camp liked the idea that no time was wasted, if the time was set for 9:30, then 9:30 it should be. Besides, if anyone came in late, the tardy ones should miss out and for this reason, to be sent home. He stood up, straightened his tie, and headed towards Sandy. He did so quickly, as to show all there, that he could follow instructions, even though he might be the president of this company someday and giving directions.

He might as well start now in setting a good example, he thought to himself and believed that everyone there, should have, or soon would have, the same view of him.

Kitty placed her mirror back in her purse and then paraded herself to the front of the line. This way, when the group arrived at the next location, that she would be the first to enter the room.

Earlier, she looked over the other women in this group, and knew that she was the pick of this litter, but still, she wanted to be first. Ben, for a moment, got a flashback as everyone stood up at the same time. The immediate reaction of everyone moving in unison, reminded him of movements in prison by the general population. Back in prison, when a bell sounded, everyone rapidly moved into or out of a room, as not to have a guard jab him with a nightstick for being slow.

'Same crap here as in prison. This job sucks already,' he muttered softly to himself.

However, Ben was not in a hurry, but he did make it a point to get in behind Kitty, who happened to have a nice butt to look at. He was most pleased that he did not fall in behind Lisa, as there was no need to get into line and not be able to see past her. On a side note, it was a good thing that he had hooked up with a hooker last night, cause if not, Lisa would be looking just fine right about now, and he would not have complained if he did fall in behind the, 'big behind.'

Alice took the pictures of her grandchildren that she had out talking too, and placed them back in her wallet and headed up to line.

Billy Bob and Bob Billy stood up with the oldest, Billy Bob taking the lead. They fell in behind Alice, which was almost on purpose. With Alice being short, they could easily see over her and keep an eye on Ben, whom they could tell was keeping an eye on the girl that was in front of him.

Rose Marie wanted to blend in and felt that it was too soon to work at standing out in the group. She simply moved into line without cutting anyone off, just wanting to blend in with the flow. Jerry, stood up right away, but took his time getting in line because he wanted to be at the end. He hated to be the first at anything.

Eddie got up and made it in line, making a nice jester by letting

Alice pass by in front of him. Eddie noticed how there was no real order on how everyone lined up. It did not matter to him that they were not lined up by height or rank, everyone just got in line. Civilian life was going to be easy. He was even polite to let in the two brothers that seem most eager to get in line in front of him. Steven jumped up and got to attention. He looked to see before he moved, just how the line should be formed if by height or rank. No one seemed to care about this, but him. He did not like the idea that there was no order in this line formation. How did R.E.A. International expect things to run properly if you could not control something as simple as forming an orderly line.

This job sucks already he thought.

Lisa got up and had to make a decision on how to get to the line. No need for her to bump into tables and chairs with her fat ass if she could avoid it. With that in mind, she bitched to herself and walked the long way around to fall in at the end of the line.

She was also aware that if this was a long walk, that it was a good idea to stay at, the end of the line as not to slow down everyone behind her. She hated getting into lines and this was just another reason she bitched to herself.

Burt made little car noises as he got up and started across the room. More car noises as he got up and made his way across the room, and then a breaking sound when he stopped. He had planned to follow close as if he was drafting. However, in line, he was standing a little to close to Steven, drafting or not.

Steven looked back at Burt, expressing that maybe; he was a little too close. Burt did back up a little after realizing that this guy considered it tailgating, and not drafting. However, for Steven, he liked the idea that Burt was close behind him, just not too close. He thought back at the times when he was learning to march, that standing, 'nuts to butts,' was the correct way to stand in close formation.

Ben noticed the look between Burt and Steven that was clearly about this line up of theirs. He thought to himself,'Great, a little queer is in our group. If he was to get up on my ass like that, I'll shove a broom stick up his.' The anger of his soon dissipated as he looked around and took another glance at Kitty.

Joe-Joe got up, all the while not taking his eyes off the TV. He did not like missing anything on the tube.

The line was all formed up with no one saying a word. Sandy paused a minute to see that everyone was accounted for and looking at her for instructions. That made her smile even more as she took notice how everyone was so compliant with their instructions.

Just as she opened her mouth to speak, Lisa farted and with her standing next to the wall, it was loud, and echoed a few times. Ben, having been in this type of situation before in prison, suggested to Sandy, "Let's get moving before we all pass out."

Lisa, having been in this sort of circumstances, a number of times, by habit she looked back at the wall and then up at the TV as if the explosion came from somewhere, anywhere besides her. It did not fool anyone and this only added another thing for her to bitch about later.

Sandy, not wanting to lose control of the situation, ignored what had just happened and politely said, "Follow me please."

The group of fourteen did as instructed and followed Sandy out of the waiting room and down a long hallway, a very long hallway. As expected, Lisa found it hard to stay with the group, or maybe it was the group trying hard to stay away from her.

Sandy was watchful of this group as she would occasionally look back to see if the group stayed together. Lisa was a little distance behind everyone as she was bringing up the rear. You always knew she was there and there was no reason to turn around to see for yourself. You could hear her legs rub against one another with each, and every step.

The long walk caused Billy Bob to say to Bob Billy, "There is a lot of hallway here and with only a few doors, this will be an easy place to keep under surveillance."

Jerry did not like this hallway for fear that if he was hired, that they would use him to paint it and it would take weeks to complete.

It did not take long, and Lisa was starting to tire. That added additional items for the new rounds of bitching to herself, that heated up as her legs heated up from all the rubbing. If this walk was to last much longer, her legs just might burst into flames. With all that rubbing, there was never a need to shave her legs from the knees up.

Kitty was worried that her hair might be messed up while walking down this long hallway. There was not much of a breeze, but even a little breeze would off set the balance of life in her little world.

Sandy came to a halt in front of a rather large door, a safe type of door, a safe door that you would expect to find in a bank. Ben had visions of tables and tables full of money inside just waiting for him to grab a hand full.

Joe-Joe knew that there would be poor or no TV reception behind that big door.

Naturally, Billy Bob and Bob Billy wanted very much to know the combination of the lock. It did not matter to them what was behind that door, just that it needed guarding and that they had the combination.

Once everyone, except Lisa, came to a halt, it was quiet. The sounds of fourteen sets of shoes tramping down the hallway had ended. The only sound now was the footsteps of Lisa and the rubbing of her thighs. At least she was not farting her way down the hall.

Sandy opened the huge door with surprisingly ease. Inside was a freshly painted room, about 50x50 feet with four rows of 10 chairs. These were the chairs that you would find in a classroom with the little desktop attached.

Sandy instructed everyone to take a seat. Jerry headed for the back row along with Ben, Billy Bob, and Bob Billy. Kitty headed for the front row along with Van Camp. Everyone else made there way in the remaining two center rows.

After everyone had taken their seat and apparently made them selves comfortable, Sandy gave one last instruction. "Please remain seated and someone will be with you shortly."

Sandy gave everyone a pleasant smile and headed out. Nothing was unusual about her departure, except for the minor detail that you could hear the sound of her locking the door behind her. There was the normal 'click' of the door closing, then two more 'clicks' of what appeared to be locking mechanisms.

The first person to speak out about the locking of the doors was Ben. He said, looking over at the Brown brothers, "What's this? They need to lock us down?"

Billy Bob responded with,"Maybe they don't want us roaming the hallways without a hall pass."

Jerry added in his two cents, "Nah, the jobs here are in such high demand that they want to keep the late people out."

Joe-Joe joined in with, "Damn, and no TV."

Kitty just sat there and worried that the room temperature and humidity would rise. If they did, that would put negative vibes on her hair and makeup.

Eddie and Steven did not care one-way or the other. They were in a safe and secure environment.

Lisa had thoughts that if she were to fart again, that someone would surely die.Alice, along with Van Camp, were also thinking that if Lisa were to fart, that they were going to die. For Burt and Jeff, they did not notice anything unusual about this room, and if they had, they would not care.

CHAPTER 6

THE LONG WAIT

T HE ROOM, OR SAFE AREA, was nothing special, except for the fact that there were no windows, only the one door and that was locked from the outside. There was a simple desk up front from where Sandy had stood beside, giving instructions.

This room just did not seem to fit in with the rest of the complex. In some ways, this could be an examination room not allowing for any outside openings. One would have thought that there would be a large mirror, doubling as a two-way mirror on one of the walls.

Steven, recalled his time onboard a coast guard cutter, and noticed the similarities that this room had with compartments onboard ships. If this room was to fill up with water, then nothing would leak out, he thought to himself.

So here it was, fourteen potential new-hires sitting in a room, a safe and secure room, and waiting for someone to check back with them. A few were expecting that they would be given tests, oral or written tests, forms to complete and or company policies to be listened too. Others just daydreamed about anything but test, oral or written, forms to complete and the boring task when listening to company policies.

As time when on, some would turn around, or lean forward,

to speak to whomever it was that they were facing. Conversations came up with questions as to ones name, what positions they were applying for, and what do they think would happen next, and when.

For the first 10-15 minutes or so, no one seemed to mind. It was just taken in stride until Jeff spoke up and said to no one in particular, "Maybe no one else is here but us and the receptionist."

"That can't be," bitched Lisa as she shifted in her seat.

Jeff responded with, "Did you see anyone else on your way in? "No, but there were cars in the lot," came a quick addition to this conversation from Bob Billy, with Billy Bob shaking his head in agreement.

"True," was the response from Van Camp, who wanted with passion to join in on this exchange as he maneuvered his way to take control of this situation, and then to take the lead in this, little chat. "Yet, I do not recall seeing anyone else on the lot besides the few of us."

"Everyone is working," joined in Alice.

Rose Marie said, "They know we are here. They might forget about one of us, but not a group of this size."

Ben added, "Working, I don't even know what this company does. Does anyone know what they do here?"

No one said a thing; no one had an answer except for Van Camp. "It's a factory because you can tell by the size of the building."

"That's right," chimed in Burt. "I noticed that they had a large loading dock on the east side of the building."

After all that was said, everyone sat back and just took it in stride that they had to wait in a factory place. No one wanted to cause a scene by disagreeing with what was agreed upon, not now before anyone was hired.

Thirty more minutes go by and the group got a little restless. Nothing was said and before long, thirty additional minutes went by. Ben was well adjusted, to just sit there and do nothing. For him, it was like prison life.

Lisa needed to find a rest room, as she simply had to go. Gas had started to build up in her stomach and she needed to fart to relieve the pains that will soon follow.

She moved side to side in her chair, allowing different parts of her butt to hang over the side. Those near her were watching with much caution as the Brown brothers made little jokes between each other. No one could hear what they were saying, but everyone could easily hear them laughing and it was assumed that they were talking about Lisa.

Jerry was enjoying this free rest time, as if this was study hall and his only concern was if he was going to be paid for his time here. Joe-Joe did not care one way or the other about this down time. Eddie took this free time as if he was standing guard duty, with nothing to watch, other than watching Kitty.

Kitty spent her time noticing the ones who noticed her, and she liked it. It didn't make no mind to her that guys noticed her. That's why she kept herself looking like she does. She did have a deep fear that in her senior years, she would get fewer looks, and if so, that she might as well bank a high number of hits now while she can.

Eddie, Burt, Jeff, Joe-Joe, Ben, and Steven were sitting up with their eyes closed. Billy Bob, Bob Billy, and Jerry also had their heads down on the desk and it was assumed that they had their eyes closed to.

The ladies, along with Van Camp, had dozed off. Even for just a second, they were still out.

Van Camp realized that he had fallen asleep and quickly awakened himself. He looked around to see if anyone had noticed him, and no one had. Even the ladies had their eyes closed and he believed that he only had them closed for a moment, not even a full minute.

Van Camp went right into his managerial mode, and started to make a mental note on those who did fall asleep and to give them a score. The ones with their heads down on the desks, they would receive the highest score. Sitting up with your eyes closed, you received the next highest score. He did give the ladies a little slack as he felt that they were weaker than men, and needed the extra rest, but they still received a few points.

Van Camp did assign himself a couple of points, but only because he was only out for a second or two. Certainly, not long enough to score above the women.

One by one, everyone started to stir around, almost as if a silent alarm had sounded.

Van Camp noticed something very odd in the way men and women woke up. The men would rub their eyes with great vigor, whereas the women did it, lady like. Just a little touch as if not to mess up their makeup. Kitty looked as if she didn't actually touch them, but hovered around her eyes going through the motions.

Lisa needed a trip to the restroom along with Kitty and Rose Marie. Alice would tag along when one of the girls got up to go. Thirty more minutes go by, and now, it was starting to take its toll on everyone except the men. The men were well rested and it was fine with them if they had to wait a little longer.

Lisa squirmed a little, as she shifted her weight around some to relieve the pressure on her butt for sitting so long in one spot. Add to this, she was really in need to make a rest stop. She was doing rather well in keeping her gas to herself, but nature was telling her that a 3.5 quake along with hurricane winds are due soon.

Because Van Camp had seemed like someone that could be in charge, also, he was the only male that had his eyes opened; she looked over at him and asked, "Any idea on what is taking so long?"

With a huge smile on his face giving the impression that he was in a good mood and was pleased to answer her question, but in reality, he liked the attention that he was getting, responded with, "Not sure, but I agree with you, it has been a long time to wait without anyone giving us an update."

This conversation awakened most of the guys except for Billy Bob, Bob Billy, and Jerry, as everyone was looking at Lisa to see her response.

Lisa shifted a little more and it was apparent that she had to go, before she had to, let it go.

Van Camp took the high-ground on this and as he stood up, making an effort to create some noise to wake those who were napping, and announced that he would go and see if he could find anyone that was available.

Lisa wanted to go with him but before she could raise her hand to catch his attention, Van Camp was out and away from his seat and heading towards the door.

All eyes are now focused on Van Camp, and that was just what he wanted. He knew that he would be a hero after he cleared up their problem with being left alone for such a long time. He was already thinking about what to say, as everyone would thank him individually. He may not be a leader in this company yet, but for now, a leader with this small group is just fine.

His big ideas and big head were soon deflated when it was reconfirmed that the door was locked from the outside. Van Camp was clever enough not to make his disappointment apparent, but acted as if he knew that it was locked, but was just verifying that it was still locked before he started to bang on the door.

At first, his knocking was polite, just loud enough to be heard by anyone walking by.

Ben suggested that he,"Bang on that damn door man. We've been here long enough. No need to be nice about it."

Well, that earned him a few more points from Van Camp, even with him being correct. As if he did not hear what Ben said, Van Camp knocked again, only this time, just a little bit harder.

He did not want anyone to think that he was taking instructions from Ben.

For Ben, he had about enough of this sissy-ass knocking on the door. He got up and made his way towards the door as the Brown brothers stood up to join him.

The three of them arrived at the door at the same time with a single purpose in mind, to get someone's attention. Van Camp made a face as if he did not approve of what they had planned and by his actions of stepping away, made it clear to everyone that he was not going to be a part of this.

As you would imagine, the three of them banged on the door.

Not many times, but enough in volume and numbers that it should have been heard all the way back to the reception desk.

All was quiet now, as the three of them listened for any sounds coming from the hallway. For everyone else, they may not have approved of the way they were banging on the door, but they knew they were right in trying to get someone's attention.

Everyone listened, and nothing, not a sound at all in their efforts for a response. The three of them banged on the door again and this time, it was harder with many more hits. They stopped and listened once more, and the results were the same. Some fear was starting to creep into the group. Lisa was pissed and started to bitch. "No way do I want to work for a company that forgets all about you."

Rose Marie was not pleased as well. She did not want this interview to take longer than an average day at work. Her cats knew about what time to expect her home and she did not want to disappoint them.

Kitty needed to fix her hair and tried to maintain her smile. She had never gone this long before without a little touch up to her hair and makeup. She was afraid of what she may look like if this takes more time.

Van Camp sat himself down because he wanted to be seen sitting when the door opened up. He did not want any company personnel to see him at the door contributing with all that banging noise. Let the common employees take the credit for making that racket, he thought.

Still, no response as Eddie, Steven, and Burt made their way to the door. Then, Burt, Jeff, and Joe-Joe fell in behind them. For Kitty, Alice, Lisa, and Van Camp, they sat patiently with nothing to say.

Eddie, the x-marine did some soft knocking on the dry wall as if looking for the locations of the studs. Jerry did not know why he was doing this, so he asked, "What, you looking for another way out?"

"That would be affirmative. If they won't let us exit by the door, then we'll make our own doorway."

Joe-Joe, without using his head or common sense, pointed to Lisa and said, "How big a hole do we need to get her fat ass to fit through?"

Everyone, without thought, gave a look towards Lisa. Lisa, pissed at this, decided not to bitch about it. She responded with, "Don't worry about me. Send that skinny guy out first, and he can unlock the door from the other side for all of us."

She was pointing towards Jeff, who by his physical size, was the smallest of the lot.

Steven, thinking that busting a hole in the wall might be a little much, commenced to bang on the door some more. Others joined in along with some yelling.

This went on for a few minutes before they stopped and listened. Ben and Burt placed their ear up against the wall and they listened some. Nothing, still nothing, nothing at all and it looked hopeless.

Alice, who up to this point, had said nothing, spoke up with Rose Marie in agreement, and said,"Maybe they forgot about us. Everyone went home."

Joe-Joe was pissed that he was missing his shows, and Van Camp was busy thinking of what to say to the president of the company when they did get out. In some ways, he felt that this was setting a bad taste in his mouth, well, not that bad as he was looking for a job, and would overlook this if he were hired.

Getting back to the door, still no answer. Again, all the guys started to bang on the door and yelled some more. Van Camp wanted to join in, but felt he looked more important sitting where he was rather than manually banging on the door and walls. No need to work up a sweat and dirty his, expensive, clean, starched white shirt.

Steven, initially thinking that breaking down the wall was a bad idea, now believed this to be the only way to go. He spoke up, and said, "Let's take a vote on what we should do next. We can continue to bang on the door, or we can bust the wall down."

Everyone agreed, except for Van Camp, that drastic action was required, but moreover, not that drastic that they need to bang a hole in the wall. He was going to speak up and say something, but noticed how everyone agreed with what they wanted to do; even the ladies had voiced their opinion.

This time, a few guys started to do the, tap-tap on the wall to find the spaces between the studs. Joe-Joe did not help, because he had no idea how to tell the difference between a stud tap-tap, and a no-stud, tap-tap. Jeff did not want to mess up his hand by knocking on anything. Burt stepped aside, as there was not enough room for them, and him.

They just wanted to get someone from R.E.A. International to acknowledge that this little group was there, locked in, and apparently ignored, or worse, forgotten.

Ben announced that he had found the space between two studs. Steven and Billy Bob re-tapped the same location and concurred that they had a place ready to attack.

Their next decision was how to make the hole, and who to send through it. Jeff was chosen by default by his small size. Alice was smaller, but none of the guys wanted to send a lady when Jeff was right there and most willing.

Steven, wanting to prove that he was a, macho kind of guy, said, "I'll just punch it with my fist."

A few of the guys looked over at Eddie because he was bigger and meaner looking as if he would be the one that was better suited for this task.

Ben just smiled and suggested, "Let him get started, and I'll finish it up."

All was in order and Van Camp was not drawn in, and he wanted so bad to be involved. He gave it some thought and decided to say nothing and stay right were he was. By being this far away, he would avoid getting any of the dry wall debris and dust on his nice suit.

Steven, now giving his task a second look, decided to change it up a little. He spoke to the group of guys nearest to him and said, "Before I go and destroy a perfectly good wall, lets do one more round of banging on the door and yelling our lungs out." The group seemed to find this an excellent idea and it was at this time that Van Camp stood up and said, "That's a good idea, go for it."

Billy Bob and Bob Billy looked at him and gave him a look as if suggesting,'who asked you, sit back down.' Then Billy Bob said to his brother in a soft voice, "Let's get that fat girl, and have her run into the wall a few times."

Bob Billy answered with, "Why not just back her big ass up against the wall and she can fart-blast her way threw."

Alice overheard them and gave the two of them a dirty look. This was not a dirty look to tick them off or anger them. Just the sort of look that a parent in church would project towards a misbehaving child to, 'knock it off.'

As if on cue, the guys closest to the wall started to bang on the wall as the ones near the door, started to bang on the door. Together, everyone was yelling, even the women added in some volume. As for Van Camp, he was recovering from the looks that everyone gave him and now thinking of how to join in.

This went on for a few, maybe three minutes. Then all was quiet as they listened for some response, nothing, not a single sound from the outside.

Billy Bob leaned over to his brother, and said; "Now this be an easy place to guard. Just lock everyone up and allow nobody to walk the halls."

Bob Billy answered with, "Yeah, that be true as long as they don't lock us up. Know what I mean?"

They agreed and knock knuckles as Steven took in a deep breath as if he was some kind of, Kung Fu champion that was about to bust up a few cinder blocks.

In reality, Steven was hoping that someone would step up with a better idea or take his place, neither one happened. He was now the focus of everyone.

CHAPTER 7

THE BREAKOUT

STEVEN TOOK UP A POSITION just to the left of the door. He double-checked then he re-checked the position of the studs. No need to hurt himself more than needs be. Just as he took a stance and prepared for the first hit, Joe-Joe said, "Why not use one of the chair legs?"

Everyone looked over at him waiting for him to explain his suggestion. "Yeah," he spoke out with pride. "MacGyver, episode number seven, he took the legs off a chair using a dime as a screwdriver. It can be done."

Everyone looked at him, as if he was not, the smartest person of the group. Every seat/chair in the room was the ones you would find in classrooms. The legs were not attached to the seat; the legs were made in one piece as part of the base of the chair. There were no legs to say, which could be unattached.

Just as everyone was to turn back to Steven, he, Joe-Joe, spoke up and added, "Not those chairs, the one up here."

He had taken the one chair from behind the desk at the front of the room and turned it up side down on top of the desk. Immediately, he extracted a dime from his pocket and started to unfasten one of the legs.

Steven, who was most grateful, made his way to Joe-Joe who

handed him the first leg off the chair. Joe-Joe continued and soon, all 4 were legs off.

During this time, no attempt was made to open a hole in the wall, nor was anyone banging or yelling. Joe-Joe made his way to the door and the legs were all taken from him. Steven had the first leg, the Brown brothers snapped up one each, and the fourth leg was taken by Eddie, who said to Joe-Joe, "You did your part, take a break, and let us finish it up."

He agreed and took a seat, as he really wanted to rest his hand from all that unscrewing he just completed.

The four guys, now holding a chair leg each, converged next to the door. Without saying a word, they visually agreed on the spot that should be opened.

Steven spoke up and said, "On three. Ready, one, two, three." And with a single purpose in mind, the four guys, with encouragement from those around them, prepared to poke a hole in the wall.

Just as Stephen was about to start, Bob Billy asked. "Do we hit on three, or do you say three, then we hit?"

Stephen lowered his chair leg and explained, "On three. I say one, two, and then we trash this wall on three."

Still with another question, Bob Billy asked, "We hit the wall at the same time you say three?"

Van Camp, having been out of the loop on this adventure, added, "I'll count. I'll say one, two, and smash the wall on my count of three."

No one cared that Van Camp had worked his way into the program, everyone just wanted to get out of this cell.

With their hands raised, and anticipating a quick start to the count, it was time to breakout.

As planned, it was one, two, then three with all four hitting the wall as if this was synchronize swimming.

It was surprisingly easy for a room that appeared to be sound, water, and escape proof to be destroyed so easily. A small hole was created, and after some debris was removed, they started working to make the hole bigger.

In no time at all, they had broken through. As if this was, an agreed upon stopping point, everyone, and these four in particular, stepped back to admire their work and to listen in on any sounds coming from the hallway.

As before, no sounds, nothing. With this opening, Eddie was able to stick his head in the hole and peak out at the hallway. He did not see anyone, and with that, he started to yell, "Anyone out there? Come let us out."

This went on for about a minute and it was surprising apparent, that no one was out there. This realization was followed by anger and the demolition team continued to break out by making the hole larger.

With four guys banging away, it did not take long at all to create a space large enough for Jeff to escape. Just as there was enough room to exit, he did.

"Don't you forget about us," bitched Lisa, as she tried to remember where the rest room was. As she had to go, as soon as she got out.

Just as Jeff breached the hole, high-fives and big smiles were plentiful. Everything was looking great until they could hear Jeff banging on the door, trying to get in.

"Open up," shouted half the group.

"I can't," was the reply from Jeff. "I need the combination."

"Run down to the lobby and find some to help," directed Van Camp.

Without waiting for additional instructions, Jeff said, "I'll be right back."

Ben, after hearing Jeff running away, said, "I ain't waiting on nobody." With that, he commenced to make the hole a little bigger for himself. Others took the hint and before long, the hole was plenty big.

After Ben and the Brown brothers escaped, Eddie suggested, or commanded, that the women should go next. With that, all the guys wanted to help Kitty out. Rose Marie was next, as she was not as old as Alice and one-third the weight of Lisa. For Alice, she was a nice old lady, and she was given more care as she made her way out.

Lisa bitched up and said, "I'll need a little more room."

Van Camp, wanting to be a good guy, or wanting to give the

impression that he was the captain of a ship, and that he would leave last, suggested, "I'll stay back and help her out."

No one argued with him and quickly, they singled filed themselves out. A little more excavating was required for Lisa.

Eddie and Burt were working on the sides of the hole making it just right, and not wanting to leave it too small, or make it too big and embarrass Lisa. Rather like because, you do not guess at a woman's age or weight, or in this case, her size.

When they visually agreed that the opening would work, and by the smiles on their faces, they motioned Lisa to move her fat ass over and to make her first try on getting out.

Burt and Eddie were still in the room, and they could not take their eyes off Lisa's huge butt as she bent over. At least, if Lisa needed a push, there would be enough room for three people to get in behind her behind and push.

The hole needed a little more space, as when Lisa bent over, her sides speared far and wide. The hole had the height, but not the width.

With Van Camp's help, they all gave her a big gentle, but firm push. Besides, if she were to become stuck in the wall, they would be locked in, for a second time.

That thought was not as bad as the thought of being stuck in this room, and seeing Lisa's butt stuck in and sticking out of the wall.

Van Camp was sorry now that he had spoken up, to take up the rear, and what a large rear it was. Lisa did make it past with only a little difficulty, as she only rubbed on three sides of the hole and not all four.

Van Camp got the surprise of his life when she was unable to hold it in any longer. As expected by her, and not Van Camp, she cut one loose that almost knocked him down. Not so much from the force, power, or odor, but by the surprise that a human being would be able to make such a sound.

Well, Lisa made it out okay as Van Camp picked himself up. He double-timed his way out into the hallway. Once outside, he was able to breathe again. Van Camp reminded himself that once he made it to a restroom, that he would wash his hands and face once real good, and wash his nose twice.

In the hallway, everyone mingled with each other with some small talk. Jeff returned and announced, "No one is in the lobby."

This previous small talk from the group, started to become a little louder and intense. Van Camp seized the situation and instructed, "Let's stick together and make our way back to the lobby."

With no one else having a better idea, and because it did make sense, they singled filed themselves down the hallway, the same way they came in.

Lisa, Rose Marie, and Kitty at the same time asked the group if they would wait as them made a stop in the rest room. Van Camp, wanting to stay in charge, suggested, "We'll all make a pit stop."

This latest direction of his was made feasible, as they were approaching a set of rest rooms. After just a few minutes, the group was together again. Normally, a rest stop like this would have taken longer, but apparently, everyone was in a hurry to move this adventure along, and not to be left alone.

CHAPTER 8

WE ARE ALONE

THE GROUP SINGLED FILED DOWN the hallway as they headed back the way they came in. No one said anything to one another as each in their own way was listening for any sounds of people. In addition, no one wanted to be the last person in line in fear of losing the group. Even Lisa kept up.

Approaching the lobby, Van Camp spoke to the group, and said, "This is no way to treat potential excellent employees. I will give them a piece of my mind."

For those who heard what he had said, felt good about that, even after what they had just endured. 'Potential excellent employees,' did make them feel special, but Van Camp was speaking about himself only, and not about any of the common workers, that he had just spent time with today.

Ben paid Van Camp little attention as he made his way behind the secretary's empty desk. Being as obvious as he was, he believed that everyone there would think that he was looking for a phone. He had anticipated that they would not think that he wanted to find an unattended purse.

Bob Billy knew exactly why Ben had made his way there and made it a point to say aloud for everyone to hear, "Looking for the phone?"

Rose Marie walked by the reception desk and noticed that there was a cat calendar on the wall. It was one that she had not seen before, and that surprised her more than the fact that no one was around. And, with no one around, she might consider taking the calendar.

She had never, in her life taken anything before that wasn't hers, but if this place was empty, as say an abandoned ship, left adrift, then whoever arrives on scene first, has rights, and salvage rights will apply.

Ben knew that the jig was up and he, without any quick movements, made his way to the other side of the room having not finding a phone, or purse. He did make it a point to say for everyone's benefit, "No phone. You would think there would be a phone there."

Everyone else took a seat, as if waiting in the lobby, was better than waiting in the other room. Lisa found the same large chair from earlier. Joe-Joe, Jeff, and Steven took the same seats they had when they first arrived. The Brown brothers along with Jerry and Burt, had seats in the back row. Kitty and Alice sat up front along with Van Camp as Eddie stood up against the near wall.

Joe-Joe looked up at the TV and after a few minutes, noticed that the same commercial, the one about how Countrywide can reduce your monthly mortgage, played repeatedly. He paid this no mind, but thought it to be odd, or maybe, this was a slow news day.

Van Camp made it a point to sit up straight as not to show that his butt was dragging. Everyone else, except for the ones standing, slouched in their chairs. If you were to walk in the room and at first glance, decide whom you would want to hire, only Van Camp looked alert, as if he gave a shit.

For the next ten minutes or so, no one did anything. They believed, because they were in the main lobby, that someone would eventually walk by, but nothing happened.

Billy Bob mentioned to Bob Billy that he was going to take a walk down the hall for a look-see. Bob Billy agreed that to be a good idea and mentioned that he would take a walk in the other direction.

Steven, overhearing what they were talking about, looked over at Eddie and said, "Why don't you and I check out the parking lot?"

Eddie responded back with, "Yes sir. Can do." Eddie did not

mean to respond with 'yes sir,' but it was a habit and not meant to put Steven in a superior position.

Steven made eye contact with Billy Bob, and said, "We'll check the lot. He'll go one way, and I'll go the other."

As Steven spoke, he pointed towards Eddie to indicate that it would be the two of them. He added, "What do you say we all meet back here in, say, in no more than five minutes?"

No one said a word, but all agreed by shaking their heads up and down. With a plan in place, the four of them left the lobby area.

Van Camp was just fine sitting where he was. Kitty and Lisa had no intention on straying away on their own. Let the guys do it, they agreed.

Jerry was too lazy to spend two and a half minutes walking one way, and then doubling back, just to end up back here. Burt, Jeff, and Joe-Joe, liked the idea of those guys working out this look and see routine, and leaving them alone.

After a minute or two, Joe-Joe made aloud his thoughts about the TV. "Check it out," he said loud enough for everyone to hear, but not scare them. "Fox news keeps replaying the same commercial over and over. Enough already with getting a first, second or third mortgage from Countrywide."

As everyone looked up at the TV, Bob Billy returned. Van Camp spoke up, as if he should be reporting to him, and asked, "Did you see anyone?"

"Nope. Not a single person."

"You weren't gone very long," he questioned.

Bob Billy looking at Van Camp indicating that he did not know that someone had died and left him in charge, answered, "Well, if you must know. The way I went, soon turned into a dead end. All the doors that I passed, that were not locked, I looked inside. The ones that were locked, I knocked and no answer."

After a short pause, he added, "Nothing. No answers and still, no one in sight. From my side of the building, it was empty."

With that news, no one got too excited. With only one out of four reports, that was acceptable news until the others return. Before anyone could muster up a question, Billy Bob returned and had similar news. After he was asked, he apologized for not opening doors along his way.

Now, this started to worry a few of them. The only person really upset about this was Kitty, as she had kept herself looking good for this group of guys, and none of them had a job. She wanted to impress someone, anyone of importance in this company.

Outside, Steven and Eddie returned about the same time and met up at the main door. Both of them had a look of disappointment. At first, neither one wanted to say anything to the other anticipating that the other would say that he had met up with a few people, at least with one person.

Eddie spoke up first and said, "I didn't see a thing. Not even a moving car or truck."

Steven scratched his head and said, "Same for me. No people and no traffic. I just don't understand it."

"Might as well head back with the news," suggested Eddie, as he turned, headed inside, and added, "Those two black guys must have found someone."

"Hope so, if not, then what," questioned Steven.

"Don't know. Never been in this situation before. This must be a trick. Maybe even a physic test of some kind given by the company. You know, to see how we respond to crap like this."

"That will be great, only I wish they would soon finish up so we can get hired or send us home."

A moment later, Steven and Eddie returned and they walked over to the Brown brothers. There was not a single smile between then, just serious frowns of disappointment. Nothing really needed to be said, as it was obvious that no one found anyone.

As the four of them faced each other without anything to say or ask, Van Camp then joined them and said, "You guys," he questioned, looking at Steven and Eddie. "Find anything?"

Before anyone could respond, Joe-Joe added, "Check it out man."

Everyone looked over at him as he pointed at the TV, "Same commercial, over and over."

Not wanting this guy to take over the conversation, Van Camp suggested, "Then change the channel."

"Ain't no channel to change. Close circuit," he responded as if everyone should have known that.

Everyone else in the room just looked to each other, as if the other person would have an answer, which no one did.

Kitty stood up and said, "This has got to be a joke. I'd bet that there are cameras all around us to see how we would respond."

A few nodded their heads slightly, showing approval while the others looked around for cameras. There were no cameras and the commercials for Countrywide kept on playing.

Burt and Jeff who had up to this point, done nothing, started to talk to each other. "Great idea," said Burt to Jeff.

With that, everyone else looked over at them, expecting to be let in on what this great idea of theirs was.

Burt, realizing that everyone was looking at him, swallowed, and said, "Okay, you guys did not see anyone. So let's all fan out, find telephones, and start making calls."

"Who we gonna call, Ghost Busters," joked in Joe-Joe.

Normally, this would have gotten more laughs except now; this had gotten serious, no longer a joke.

"That made sense," added in Van Camp. "First one to fine a phone, dial 0 for the operator."

Ben mentioned, "There was no phone behind the desk."

"No problem," Bob Billy broke in. "A few of us will head out, find a phone, and make some calls."

Everyone shook his or her head as if this was a plan that just had to work. Except for Lisa. She added, "And if you don't get an operator?"

Burt responded with, "Then you should dial 911."

"That is only for emergencies," reputed Van Camp.

Lisa gave him a dirty look and responded, "If you can't find anyone here, and you can't find no one on the phone, then 911 be an emergency."

Burt and Jeff looked at each other, and Jeff said, "We'll head out and find a phone. Whatever the results, we will be gone no longer than five minutes."

Steven, Eddie, Billy Bob, and Bob Billy all seemed to agree with them at the same time. They simply sat down and Eddie said, "Hope you have better luck than we did."

Without any additional fan fair, they left the room and headed in different directions on a mission to make a phone call.

Just as they left the room, Joe-Joe said, "There was an episode on the Twilight Zone that started out like this."

"How did it end up," Alice questioned.

Without moving his head to face her, and adding fear to his voice, he answered, "The world had come to an end, and they were the only ones left alive."

"For real," questioned Kitty, and she was serious.

Ben quickly responded, "You dumb ass. That was a show."

After he said that, he wished that he could take it back. He had no problem talking that way towards a man, but not to a goodlooking girl that he hoped would find him attractive.

She gave him a dirty look, and then responded, "I know that. It's an old science fiction show and I was trying to lighten up our situation."

"Sorry, I should not have responded that way. I am just a little upset with the way things have turned out today."

Kitty accepted his apology, and for that, Ben was most grateful. Not very often had he ever apologized to anyone for anything. For this situation, it felt rather good. Maybe, he would do this more often. Sure beats getting into a fight.

The Brown brothers were joking to themselves about, if this was the end of the world, that they would only have four women between them. They had it all figured out, Lisa would be used for warmth on cold nights, and if they ran out of food, they would eat her.

Alice could be used to cook and clean, leaving Kitty and Rose Marie, to have many children and to provide entertainment.

Lisa heard them giggling and she strongly assumed that they were talking about her. That pissed her off and she gave them a dirty look. For the brothers, dirty looks only promoted their laughter.

The room fell silent for a little while. Only the Countrywide commercial could be heard, and it was still repeating itself.

A few minutes go by and Burt and Jeff had not returned. Everyone felt that the longer that they were gone, the better the odds were that they found someone or something. A few minutes more go by and Joe-Joe walked away from the TV and peeked out into the hallway. He looked both ways and listened.

"Hear anything," asked Alice.

He held up his hand indicating that it would be helpful if she kept silent, as if he had heard something. Right when it appeared that he did, he turned in the other direction to listen. Each time he would change direction, everyone seemed a little more disappointed with his results.

Five more minutes pass and still, they did not return. Steven said to Eddie, "Should we organize a search party?"

Joe-Joe heard them and said, "Don't send me to find them."

He looked back in the room at the group, and finished with, "There is no sound out there. No sounds at all, just ain't normal. I should at least be able to hear them walking around and some phone conversations, but nothing, nothing at all."

This was not cool and even the hard-core guys seemed uneasy. It was not so much being alone, it was the, 'not knowing,' why they were alone.

Kitty, not being as brave as she tried to appear to be, walked over and sat next to Alice. They looked at each other, and without words, they agreed to stick together. For Lisa, she was pissed that they did not walk over and sit with her. The last thing she wanted to do, was to be the only one in a room walking around looking for a seat. It always drew too much attention to her and that ticked her off. She needed things to bitch about and right now, there were plenty of things for her to bitch about for the rest of the day.

However, with ten men and only the four of them, Lisa decided to make the move. As if a large ship had left the pier, she made her way over to sit next to Alice.

Van Camp noticed this, but had no idea what he could say that would include him in that little group. He did make it a point to shift in his seat so that it would allow him to be in a better listening position should they have anything to say to each other.

Another five minutes go by and still there was no news from Jeff and Burt. With that, the group started to get restless.

It was determined by Steven, Eddie, Billy Bob, and Bob Billy that they would be the rescue party members. It was also decided, that it was best that they stayed in pairs and only go out for one minute at a time, and then return.

If, when one pair returned and the second pair did not, that the first pair would venture out looking for the missing pair.

All this seemed to be a little crazy, but taking in consideration what had transpired so far, these moves appeared to be the correct actions to take.

As the four guys readied themselves mentally for this new adventure, the ones remaining behind felt lost in many ways. Yet, with no other ideas available to them, they had no choice but to sit tight and wait for them all to return. Moreover, if they did not return, well, that was not discussed. They just had to come back, all of them.

Okay, off they went. Two of them turned left and two went right with Joe-Joe standing in the middle of the hallway. Joe-Joe was looking both ways, not wanting to let either team out of his sight for more than a second or two. Before long, Joe-Joe came in from the hallway and said to the group, "They are out of sight."

"Anything," questioned Van Camp, as if he was speaking for the group.

"Nope. When they came back into the hallway, they would look at me and shake there heads telling me no, nothing."

Wanting to put a positive spin on this, Alice spoke up and said, "They just got started. Give them a few more minutes."

As a few more minutes passed by, everyone started to form

little groups with soft conversations. Alice wanted to show off her grandchildren's pictures, but thought against it at this time.

The remaining guys huddled together and could only muster up a little small talk about sports and super models.

Of all the conversations, nothing was that important that it could not be interrupted by news from the returning search parties.

A few more minutes later, all four of them returned at almost the same time. Everyone gathered around them to hear the results.

Steven spoke first. "No one is around. We did find a few phones, we dialed 0, and it went to voice mail."

"Did you leave a message," questioned Lisa.

"Yeah," quickly responded Steven.

Eddie interrupted this friendly conversation and added, "I did the same on other phones that I found. Dialed zero and no answer. I went as far as dialing 911."

Van Camp was most anxious to hear this part, he asked, "What did you tell them was our emergency?"

"I didn't tell them anything."

"You just hung up," snapped back Van Camp.

"No. I just didn't hang up. I stayed on the line for a few minutes, and no one answered. I felt that we had a problem here and I wanted help. You know, maybe there was some evacuation here or something," Eddie snapped back. Not in a mean way, more like, let me finish.

"Sorry," responded Van Camp. "It's been a long day and I appreciate you going out there helping us all."

"No answer there. It just kept on ringing. It never asked for a message."

"Then what?" asked Van Camp. Only this time, more politely.

"I placed the phone down and let it continue to ring. I did not hang it up. Figured that eventually they would pick it up and with no one on the line, they'd most certainly send help. Or at least send someone to see who made the call and why."

Steven added, "I did the same thing. Called 911 and left the phone off the hook as it was ringing and ringing."

After they spoke, Steven and Eddie looked over at Billy Bob.

Not to ignore Bob Billy, but Billy Bob was closer and looked as if he had something to say.

"We did the same damn thing you guys did. No answer anywhere," announced Billy Bob.

Bob Billy spoke and added, "Me too man. Only I did not dial 911. I dialed my girlfriend's cell and it went to voice mail."

"Did you leave her a message," questioned Van Camp, again as if he was in charge and everyone had to report to him.

Bob Billy gave him an obvious facial expression that he did not recognize Van Camp. Not recognizing him more, than a fellow person that was also looking for a job.

"Yeah, if you must know. Just to call me when she got the message," he responded, looking at everyone except Van Camp.

Van Camp did not like his answer, nor did he like his attitude.

Continuing, Bob Billy said, "I made a few other calls with the same results. Either the phone was never answered, or it went to voice mail."

Billy Bob added, "I even called our mom, and she is always home and she always answers the phone. No answer."

Everyone that was standing took a seat and everyone that was sitting, except for the women, stood up as if their thinking would improve with their new positions.

No one wanted to say anything, nor did anyone have anything to say or ask. Naturally, with the room so quiet, except for the low volume on the TV, Lisa had to worry also on how to hold in another gas explosion. With that in mind, she just bitched silently to herself.

So there they sat, fourteen potential new hires with not a single clue between them on what to do next.

CHAPTER 9

HOW ALONE ARE WE?

JOE-JOE WAS THE FIRST TO break the silence. "For me, I want to go home."

Jerry, the lazy kid, added in his opinion. "Me too. If they want to ignore me, then I'll just send my ass on home."

His only issues were that his Dad would not believe him. Yet, it did not matter, as this was one story that he was not clever enough to make up on his own.

"Yeah, you guys make sense," Burt joined in. "I just want to get in my car and head out. There are other jobs out there."

Van Camp stood up and said, "What a waste of our valuable time. If they treat us this bad when this was a time to impress us, can't imagine how they will treat us after we are hired."

Van Camp purposely added in the 'our' and 'us' part to make him seem as a team member, and not as a team leader.

Ben did not say a thing, as he had nowhere to go, so, he would just listen in on everyone else.

Kitty's only thought now was to fix her hair and head out without saying a word. All she needed was a cup of coffee from Starbucks.

Rose Marie knew that her cats needed their daily attention.

Whatever they decided to do is fine with her. Only that, if it were to involve her, let her do it after she feeds her cats.

Lisa just sat there and bitched aloud to herself. This was just another thing that pissed her off.

Jeff, Eddie, Steven, along with Billy Bob and Bob Billy, stood up and gave the impression that they all had exiting this place in mind.

Alice walked up to the, sign in log, and signed herself out.

No one had a smile on their face, just a tired, downtrodden look as if they had been made a fool of, and then ignored.

Joe-Joe, recalling an old movie, 'Night of the living dead,' where only a few people were alive, and the ones were dead, wanted to eat those that were alive, spoke up and said, "Is everyone sure that they want to venture out there alone, not knowing how, what, and why we are in this predicament?"

What he said seemed childish and not part of a normal, serious conversation, except for the fact that they needed to know how, what, and why they were in this dilemma.

Kitty, expressing fear, came back with, "What should we do?"

Alice said, "Grow up little girl. The world did not come to an end, and if it did, do you think that they would leave it to all of us?"

Lisa spoke up, and said, "Look, there is something that we have all forgotten about."

Everyone looked at her expressing that, okay, if you have something important to say, then go ahead and say it.

Well, she did. "We all have cell phones, right? Okay then. Let's all go outside, together, and make a few calls. When we get a hold of someone, anyone, ask them if anything unusual has taken place in this area."

Approving nods came from everyone and if on cue, they all singled filed out to the parking lot. Once there, everyone looked around for people and or traffic before making their calls.

Lisa was almost right. Everyone had a cell phone except for Ben, Joe-Joe, Eddie, and Steven. The ones that did have a cell phone, were phoning away.

At first, you could imagine that a few of them had reached

someone, only to realize a few seconds later that they were only leaving voice mails.

This exercise was turning out to be very productive, but not in a positive way. There was just no way that with all these calls being made, that no one was answering.

Frantically, more calls were made with the same results. Everyone was getting voice mails. Bob Billy announced, "I have a busy signal, I have a busy signal."

His brother Billy Bob looked over at the number that he called. With disappointment, he said, "Shit, shit, shit. I was leaving that number a voice mail. No wonder it was busy."

Bob Billy then dialed another number, when he heard, "hello," he got all excited and started to yell, "I have someone, I have someone."

Billy Bob looked over at him in anger, disappointment, and embarrassed, then said, "You dialed my number you ass hole."

Half the group found this to be funny, the other half were a little ticked that their hopes were raised then dropped, and all in one second.

Reality was setting in, along with some fear. Not so much the fear that they were alone, but fear that their loved ones were not available for reasons unknown.

While everyone was calling and calling, Ben and Steven had stood side by side looking around for any movement of people or traffic.

Jeff thought he had a good point and said, "No sweat, we just can't make a phone call from here. You know, no cell towers close by."

He felt good with the point he gave, but Joe-Joe soon chopped it down. "If that were the case, then no one would be able to reach any voice mails."

Everyone's short-lived smile, was reduced to a sad one. Like winning fourth place at a competition that only gave medals to the top three.

Slowly and painfully, the numbers of cell phone calls were dropped until everyone had finally given up and placed their phones away. This short battle was over and they had lost, and even with all the evidence that they were alone, it was simply impossible. No way, no how, not now, not today, not here, and not to them was any of this acceptable.

No one made a move towards his or her car to leave. Burt took a brave step and said to the group, "The only answer here is that there was an evacuation in this area. Of course no one was around to answer our calls."

"Nope," chimed in Alice. "I called for my family that lives in Washington State. Same as the other calls, voice mail."

Rose Marie did not have any family nearby, and the ones out of state, well; she kept their numbers at home. There was no one for her to call at work, as she did not have a job and didn't want to call them anyway based on how she left the company.

Eddie added his findings, "Me too. I called a number in Texas and it was never answered."

Ben wished that he was back in prison were there were no surprises to the mundane schedule of prison life. Guards and fellow inmates were always around. In prison, you are never left alone. Kitty started to cry, not heavy crying with lots of wailing, but just enough for everyone to hear her. Normally, when a girl started to cry, there was a feeling that everyone should comfort her some. Only this time, everyone knew why she was crying and they all felt like crying also.

Well, not everyone, the guys had little compassion for a crying girl and thought that it took away the real concern that they were all facing right now.

This odd collection of fourteen people had a common problem, as they had never experienced anything like this before. Nothing like this took place while in prison, in the military, baby sitting, interviewing, or in daily life situations. Only in books, movies, and old tales had this magnitude of a problem ever existed. Even then, it was always fiction.

The question for the group was, what were they going to do now.

CHAPTER 10

WHAT DO WE DO NOW?

T HE REALIZATION THAT THEY WERE really, really, alone had sat in. Not that they were the only ones left in the world, but in this building, in the nearby area, and without outside communications, they were about as alone as alone could be.

Fear was slowly starting to get out of control. The ones talking wanted to talk louder so that everyone would take their side. Others, added in their points and counter points, but nothing was resolved to anyone's satisfaction. Not that it could be.

There was conversation of going home with equal amounts of talk of staying put. Van Camp, seizing on the opportunity, spoke up and announced loud enough to quiet everyone, said, "Let's take a head count on who wants to do what and when."

Ben was the first to speak up. "For me, I'll just stay here a while." He had no place to go anyway.

Alice had her hand up as if asking permission to speak. It was not that Van Camp recognized her, but it was that everyone else noticed her hand up, and politely waited their turn.

"I am going home. Then I will check up on my grand kids."

Ben spoke right back, and said, "When you get home, and find no one there, come on back here."

Van Camp wanting to take credit for that idea, dismissed Ben, and said, "Okay, let's all head back home, and if we don't find anyone, come on back here."

Joe-Joe, missing the first half of the conversation, asked, "How long should we stay home before we come back? Will we get to finish our interviews then?"

Then Billy Bob answered Joe-Joe with, "Yeah sure man. Go home, make a few calls, and look around for people. Then be back here in two hours."

Bob Billy nodded approval, and added, "Same for the two of us. Back here in two hours if we find nothing at our place."

Joe-Joe, looking more confused, asked, "What are we looking for?"

Van Camp believing that he was joking: ignored him and confirmed what the Brown brothers said. "Back here in two hours." "What if we find something," questioned Jeff. "Come back anyway?"

"Yeah," were the quick responses from Steven, Rose Marie, Burt, Eddie, and Kitty.

Still looking confused, Van Camp instructed Jeff to, "Come back. If you find something, it would be good for the rest of us to know about it. Don't you think?"

The group had a plan. Not a very complicated plan, but they were fearful of this plan just the same. They were fearful of the unknowns that awaited them.

Without any ceremonial fan fair, long good byes, etc, they separately made their way to their cars, all except for Ben.

For those that thought that he had no one at home waiting for him, which was why he decided to wait, they all were wrong. From his point of view, a place this size must have plenty of purses under, on, and in the desks. He would have two hours to search them out, and he would find them with no one to catch him in the act. His first full day out of prison was already a payday for him.

Burt, the professional driver, was the first off the lot. Kitty, Alice, Jerry, and Eddie soon followed him. Behind them was Steven in front of Jeff, Joe-Joe, and then the Brown brothers.

At the end of the line was Lisa with Van Camp last. It was his intention to be the last off the lot, but he was not counting on Lisa taking so much time, herding her way to her car.

Again, Van Camp wanted to be the last one to leave. And if anyone was going to be the captain of a ship, he was qualified. Also, he did not want to appear too anxious, in his departure.

Once out of the parking lot, there was only one road out to the main highway. This road was not an interstate, limited access road, but a four lane rural road with a grass medium. Route 13 to be exact, which ran north and south in Delaware.

To turn left, or north, there was a traffic light. For anyone turning right, it was a simple task of yielding into the southbound traffic lane. Most everyone had stopped at the light, as they were the ones heading towards Glasgow, Newark, and Wilmington.

For Steven, Alice, Rose Marie, and Jeff, they headed south and entering the highway was not a big deal. In fact, there was no traffic for them to blend into for southbound.

The first to reach the light was Burt, and being a professional driver, he pulled right up to, but not on, the white strip that indicated where one would stop for a light to allow pedestrians to cross and to give incoming traffic adequate room to make the turn. This light was red for a very long time. In fact, it was red for such a long time, that Burt started to inch up as if this would hurry things along for him. No traffic was on the road, as nothing was going north or south on Route 13, and that made the time waiting for the light to change seem even longer.

With no traffic on the road, no one had yet to comprehend the significance. For the group heading south with Steven in the lead, Steven started to notice the high number of cars that had pulled over to the side of the road and left abandoned. With that many cars deserted, there should be a few people milling around he thought.

Trying to reason this out, it seemed that the population was evacuated and placed on buses to cut down on the number of cars on the road. The longer he drove, the more cars there were on the shoulder. With the cars pulled over neatly as they were, it did give the impression that his perceived evacuation was orderly. Alice, who was behind Steven, also noticed the abandoned cars, trucks, and vans along side the road. She slowed down a little and tried desperately to see if anyone was walking around. In doing this, she was not watching where she was going and by the time she looked forward, she had almost crashed into Steven. Jeff, on the other hand, was looking for people as well as keeping an eye on the car in front of him. Even with that, he almost ran into Alice.

At the next red light, Jeff pulled up along side of Alice and asked, "You okay?"

She rolled down her window and answered, "Yes and no. Where is everybody?"

Steven noticed that the two were talking and wanted to be a part of the conversation. He pushed in the hazard light button and exited his car. He headed between the two of them and asked, "What's up?"

Alice spoke first, and said, "No people, there are still no people around."

Steven, before he responded, gave one more look around. "No. Nobody. I don't see anything but a bunch of empty cars on the side of the road."

Jeff added, "Looks like everyone just pulled over and disappeared."

Before Alice started to cry, Steven suggested, "My guess is that everyone was evacuated. You know, a bus pulled up and everyone got onboard. No need to fill the highway with a lot of cars when a few buses can do the trick."

Jeff and Alice took Steven at his word. That just had to be the answer as there could be no other. Alice reasoned in her head that if this was the 'End Times,' that there would be some people left behind.

With nothing more to discuss, Steven got back in his car and after looking both ways, he ran the red light.

Alice, a little more hesitant, ran the light also along with Jeff close behind her.

Rose Marie did not get out of her car to join in on their little chat. Just as she was about to do so, Stephen returned to his car. After everyone ran the light, Rose Marie followed their example.

Back at R.E.A. International, Ben made a few desk checks, looking for anything of value before heading back to the lobby. He found nothing worth stealing, as he had no need for supplies of paper clips, pens, and staples. He believed that with the absence of purses, as they were usually found in bottom desk drawers, that everyone had simply left the building instead of disappearing into thin air.

Once back at the lobby, he looked up at the TV and noticed that the same commercial from Countrywide was still repeating. With nothing to do until they returned, he moved a few chairs around for comfort and decided to take a nap. In the back of his mind, he wondered if they would return, with good and or bad news. If not, hopefully, an employee would certainly return to work. Then again, if no one came back, then he would have a good shot of getting a job as he was the only one of out of fourteen that was still here.

At the light, seven cars sat patiently for the light to change. Burt was in the first car with Van Camp taking up the rear. Between them, in order, was Kitty who was fixing her hair in the rear view mirror.

She was followed by Jerry, Eddie, Joe-Joe, the Brown brothers, and Lisa.

Burt was getting restless with the length of the light. He believed that with no traffic on the road, that it did not matter if he ran the light or not, however, the last thing he wanted on his driving record, was a ticket. On the other hand, not only was there no traffic, there were no cops. That argument seemed to satisfy him, but on the flip side, if he did run the light, he would be the only car on the road and most easily to notice and catch. With that reasoning, he sat in place.

Everyone behind him seemed content to wait, a little longer. The Brown brothers had no patience and wanted Burt to, just run the damn light. From where they were located, they could clearly see that there was no traffic. So why wait?

Billy Bob said to Bob Billy, "Just go around them. That light ain't gonna not change."

Bob Billy did not answer; he merely pulled to the right and drove on down the shoulder. At the light, side by side with Burt, he yelled over to him, "For us. We are out of here."

Before Burt could respond, they had crossed the road and headed north on 13. Joe-Joe followed the brothers and did the same. When he came alongside Burt, nothing was said, as Burt headed north across the intersection.

While Joe-Joe spent time looking both ways, Kitty and Jerry crossed the road ahead of him. Because he did not want to be left behind, Joe-Joe shot across the highway. This was followed quickly by Eddie, Lisa and after coming to a complete stop; Van Camp made his way north after running the light.

This loosely placed convoy was now headed north on 13. They all noticed the same things as the southbound group observed, that the cars had pulled over to the side with no one in sight.

The Brown brothers were flying on down the highway, with one driving and the other looking around for anybody. For a mile or two, nothing was said as they both saw the same thing, much of nothing, and no one.

Bob Billy slowed down and started to spend more time looking than driving. He said, "Ain't nobody here."

"Don't like it man. This is scary," responded Bob Billy.

Burt, who never went over the speed limit, had slowed down a little to spend more time looking around. He was impressed with the idea that everyone had pulled over and left their vehicles off the road completely. From his thinking, it appeared that this was a well-coordinated, planned exodus.

Kitty, Jerry, Eddie, Joe-Joe, along with Lisa, drove and looked, and drove some more, and looked. Each were thinking to themselves as to what had happened. Everything from the End-Times, alien abductions, to some kind of weapons that vaporized everyone, after allowing them to pull over, and park their cars, to a huge magic trick.

Joe-Joe spent time remembering the last time that he got high, hoping that his mind was playing tricks on him.

For Van Camp, the longer he drove without seeing anyone, the more he imagined that he could be the new leader of the world. He spent more time daydreaming about his acceptance speech than his driving and looking for human life. It didn't really matter to him where everyone was, just that this was a good time to spend on his first set of rules, or laws, that he would impose on those that were left behind, or just plain left out. His current situation was not under his control, but his future situation would be.

For this group of travelers, this will be a long, lonely drive home.

CHAPTER 11

HOME ALONE

Alice was the first to arrive at her home. As expected, no one was there. She immediately went to her phone and hoped for messages, and there were none. She quickly turned on the TV expecting to see CNN or Fox News reporting on today's stories. She had cable TV with over 250 channels and the only thing that came across on all the channels that she checked, was the same screen, with the message, 'We are having technical difficulties. Please stand by.'

She said to the TV, "No, no, no. Give me something."

For Alice, this was panic time. She went back to her phone and started to call everyone she knew, beginning with family members. As expected, the phone either went to voice mail or just kept on ringing.

A few more calls, and to the ones out of state, she received the recorded message of, 'All phone lines are busy at the present time, please try your call again later.'

With this news, she started to shake uncontrollably. Quickly, she took a seat on her couch with her phone in one hand and the remote for her TV in the other. As her shaking came under control, she kept redialing her children's numbers and changing channels on the TV desiring to make a connection with anybody, somebody, soon.

Jeff headed back to his job because he had only taken ½ day off for this interview. He did not see the need to head home first, or to even head home at all. He knew he had to work the second half of the day and his job was more important than seeing if anyone was at his house. If his parents were there, they knew that he would not be home until the normal time.

He pulled into the parking lot where he worked and noticed that there was the normal number of cars there. Other than no one on the streets or in the parking lot, his workplace seemed like a typical workday.

It was not until he made his way to the second floor, passed the empty reception desk, did he really appreciate the seriousness of his problem. No one, not one person was at their desks working away on their computers. The conference rooms were empty as well as the break areas. His workplace always had people running around, even on weekends.

"Houston, we have a problem," he said aloud to himself, hoping for a response before he made his way to his desk to check his e-mail and voice mail.

No voice mails, but he did have the usual assortment of spam e-mails. He would not normally open the spam ones, but today he did. Not sure why, but it seemed to be the logical thing to do. As Burt was driving and looking, he viciously scanned up and then down on his satellite radio. Not a thing other than the message, 'Acquiring signal,' was displayed.

Even without traffic, he continued to cross intersections with caution. Others in his convoy would pass him, but for Burt, he was going to follow the rules.

All the empty vehicles on the side of the road gave him something odd to think about while driving. If the keys were still in them, then why not upgrade. You could simply drive around in the vehicle of your choice, and instead of filling up on gas, select another one. Besides, in his mind, any car with the keys inside simply gave you permission to steal them. Certainly, Burt did not think that to be such a great idea.

Burt arrived at his apartment in a few minutes. As expected, there was no one around. Before he walked into his building, he gave a quick glance towards the park across the street. The small playground there always had children playing with their parents close by. Today, nothing, not a single child or parent in sight.

He opened his mailbox expecting to see his electric or phone bill. They always came in about the same time and they were supposed to be there today, they were not.

In his one bedroom apartment, there was nothing waiting on him. No family members or pets and he did not have an answering machine to check.

Burt turned on the TV and while it warmed up, he made a trip to the bathroom. Next, and before sitting down to watch TV, he grabbed a can of Diet Coke from the frig. He did not have cable or satellite TV, but large rabbit ears that could pick up Philadelphia stations to the north, and with some movement to the antenna, he could tune in to a few Baltimore stations to the south. Today, there was nothing but static as he checked all the channels. He thought that there might the emergency notification broadcast that would flash by like when bad weather was approaching.

He made a number of calls, including some 911 and 0 for the operator, but no success. With the logical things to do out of the way, he took a seat on his balcony to clear his head.

Kitty arrived at her apartment where she had a roommate. The roommate would not be home at this time of the day. She hoped that today, she would be there.

She gave her roommate a call at her job and only received the normal, 'I am here today, but I am away from my desk or on another line. Your call is important to me, so please leave a message at the tone. If you need immediate attention, press one.'

Kitty pressed one for the operator and as expected, she did not get an answer. With the way things had been going for her today, she was not surprised. Even though she knew the results, she made a few calls to family and friends and as expected, zero, zip, zilch, nada.

The TV was turned on and as expected, zero, zip, zilch, nada. She made a trip to her bedroom that had two windows on different walls. This way, she was able to see out two directions, east, and south. She looked for traffic, people and for anything else, which might move. started thinking that if, everyone was gone, that there might be a fire burning, out of control, somewhere in a city this size, again, zero, zip, zilch, nada

Lisa was not only looking at all the ca rs and trucks on the side of the road, but also looking for a Dunkin' Donuts. Being alone was one thing, but being alone and hungry was not acceptable. However, those two items were very acceptable, as additional bitching material.

At the first Dunkin' Donuts, they had the doors locked. There were a few cars there, but no one around and no one inside. She bitched her way back to the car and headed out seeking another donut place. She had a mission, not one to fine people, but one to find food.

A few blocks later, she found one and it was unlocked and empty. Behind the counter, she began to place one of each kind of donut in a large bag. She did not want to waste time boxing up the boxes, as this was a grab and bag operation.

She filled a second bag with bottles of sodas making, it a point not to take any diet ones. She was disappointed that they did not have any Jolt sodas left.

Back at her apartment, this bag lunch, turned out to be lunch, and dinner. She wanted very much to finish off what she had, because donuts would not be good enough to eat later. Half way into her bag of dozens of donuts, she toyed with the idea of stopping, but figured, why. If no one were around to make more, then tomorrow the world would be out of donuts. That was about as sad to her as not having anyone else around.

After she was stuffed and with layers of sugar on her lips, chin, and all ten fingers, she decided to plop herself down into her double wide recliner that was motorized to recline. The motor did not need to work as hard to recline her chair back, however, when it came time to get up, the motor would struggle a little, but in the end, would bring the seat back to the upright position.

She reached for the TV remote and was unable to hang onto it. Her sugar-stained fingers were not able to grasp it securely and it landed on the floor. It would be a simple thing for her to motorize the chair up for her to get out and to retrieve the remote, but she knew that once she got back into her chair, that it would be five minutes or more before the motor would be cool down enough to safely move her fat ass again. With little regards for cleanliness, or to watch TV, she took a nap with dirty hands, lips, and chin and without an update about life on earth.

Jerry returned home and knew that his mom would be there and that his dad would be at work, yet, in the driveway, both family cars were there. His first thoughts were that what ever happened, that his dad had hurried home to be with his mom. With that thinking, he was thrilled that the first two people he saw that were not gone, would be his parents.

Inside his house, no one was around. Each time that he yelled for his mom or dad, there was no response. The TV was left on, and so were most of the lights, but no family.

The absence of people on his way home, was a minor thing. With his parents gone, and gone without leaving a note, this was a major, big time problem for him. He found himself alone from his parents and knew then that he should have paid them more attention and to what they were trying to tell him.

He called their cell numbers with a planned speech on how much he loved and appreciated them. However, when he called his Dad's number, it rang and rang. While it was ringing and ringing, he heard a phone on the kitchen table ringing. He ran to it and answered it excitedly, "Hello!"

It was his Dad's phone. He had his Dad's phone, but no Dad.

Jerry then dialed his Mom's cell. Same thing, when it did ring, his Mom's phone was on top of the microwave. Like with his Dad, he had his Mom's cell phone, but no Mom.

It was not like either one of them to leave the house without their cell phones. It was as important to them as taking your car keys. Not only did he not know the whereabouts of his parents, he had no way of contacting them.

With a need for something to do, other than crying, Jerry dialed his home number using his cell. Thinking that if, someone was home, and that he missed them, that they would hear the phone and answer. If not that, that there would be a phone message for anyone that called. There was nothing, no answer, and no messages. At this point, he had no idea of what to do next.

Eddie, after a few miles north on 13, pulled over to the side of the road. Steven noticed this and pulled in behind him. Eddie was initially headed towards Patuxent River Naval Air Station, but decided to turn around and head towards Dover. Dover Air Force Base was much closer and he had seen enough of empty roads.

As he looked in his review mirror to make his U-turn, he noticed that Steven was walking up to his car. The car was then placed in park, followed by the rolling down of his window.

Steven looked in, and asked, "You okay?"

"Yeah. I was heading back to Pauxent River Naval Air Station, but decided to head down to Dover instead."

"Patuxent River," questioned Steven.

"Patuxent River Naval Air Test Center, down in Southern Maryland. I was discharged from the Coast Guard the other day."

"No shit!"

"Really," said Eddie, with a surprise look.

"You didn't notice my haircut," joked Steven.

"Not really, but remember, I've been around those buzz cuts for years now," responded Eddie.

"I was a marine. I got out the other day. Same place, Patuxent River.

Both men seemed pleasantly surprised to have a fellow military buddy in the same boat. Yet, they did not remember that they meet yesterday, same haircut or not.

"Shit man," announced Steven. "I was heading towards Patuxent River Naval Air Station also, but I like your idea better about Dover."

"You can follow me or hop in," suggested Eddie.

Steven thought for a minute, and answered, "I'll follow you down. We might need to have our own cars when we get there." "No sweat. Stay on my six and we should be there in thirty minutes."

Steven gave him the thumbs up and headed back to his car. The two of them made a U-turn and proceeded south on 13 towards Dover.

Thirty minutes later, they turned left onto the base and approached the main gate driving slowly side-by-side. The gate was unmanned and opened.

Steven stopped first, just short of the gate. Eddie pulled closer to him and with their windows rolled down; Steven said with concern, "There are always marines at the gate. Where are they?"

Eddie did not say a word; he looked around anticipating armed guards rushing them with weapons drawn.

They stayed in place, neither one wanting to be the first to drive onto a military base without permission. They had both thought that if people were anywhere, that they would be here. Not necessary civilians, but a military base should be active, very active with military personnel.

Steven looked over at Eddie and said, "I'm heading in. Need to find HQ. If no one is there, we should head towards the control tower next."

"Agree, but let's drive slowly. No need to have anyone thinking that we are the bad guys. Know what I mean."

Steven shook his head yes and took the lead. Eddied pulled in behind him, but not too close. Finding HQ was easy as the base had roadside directional signs clearly marked.

It was almost a five-minute drive to cover the distance from the main gate to HQ, driving slowly, at ten miles an hour. They both pulled right up and parked in two spots that were marked for flag officers only. No one exited right away, but spent time looking into each window and doorway. They saw nothing at all. They were expecting gun barrels peering out each window, but there were none.

After a long minute or so, Steven exited his car and stayed in place after closing his door. Eddie on the other hand, stayed in his car and laid on the horn.

The horn scared Steven for a second, but after he recovered, he responded by opening his car door and laying on his horn.

Thirty seconds or so, they stopped and waited for something to happen. Nothing did.

Eddie got out of his car and joined up with Steven. Nothing was said as they walked side by side to the main door. In the lobby, there were plenty of flags, photographs on the walls of military personnel, a well-polished floor, a number of clocks on the wall indicating times from around the world, but no people. With little reason to hang around, they made their way to the control tower. No need to search for signs for directions, as the control tower was the tallest building on base.

At the control tower, they were met with the same results, no guards on duty.

Eddie asked, "Heading up?"

Steven pointed up, and asked, "Way up there?"

"Yes sir, even if no one is up there, there will be plenty of radios." Steven, not wanting Eddie to be in charge of this operation,

added, "Yeah, we will also have a great view of the area. We'll be able to check a lot out from up there."

Eddied smiled approval and headed towards the stairway. Up in the control tower, there were plenty of radios. The ones that were turned on, had nothing except for a lot of static.

Steven picked up a pair of binoculars and began systematically to scan the base. Eddie found a pair of his own and joined in with the search. Both men knew the importance of a through check, and a most through check was performed.

"See anything," asked Eddie.

"Nope. Didn't expect that I would."

"Me to. After we drove thirty minutes on a major road and not seeing anything, I didn't think that we would find anything here."

"Got anybody you want to call," Eddie asked after a few more minutes of scanning the base.

"Yeah. I'm going to try to call Patuxent River. Just maybe I'll get an answer."

Steven made his way over to a desk and took a seat. After making a few unsuccessful calls to Patuxent River, he slammed the phone down.

"Let me guess," joked Eddie. "Nobody was home."

"You have any ideas on this," asked Steven.

"No. Not a single idea at all. If you were to tell me about this, I'd think that you were crazy."

Steven said with hope in his voice, "If one of us had a pilot's license, we could fly our way out of here. Don't know where we would go, but away from this area for sure."

With disappointment, Eddie suggested, "Maybe we should report back to R.E.A. International to see if any of them had better luck."

"I'll need some gas first before we head back." Steven answered sounding defeated.

Joe-Joe made it home without incident. His first action was to view the tapes that he had set to record this morning while he was at the interview. As assumed, and with disappointment, the tapes had recorded nothing but a blank screen, as if the VCR channel was set in error. He presumed, whatever happened, it happened on or before 10am.

His next move was to view all the channels on the TV and radio attempting to pick up any signal. Nothing, the airwaves were empty. Not even that one station that you would always pick up from some preacher out west talking about the End Times. Maybe his time was up also.

His next move, the same as the others had done, was to make a few cursory calls to other family members and friends. Again, without success. There was only one thing that he could do successfully right now, and that was to fix himself something to eat. With a little scrapple and two eggs, lunch was only minutes away. Cooking took his mind off life and TV and this was a good time for it.

The Brown brothers lived together in public housing in Wilmington, DE. They took care of a very little, two-bedroom apartment. When they moved in, the walls needed fixing and painting. The tile around the shower needed to be replaced and they took it upon themselves to do the fixing and repairing on their own. The superintendent of the building would often display their apartment to anyone that wanted either to move in, or to do a story for the news or completing a government report about public housing.

In this building, and in this neighborhood, people were everywhere 24/7. There were always a small crowd around the main front door and lobby. There never was a time that you rode the elevator without someone else.

Not today. As with the 20-minute drive from Middletown to Wilmington, no one was around. Billy Bob mentioned, "There is a good side to all of this."

"Like what," asked his brother.

"Today, today there were no shootings."

Bob Billy could only respond with a smile. He knew how true and sad that was. As security guards as a profession, they kept up to date with the crimes in their building. Most everyone who knew them, knew that they legally carried guns and had no problem with defending himself, or anyone else nearby that needed assistance from the bad guys. Shortly after they moved in, crime dropped and stayed down.

"If this is true and does not change, then you and I are out of a job," Bob Billy added.

This only got a nod from Billy Bob as the two of them walked into the lobby and pressed the button for the elevator. A habit of theirs was not to face the elevator door while waiting, but to turn around to scan the area, an old security guard habit. Only this time, it was hard to scan effectively as they had no one to scan.

"Going to miss this place little brother," said Billy Bob.

Bob Billy, answered with, "Remember when we first moved here, the toilet kept running and our car would not start."

Billy Bob, did not respond, he was busy holding back tears.

It was a quick ride to the 22nd floor and once in their apartment, they knew that there was nothing for them to do there after they made a few calls, but to return.

Van Camp pulled into the driveway at his townhouse and opened the automatic garage doors. Instead of pulling into his garage, as he normally did, he decided to leave his car in the driveway. This way, if anyone were around, they would see his car and possibly search him out.

Exiting his car, he took a slow look around, and the same as every place else, no one. Not even the barking dog that was always in his neighbor's window when anyone was in front of his house.

He took a few steps, stopped, and looked around again. Not really expecting to see anyone, but he did not want to miss anything either.

As he habitually did, Van Camp performed his 'return home rituals.' Check for mail, pick up the newspaper, turn on the TV, and look for the red, blinking light on his answering machine. Today, there was no mail, no newspaper, and no blinking red light indicating messages.

For Van Camp, this was just as strange as not seeing anyone around. He had always gotten a daily newspaper, always gotten mail, and there were always messages on his answering machine. Mostly, the messages on his answering machine were from telemarketers. He made it a point not to have his number added to the national, Do Not Call, registry. He liked getting the calls, so that he could take charge and tell them 'no.'

Being that he was widowed with no children, and having no other living family members, he had no one to call. There were the few friends and previous co-workers that he could call, but he did not want to call them. No need to have them know that he had no idea what was going on.

Turning on the TV was his next move. He had satellite TV and the only thing on his screen was the message, "Trying to connect to a satellite. Hit ENTER, to cancel."

He made his way to the kitchen and walked out onto his back deck. He did the same as he did out front; he looked around slowly and saw no one. Once back inside, he sat in front of his TV and stared at it for a little while expecting a connection to the satellite, expecting it to happen just because he was there.

Van Camp is lost. With no mail to read, no paper to peruse, and not a single phone message to delete, he had to decide what to do next.

All the way home, Rose Marie was crying. Yes, the world was empty of people, and she had hoped that all of her previous co-workers went first, to wherever it was that they were taken too and that they had suffered. She did not care how or how much they suffered, but only that they suffered something.

It did not cross her mind that anything had happened to her cats because she believed that whatever happened, happened only to people. With the world empty of people and with her being left behind with only her three cats, life would be just fine. As she drove home, if the lights were red, she would stop, look both ways, and proceed. Other than going around a few abandon cars left in the driving lane, her drive home was nothing special.

The only things special to her right now were, in no particular order, Grace, Dulcinea, and Dahlia.

For Rose Marie, this was the first time in many years that she entered her home and found that the cats were not there to greet her. Even with the doors locked, they were still gone. She did not know what she missed most, the cats being gone, or no one there to greet her. The complete absence of the friendly appreciative sounds of cats purring was easily missed.

She realized that calling their names would not make things better, she called for them anyway. Rose Marie was under the small, very small, hope that they were there, hiding or that they had not gotten to her yet.

Even with the facts clearly stacked against her, she still had to take a quick tour of the house. Maybe something would give an answer as to what happened. Not necessarily to everyone here in Delaware, but possibly what happened to her cats, her feline friends.

As disappointingly expected, nothing was out of place. Food and water bowls were at normal levels; their toys were spread around the rooms as if they were here all day, playing. They were simply gone and that was something that Rose Marie was now struggling to comprehend.

After a very methodical search of her home, followed by a second thorough search, Rose Marie came to terms that they were gone, not dead, but gone. With no reason to stay home, alone, she packed a few things, and headed back to R.E.A. International.

Trying to find something good about this situation, she surmised that by not finding her three cats, that there was the possibility that they were very much alive. Second, by not finding their bodies, that there would be no need to bury three more cats next to the one that just died, and was recently buried.

With the situation the way it was, she hung up her interview suit and dressed in comfortable jeans and top. Of course, it was a sweatshirt top with a photo of her cats on the back. Along with a few personal items that she packed into an overnight bag, she included a bag of cat treats. This was in the event that she came across her cats, or if she had to settle for any cat, or even a stray one or two.

CHAPTER 12

THE RETURN TRIP

Back at R.E.A. International, Ben has completed his second search for money and other items of value. It was now time to go back to the lobby area to wait for the return of the others. He had found a few purses and some cash. Not sure where or how he would spend it, but it was the thrill of stealing.

In addition, he found a few set of car keys. The ones that had key-pods and were recognizable, he took.

With cash in hand, along with some car keys, He made it to the parking lot to find himself a car or two. It was a simple task to set off the alarm, and then find the car.

His first hit was a minivan. Nope, that would not do. Next, he found a Ford F150 old piece of crap pickup truck. On his third hit, he lucked out with a Chevy Malibu. A nice Malibu, and now it was his.

Jeff after opening and reading his e-mails, figured that there was no reason to head home. No one will be there anyway and he might as well head back to R.E.A. International.

After he returned to his car for the drive back, he drove around the building parking lot twice; just on the slim chance that he might see someone as alone as he was. At this time, it was confirmed in his mind that he was alone. With the need to be with other people, Jeff headed on back.

The drive for Rose Marie was almost uneventful. With no traffic to fool with, only the occasional car abandoned in the driving lane, she made good time. She was a good driver with a clean record of any accidents or tickets, not even a parking ticket. However today, right now, she was not totally focused on her driving. If there were the normal traffic to maneuver around, she probably would have crashed.

Every time she passed an animal place of business, she broke into tears and lost focus on her driving, almost driving into a few parked cars on more than one occasion.

She had never noticed before just how many animal businesses there were. Just between her place and R.E.A. International, there were two animal hospitals, one animal wellness center, an animal insemination service, one animal shelter, two places for animal training, one animal removal service, and a place for pet adoptions, pet boarding, a pet cemeteries and crematories, and pet breeders. Not to forget the pet supply stores, pet grooming, and a billboard sign for pet photographers, with pet health care plans, pet nutrition's, and plenty of pet shops to buy supplies and more pets. Another billboard for pet sitting and exercising services, and a pet transporting company. And of course, there was cable TV, with the animal channel and the pet physic.

Every time she saw anything about animals, she thought about her little family of cats. Even when she tried to focus on something else, it did not help. She had thought about going to the grocery store for a few items but remembered that aisle 6 at the Acme, was entirely for animals. On one side, strictly for dogs, and the other side, for cats. Other pet supplies, like birds and fancy rats, had another aisle of their own.

With her needing a few items, she decided not to visit the Acme, but to venture into Happy Harry's for a few girl items. That was almost a success until she passed the book section and noticed books on cat breeding, dog care and dog stories. Quickly she left that aisle and headed to another where she came across pet supplies. Animal brushes, shampoos, nail cutters, and even a box of dental cleaning supplies. Even with her having good cats, they would scratch her up if she ever tried to floss their teeth. Yet, just to have her cats with her would be well worth the scratches. With girl supplies stashed into her purse, she headed out of Happy Harry's for the last few miles back to R.E.A. International. For the remainder of the drive, she looked only at the road ahead, not wanting to see anything else that was animal related. This worked out fine until she passed two signs, one warning about a deer crossing ahead with a second sign about duck crossings.

Steven pulled up to the base gas station with Eddie right behind him. Both men filled their tanks as they continued to scan the area without saying a word.

With their tanks topped off, they drove a little faster this time towards the main gate. Steven took the lead as they headed north on 13 towards R.E.A. International.

Alice had spent so much time redialing and changing the channels on the TV, that her hands and fingers started to ache. She knew that if she kept this up any longer, that blisters would soon form on her fingertips.

Again, she started to shake uncontrollably. It was at this point that she eased back on her sofa and fell into a short nap. She did not pass out, just fell slowly back, and closed her eyes, which resulted in her body shutting down for a short time.

An hour passed and she awakened in a most confused state. It was still daylight outside, but it was as quiet as nighttime. After a trip to the bathroom and a review of her situation, she made herself a cup of coffee, resumed the redialing, and channel surfing without success.

She wanted to stay put here, in her house anticipating a call from her children, as they would surly be checking up on her. However, after thirty minutes of redialing, an hour nap, followed by another thirty minutes of redialing, it appeared to be hopeless.

Alice then washed her face, redid her makeup, and headed back.

Burt had had enough of this isolation. He did not mind living alone, but this was not what he had in mind. He changed his clothes into something more comfortable, and decided to make his way back to R.E.A. International. In just ten minutes, he was already out the door and heading south on 13.

Kitty, not wanting to be alone, and with the knowledge that back at R.E.A. International, she would have company. She grabbed her overnight case, packed it with some clean underwear and makeup.

It was not but a few minutes later that she had left a note for her roommate, was packed, and out the door.

For the drive back, she took her time and made a stop at Starbucks. She made enough coffee to fill the large 32-ounce cup, and it did not cost her a thing. In the past, she could not afford the 32-ounce cup of her favorite brew, but today, she had one.

With coffee in hand and static on the car radio, she headed back.

Jerry knew that returning to R.E.A. International was his only logical next step. He hoped that others had better results than he did, or at the very least, someone had an answer about the whereabouts of the people in this area.

He grabbed a soda and his car keys along with his cell, and headed back to join the others.

Joe-Joe completed his meal, washed up the dishes, and did another look at his TV with no improvements from earlier. His decision of what to do next was simple, head back towards a place that had people. This was not his choice of a group of people to be with, he would have picked another group of people, but this way, he would not be alone. The only drawback was, that there was only one TV, with one channel, for everyone to watch.

With nothing to do, the brothers changed into more comfortable clothes and shoes. Without saying a word, they retrieved their handguns along with some shells. They each had an ankle holster on their right leg with additional ammo in their left leg ammo holster. The brothers had no idea on what they could anticipate, but needed to be prepared.

Back outside, they made a pit stop at the first gas station that they passed on their side of the street. Not expecting anyone to monitor what he or she was doing, Billy Bob filled the tank while Bob Billy stood in front of the license tag. He figured that if anyone was to report them for stealing gas, that it would be harder to do if they were unable to read the tag off any security cameras that might be around filming.

With a full stomach and an hour nap, Lisa was ready to bitch to the world. She is ready to start bitching about the expected donut shortage. And now, she has no one to bitch at, and that is a bitch-able item. She did bitch a little to the TV because there was nothing on any of the channels. She bitched a little more when she found out that the Food channel was bare.

She made a few additional phone calls with predictable results. Then it was decision time, as she had to decide to bitch some more to herself, or to head back to R.E.A. International and bitch at those that were there.

Going back there made more sense and she knew that she would be passing the same donut shop on her return. Only this time, she would take two bags of donuts. She supposed that if she had to share them once she got back, that there would be plenty.

Being without direction, to give or take, Van Camp was out of place with reality. The only thing that he could plan was to return to R.E.A. International and to join back with the team, if anyone came back. Not his first or even second choice, but he had no other choices. To say at home without mail, newspapers, phone calls, and TV, would make him very lonely. Besides, he would need someone to boss around that would appreciate his ability too effectively manage.

Thinking of what to do next was a good plan. He set out to pack a suit case with what he believed would last him a few days.

A nice suit with a power tie was first to be packed along with business casual slacks, golf shirt, and a few business cards.

Within thirty minutes, Van Camp was on his way back to R.E.A. International.

CHAPTER 13

THE REUNION

B EN LOOKED AT HIS WATCH. He did not know why he kept looking at it, as he had nowhere to go anyway. Maybe it was because he was anticipating the return of some of the interviewees. Yet, somehow, in his mind, he needed to have an idea as to when he would leave and head out himself, if no one did come back.

Then, giving this some more thought, he figured that if no one came back, that they disappeared also? Then what, would it be better for him to stay where he was, alive, rather than to venture outside to an unknown fate?

Granted, it had only been a little more than an hour, but he was getting restless. In prison, killing time was not very easy, but you did it with plenty of people around. Funny, he thought, how he wanted so much at times in prison just to be left alone, with a little peace and quiet. Now, here he had all the peace and quiet one man could take, and nothing that he could do about it. He could not con his way out of this situation. He looked at his watch again and just sighed.

Kitty was the first to return. She entered the lobby and noticed that Ben was the only one there. This frightened her, and it clearly showed on her face. She did not trust the way he looked at her while she was with a group, and now, they were alone.

Ben, accustomed to making women fearful of him, felt bad this time. He responded to her with a big innocent smile and made it a point not to approach her. That disarmed her slightly, but she kept up her guard.

"What did you see while you were gone," he questioned, from where he was.

Regaining her composure, but keeping her distance, she recounted her trip home and back without much detail.

Wanting to defuse her even more, he said to her, "I stayed here because I don't have any living relatives to call or visit."

He made it a point to look sad and continued, "I'm from out of state, and left all my friends phone numbers back at my place. With nowhere to go, I wanted to wait here. You are the first one back."

Relaxed a little more, but cautious, she took a seat near the door and did her best to hold back the tears. She felt alone now and started to cry a little.

Before he could ask anything else of her, or to make a comment to ease her crying, Burt arrived. Burt relayed the details of his trip to them and found it to be disappointing that Kitty had the same results.

Then Ben and Burt moved and sat next to Kitty as her crying continued. Kitty looked up at them and asked, "Do you think anyone else will come back?"

Burt answered with,"They should if they found out what we found. No way would I want to be out there very much alone. No way. I'd come back here for sure."

Kitty and Ben looked at him in agreement.

Next to return was Van Camp. He had anticipated that with his return, that everyone would be there already. This way, he could make an entrance appropriate of a leader. However, with just the three of them, he would deal with it in a different way. He would simply, and skillfully, change his plan of action to welcome back and interrogate each one as they return. Either way, he would emerge as their leader.

Burt and Kitty compared their stories with Van Camp as he explained it in more detail than was needed. No one cared about his mailing address, the size of his house, the grand view from his deck, and that he packed another suit and brought it with him. Jeff came in next with Joe-Joe close behind him. Van Camp directed them where to sit, leaving him in the only chair that faced the group. For him, it would be easier to control the group with all of them having to look his way.

Van Camp asked Jeff, and then Joe-Joe, if they would briefly describe their events. Before they could start, Jerry and Alice walked in and sat down behind Van Camp. This unsettled him, as he had to move his chair to a more prominent position of importance. Everyone noticed what he was doing and gave him no mind. Individually, they felt that it was just not important enough for anyone to be in charge of people repeating the same story to each other. They were not at school or work, and Roberts Rule just does not apply here. They were alone in the world right now and it was not the time to appoint a king.

Alice had a hard time saying anything, as she would break down and cry. Kitty placed her hand on her shoulder and said in a soft voice, "It will be okay. You are not alone on this. We all have the same story."

"But my children. What happened to my children," Alice asked, knowing that no one had an answer.

Van Camp did not care for the crying crap and spoke up to change the subject. "Has anyone else returned?"

"No man, just us. I've been here the whole time," answered Ben.

Jerry arrived right at that moment. He looked around at everyone expecting better news from them than what he had to share. However, the news was the same, no one saw anyone. Not even evidence of what might have happened.

For a moment, everything was quiet as no one had anything else to add. Nobody felt like adding more bad news, to their collection of bad news.

Right then, they all could hear the familiar sound herding down the hallway towards them. It was Lisa with her legs rubbing away very hard at each other as she plowed herself down the hallway.

Kitty and Alice paid it no attention, but the guys had a laugh between them. Van Camp thought it to be funny, but beneath him to laugh with the group. He would do so only around senior management and only then if the one most senior, laughed first.

She came in looking as tired as can be. Ben had hoped that she would not return, as he believed that she would just hold up anything they wanted to do. Then again, if they were going to starve and had to turn to cannibalism, she would certainly feed the whole group for a few days.

Once he noticed that she had donuts, he fell in love. Not with her, but with her donuts. Before she could fill anyone in on her trip home and back, he grabbed one of the bags out of her hand. He did this quickly, but he was not rude about it.

"Sorry," he explained. "I'm starving and I love donuts."

She plopped herself down at the nearest couch, took a deep breath, and said, "You are most welcome."

With both of his cheeks puffed out with a mouth full of donuts, he shook his head, indicating acceptance.

With Lisa still out of breath, listen as everyone gave bits and pieces of their little driving home adventure. She would just nod her head and commented, 'Same thing happened to me,' and 'yep, I saw the same thing, plenty of nothin.'

Overall, she was too tired, ticked off, and pissed to bitch about it. She just sucked down another donut.

Rose Marie came in and quietly sat down. She was not in the mood to share about her drive home, but was more interested to hear the stories of others. She felt that if she were to mention anything about her cats, that they might turn against her as they did at her last job. Besides, people here have lost family members, people family members, and not pet, family members. At least, it was not that big a deal to be looking as if she had been crying, as everyone had that look of having been crying, or the look of holding it back.

Walking in close behind her, came Billy Bob and his brother Bob Billy. Together, they explained the details on their trip home. Mostly on how vacant it was in town. As Bob Billy helped himself to a few donuts, Bob Billy asked if anyone had a different story.

Naturally, no one did and Van Camp, wanting to show that he could ask the important question, asked, "Are we still missing two guys?"

Everyone looked around trying to figure out who it was. Kitty was the first to respond. "Yeah, it was those two guys that had haircuts like they were police officers, or maybe they were in the military."

"I don't know their names, but you are right, we are missing two guys," Jeff added with Joe-Joe and Burt in agreement.

"I sort of wish they were here," explained Kitty. "You know, military guys know how to survive and all that. And if they are policemen, they could protect us."

"Protect us from whom, jokingly asked Ben, believing that she said that, because of him.

"Anyone bad, I guess," she answered with some embarrassment, not wanting to indicate him.

The subject was dropped as everyone compared notes between themselves about what was currently going on. When it was found out that Jeff went to work, and not home, it caught everyone off guard.

Alice felt anger towards him for she could not believe that anyone could be in this life-changing situation, and not go home. She made it a point not to say anything about it, but kept it to herself. It was okay that Ben had stayed, because he explained that he had no one in the area and that he was living alone.

Joe-Joe walked over to the TV and switched it on. Ben had turned it off earlier and Joe-Joe wanted to see if the commercial had worn itself out, or if anything else was on. This time, the TV was all-static. No sounds, no news, and no commercials, just static.

Van Camp stood up in front of the room and announced, "Does anyone have a suggestion on what to do next?"

Everyone looked at each other, believing that someone, besides them, had an idea, suggestions, or questions. They had as many ideas, suggestions, and questions as they saw people outside this room, zero.

"We'll need a place to stay tonight," Burt said aloud to the group, and he made it a point not to look at Van Camp.

"Someplace to eat," Lisa added, and then wished that she did not say that. Everyone gave her looks as if suggesting, just step outside and you can graze on the front lawn you fat cow.

No one there was picking on her because she was heavy; it was because she was so, unnaturally heavy. Some thought that anyone that big should be performing in a circus, or as a part of a research center.

Burt spoke up again, and suggested, "There is a hotel a few blocks from here. I believe that we should stay together. We should check in and get a room, followed by a good nights sleep."

Others in the group started to add in their approvals with nods, and saying 'yes, good idea,' as Van Camp attempted to move the conversation and decisions back towards him.

Before he could speak up, Jeff suggested, "Yeah, good idea. We can then meet in the hotel lobby first thing in the AM to discuss and decide what we are going to do next. No need to go home just to come back here. We should stay together."

Everyone agreed, and now, there was a plan. Van Camp wanting to get back into controlling the planning stage, said to the group, "9am. How does 9am sound for getting together tomorrow morning for a little meeting?"

"What about the other two guys," questioned Kitty?

Ben was just fine that they had not returned. He did not like the fact that one, or both of them, might be a cop. If he had his way, he would replace them with two girls that looked like Kitty. If you had to repopulate the world, might as well do it with young, hot looking chicks.

Van Camp was also okay with them not being there. No need to have any additional male competition than there needs to be, especially anyone that had jobs of authority and understood the management of people. If he had his way, he would replace them with two girls that looked, and had the maturity of Kitty, as young people were easily directed to follow instructions from anyone in authority.

Kitty and Alice both felt that no one should be left behind, especially if they could be helpful supporting the survival of the group. Without saying it, it was apparent that they wanted the safe return of those two.

Everyone else felt the same as Kitty and Alice. Jeff spoke up and said, "Let's give them sometime to get back."

Lisa wanted nothing more than to check into a hotel and get some rest. A good nights rest only after she checked out the kitchen to find the dessert tray, and to sample most of it before it goes bad. She only had a half-filled bag of donuts left and that would not last her too long.

"Why can't some of us find this hotel, and some of us wait here," Lisa asked the group. Like the others, she looked around at everyone and ignored on purpose, Van Camp.

Van Camp was quick to pickup on this and knew that he had to take a stand, and to take it right then. Quickly, he formatted a plan in his head that would be easily followed and clearly make it his own idea.

"I have a plan. What do you all think of this," he asked the group, while making it a point not to stand, trying not to give the impression that, he wanted to be in charge. Well, not in charge just yet.

"What do you have for us, old man," asked Bob Billy.

Van Camp did not like the title, 'old man,' but decided to deal with that later. "Why doesn't everyone just go and check into the hotel right now. I will stay here for a few hours and wait on them."

Not waiting for anyone to respond, and most importantly, to give something for Bob Billy and Billy Bob to do, he added while he pointed to them, "At the hotel, you guys can write down everyone's room number and leave it at the front desk. Also, next to each name and room number, write down their cell phone numbers." Bob Billy, not being to quick to catch this ploy, said, "Cool man. I can do that and I'll find a copy machine and give everyone a copy so that they can add the numbers to their cell phones." "We should have the ability to stay in contact with each other," Van Camp proclaimed.

He was happy that he scored a few points this time, continued with, "I like it," as if he needed everyone to know that he approved it.

Everyone was satisfied with this plan. It was not complicated and they would stick together. They would then have time alone, with everyone near by, to reflect on what was in store for them now.

"But before you go," he said looking at Bob Billy, "let me give you my name and cell number for our list." Van Camp was very pleased with himself for that quick action of his, because that should put his name on the top of the list.

Bob Billy now realized that he had been conned into doing something extra for Van Camp, and ended up allowing him to have all the credit. In the back of his mind, he made a mental note to create a new list, and to place his name at the bottom, with his name first, and his brother's name in second place.

Joe-Joe was the first to make his way to the door. It was not that he wanted to be first, he just wanted to get to his hotel room, so if he was unable to pick any TV shows, that he could order some movies to watch all night.

"Okay then, we have a plan," proudly announced Van Camp. He wanted to make it clear before everyone left him there, on his own.

A few of them acknowledge him as a planner, but everyone knew the plan, and that it was not all that complicated.

Slowly, they left the room with Lisa taking up the rear. The only thing that made Van Camp sad, as they all left the room, was not the fact that this might be the last time that he will ever see any of them again, but the fact that the last thing he saw was Lisa's big ass butt, swaying back and forth as she left the room.

Once everyone was outside, and in the hallway, instead of everything getting quiet as everyone left, Van Camp could hear some celebrating coming for the hallway. Believing that maybe they saw some people, he rushed out to the hallway to join them. In the hallway, Eddie and Steven had returned. As expected, everyone had asked them questions after questions, as if they were the only ones that made it outside and back. This went on for a few minutes until everyone was satisfied that they had nothing new to report, other than they had visited a military base, an empty military base. With this knowledge, it became more evident that something bad had happened to the state of Delaware,

if not, the United State, and if not that, then the whole world.

After Eddie and Steven were filled in with the plan, they agreed that this was a good idea that made sense. Their recognition and approval, gave the plan more credibility, at which prompted Van Camp to have the strong desire to say, 'that was my plan.' He decided not to say anything about it, but, he did make it a point to mention to them that he had volunteered to stay behind, and wait for their safe return.

Eddie looked over at him, and with some appreciation, thanked him. Steven only gave him the thumbs up, that no one else saw, but Van Camp, and that disappointed him. He wanted recognition that everyone would witness and remember.

They had directions on what to do next. Not complete directions because not everyone knew where this, near by hotel was.

CHAPTER 14

THE HOTEL

THEY ALL MADE THEIR WAY to their cars in the parking lot. Burt assumed that not everyone knew the location of the hotel. He figured that because he would be picking out a new car soon, he stood on the hood of his car, not worried if he were to scratch or put a dent in it. With the waving of his hands, he got the attention from everyone.

"If you don't know where we are going, pull in behind me," he announced.

Van Camp was pleased that Burt had done this, because he wanted to get to the hotel first, now that he does not need to stay behind waiting on those two guys. If he were to get there first, and beat the Brown brothers, he would be the one to find paper and pen, and start the name and phone number list. If he were able to complete the list, then he would be the only one in the group that could identify each person by name. Until now, no one had offered up his or her name. Van Camp was in his element now, his zone, he was taking names and kicking ass. Not to mention that he wanted time to select the nicest room, as that would be most appropriate for a manager in his position. By getting there first, he would be able to do all those things by multitasking.

In no time at all, the convoy of eleven cars had lined up without incident. With no other traffic to be concern about, getting in line, one behind the other, was a simple task. For some unknown reason, everyone had turned on their headlights, as if in a funeral procession.

Van Camp had already taken off. He did not wait around, as he knew; everyone wanted to get in behind Burt.

Ben, in his new Chevy Malibu, checked on how much gas was available, and then to set the radio to country/western.

The hotel, a Holiday Inn Express on Route 13, was a few blocks away on the southbound side. Van Camp moved quickly to the lobby and found paper and pen. He promptly headed up the line pad of paper with the headings, Name, Cell Number, and Room Number. His name was on the first available line, not leaving a chance that anyone with the last name that was before his alphabetically, would be on top of his.

His next task was to find a room key for himself, and he remembered that rooms in this type of hotel were all the same. Yet, he wanted to be special, so he looked at the hotel floor plan with room numbers, and selected for himself a room next to the lobby. If there were going to be any meetings or get-together, he wanted to be near the action.

As everyone started to arrive, he greeted him or her, as if he was at the head of a reception line. However, this backfired on him, because once he gave them his name, and asked theirs, everyone asked for their room number, as they thought that he should have assigned them a room. Van Camp did not believe that, that was his job, and that one of the girls should step up and be a receptionist, and to set that up for him.

The first thing that Rose Marie noticed was the sign on the front desk that stated, 'No pets.' For her, already she did not like this hotel. She asked herself, 'What if a blind person came in and needed a room for him and his Seeing Eye dog.'

She frowned a moment and then answered her own question, 'There would be no problem as the blind person would not be able to read the sign.' Okay she thought, this place might be acceptable for her.

Jeff, the computer guy, walked in behind the front desk and started to bang away at the keyboard. It appeared initially that he knew what he was doing, but in reality, he needed a password. By now, everyone had arrived in the lobby. Alice had made her way over to a bank of phones along side one wall and started to make a few calls. She realized that she still might not get anyone, but thought she would try anyway.

Jeff threw up his hands and admitted that he was unable to log into the hotel's system. "Sorry guys. Unable to get in."

Joe-Joe asked, "How will we know which rooms are available?"

Ben chuckled a little and answered him with, "And just who might that be? You think that everyone that we can't find has checked into this hotel?"

"Oh yeah. I see your point," he sheeplessly responded.

Van Camp saw an opportunity to take control and said as he held up a set of keys. "I believe that I have the master keys here."

He held them up and allowed everyone to see what he had and that what he had, would save the day.

"I'll check on a few rooms and find the ones that are already cleaned," he said. Then asked, "Anyone want to help?"

Kitty spoke right up, "I'll help you."

Van Camp looked pleased that she volunteered. He thought that she would be doing a woman's part in assisting him, and in reality, she wanted to first, pick a room that was near the lobby. She had no desire to be up on another floor, far from everyone.

Steven, Burt, and Eddie walked over to the gift shop that was opened and all lit up. Behind the counter, they looked for toiletries for their stay. Joe-Joe followed them in and found himself a copy of TV Guide.

The others took a seat in the lobby and were just happy that someone was getting them a room. The seriousness of their true situation had not hit them totally. Everyone felt that tomorrow, everything would be back in order and that just maybe, they were having a dream.

Alice completed her round of unanswered phone calls and took a seat with the others. Returning from the gift shop, Burt informed everyone what he had and why. Those who had not made a trip to the gift shop got up and did their own shopping.

By the time this shopping spree completed, Van Camp and Kitty returned. Van Camp allowed Kitty to read off the names and assigned room numbers. There were enough rooms available on the first floor for everyone.

Van Camp suggested, "When you do leave your room, don't let it lock behind you. Put something in the door way so it does not shut."

"Don't lock it," questioned Alice.

Seeing the fear in her eyes, Van Camp answered her with, "Only when you leave your room. Once you are inside, sure, lock it. I only found one master key."

She seemed fine with that answer. Kitty was shaking her head in agreement with Van Camp to reassure Alice.

Kitty added, "I'm going to make copies of this list for everyone."

For the group, the fundamentals were taken care of. They were together, they had a place to stay, and that they, sort of, knew each other.

Kitty returned from making copies and handed them out to everyone. The lobby seating area had the perfect set up for fourteen people to sit around in a group. There really was not a back row or a seat where you could not clearly see everyone.

Kitty was the last to sit down after she passed out the copies, she spoke up as if she was in charge, and said, "Why don't we go around the room and introduce ourselves."

Van Camp did not like the idea that Kitty took the initiative to start this, however, he did like it when she volunteered to walk with him to check on the rooms. It was appreciated when she made the copies and gave them out, but that was enough. He was there to handle the introductions, naturally, after he announced himself and his work history.

Just as Van Camp was about to open his mouth, Kitty spoke right up, and said, "My name is Kitty."

Before she could add in any more, Van Camp announced, "My name is Van Camp."

Ben, not wanting to hear anything from Van Camp other than his name, interrupted him and asked, "First name man. What is your first name?"

Van Camp looked shocked that he was interrupted, he would have said something, but Steven stood up and said, "My name is Steven. Until the other day, I was in the Coast Guard."

Leaving Van Camp out all together, Ben finished up and said; "Now that is more like it. My name is Ben."

As he sat down, Billy Bob and his brother stood up and he said, "My name if Billy Bob and this is my brother, Bob Billy. Until the other day, we were in security."

Jerry stood up next. Not because he wanted too, it was because he was sitting next in line for intros.

"My name is Jerry. Glad to be here."

Jerry sat back down as Alice, said while still sitting, "My name is Alice, and I miss my children and grandchildren."

Lisa was glad that Alice stayed seated, because she had no desire to get her big ass out of her seat. "My name is Lisa."

Burt stood up and said, "Hi. My name is Burt."

He sat down as Jeff stood up. Jeff only said, "Hi. Jeffery Harden, you can call me Jeff," as he waved a little wave before he sat down and stared at the floor.

Eddie stood up and after he realized that he was at attention, relaxed a little and said, "Eddie. I'm an x-marine."

Joe-Joe stood up quickly and before he sat down just as fast, waved his hand and said, "Joe-Joe."

"Rose Marie, my name is Rose Marie. Glad to meet everyone and I hope we can get along."

Once she said that, she wished that, she could take back the part about, 'getting along.' These people were not co-workers and no matter what she wanted as far as everyone getting along, this was it. At least this was it, for now.

Ben, after he realized that everyone had given his or her names, looked over at Van Camp and asked, "So big guy, what's your first name?"

Trying to look studious, he responded, "Richard."

"Okay Dick," snapped Ben. "Since it appears that you want to be in charge here, what do we do now Dick?"

Van Camp did not know which caused him more alarm, being called Dick instead of Richard, or being asked a direct question for which he was not prepared. Because he had not yet given this any detail thoughts on what to do next, he quickly regrouped and said, "Let's review our situation."

This did cause everyone to give him the attention that he desired. He only wished that he had a white board, or flip chart to make notes.

Right when he thought he had everyone's attention, Joe-Joe asked, "When do we eat? I'm starving."

Before he could redirect the meeting flow his way, Jeff, Steven, Ben chimed in and agreed, "Let's eat."

Lisa added, "Let's eat and meet back here later."

In order for Van Camp to regain control of the flow, he knew that he had to join in with so many now focused on eating.

Van Camp suggested, "I believe that there is a Salad Shop across the street."

Lisa snapped, "Salads?" As this made her happy.

Kitty stood right up, "Sounds great. I'm in."

Everyone agreed that, that they now have a plan.

CHAPTER 15

THE FIRST SUPPER

For the trip to the Salad Shop, everyone doubled up with three and four to a car. Like everyplace else in New Castle County, Delaware, there was no one around.

It was a simple task for each person to make their way behind the counter, and fill their plates. Getting drinks was just as easy. After a few minutes, everyone was seated with salads and drinks. Coffee and soda was cold.

For their first supper together, small talk went on very well with this odd collection of people. It was a little easier for everyone to talk now that it was realized that everyone there were in the same boat. Moreover, that they knew each other's name this time.

It did not take long before Lisa made her way for seconds. She was then quickly followed by Steven, Burt, Jeff, and Ben.

Nothing was spoken about their status. It was assumed that once they returned to the hotel, that directions on what to do next would be talked about then. For now, it was, where are you from, married, children, and what you did before you applied at R.E.A. International.

It was starting to get dark outside and it seemed more pressing to return to the hotel. Van Camp stood up and addressed the group.

"We should head back soon. What do you say we meet back at the hotel lobby?"

No one responded verbally to him, but made their approval by getting up and heading back to their cars. Thirty or so minutes later, almost everyone had taken a seat back in the lobby after they had time to check in to his or her room, and freshened up. Naturally, with Kitty having been outside, she had to retouch everything from the neck up.

Rose Marie stood up and did a quick head count and noticed that they were two people short. Ben stood up beside her and came up with the same count.

"We are short two people, any idea on who," she asked the group.

"Yeah, answered Burt, "It's those two military guys."

Before anyone could offer suggestions on where they were, or volunteer to go and find them, they heard the sounds of dishes clanging together. They all turned their heads in that direction and sure enough, here they come with smiles on their faces.

They were pushing two room service carts. The first cart had a large coffee pot on it. That was surrounded with cups and saucers, with piles of sugar and creamers. They apparently had been even more thoughtful as the second cart had an assortment of sodas with cups and a bowl of ice. In addition, there were bags and bags of chips and pretzels.

For a moment, this placed a smile on everyone's face. Everyone except for Van Camp, as he wished that he had thought of it first. In addition, if he did, he would have assigned Alice, Kitty, and Lisa to that task, not to the military.

Apparently, Steven and Eddie had taken a liking to each other and felt that they all could use some hot coffee. It would appear that they would make a good team like the Brown brothers.

"A meeting is not complete unless you have drinks," said Eddie with a smile.

Instead of an orderly movement of people, they mingled up and filled their cups with ice, soda, and or coffee. Van Camp on the other hand, would rather call them up by table number, or in alphabetical order. With him losing control here, he figured that he might as well have a cup of coffee with them.

Instead of everyone grabbing a drink, and returning to their seats, they hung around the coffee cart and continued their conversations that they started at the Salad Shop.

This went on for a few minutes, well, almost half an hour before a few of them noticed that Alice yawned. Naturally, this caused a few of them to join in with a yawn of their own, because nobody really wanted to get into a conversation about what they were going to do next. It was much easier just to sip on your drink and continue with the small talk.

Yet, everyone did finally take his or her seat and all was quiet. Some waited patiently assuming that Van Camp would speak first. Van Camp on the other hand, was not going to speak first in an attempt not to turn people against him, as the, 'self-appointed leader.' He could wait until the correct time.

Ben wanted to speak up first, but he did not have anything to say, ask, or suggest. So, he kept still.

Rose Marie did not want to say anything because she felt that she had done enough already and wanted someone else to step up. Kitty, being cautious, paid close attention, and she did not want to add anything. She did however, tried to figure out who might end up taking the lead, as in the manager or head honcho, and no one really stood out.

Jerry spoke first. This was uncharacteristic of him, as he would rather watch TV and follow the crowd, but now, he was tired and wanted nothing more than to fall asleep watching TV. "Look, we are all stuck here. Everyone in the world has checked out and left us behind. I have a full stomach and I am tired. I want to go to bed and believe that when I wake up tomorrow, you folks won't be here."

Most everyone shook his or her head in agreement. He was right; the peoples of the world have gone.

Jeff added in, "I agree. It's almost 10pm and nothing is going to change between now and tomorrow morning. If it does, at least we will be rested enough to handle it."

Alice questioned, "Do you think that we will all be here tomorrow? You know, disappear like everyone else."

Van Camp saw were this was going. Soon, if some of them did not get to sleep, there would be panic. He suggested, "Does everyone agree that we just check into our rooms and discuss this tomorrow?"

A few head shook up and down in agreement, as the youngest few, wanted to stay up and work this out.

Jeff said, "Why don't the one who want to go to bed, go to bed. The ones that want to stay here and talk, then they can stay here and talk."

Van Camp seizing the moment, said, "I like your idea. Should we set time aside for us to meet here tomorrow morning?"

Everyone agreed that anyone could choose what he or she wanted to do next. However, it was impossible to set a time that everyone could agree. Some wanted early, 8am, others wanted to sleep in and make it 10am.

So, for the next few minutes, times of 'on the hour,' 'half past,' and 'quarter after' came up for every conceivable time from 8am to 10am. After some debating, 8:30 seemed acceptable for everyone. The ones that were tired and were not in the mood to discuss anything else, headed to their rooms. Kitty, Alice, Lisa, Jerry, Joe-Joe, Jeff, and Burt were the ones that headed off to bed. Joe-Joe was the first to reach his room. Before he washed up, undressed, or even checked out his room, he turned on the TV. Nothing was on and he was not able to order an in-room movie. He was more upset with that problem than the larger issue that everyone in the world had possibly vanished. Knowing that tomorrow would be a busy day and that there was nothing on TV, he was soon in bed and asleep.

Once in his room, Burt decided to make a few phone calls. Along with 911 calls, he called the local and state police numbers. He went into the phone book and called the FBI and other federal agencies. Even a few calls to other government agencies such as the Post Office, libraries, and court offices. As before, no one was home. That was so tiring, that Burt fell back in bed and fell asleep on top of the covers, with his clothes on.

Jeff and Jerry had nothing on their schedule, except for a quick shower and then sleep.

Alice cried a little, made a few phone calls, and cried some more. She was afraid to fall asleep believing that she would not wake up tomorrow, or if she did, that she would be alone. She did eventually fall asleep, but it took awhile between crying and looking at the pictures of her children and grandchildren.

Lisa went to bed, pissed and bitching to herself. She was also very hungry and knew that hunger pains would wake her in a few hours. She knew that she would just pick up again, with her bitching at that time about hunger and life in general, if she woke up at all.

After brushing her hair and washing off all her makeup, Kitty doubled checked the locks on her door, hung up her clothes neatly, and headed right to sleep. She knew the importance of sleep and no way did she want to wake up tomorrow morning looking all red eyed and tired. Even being the last good-looking girl on the planet, she always wanted to look good.

Rose Marie, trying to understand that the loss of her cats could not compare to those who had lost family members, headed to her room for her private pity party. Her cats were her family and if she wanted to grieve for their loss, she could and would.

Six of the remaining guys, stayed behind. Van Camp stayed because he did not want to miss-out on anything that was talked about. He was tired, but he just had to stay.

Ben wanted to stay up, not to be entertained by any major discussion group, but he felt like it, and no prison guards could order him to return to his cell.

Billy Bob and Bob Billy were nighttime security guards and staying up was their thing.

Eddie and Steven's military careers had made it the norm for them to be up for hours and hours at a time.

With a second cup of coffee, or a refill on their sodas, the group moved their chairs closer to each other.

Ben directed his question towards Steven and Eddie. "Do

you think that something military happened? Secret weapon or something?"

"No man, no idea," answered Eddie.

"Nope. No idea also. Besides," continued Steven, "If I had known that this was going to happen and it was a military thing, I'd never gotten out."

The group shook their heads in agreement as Bob Billy asked, "Anybody have a guess on what happened?"

The group again shook their heads, only this time, it was back and forth indicating, no.

"For tomorrow," started Van Camp, "does anyone have an idea on what we should do?"

Ben took a deep breath and responded, "Take another look around for people."

Eddie spoke right up with, "Like we did earlier, a few of us set out and drive half an hour in different directions, then return."

Steven had a point and said, "Let the ones that have phone numbers of those out of state, make some calls."

Billy Bob mentioned, "Someone should look for food and water for us. That Salad Shop across the street won't be any good after tomorrow."

Bob Billy asked, "Is there anything we can do now instead of waiting until tomorrow?"

No one had an idea or suggestion, but Van Camp did make a point, "It might not be safe to venture out at night."

No one had a reason to disagree with that, but no one thought that to be a good enough reason not to try.

Ben looked over at Steven and Eddie, and said, "You guys didn't see anything down at Dover Air Force Base?'

They both looked down and shook their heads, as Eddie answered, "Empty. Not a single person around. Just like on all the highways, it appeared as if everyone parked their vehicles and boarded a bus and left Dodge."

Steven added, "Planes were neatly parked with no evidence that something happened to them. We even made it to the control tower anticipating some hint of what had happened."

Eddie slowly shook his head, and said, "Nothing, no radio traffic."

We had an excellent view from the control tower," Steven explained. "The whole base was empty."

For a few moments, everyone was still, heavy in sorrow, disbelief, and at a lost for anything to say.

Van Camp, wanting to appear strong, summarized, "So you guys think we should scout the area once more and make some additional phone calls?"

No one had anything to add. It had been a long day and it was too late for any heavy discussions. So for the rest of the night, they hung around and did some talking, found a deck of cards in the gift shop and played some poker. Two or three hours later, one by one, they would head to their rooms. Each one walked back to their rooms with their heads held down low, anticipating a long day tomorrow.

The Brown brothers were the last ones left. They decided that before they headed to their room, that they would walk once around the building. They made it a decision not to walk around alone, but to walk together in fear that one of them might disappear into the night.

Van Camp, after a long, hot shower, sat down at the desk in his room, started to take some notes about today's activities, and to map out plans for tomorrow. Realizing how some viewed him, he made it a point not to add names to his list of Things-To-Do. He felt that with this group, he could be in charge without really being in charge. It would be a challenge, but he could pull it off.

The only problem he had was that he ran out of paper before he ran out of ideas. Feeling a little frustrated, he made a mental note to continue this chore tomorrow after he found a larger pad of paper, and not just a few sheets that all hotel rooms provide.

Falling asleep for Van Camp was easy, to him, sleep was a manageable thing, and he could manage anything.

Ben took the longest shower that he had taken in many years. This was the first time in a long, long time, that if he dropped his soap or wash towel, that he did not worry about what or who was behind him.

When he did fall asleep, he slept like a baby.

For Steven and Eddie, it was by the book. Both men neatly hung up their clothes, took a quick shower, and went directly to sleep. No TV channel surfing, no radio playing, and no smoking in bed. Neither one of them smoked, but if they did, they would not smoke in bed. At nighttime, the Smoking Lamp was out.

After the patrol around the premises, the brothers checked into their room that had two double beds. They talked a little after the lights were out, but only to remember their past when they were little kids.

They both made it a point not to bring up what happened today or what might happen tomorrow. For the first time in their lives, they both told each other how much they loved one another. There was the fear in both men that they might not wake up tomorrow.

Chapter 16

DECISIONS, DECISIONS, DECISIONS

A S EXPECTED, AT 6 AM, EDDIE, Steven, and Ben were the first ones to wake up this morning without having to set their alarms.

Ben was happy that he was getting up and that he was not in prison, but disappointed that he did not have a hooker with him. He knew that Kitty, as a hooker replacement, looked hot right now, then Alice and Rose Marie would do after a few weeks, and after all else fails, Lisa would be just fine with him.

After he dressed, Ben made his way to the gift shop for something cold to drink and a candy bar.

Steven and Eddie met up in the hallway about the same time heading towards the lobby. Together, they decided to retrieve and restock the coffee cart. They both knew the day could not begin properly without a large pot of hot, fresh coffee.

As Ben passed them in the hallway, he asked them where they were going and he decided to join them. With luck, he could find something more than candy bars for breakfast.

Van Camp was awakened by the sounds of those guys talking and pushing the coffee cart towards the kitchen. He knew that he had to be apart of their activity as he quickly got up, shaved, and dressed to find them.

Lisa bitched a little, as she was somewhat surprised and disappointed that, she was still alive. She felt that if she woke up dead, that she would be just fine with that.

Billy Bob was the first to wake up because he heard the men talking in the hallway. He got up and shook his brother Bob Billy, encouraging him to get up. "We made it through the night."

Bob Billy rolled over and said, "Damn, we did it."

"Yes sir," Billy Bob answered as he made his way to the bathroom.

With showers going, people in the hallway rolling carts by and talking, almost everyone that was asleep, were now getting up. No one wanted to be left alone any longer than need be.

Kitty, Alice, Rose Marie, and Lisa were up and fixing their faces with what little makeup that they found in the gift shop last night. It was not much, but it was sure better than having none on at all. Well, maybe for Lisa, as she was so ugly, that there was not enough makeup in the world to give her any improvement, except for a full-face mask. It would be an improvement if she had on the mask of Richard Nixon.

Burt and Jeff also heard the commotions in the hallway. With little delay, they were up, dressed, and in the hallway making their way towards the lobby.

Jerry and Joe-Joe were still asleep and easily ignored the noise just outside their rooms. For the two of them, it was not yet time to get up.

Before long, the coffee cart had returned filled with coffee and donuts to the lobby to be greeted by everyone except for Jerry and Joe-Joe.

Van Camp picked up that they were two people short after a secretive headcount. He took it upon himself to knock on their doors to get them moving. Even though it was only 6:30, two full hours before the planned meeting, he felt that it was important that everyone be up at the same time. He did not like repeating himself to anyone that came late, especially, ones that slept in.

Without saying it to anyone, he wanted to make sure that those two, Jerry and Joe-Joe, were still around because they seem easy to manage.

He returned to the lobby, and after he made himself a cup of coffee. Van Camp then let a few people know that he had made a headcount and taken it upon himself to get the last two boys up and that soon, everyone would be here.

It took but a few minutes for Jerry and Joe-Joe to join them. They seemed disoriented and looked as if they could have used a few more hours of sleep.

CHAPTER 17

THE PLAN

T HE CONTINENTAL BREAKFAST CONTINUED AS no one wanted to stop the small talk, no one wanted to step up and start the meeting, no one especially wanted to discuss yesterday, and most certainly, no one wanted to talk about today's much unknown activities.

As the talk died down with fewer and fewer things to discuss, people slowly started to take seats in anticipation of their meeting. Once everyone was seated, they simply looked at each other expecting that someone, anyone but them, to start a conversation.

Van Camp wanted to start out following Robert's Rule for the meeting, but decided against it because he did not believe that anyone knew about that except for him.

Ben looked over at Van Camp and said, "So Dick, you want to start this party up?"

Van Camp did not want to start out this way, especially being called Dick, and not Mr. Van Camp. However, now that he had everyone's attention, he might as well.

"Okay, we made it through the night and we didn't lose anyone," he started out saying as everyone looked around, as if double-checking his count.

"Last night," he continued, "A few of us stayed up late discussing what we might want to do today."

"Who stayed up," questioned Lisa. In reality, she was bitching about people talking about her behind her back, but she was able to pull it off as if that was a question that everyone wanted to ask anyway.

"Good question. I should have mentioned that first," apologized Van Camp.

"There was Steven, Eddie, Billy Bob, his brother Bob Billy, Ben, and myself." A short pause for effect, and he added, "Nothing was set in place and nothing was assigned to anyone. We collectively considered what we should do today."

Lisa wanted something else to bitch about, so she asked, "So, who is in charge?"

"We did not discuss that, it never came up. We are all in the same boat. We only talked last night about what we might need do as individuals, and as a group," concluded Van Camp.

Ben spoke up and added, "We can tell you what we came up with. Then if we agree, decide who wants to do what."

Van Camp stepped back in and said, "We never discussed who will do what, just that we had a few things as a group, needs to be done."

"What to you want me to do," bitched Lisa.

Ben leaned over to Eddie, and said in a whisper, "She can hunt for food. It appears that she is good at it."

Eddie tried to hide his response, but was unable to do so.

Steven looked over at him, and asked, "What did he say?"

Eddie leaned over to Steven and repeated what Ben said. As predicted, Steven found it very funny and he too was unable to hold back a big smile indicating that he enjoyed what was said.

Lisa, pissed about this, bitched, "What's so funny?"

Van Camp figured out what was said, and wanted to get the meeting, or this get-together, back on track, interrupted this debate and said, "What we discussed was, one, to take another look around for people. A few, maybe four people, would take off and drive thirty minutes away from here in different directions. Then come right back."

Everyone shook their heads, believing this to be a workable plan.

"Two," he continued, after looking around to see that everyone was paying attention to him, "A few people could start and make some more phone calls."

Ben added in his two cents, "If anyone has phone numbers of people not in Delaware, then we should call those numbers."

Everyone shook his or her head in agreement.

"And Three," Van Camp concluded, "We need some supplies such as food and water. Others could do a supply run."

"What else did you discuss," bitched Lisa.

All six of those who stayed up late looked at each other as if there might have been something else. There was not, and Ben answered her with, "That's all. Like the man said, just some thoughts on what we should do today. No decisions were made, no direction was given, and no one was the head man."

Not giving Lisa time to bitch at them again and disturbing the flow of the meeting, Van Camp asked, "We need four people who are willing to head out and drive for thirty minutes one way, and then return. Only to be gone an hour or so, max."

Kitty spoke up and volunteered. Not that she wanted to be, all that helpful, but while out, she could stop in a drug store and restock on makeup. "I'll go. Can I take someone with me?"

"Sure, why not," quickly answered Ben, hoping and expecting her to ask him to ride shotgun with her.

Kitty looked over at Alice, and asked, "Want to go with me?"

Alice was delighted to be asked and she wanted very much to do something that would help the group. Hanging around the hotel and making more phone calls was not something she felt like doing.

"Can I join you ladies," asked Rose Marie, not wanting to stay in the hotel, not wanting to go home, and not wanting to venture out on her own.

Kitty smiled, and said to the group and Rose Marie, "Good.

Alice, Rose Marie and I will head north on Route 13 for thirty minutes."

Wanting to keep things moving, Van Camp asked, "Who wants 13 South?"

Eddie and Steven at the same time, raised their hands. Ben recognized that this to be a good pair to head south on Route 13 towards Dover Air Force Base. He said, "You two should go south on 13 together. You can make another stop at the Dover military base."

Steven looked over at Eddie, and said, "I'll drive, and you can ride shotgun."

"Can do," was the reply from Eddie.

"Okay now, we have north and southbound 13 taken care of. Does anyone know about anything east or west of here," questioned Van Camp.

Bob Billy spoke up, and said, "I don't know no nothing about no east or west, but my brother and I can drive up and look around downtown Wilmington. It's not north or south, or even east or west, but Wilmington is a big city, and we know our way around. Let us make that run."

It was logical and Ben, along with Van Camp, nodded their heads in agreement and approval. Besides, it made sense that they would double up for their search.

Ben spoke and suggested, "We should check out local jails."

Everyone looked up at him as if asking, 'Why?'

Noticing this, Ben replied, "From what we can tell, what ever it was that took everyone away, it looked orderly."

Waiting for more clarification, or a good reason, the group gave Ben their attention.

"There are a lot of people in jails around the country. If there was an evacuation, you must let everyone out, guard them, then take them someplace else, and lock them up again."

"An easy task," added Van Camp, staying in the middle of this conversation.

"I'll get the phone book and figure out the nearest jail," Ben added.

"If you find anyone, what will you do," questioned Kitty.

Confused, Ben answered, "Didn't think that part out."

"We don't need murders and rapist in this group," she added. Everyone shook their heads in total accord. "Okay," said Ben. "I'll check it out, being careful not to lock myself inside. If I find anyone, I'll keep them there and come back."

Then, trying to look like a good guy, Ben added, "If someone is locked up, I'll see that I get them some food and water."

Everyone agreed with his plan. Giving this some thought, Ben started to hope that he would find some women that he would let loose. Besides, Kitty can't always be shared.

The smile on his face soon dropped to a frown as he anticipated that if he found any women, they would be convicted felons, murders, and hookers. He was sorry now that he had mentioned this.

"Let me go out and get some supplies," suggested Jeff.

"Me too," came a request from Joe-Joe and Burt.

"Okay," responded Van Camp, but let's first take care of who will search east and west."

Jerry, wanting to do as little as possible, spoke up and said, "I'll go east. I won't be going all that far before I run into the bay, but I can spend time looking around at all the docks that I come across."

"Splendid," answered Van Camp.

"There might even be a boat or two in the water," added Jerry. "Great," responded Van Camp. "I'll head west." He really did not want to leave the hotel, but he had to do something. "I'll stay and make a ton of phone calls," added Lisa.

"Okay," announced Ben with a sense of accomplishment. Van Camp quickly added in, "All we need now is supplies from Jeff, Joe-Joe, and Burt."

Jeff spoke up first with, "Radios, CB radios, flashlights, portable TV's, plenty of batteries and a generator or two. I can probably find most of that stuff at Radio Shack or Lowes."

Those items were something that no one had thought of and Ben showed his approval by giving him the thumbs up.

Burt added in his two cents. "I should try and find some tools."

"Tools," questioned Van Camp.

"Yeah, tools," was a quick response by Burt. "If we need tools, it would be good if we had a trunk full of tools and stuff. Things do break down, and we don't know how long we are going to be on our own. We certainly can't call anyone to come over and fix it."

Van Camp acknowledged him with a broad smile, and responded, "You are right. It's still hard for me to accurately realize just what kind of predicament that we are in."

Everyone was now looking at Joe-Joe. He did not appear to be, all that smart, and that it was going to be hard to tell what items he would consider important enough that he should collect for the group.

Joe-Joe felt that he was placed on the spot, and he took a minute before he responded. He knew enough that he governed what he says and that what he says, will govern him.

I'm going to get a DVD player and some DVD's. A mess of can goods and anything else that does not require to be kept cold."

"DVD's," question almost everyone there at the same time.

Feeling a little pressed to justify himself, he boldly spitted out, "Yeah, DVD's."

He looked around to see that he had everyone's attention, and continued, "At night, every one of you probably watched TV. Now that we don't have any TV, I will supply the entertainment for us in the evening."

Seeing that everyone wanted to team up against him, Van Camp stepped in and said, "You know, that makes good sense to me."

Everyone stopped thinking of how to jump on Joe-Joe, and turned their attention to Van Camp.

"We still don't know what is going on here, and no way, do we know for how long."

Looking around for effect,"We can meet like this every night and every morning, but as you can imagine, that will get old soon."

"Yeah," Joe-Joe stepped right back into the conversation. "Along with can goods, I'll find a place with fresh bread and fruit. I won't be spending all day picking out DVD's."

At this point, everyone seemed pleased that they had a plan and it appeared that the assigned projects were evenly spaced out.

Lisa, trying not to bitch this time, asked, "Should we meet back here in a few hours or so?"

Everyone shook his or her heads in agreement."Let's make it noon time, right back here."

Wanting to crack a joke, Ben suggested, "Get back sooner, and we can watch a movie provided by Joe-Joe."

This got a few chuckles from the group and a big smile from Joe-Joe who now considers himself a team player.

CHAPTER 18

EXECUTING THE PLAN

E VERYONE GOT UP SLOWLY AND hung around for a short time talking to one another. The seriousness of their situation, the unknown reasons behind the lost of family, friends, and co-workers had not yet fully hit them.

Alice seemed to be the most affected along with Jerry. For the rest of the guys, they did not want to be the first one to break down. At least, not in front of anyone.

Kitty did not want to cry and mess up her appearance. Having red and puffy eyes was not attractive and too difficult to cover up with makeup.

Lisa, not having any family or friends, well, no close family and close friends, did not feel a loss. The only response she had was to bitch about it to herself. Bitching to others was useless because they were all in the same boat. Nevertheless, given enough time, she would be up at full speed bitching about bitching stuff to everyone in no time.

Kitty, Rose Marie and Alice teamed up and agreed that after one more trip to the bathroom, they would meet up out front where Kitty had parked her car.

Minutes later, the girls were headed north on Route 13. As before, nothing was on the road. They flew past intersections not taking the time now to look both ways first, even if the light was red.

Alice asked, "Why are you in such a hurry?"

"Well, we only have thirty minutes to head this way. Yesterday, almost everyone was on this road and found nothing. I figured that I would head out even further north on 13 and cover more area."

"Okay. I see that," said Alice, with Rose Marie shaking her head to agree.

So north on 13 they went until it joined in with Route 40 and they crossed the Delaware Memorial Bridge into New Jersey. They only went for a few miles and they turned around in the medium. Kitty did not want to take a chance getting off the highway and not finding her way back on.

Coming back across the Delaware Memorial Bridge, Kitty stopped at the top of the bridge. She got out, just to look out at the river, hoping to see a boat or two. Nothing, just like the roads, nothing was sailing today. Sadly, she returned to the car and mentioned to the others, "Nothing in Jersey."

After everyone was gone, with Lisa sitting behind the front desk in the lobby, Ben, with master key in hand, made a detail search of every room on all the floors, except for the first floor where everyone was staying. He even checked all the hall closets and supply rooms. He did come across a few purses, which he quickly examined and took all the cash. There was not much, but he took it anyway to pay for his trouble. He did make it a point to put the purse back in place as if it had not been ram shacked. Every closet in every room was examined. When he came across men's clothes, he checked the size. If it were his size, he would take it and pile them at the end of the hallway to retrieve later.

Lisa had a system going. She would make a call, get no answer, and bitch. Make a call, get no answer, and bitch.

After twenty or so calls, she would make a call; get no answer, bitch, and then slam down the phone. Again, make the call, get no answer, bitch and slam down the phone.

Before long, the phone no longer worked. Not sure if she banged it, or that she had bitched it to death. Either way, the phone was out of order now.

With nothing to do, she made her way to the gift shop for a light snack. A light snack for her would consist of four or five bags of chips, two or three candy bars, washed down by two or more sodas. Naturally, they were not diet sodas, just sugar filled, with high calories and a high-carb count kind of sodas, with no nutritional value. However, this made her happy and it did cut down some on her bitching.

As she took a seat in the lobby and started in on her snacks, Ben returned wearing a new suit. He took a seat beside her, placed his feet on another chair, and said, "Wake me when the others return."

"No problem," she answered. "If you are awake when they come in, you can wake me."

He looked at her and smiled. Within minutes, she had sucked down her treats and leaned back in her chair to nap along with Ben. Jerry needed gas for his car before he could venture onto the back roads off 13 towards the bay. He found a Shell station and was pleased that he was able to fill his tank as the pump accepted his debit card.

While he was pumping gas, he walked into the station for a candy bar and soda for the ride. Once inside, he noticed walls and walls of cigarettes. If he were a smoker, he would be in heaven right now. He could easily fill his trunk with all that he could carry and it would not cost him a thing.

He remembered that his mom smoked Misty Lights 120s. He went ahead and grabbed a dozen or so cartons of smokes for her, in the event that they were to get together. He was both happy about getting the cigarettes for her and sad that he might not see his mom again.

With a full tank, a diet coke, Snickers bar, and cigarettes, he was off to explore the back roads off Route 13 towards the bay.

It was not long before Jerry could see the bay and Route 9. Delaware Route 9 pretty much stayed close to the water as it snaked its way north and south paralleling the bay.

He was not that familiar with Delaware, but he knew that he

could travel in either direction and come across small towns and docks. He decided to travel south for no more of a reason that it was easier to turn right, than to turn left at this particular intersection.

It did not take long before he drove past a few homes and a post office. As before, no one was around. He only slowed down, as he had no reason to come to a complete stop. A few times when driving very slowly, he would lay on his horn, trying to attract attention.

A few more miles down the road, he came across an area that allowed for the parking of vehicles and their boat trailers. This was a public boat ramp and parking lot. Even though there was no one around, he decided to pull up to the dock for a look. There were a few trucks with boat trailers hitched to them. Some had boats, and others, jet skis, and a few trailers were empty.

He walked onto and out to the end of the dock to get a better view of the bay. He looked up and down the bay anticipating seeing some boat traffic. He knew that sea going boats traveled this way heading towards the ports of Wilmington and Philadelphia. However, just like the highways, the bay was calm and very much empty. Not even a sailboat could be spotted.

Then a cool idea hit him. If they had to travel any place, instead of a convoy of cars and vans, why not take a boat. Just stay along the shoreline. You might not be as fast getting places, but where do they have to go right away, any way.

Jerry looked at his watch and realized that he had been gone almost an hour. He then decided to hurry back. He did not want to miss anything and secretly worried if anyone would be there when he returned.

Driving real fast up Route 13 towards Wilmington, the Brown brothers joked and made fun of everyone. There were jokes about Van Camp and how they nicked name him, The-Man. This was very disrespectful and they knew that he wanted to be the new king, god, emperor, or Indian chief of this small group of survivors.

They made fun of Lisa's fat ass. They even commented how many of their guy friends have loved women with big butts, but agreed that she would need two or three men to keep her happy. They did not trust Ben, and vowed to keep an eye on him always. They agreed that Kitty was hot, and took bets on who would get her first. Not that they would do anything without her approval, but if the world was to continue, they would need her to make plenty of babies. Rose Marie came in at a close second for having children. Alice was old, but would do while Kitty was pregnant.

They saw both Eddie and Steven as gung ho, military, by the book, ass holes. Yet, they knew that these two guys were needed to help them survive. Besides, if one of them were to be in charge, they knew that those two military types would follow orders.

They saw Jerry as a lazy kid and Joe-Joe to be the idiot of the group. They were not too sure about Burt and Jeff. They knew that Jeff had some computer knowledge, but nothing more than that. Their conversation lasted all the way up to Wilmington. They drove first through areas that they were familiar with looking for friends and family. Then they drove downtown believing that there would be people there. Nothing was out of order and no one was around.

They made a quick stop back at their place to grab some clothes. Once back in their car, it was a stop at the gun store on Route 13, just south of Wilmington. They needed supplies.

They were able to break into the gun case of assault rifles, but they did not find the key to unlock the cable that kept them secure, in the event, someone broke into the case.

Instead, they found a few rifles, handguns, holsters for the handguns, and ammo, plenty of ammo. So much ammo was seized that it almost filled a large canvas bag.

Billy Bob knew enough about guns to add in some maintenance items.

Bob Billy, thinking that his brother was smart to pack away cleaning supplies that he had to think of something besides guns and bullets. What he added to the bag was targets.

Bob Billy tells his brother, "We'll need these targets. No need to be supplied with all these guns and ammo and end up being a lousy shot."

"like it," smiled Billy Bob.

Now that they were armed to the teeth, they headed back.

Burt pulled over to the Home Depot store parking lot in Glasgow Delaware. The lights were out inside and the automatic doors did not open. He was about to walk away because they were closed, and remembered, all the stores in Delaware were closed today.

Looking for something to bust the doors in with was an easy find. Not far from the doors, was a pallet of cinder blocks. It only took one try to break enough glass for him to slip into the store. Just inside the door, at the first register, was a display of large flashlights, the square ones, with batteries. Next, he found a cart and placed two flashlights in the front, that acted as headlights, as the store was dark, without the power for the lights. Then he was off to find tools, gas cans, and anything else he believed to be a good idea.

To make his search easier and quicker, Burt grabbed packages of tools. The ones that had complete sets of screw drivers, hammers, nails, screws, etc. Plenty of electrical and duck tape, and two generators. The generators were small units, and probably would not run very much at one time, but having two should be fine.

At the lighting department, he grabbed a few large spotlights with more flashlights and plenty of batteries. Walking back to the front door to unload what he already collected, he noticed the locks that were on sale. He did not see any reason for locks, but that spurred the idea to get lock cutters. That item would surly be needed.

He placed two of them on his cart and then loaded empty gas cans that he found near the lawn mower section of the store. With the gas cans, he would need gas. He would get that later, but thought he would need a pump and same hoses. He figured that if the gas pumps are not working, then he could pump them out of the tanks. So he found a few pumps and two, fifty-foot garden hoses. These hoses were not designed for gasoline, but that was all that they had.

Even with his cart full and knowing that what he had might not fit in his car; he made room for one of those small gas grill, the ones that use the little propane tanks. He grabbed two grills with a dozen of those propane tanks.

This was not a required item of his, not yet anyway, but he got it just for the small chance that he could get everything else in his car.

Well, his car was able to hold everything but the grills and a tank of gas. Not a big deal, he could always come back later and get a bigger grill with more than a few tanks of gas.

With his tasks completed, he headed back.

With Steven driving and Eddie riding shotgun, they headed south on 13 towards Dover and Dover Air Force Base. Eddie thought it would be a good idea to stop off first at the Dover Mall, just a few miles short of the main gate to the base.

"The mall," questioned Steven.

"Couple of reasons. One, if people are around, they would be there packing up on supplies. Two, is there any supplies that you think we should get?"

Steven gave this a minute, and answered, "I could use a change of clothes." After another minute, "I could use a suitcase of clothes."

"Yeah, we might as well get a few things that we need before we head back. As for me, I could use a toothbrush and toothpaste. There is plenty of soap and shampoo back at the hotel,"

Steven following up with what Eddie had said, and added, "I'll pick up some extra toothbrushes for the group."

Eddie responded, "You're a good man Charlie Brown."

This placed a smile on their faces as they pulled into the mall. When Steven appeared to be looking for a parking space, Eddie spoke up and said, "Don't park way out here. Pull up to the door." "Oh yeah," chuckled Steven in response to what Eddie said.

"I'll do better than that, watch this. I saw this done in a cartoon one time. I think I can do it."

That statement caught him off guard, as he had no idea what he was going to do. It was soon explained as Steven pulled right up on the sidewalk and parked right at the door. Fifty or so feet closer than if he had parked at the curb.

"Be sure to lock it when you get out," suggested Eddie.

Steven was about to lock the car door when he realized that Eddie was joking. "You a funny man," joked Steven.

Once they marched inside, both men got serious and scanned the mall for anything out of place, before they started their patrol. Nothing was said as they both, automatically, walked silently with one on each side, heading towards the other end of the mall.

Because they were military, not walking side by side, but walking on opposite sides of the hallway, was natural to them.

At the doorway of each store, they would stop, look, and listen. With nothing to see or hear, they would make their way to the next store and repeat it once more on both sides of the mall.

At the end of the mall was Sears. They took a seat on the bench that faced back in the direction they just covered.

Nothing was said because there was nothing new or different to report. Surprise, surprise, the mall was empty.

They sat there for a minute or two before Eddie walked over to the Auntie Anne's Hand rolled Soft Pretzel stand, that was in the middle of the mall, just a few feet from them.

"My treat," he said to Steven, as he made his way behind the counter. "Sorry, no soft pretzels today, but I do have a few, hard ones."

"I'll take you up on that fine idea. What will it cost me?"

Looking up at the menu with the prices posted, Eddie announced, "That will be 2 for 2 dollars."

"You take credit," joked Steven.

"Don't think so. Look, you don't have a job, you don't have a place to stay, and you are an x-marine hanging around an x-coast guard guy. I see that you keep bad company. So, to answer your question, no credit for you today."

This created a laugh before he responded, "Look, just call my bank, they will verify that I have plenty of money."

"I'll call later. Phones are not working right now."

With this little joke out of the way, with two pretzels and a soda each, they walked back towards their car with a stop over at JC Penny's men's clothing department after they pulled out two suitcases that were on display.

With suitcases full of new clothes, and a quick stop at the drug store for more supplies, they headed towards the air base. As expected, their car was still in place. They did not get a parking ticket, nor was the car towed away. The drive to the base only took a few minutes, and this time, they did not stop at the main gate.

The control tower, they agreed, seemed to be the most logical place to start. Up the stairs they go, with the same results as their first visit. No one there, no radio traffic, and no one in sight.

Both men took binoculars and scanned the area hoping to find something, anything, everything, that could shed some light to what has happened. Nothing was seen near or far. They're as no automobile traffic, no plane traffic, and no people traffic in sight. Steven completed his search first and placed the binoculars down. Eddie stopped when Steven did, only he held onto the binoculars. He placed the strap over his neck, and had plans to keep them.

Steven took the hint that it would be a good idea to keep his, picked it back up, and placed the strap around his neck.

Then it was off to HQ for a second look. Yet, once at HQ, it was found still to be empty, with nothing out of place.

It simply looked as if everyone got up from their desk and walked outside. Computers were still turned on, coffee cups and soda cans, half-empty, were still on people's desk.

Eddie walked up to a white board on the wall that displayed flight information into and out of Dover. Each row had listed the plane type, tail number, destination, or arrival from, along with cargo notes. There was even a column for additional comments, and that column was empty.

"What are you looking for," questioned Steven.

"Not sure. Anything that might be important."

After a short pause, as he continued looking at the chart, Eddie said, "Nothing here but normal stuff. Flights in, flights out, times, and cargo information."

"What did you expect to find," pressed Steven.

"Don't know, just thought something would stand out. Maybe a lot of flights hauling people away. Search operations, or plane crashes."

As Eddie continued looking at the chart, Steven peeked into

the 'in' and 'out' baskets on the counter. "What are you looking for," asked Eddie.

"I'm looking for the same sort of things you tried to find on your board. In addition, I found the same things, nothing. Nothing at all."

"Want to check out the barracks," asked Steven.

"What for?"

"To see what was left behind. You know, if all the rooms are filled with stuff, and looked lived in, then they plan to come back. On the other hand, if the rooms are empty, then they moved them away," explained Steven.

"Okay," responded Eddie, as he made his way back to the car. "Good idea."

The barracks was easy to find. Just look for a hotel type building, three or four stories tall. Minutes later, they pull up to a court that had four buildings.

Eddie said, "I'll check those two and meet you back here."

Steven only had to respond with, "Gotcha, no sweat."

Both men made their way inside. Five minutes later, they both met back at the car with the same results. Some rooms were completely empty, and some looked recently lived in. They agreed that their conclusion told them nothing new.

Disappointed, they headed back to the hotel.

Steven mention, "You know. If we had stayed in the military, we might have ended up missing like everyone else."

"I can see that," Eddie agreed.

Jeff drove down Route 13 and slowed as he drove past the strip malls. He was looking for a Radio Shack, CB store, or a store that sold marine equipment. All of which sold radios.

It was not long before he saw a Radio Shack on the other side of 13. He did not see a reason to drive down the mile or so to the next intersection to turn around, so he darted across the medium. There was a parking space right at the front door. He backed in and popped his trunk.

Once inside, Jeff grabbed over a dozen walkie-talkies with a supply of batteries. Next on his list were scanners and powerful flashlights. With these items piled in his trunk, he noticed that he had plenty of room for other supplies.

Back inside the store, instead of items that were essential, he picked up a few luxury gadgets. He grabbed a dozen or so, hand held battery operated games. Games to play chess, poker, and solitary, along with a few space invader games, and a few boxes of batteries.

After he loaded up the trunk until it was full, he went back inside to look for anything else that might be worth taking. He did not see a need to get cell phones, because everyone had one already. No reason to load up on TVs, or stereo equipment, if you cannot use them. However, he did see the value in some tools that were on the shelves. Along with pliers and wire cutters, he found electrical tape and soldering irons.

These items were loaded in his back seat and because he still had room, he went back inside. He had walked right past the computer laptops and did not notice them. This time, he picked up three laptops that were on the bottom shelve. As he made his way to the door, he noticed a few weather radios. He figured that predicting the weather would be a good thing. Assuming that someone was there to do the, predicting.

Now that his car was loaded, he headed back after a stop at Subway for a cold cut sub and drink.

Van Camp, with some hesitation, left the lobby for his turn in scouting the countryside. He wanted to stay behind to coordinate everyone's efforts, but decided to follow the examples of the others. In order to be a team leader, he knew he first had to be a team player, a good team player.

Before he left the lobby, he made it a point to tell each person, "Good luck," and to, "be careful."

Shortly after he pulled out of the parking lot, he remembered that he should have taken his cell phone. He had the phone list with him, but no cell phone.

"Damn it," he mumbled to himself. "Haven't gone a mile yet and already I left out an important function."

Then he quickly recovered and proceeded westward determined

to find something positive to report about when he returned. Cell phone or no cell phone, this trip of his would be successful.

Van Camp headed north on 13 until he came to the first major intersection. He turned left and drove west for fifteen minutes or so. As before and as with others, there was nothing and nobody. Cars were neatly pulled over to the side of the road and abandoned.

He also drove past a few horse farms after he crossed into Maryland. Same thing, no people, and no animals. Wanting reinsurance for himself about the animal part, he pulled into the very next horse farm.

Summit Pond Farm was the sign posted at the driveway. He stopped short of pulling in and made sure that there was a barn. A decent size barn that would house horses, or other farm animals. There were two barns, large ones. With a plan, Van Camp drove slowly towards them. With his windows down and CD radio turned off, he listened for any animal sounds that were common to a farm. He had unwittingly given up looking for people, but now he had his focus on animals.

He had not heard a thing, not that he was surprised, but he felt that he should have heard something, at least a dog barking to greet him.

He parked between the two barns that were about fifty feet apart. He got out slowly and before walking to the barn on his left, he looked around carefully and saw nothing. Nothing but farm buildings and farm equipment.

Once inside the barn, he found it empty. There were the smells and odors that were normal for farms. The barn was clean, but not completely. There was the occasional pile of horse and or cow crap on the floor, but for the most part, it appeared to have been cleaned most of the time. He did pick up that there were no flies. He thought that there were always flies in barns.

With this discovery, Van Camp knew that not only that people have disappeared, but so were all the animals. They were gone and nothing was left behind. No way, could there be total evacuations of all the people and all the animals in the span of one day. This find of his created more questions than answers, and in some ways, wished that he never discovered the disappearance of all the animals.

Van Camp then looked at his watch and realized that he should be headed back. He really wanted to get back right on time, not too late to miss out on what was said as people returned, but not to early to give the impression that he was unable to follow directions of thirty minutes out, and thirty minutes back.

Joe-Joe headed out and made his way to the Acme store not far away. He picked this particular Acme because there was a Blockbuster video store close by.

Inside the Acme, it was all can goods. Even with the power on to keep frozen food frozen, and cold items cold, he knew that there might not be a place to store them at the hotel. Even if there was, he had no idea on how long they would have power.

With a grocery basket full of can good, he left this basket near the front door and searched out items that had a long shelf life. Noodles, can soups, spaghetti sauce, crackers, cookies, and like items.

After he loaded the car, he wanted to fill the car completely, but not overload it with weight. Paper was his next item, not newspapers or magazines, but toiler paper, the good kind, and paper towels along with paper plates.

Happy with his shopping, it was then a trip to Blockbusters. Once inside, he walked down the aisle that had all the new arrivals. He got one of each. Next, he headed to the TV show collections. He picked up all the seasons for Survivor, Gilligan's Island, MacGyver, and American Idol along with, So You Think You Can Dance.

Next, was a trip to the Time and Life, 'Fix it yourself,' collection. To Joe-Joe, these were excellent items to have, whether you were at home, or alone in the world. This was good stuff and he had enough. Time to head back.

Ben, in his new car, drove towards Gander Hill Prison. He had no idea on what he would find, but he would be okay, if he did not find anyone.

Yes, he had friends in prison, but you can't keep prison friends,

friends once you are out on parole. There were a few guards that he got along with, but not well enough to be friends on the outside.

As he neared the main gate, he slowed down and stopped a few feet before the gate, a gate that was never left opened.

Ben got out and looked at everything. He checked out the guard shack by the open gate, the guard towers, and all of these are normally manned 24/7, but not today. Before he got back into his car, he blew on his horn, hoping to get anyone's attention. It did not.

Back in his car, he only drove far enough, and left his car parked in a way, that if the gate were to close, it could not with the car there.

Once out of his car, he decided that he would not venture too far into the complex. He knew the place well enough and he did not have the fear of getting lost, but a fear of a door closing shut and locking him in.

From one stairway, he was able to see into the main yard. Normally, on a day like this, there would be dozens of convicts and guards milling around. Again, as expected, no one was there. For Ben, he had spent about as much time in here as he wanted. With quick moves, as if he was escaping, Ben made his way out and into his car.

After backing out, and making a U-turn, Ben got out of his car one more time to look back and see if he could pick out anything or something new. It was good that he did, because he noticed that a few, if not all, of the prison buses were parked in the lot. If the prisoners were moved, they did not use the buses.

For the first time in his life, he was scared. He was not going to let it show, but he was scared. Scared of not knowing anything about what had happened, and if this was a scam, it's a good one and that scared him too.

With mission accomplished, Ben had nothing else in mind, but to return to the hotel with this grim, but expected news.

CHAPTER 19

HEADING BACK

After only a short drive north to New Jersey, Kitty, Rose Marie, and Alice were headed back to Delaware. They assumed that the others that took similar drives would repeat their findings of finding nothing.

Kitty did remember to make one quick stop at the Happy Harry's Drug Store for her makeup re-supply. Alice like the idea and once inside, she took one of the shopping baskets and filled it up. The only non-makeup item Alice placed in her basket, was a camera. She had wonderful thoughts of showing her children and grandchildren her adventures when they all got back together.

Rose Marie, out of habit, walked past the pet section of the store, but did not get anything.

With the shopping spree for the ladies completed, it was back in the car for the return trip.

With disappointment about his find, Jerry headed back, all the while hoping not to get lost. He wondered that if he did get lost, and or if he were gone a long time, would they come looking for him.

Then Jerry remembered that he had his cell phone on him, and that made him happy, but then he was again sad, as he did not have an of their numbers. He had left his list back in his hotel room. A mistake he would not repeat.

So now he was sad once more, then he was happy again because he knew that someone there had his number and surely, someone would try to call him if he did not return.

Feeling better, he could focus on finding Route 13. Once he found 13, he had to decide if he should head north or south. He had lost track just how far he had driven on 9.

Ten minutes later, he saw signs for 13. At the intersection, signs were posted. Dover left, and Middletown, Wilmington, right. Great, he knew that he needed to turn right, all was good. Billy Bob and his brother collectively decided that they had been in Wilmington long enough. Bob Billy said disappointingly,

"Wished we would have found something, you know."

Billy Bob only shook his head in response. Bob Billy added, "Not even the animals are here. No birds, dogs, nothing."

Wanting to put a happy face to this conversation, Billy Bob spoke up and said, "We should have seen dogs. You know there are more Pitt Bulls in Wilmington than people."

This got a smile from his younger brother, but that did not last long as he started to realize that they were apparently the only two black people left in the world.

Bob Billy sadly said, "We will be celebrating Kwanzaa by ourselves this year. You know that will be hard. Kind of sad."

"True," quickly responded Billy Bob, "But next year, we can replace Martin Luther King, Jr. day, with our own day."

"I like it," Bob Billy said with laughter in his voice.

Bob Billy added, "When we get back, we will report on what we did not find and announce the birth of a new holiday."

At that moment, these two did the high five, well, as high of a five as you can do inside of a car. For a brief moment, they were as happy as can be.

For the rest of the ride back to the hotel, they kept to themselves, recalling their short lives together and contemplating on what will become of them now. Their own holiday, or not.

Burt's car was over loaded with tools and gasoline. This was quickly resolved as he made a stop at the Hummer's new car showroom on Route 13 and 40. He always wanted a Hummer with all the bells and whistles. Sure enough, there was a bright yellow one on the showroom floor. This one had more than everything you could possibly want on it. The keys were already inside. All he needed now was to get it out of the showroom, load it up, and to fill the tank.

A minute later, he figured how to get his new Hummer outside, and wasted no time with this task. A few more minutes later, he was loaded up and heading south on 13 looking for a gas station.

It worried him that he might not be able to fill the tank and the gasoline cans that he had with him. It was not until his second gas station try, did his credit card work at the pump. He was one happy man and he said aloud to himself, "I am the happiest and luckiest man in the world."

His happiness dropped quickly as he remembered his current situation. It was not hard to be the happiest man in the world when there were apparently only nine other men in the world left. Instead of being sad over this, he said even louder to himself, "What the hell, I have a brand new, fully loaded Hummer, and I did not spend any time with a sales person and finance manager."

With his tanks topped off, he headed back to the hotel.

Leaving the base with much sadness, Eddie and Steven headed out. For the ride back, they spent the time bragging about their military service. Each one trying to outdo the other with assignments and medals awarded. For the most part, they were even up, but neither would admit it. The drive back was uneventful as was everything else.

After his sub from Subway, Jeff drove back as fast as he could. This fast driving did not last long as he noticed that everything in his back seat and trunk were being knocked all around. It did not make sense to him to grab all this stuff, just to bring it back all busted up. He slowed down and drove reasonably back to the hotel.

Van Camp made one quick stop in the second barn before he headed out, just on the small chance that there was something to be found. There was not, and it was back to his car for the silent, sad ride back to oversee his subjects, or so he thought.

Joe-Joe, with his carload of entertainment and can goods, headed back to display his selections from Blockbuster. With the exciting news that there would be no late charges, if they were not returned in six days.

Then he realized that he needed some DVD players. It was a quick u-turn back into the lot with a stop in front of K-Mart. It was a Super K-Mart, so finding DVD players should be easy and plentiful.

After Joe-Joe loaded up a couple of DVD players, he smiled approval for his work and headed back to join the others.

CHAPTER 20

THE RETURN

I N THE LOBBY, LISA AND Ben were deep into their naps. At one point, Ben had opened his eyes and found that he was looking straight at Lisa. Initially, he assumed that he had picked up and slept with the biggest and ugliest hooker in the world. After giving this some thought, he realized that he was almost completely right. She was the biggest and ugliest person left on the earth, but not a hooker. Moreover, if she was a hooker, she could only make sales to blind guys.

He then wondered how long he would need to be alone on this earth with her before she started to look acceptable. After years in prison, and wanting to be left alone, he changed his mind after looking at her a second time. He wished to himself for the safe return of everyone. Even those two brothers, that he believed did not trust him.

Rose Marie, Kitty, and Alice were the first to return. Alice went directly to her room to unpack her bag of goodies and to attempt a few more calls home.

Kitty also made it to her room to unpack, re-make her make-up and hair before returning to the lobby.

Rose Marie made her way to the lobby after she got a soda from the gift shop. She enjoyed the ride with her two new friends, but now realized that they might be her only friends for the rest of her life. Rose

Marie still likes cats better than most people do. Alice spent about the same time calling home as Kitty did with her makeup and hair. They met up with each other in the hallway and headed to the lobby. There, they joined up with Van Camp as he was talking with Ben and Lisa.

"Are we the only ones back so far," questioned Van Camp.

"I believe so," answered Kitty.

"Find anything," asked Ben looking at Van Camp.

"Not a thing. Not even animals," he answered.

With no one having anything new to add, they sat there looking at the floor. With his small group, Van Camp took a bold step and instructed, "We should wait until everyone returns, then have our fact finding meeting."

Ben did not like him to take charge as he did, but he did not have an idea right then of his own, and if he did, it would be the same as what Van Camp just said.

Lisa, having nothing to say, closed her eyes and ignored those around her. Van Camp talked a little with Kitty and Alice as Ben made his way to the men's room.

Just as Ben returned, so did Jerry, Burt, Steven, Eddie, and Jeff. A few of them went first to the rest rooms, some made it to the gift shop, as others took a seat and joined them.

Small talk was in session between everyone, when Joe-Joe, Billy Bob and Bob Billy returned to the hotel.

After the brothers stopped off at their room to unload their ammo, they joined right in and wanted to start a meeting. If this was the time to get things moving, they knew that they could do it.

"Is everybody here," questioned Billy Bob to the group.

Everyone looked around as if they were each doing a head count. It appeared that everyone was there. Ben did not want them to take charge of the meeting, and he did not want Van Camp either. With that, he stood up and said, "I believe that we are all here. We should go around the room and see what we found."

Van Camp noticed the power struggle between Ben and Billy Bob, and decided that he would not do anything right now, but would volunteer to go first.

Van Camp stood up and to the side of the group, making it a point not to stand near those two. He started, "As you know, I went west for thirty minutes. As before, I saw nothing. I did make a stop on a farm."

"Farm," questioned Ben. "What the hell good was that?"

"Good question," was his reply. Van Camp continued, "I was passing a number of horse farms in Maryland and noticed the absence of animals. I felt that it needed an investigation."

After a short pause, he continued, "When I came across a large farm with two barns, I drove up to them."

Everyone was quiet now. They saw the importance of why he did, what he did.

Continuing, "The barns were empty of animals. If the people were evacuated, as some of us think, so then were all the animals. Another thing that I noticed, was that there were no flies."

"Flies," questioned Joe-Joe.

"Yes, flies. The barn had piles of animal dung and there was not a single fly flying around it. No birds, no dogs, no cows, and no horses. I found that to be most interesting."

Bob Billy spoke and said, "Yeah man. No animals. When my brother and I were in Wilmington, we picked up that there were no animals around there either. No pigeons downtown and no dogs in the neighborhoods."

This seemed to be a more serious find than not finding any people. If something bad happened, there would at least be bodies.

Burt asked, "Has anyone checked a hospital yet?"

No one responded, and then Burt asked, "There must be people there that were too sick to move, and if there are, them some of those people should still be there."

Everyone agreed to that, and Kitty asked, "Where is the nearest hospital?"

No one responded right away, but Bob Billy came back with, "Christiana Hospital in Newark. It's a big hospital and I can go and check it out after this little meeting."

Ben spoke up and asked, "When you go, can I go with you? I don't feel like hanging around here any more than I need to."

"Sure. Did you find anything at the jail house?"

"Nope, no one. The main gate was opened, but everything else was locked up. I was able to look into the prison yard, and it was empty. I even saw a couple of prison buses still there. I would have thought that if they were evacuated, that it would have taken all the buses."

Van Camp decided to sit down, as he was no longer the center of attention. With that, Kitty got up. She said, "Alice, Rose Marie and I headed north and we crossed over the Delaware Memorial Bridge and headed north on I-295. We found the same conditions."

Alice did not get up, but said, "That's right. We did not see anything going up or on or way coming back. There were three of us in the car and we saw nothing but a whole lot of nothing. Nothing and no one."

Everyone shook his or her head, somberly. Lisa stayed seated and said, "I made a number of calls, and all I got was nothing. I found no one."

Jerry was so excited that when he stood up, everyone thought that he had good news. He did, and he said, "I went east and found the bay. Nothing was on the bay, nothing. I drove around and like the rest of us, I found no one."

Eddie was about to take his turn and speak, when Jerry placed his hand out, and said, "One minute, if you please."

"This is the good part," he started. "On the bay, yes there were no people, but if we must go anyplace together, we can go by boat. Head south for the winter or north to New York City."

To his surprise, no one really cared about taking any boat trip.

They wanted to stay in place until everyone came back.

With that response, he sat down and daydreamed that, when it came time to go some place, that he would go by boat, alone if that was how it was to turn out.

Ben looked over at Joe-Joe, and asked, "What did you find while you were out?"

Joe-Joe was caught off guard, stood up, and said, "I have plenty of can goods and other food items."

Others in the group thought that was premature to stock up for the winner just yet. At least, not until they knew what was going on."

"Anything else," questioned Ben.

"Yeah, I got us plenty of movies to watch."

To the group, that seemed even more useless, than carting around a ton of can goods. Joe-Joe, able to pick up his questionable actions, said, "You will appreciate them when there is nothing to do at night and you want something to help kill the time."

For a dummy, thought Van Camp, this kid had a point. "Good idea," Van Camp said, to put a positive spin on this. "There is no telling how long we will be in this predicament. A good movie now and then, will be helpful."

Others seemed to accept his choice of supplies to be acceptable, and gave it no more negative attention.

Billy Bob wanting to get back in control, said, "My brother and I spent time in Wilmington. We drove downtown, uptown, and all around town and found nothing. Like my brother said and Dick mentioned, no animals anywhere. Even all the birds were gone."

Eddie took his turn, and said, "Steven and I returned to Dover after a stop at the mall."

Billy Bob, wanting to make a joke out of this, asked, "So, was the mall crowded?"

Looking disappointed, he responded, "Yeah man. Crowded with nobody. Yet, we did pick up some supplies for everyone. Some soap, toothpaste, and stuff."

Adding to this, Steven said, "We made a stop and got ourselves a change of clothes before we went back to the base."

Van Camp asked, "What did you find there?"

"Same as before," answered Eddie. "We made another trip to the control tower, confiscated a pair of binoculars, before we check out HQ and a set of barracks."

Steven stood up and added, "We checked the barracks to see how it was abandoned."

"What," questioned Alice?

"We wanted to see how the people left. We found that in all

appearances, things were normal. Some rooms were empty, and some rooms looked lived in. The rooms that looked lived in, their things were not packed up. Some had soap in the soap dish and toothbrushes in the bathroom."

Burt wanted to brag about his new Hummer, so he interrupted Steven. "The base was empty," he asked to hurry things along.

"Yeah, but we wanted to see if we could tell if, how, and when everyone left the base."

Eddie added, "We even checked for flights that arrived and departed the base thinking that we might find something helpful, but nothing."

Not asking anything else, and after waiting a few seconds, Burt spoke up. "I got us some tools, gas cans filled with gas, floodlights, batteries, radios, and two generators."

Everyone seemed pleased that he was thoughtful enough to gather those things up for everyone.

Before Jeff started to report on his findings, the last guy to talk about his trip, Burt added, "I also got me a new car. I stopped off and got me a brand new, yellow, fully equipped Hummer."

That put a smile on everyone's face as each of them were thinking of what kind of new car or truck, they could easily pick up. Van Camp seizing the opportunity, said, "Now there is a plan.

One day, we'll all go out and get ourselves new cars."

Jeff, knowing that he was the last to talk, stood up and raddled off the list of items that he had stocked in his car.

Joe-Joe was pleased about the laptops and games and he asked, "Later, you and I can swap a few movies for a few games."

Getting back to what he wanted to accomplish, Jeff continued with, "I have CB radios for everyone. I know that we have cell phones, but soon, they might stop working."

Van Camp, having a good memory and able to summarize easily, repeated what was noted by those who went out. He gave a quick review of what supplies were collected. He fell short on what to do next.

Ben, figured that he could con everyone into following his lead, said. "We should think about what we as a group should do next."

"Well," he started. "Some of us may want to go home and sit this out. Some may want to stay here."

Burt spoke up, and added, "Then like me, I don't want to go home and be alone, I don't want to stay here, I might want to head south with anyone that wants to go."

"Go where," questioned Billy Bob.

Given this a little more thought, "I don't want to be up here when winter sets in. We may not have heat and you know that no one will plow the roads when it snows."

Everyone was quiet and taking in what he was saying. Alice asked, "When would you want to head south?" Alice was now accepting that her family was gone and she needed to survive.

"Not right away. Let a few days go by first. See if anything changes. You know, another trip to Dover, Wilmington, maybe a trip back to where you lived or worked."

Everyone was listening to this make shift plan. Van Camp noticed that, and said, "You know Burt, I like it. It makes sense."

Billy Boy added, "I'm with you. If there is nothing here, then there might be something in Florida."

"What's in Florida," questioned Joe-Joe.

"At the very least, the same as here, only warmer."

"What about our family," Joe-Joe asked.

"When you go home, leave a note. You know, something like, 'I am safe and headed to Florida.' Leave a time and date."

Organizing all this, Van Camp said, "I like it. We can pick a date to leave. Say, two days from now. For your note that you leave, give them the time, and date that we left and where we are going, and our route."

Ben excitedly added, "And don't forget to mention that you have a new car."

This got a chuckle from mostly everyone. It was not very funny, because on a side note, they were leaving their homes, family, and jobs for places and circumstances unknown.

To keep things moving, Van Camp said, "We should set up committees on things to do over the next two days."

"Committees," questioned Ben. To him, things were getting just a little to 'corporate,' for his taste. With too many committees, he would have a difficult time working a con with everyone placed in groups.

"Nothing all that official, just to see what we need in supplies, communications, vehicles, and where we plan to go."

Everyone agreed that would be a good idea. Yet, a few had no desire to be in charge of a committee, and no desire to take part, as it was much easier to follow instructions. It was assumed that Van Camp, Ben, and the Brown brothers wanted those positions with Eddie and Steven as committee members.

Lisa spoke up, and bitched, "You all can discuss what you want to discuss and decide what you want to decide, but for me, I am hungry."

She looked over at Joe-Joe, and asked, "What'cha bring me boy?"

Bob Billy said to Billy Boy, "Just throw Free Wily some fish."

"Can't do that man, all the fish are dead," Billy Bob answered.

"Shit man, we be in trouble," chuckled Bob Billy with Lisa giving him the evil eye.

Not wanting things to get out of hand, Ben needed to con something quick like.

Van Camp picked up on that also, and as the Brown brothers joked back and forth to each other, he said, "Anyone desiring to be a committee member, let's meet back here in thirty minutes."

Ben wanting to stay in the decision making process, added, "Yeah, thirty minutes. We can decide then who, what, when, and where."

The group, having heard enough bad news, slowly got up from their seats. Some made their way to the gift shop and others headed to their rooms.

"We need coffee," suggested Eddie to Steven. With that, those two were off to the kitchen to make coffee and cold drinks for the group. They took their time as they figured that they had thirty or so minutes before the next meeting started.

Lisa was the first one in the gift shop and with her hands filled with junk food, she returned to her seat to feast.

Still in the joking mood, Bob Billy said, "Next time Dick visits a farm, he can pick up a feed bag to hang around her neck."

Billy Bob was trying not to let Lisa see him laugh, as he believed, she would attack him, and hurt him. He responded to his brother with, "Shut up man. You now if she hears you, she will kick your ass and you don't have enough ammo to slow her down."

Well, that was all it took for Bob Billy. He laughed so loud that everyone turned to look at him. He just held up one hand, waved it a little, and said, "Just a private joke."

His brother just slapped him on the head and said, "Shut up."

Nothing more was said by the two of them, and everyone went on about their way, to kill time for thirty minutes.

Bob Billy said, "Ben, my brother and I will take a ride to Christiana Hospital later today. Anybody want to join us?"

Eddie turned his way and said, "I'll go. While you guys look for people, I will pick up some medical supplies."

"Good idea," encouraged Van Camp. "Is anyone here under any kind of medication?"

No one raised his or her hand, which was a good sign, thought Van Camp, but he had to consider that someone might be holding back, and not wanting to share that information.

"Good," said Eddie. "I'll just grab enough for a good medical emergency kit."

"You want some help," asked Steven. "I have some first aid training."

"Hell yeah," came the response.

Ben suggested, "We should take two cars. We might not have room for all of us and the medical supplies you guys plan to pick up."

"No sweat," Steven and Eddie responded at the same time. "We can leave after our next meeting. I'll just follow you there. I'm not sure where the hospital is."

Bob Billy joked, "Cool, when you follow us, stay close. I don't want to lose you guys in the traffic."

This got a little smile from the four of them.

CHAPTER 21

WHAT TO DO NOW?

V AN CAMP AND BEN STAYED behind as everyone headed out from
the lobby. Billy Bob and Bob Billy were going to take a trip to
their room, but decided to stay and join in with Van Camp and Ben.

As the brothers joined up with them, Ben asked, "What was so
amusing?"

They told him about Lisa and the four of them agreed that it
was very funny. Van Camp, wanting to talk down at their level, said,
"We can put her on the food committee."

Their laughter continued before the four of them sat down and
for the first time, the dominant characteristic of each one came out.
Not in a mean way, but they knew that there cannot be four leaders
at the same time.

There was nothing discussed about what they had plan to bring
up in thirty minutes, but just questions and answers about their
backgrounds and any suggestions on what had happened. This went
on for a few minutes as a friendship started to form. You would have
gotten the impression earlier that they somehow hated each other,
not true. Well, maybe superficial friends because of what has gotten
them to this point.

After about thirty minutes or so, Lisa and Jeff returned first and sat near Van Camp, Ben, Billy Bob, and Bob Billy Brown.

Within the next five minutes, one by one, everyone else, except for Steven and Eddie, started to return. For no particular reason, they sat a few seats away from this group. It started to look like a football game where the referees are huddled together discussing a flag that was thrown, while the players kept their distance.

"Where are we going to go," asked up Jeff, as he was impatient to wait for the meeting to start.

"Yeah," bitch Lisa with a nasty looking smile with potato chips in her teeth.

The four men looked at one other for an answer. Other than heading south, assuming that Florida would be the spot, nothing else had been discussed.

"Florida," said Ben with his hand out, and shoulder up, as if asking and answering a question at the same time.

"That's a big state," was the nasty statement from Lisa.

"We can decide that later. We have only talked about heading that way, not where to stop," added in Van Camp.

Seeing that this, pre-informal meeting, might turn hostile, Van Camp asked her, "Any suggestions."

"Yeah, not Miami," suggested Burt, not knowing that the question was initially for Lisa. "Too many Cubans there."

"Not now," jokes Joe-Joe.

"How about Titusville," asked Jeff?

About four or five people responded, "Titusville?"

Jeff stood up, and said, "It's a nice little town, near the ocean, not on it, near Cape Kennedy, not next to it. And, it is not too far south were it is always hot."

"And," questioned Ben as if he needed one or more additional reasons for Titusville.

Believing that he had made good points already, Jeff added in a few more. "It has a seaport that cruise ships use. It is near the space center. If what happened came from outer space, that would be the place to be. It is also just off Interstate 95."

Everyone took in what he was saying and he had their attention. He added, "Cape Kennedy is an important location. If anything was to be well protected and manned, that would be the place."

"Anyone disagree with that assumption," asked Ben.

No one did and it was easily settled that Titusville, Florida, would be their next port of call.

"Okay then, when do we leave," asked Billy Bob.

"In two days," said Van Camp and Ben at the same time. "First thing in the morning, two days from now. Monday."

Steven and Eddie pulled up and announced their return with coffee and cold drinks. Stephen and Eddie were easily welcomed into this select group of leaders that were together in front of the lobby. This was made apparent as they stopped with the cart up near Van Camp, the Brown brothers and Ben.

They also picked up that the meeting had already started without them and they seemed a little ticked. This meeting was something that they needed to be included.

As everyone took a minute for a cup of coffee or cold drink, Ben filled in Eddie and Steven about Titusville. Van Camp added that they did not start the meeting without them, it was only that they just got too talking with nothing decided.

They seemed to agree with Titusville, and appreciate Van Camp's comments. Now, a little relaxed that they were up to date with the meeting, and voiced that it was a good idea to be near a military installation.

The meeting moved into a more formal atmosphere. More questions were asked about what had happened than on what they should do now. For what they should do in two days, was pushed aside. Maybe it was realized that this was two days away and that there was plenty of time for that later.

There were no new theories of what had happened. Everyone had good guesses from a military invasion, aliens from space taking away all living creatures, and the End-Times. The reasons for them being left behind had the same theories. It was generally assumed that there might be other groups, that may have survived.

It was agreed that whenever they traveled, that all military bases should be visited.

The six of them were poised to be the leaders of the group. Steven and Eddie were content to stay idle and to see how this started out before they said anything.

Bob Billy was not going to say anything either, but to let his older brother speak.

Van Camp spoke up, and said, "Does anyone here want to do anything, go anywhere, that does not involve any of us?"

No one said anything right away. Ben, picked up on what Van Camp was getting at, added, "You know, does anyone want to go home for example. Is there somewhere you want to check out on your own? Like other family members and friends."

Alice raised her hand, and after all of them looked her way, she said, "I want to drive to my house again. Get a few things. On my way back, stop off to see about my children and grandchildren." With tears in her eyes, she continued, "I want to do this after we decide when and where we are going. I want to leave them a note."

That created a somber tone for the meeting as everyone wanted to do the same thing. Check on family, friends, and leave notes.

Seeing the importance, Van Camp said, "I agree. I want to do the same thing. I do have a suggestion. Before anyone goes off on their own, leave a note on what time you left, where you are going, and when are you planning to return."

Ben added, "We have your cell number. That will keep us in touch until the phone services stop."

She shook her head affirmatively and wiped away a few tears.

This was sad as Kitty held in her tears. Not because she did not want to show weakness, she did not want to spend time redoing her makeup.

Lisa made a comment that only the five guys up front overheard. "At least she has friends."

Billy Bob then said to his brother, "Well dah, she ate all of hers."

Bob Billy did not laugh; he felt her pain in a way. With everyone gone, he had no family or friends either.

Joe-Joe spoke up and asked, "So, we are going to sit here for two days? During this time, we can head home and leave notes that we are going to this Titusville Florida place. Do I have it right?"

At first glance, you would have thought that Joe-Joe was summarizing the meeting, but in reality, he was not very smart and wanted to make sure that he knew what was going to happen. No way did he want to be left behind, or not to pull his own weight. He knew that he would be unable to survive on his own.

The leadership group up front, after looking at each other for anything additional to add, all shook their heads in approval of what Joe-Joe had asked.

Joe-Joe, now that he was on a roll, asked, "Who has the final say on things?"

The leadership group, after looking at each again, all shook their heads displaying that they had no idea.

Jeff added, "Do we really need one person to be in charge? It seems to be working just fine the way we have it now."

The group that was seated agreed, but it was the group up front, that had wished that this particular decision were made, made in their own favor. It appeared to them that for now, that the group leadership would remain .

Van Camp wanted to end this meeting, and naturally, that he would be the one to do it, announced, "We have a few guys that are going to Christiana Hospital to check on things and bring back emergency supplies."

He looked around to see if anyone wanted to respond. He then look at the others standing beside him for the same reason. Satisfied that there were no additional questions, he asked, "Any more questions?"

"Should we meet later this evening," ask Joe-Joe.

Ben quickly took the lead from Van Camp. "Okay, we can do that. 8pm sound okay to everyone?"

Everyone shook their heads and started to leave.

Billy Bob spoke up, figuring because he was versed in security, said,"If you go any place, you know leave the hotel. Leave a note at the front desk. We don't want to loose anyone."

At this time, this small group of survivors had a plan. Nothing in detail, just hang loose for two days, and then drive to Florida. Some headed back to their rooms, some made it back to the gift shop with Lisa in the lead, and the remaining few, stayed in the lobby, anticipating that others would so, and that they would not be alone.

Burt, after unloading his supplies, stopped at the front desk and left a note. 'I am off to AAA for maps. A quick drive to my house and return. Not sure how long, but a few hours at least, but will be back before the 8pm meeting.'

Ben left a note about the four of them heading to Christiana hospital.

Steven suggested to Eddie, we should get walkie-talkies for the four of us. Eddie agreed and said, "I'll go and get them from Jeff."

Steven said, "I'll let Ben know what you are doing and I'll get the car, and we can all meet out front."

It did not take long before they were ready for the hospital run. After a radio check, they were heading north on 13.

Alice left a note just before she was to head out. Kitty asked her where she was going. After Alice told her, Kitty asked if she could go along.

Alice was pleased to have company, and she said yes. No one else left the hotel. The ones that had somewhere to go, left their notes and headed out.

CHAPTER 22

KILLING TIME

For Burt, on his way to AAA just off I-95 near Christiana Mall, he took his time. He was enjoying his new Hummer and wanted to put it to the test. If he were to break it, he knew where to go to select him another one. For a few miles on 13 North, he drove in the medium. He had time to kill and that he might as well do what he liked to do.

At the AAA office, he collected a dozen maps of each state for the ride south and twenty or so maps of Florida. Looking around the office, he found five first aid kits that were to be kept in cars. He grabbed them up along with some cruise schedules that showed arrival and departure times at Port Canaveral. He thought that maybe some cruise ships were unaffected, and if so, it would be a good idea to know when they were in port.

Alice stopped off at the different homes of her grandchildren. She showed Kitty around and made it a point to show off the pictures on the refrigerators. It was there that she left her notes that she was alive and headed south.

Her next stop was to her house where she packed a suitcase.

Kitty asked, "Is that all you are going to take?"

"Yeah," she said sadly.

On their way back, Kitty suggested, "Want to stop at the mall? We have plenty of time."

Alice's answer was a smile and a turn at the next light that headed towards the mall.

At the mall, Kitty snatched up two suitcases. She needed a large one for clothes and a smaller one for additional makeup.

This took them about an hour and they both felt at the same time, that they had been gone long enough. They wanted to be around other people.

The trip to the hospital was uneventful. Ben suggested that they split up to cover more area. Ben was pleased when he agreed. For him, it was more purses to search.

Eddie and Steven broke into the pharmacy and made away with bags and bags of supplies. They agreed that they needed more and found the supply rooms on different floors. They had so much that a gurney was used to help haul it all away.

At the cars, Eddie radioed Ben and Billy Bob informing them that they were ready to go. He wanted to know if they should wait for them, or for them to head on back.

Billy Bob asked them to hold-off for a few minutes, and that they could drive back together.

It was agreed, and ten minutes later, they all headed to the hotel. The only things that they found and collected were medical supplies. No people around and nothing to suggest what may have happened.

Back at the hotel, Joe-Joe had set up a DVD player to a TV that was found in one of the unoccupied rooms. He had the movie Cars playing. His first choice was season two of Survivor, but Lisa bitched that she did not want to see people eating raw fish and swatting away the flies.

Jerry had a front row seat and enjoyed the movie. He had nothing going on in his life right now and watching the movie killed time. He needed a few more movies to kill more time for at least two days. He was thinking, that maybe tomorrow, he would go back to the marina and find himself a boat.

Jeff spent his time behind the front desk trying to access the hotel's computer. Not necessary to assign rooms, but to go on-line and see if there was any news on AOL, FOX, or CNN. After a few hours of trying, he gave up, joined in, and watched the movie Cars.

Van Camp spent time in his room taking notes in the form of a diary. He knew that when he graduated from this nightmare, that he would write a book. After an hour or so of note taking, he took a nap before he headed towards the lobby to try to gain some votes, should there be a vote to place someone as Supreme Commander.

Rose Marie wanted to take a nap. Not that she was tired, but a nap was a good time killer for her. At home, it was something that she would do on Saturday or Sunday, as well as any holiday or vacation day she had from work. It gave her, and her cats, quality quiet time together.

Bob Billy wanted to take a nap back at his room, but decided to take one in the lobby. He wanted to be nearby should anything come up, especially while his older brother was gone.

From those that left, Burt was the first to return. He had experienced a wonderful wild ride in his new Hummer. He had kicked up so much grass and mud, that it was difficult to tell from the side view, that his Hummer was yellow. To Burt, this was not dirty; it was the result of a good day behind the wheel.

He placed all the maps that he retrieved from AAA on the front desk, except he kept one of each for himself. Burt was off to take a long hot bath, and then he returned to the lobby to do the nap/TV watching combination. More nap than TV though.

Alice and Kitty were next to return. For the two ladies, they made it to their rooms to unpack, change clothes, and freshen up. An hour later, they were in the lobby, as they had nothing else to do. They sat together and before long, they had started to form a strong bond.

After her short and lonely nap, Rose Marie freshened up and headed for the lobby.

Eddie and Steven came in just after Kitty and Alice. These two piled their supplies in the back of the lobby and took a mental note on what was there. Not that they thought someone would take anything, just to know where an item was in the event of an emergency.

Ben, along with Billy Bob, was the last to return. As they had nothing new to add, they took a seat and started up small conversations with those that were there.

It was not 8pm yet, as 8pm was hours away, but everyone was there in the lobby.

CHAPTER 23

DINNER TIME

ERE THEY WERE TOGETHER, IN the lobby still. It was not enough time to do something, and return for the meeting, and yet, it was too much time available just to hang around. Other than small talk between them, nothing was going on.

Van Camp did his best to speak with everyone at least once.

If a click was starting to form up, he wanted in.

Ben took a different approach, and tried to determine if there were any clicks starting up. If there were, he would try to disarm it. If not able to do so, he would then try to determine who the leader was. He also knew to stay on good terms with Van Camp, the Brown brothers along with Steven and Eddie. The others, sissies that they were, could be easily tricked to follow his direction. To get things moving, or just to start bitching about something, Lisa stood up and said in a loud voice, "We need to have a plan for dinner."

This was not said to be mean or to be taken in a bitchy way, she only had one way to say anything, and she bitched it.

Because she seemed so domineering, Ben thought that she would be a good ally. Not that she would make friends, just that people would do what she said, to keep her from getting mad and bitching at them. He would use her negativity in a positive way. In any case, he would make it very clear that he was not making a move on her. Not now anyway, only if and years after Kitty, Rose Marie, and Alice were found dead or missing.

Van Camp, on the other hand, saw no reason to consult with her. If she ever worked for him, he would find a reason to fire her.

Ben walked over and stood next to her. "Me too," he added as he then looked around because he wanted to get a team effort started here. He asked, "Any ideas for tonight's meal?"

No one was quick to respond. Even though everyone was hungry, they just were not as hungry as she was.

Finally, Steven spoke up, "We have a kitchen here. Let's check it out."

started to talk between themselves about food, as they were also starting to get hungry, but many lacked the experience to cook in a restaurant kitchen.

"There is the Salad Shop across the street. Everything can't have gone bad since yesterday," Kitty joined in.

Van Camp saw a chance to make a leadership move. He suggested, "If we can get someone to cross the street and get some salads bowls made up, someone to get the grills turned on, and, someone else to set up some tables, we can knock it out in no time." He waited for a few volunteers. Then, Kitty said, looking at Alice, "You and I can go over and get the salads."

Lisa, realizing that she got the whole thing started, said, "I'll go and get the grills fired up. I might need some help."

Ben said, "I'll help you. I will find us some steaks in the freezer."

Van Camp saw another opportunity, and said, "I'll get the tables set up." He did this, not to be a team player, but because he wanted to set the tables in such a formation that, he would have himself sitting in a commanding position. Van Camp had a plan and he liked it.

Eddie spoke up and said, "I'll make us some more coffee."

Steven, seeing that this might be fun, said, "I'll find us some wine for dinner. We can make a feast out of this."

The others in the group, did not know what to volunteer for, but were eager to help. For a brief moment in his or her lives, the absence of everyone else in the world seemed to be a distant problem. For now, it was dinnertime.

Lisa and Ben made a good team cooking up some steaks. Between Steven and Eddie, coffee was hot; cold drinks were cold, and the wine bottles were on all the tables that Van Camp had set up.

Next were the salads from across the street as Alice and Kitty placed large salad bowls on each table.

The ones not contributing were, Jerry, Joe-Joe, Jeff, and Burt. These guys simply took a seat and expected to be served. Billy Bob and his brother, Bob Billy, were in the kitchen getting dishes and silverware and cooking up frozen bags of vegetables. It was obvious to those that were pitching in, that some here were not team players.

Jerry and Joe-Joe noticed the dirty looks they were given and had no idea as to why. They figured that all the duties were taken care of and that they would just get in the way. Jeff and Burt quickly picked up the hint and assisted in the kitchen.

In about an hour's time, everyone was seated and enjoying there meal. It was turning out to be a fun meal because this group realized that they had to stick together. Conversations went on not only across the tables, but also across the room.

An example would be, "Is this better than the meals at the chow hall," someone would ask Steven. Lisa spoke up, and for the first time, she did not bitch, and said, "Looks like we got ourselves a Happy Meal!"

Van Camp stood up and proposed a toast. Little did he realize that he was about to screw up royally. "I desire that all of our meals are like this, one big Happy Meal."

For a few, Jerry, Burt, and Joe-Joe, they liked what he just said. On the other hand, the others were just reminded that they had lost family members and friends. That they would never enjoy another, Happy Meal, with a loved one again.

With this toast, the happy festive atmosphere had ceased. Not a very good move on his part. Wanting to recover, he added,"My thoughts were this, we are in the same boat, and it's a good thing we can start out on a positive note. We make a good team."

He looked around to see that he had everyone's attention, and continued, "The world is different now. Everyone had already lost a lot, family, friends, and co-workers. We have a plan to survive and speaking for myself, I plan to survive."

Wanting to pick up everyone's spirit, and to pull Van Camp out of his dive, Ben spoke up and said, "I agree with Dick here. We have a plan. For right now, we have a plan and a full stomach."

That remark got a hilarious comment from Lisa, "Thank you Jesus for the full stomach!"

That created a few 'amends,' and all seemed fine as the conversations picked up where they had left off.

The meal continued for another hour. With nowhere to go but to the lobby or to their rooms, no one was in a hurry to get up and leave.

The first two to get up, were Jerry and Joe-Joe. Ben recalled how these two did not help out, and that they were going to quietly leave their dishes on the table and walk away.

He tapped Van Camp on the side and said, "Those two lazy bums should clean up for us."

Van Camp also had noticed their sneaky departure. He looked at them and spoke out, "You guys want to do your fair share and clean up tonight?"

Not wanting Van Camp to take all the credit for organizing this working party, joined in and said, "I agree. Everybody created this meal and you two guys did not contribute."

Billy Bob did not want to cleanup, after he had put in his effort for this meal, added, "You two should clean up man, do your part."

The two escapees, clearly understood what those three men were saying and what was expected of them. Jerry looked as if he would rather take a nap than to pull his fair share, but Joe-Joe spoke up and said, "You are right. We'll take care of the clean up."

Joe-Joe, with a good attitude, smiled and made his way back to the kitchen with his dishes and a few salad bowls that were empty.

Jerry, on the other hand, did not do dishes when he was home, and he did not want to do them here. However, he made all the outward appearances that he wanted to help.

As he would pick up dishes, he made a little more noise than need be. He wanted everyone to notice that he was doing his fair share. Once he dumped the dishes in the kitchen, he returned and grabbed up more empty dishes and glasses. The only thing he hated more than picking up dishes, was getting other peoples food on his hands and clothes.

With the cleanup well underway, everyone else slowly made their way to the lobby with brief stops at the restrooms.

After Jerry made a few trips back and forth, noticed that Joe-Joe was washing dishes. He asked him, "Why are you washing them?"

Looking surprised, answered, "Why not? They are dirty."

"Yeah but," interjected Jerry, "There are enough dishes already cleaned to last us for another day. We are leaving in two days remember."

Joe-Joe thought for a minute, and agreed. "Great, we can clean off all the tables and pile the dirty dishes over there in the corner."

They both acted as if they were hooking school and getting away with it. Together, they cleaned off the tables, and even took the time to place clean tablecloths down, and to layout silverware for the next meal.

Then it was back to the kitchen to, neatly pile up the dishes after they were wiped clean of food. Trash was taken out and the sink wiped dry. If you were to give a quick inspection of the kitchen, the boys did a good job and should score high points for their work.

For them, it was off to their rooms to clean up and to trot on down to the lobby for a movie or two.

CHAPTER 24

WHAT DO WE DO NOW?

A FTER AN ENJOYABLE MEAL, SOME calls to the restrooms, and visits to their rooms, everyone once more was assembled in the lobby.

The congregation this time had developed into small-organized groups, as if forming into teams or clicks.

Joe-Joe picked this up and felt that it reminded him of the TV reality show, Survivors. If he had his way, he would vote off Van Camp, Ben, the Brown brothers, and Lisa. Everyone else could stay, and naturally, leaving Kitty until the end with him.

Ben watched as the groups formed and he related this to the gangs in prison. Van Camp looked around and saw this as his employees organized into project teams. Alice thought that the groups were family units. Eddie saw squads of marines with Steven placing the groups into working parties. However, for this gathering formation, it was still a click. People of like minds and backgrounds turned towards each other. The only one not in a group was Lisa. With her size, she weight about as much, if not more, as some of the teams.

Joe-Joe had an insignificant effect on the groups. With the TV on, and his show starting, a few glanced his way, and then back to the group they were involved with.

Burt was at the front desk with an unfolded map of the east coast.

He was plotting a route south. Jeff watched with much interest, a little confused that selecting a route to Florida would be that difficult. If he was asked, 'Other than driving south on I-95, what other way would you go?'

Burt looked up, and answered as if he knew what Jeff was going to ask, "You are right, the simplest and quickest way would be to get on I-95, and to stay on I-95."

Jeff shook his head in acknowledgment.

"However," stated Burt pointing to the DC area of the map, "We are not in a hurry, so we could make a few detours along the way."

"Why detours," questioned Jeff.

"Good question and I have a good answer," he said, as Van Camp and Ben walked up and stood behind Jeff. They were curious as to what was going on between the two of them.

"Washington, DC would be a good example for a detour. We could stop off at 1600 Pennsylvania Avenue, and then end up at the Pentagon," explained Burt.

Jeff realized, along with Van Camp and Ben, just how important these stops would be. In fact, agreeing so much that Ben said to Van Camp, "Do we really need to hang around here all day tomorrow before leaving the next day?"

Van Camp, after giving this a few seconds of thought, responded with, "I can see that as a good, and as a bad idea."

"How can that be bad," questioned Burt, because he felt that his plan was foolproof.

"If we leave tomorrow, for example, we might not have enough supplies," was the only quick answer that he could generate.

"Okay, lets say that we are short a few can goods or toilet paper. No problem, just as we are doing here right now, simply hit a few stores wherever we are. Besides, we can't carry all of our supplies at one time anyway."

Burt had a good point and he had developed a good, feasible plan on his own.

"You really want to leave tomorrow morning," asked Van Camp.

Ben did not have an answer right away, and when he did, Billy

Bob had joined in on the conversation. Billy Bob suggested, "Why not? If anyone must make a trip home to leave notes, there is time to do that now. And, like Burt just explained, we can pick up what we need, as we need it."

This group had all but made up their minds on leaving tomorrow morning for Washington and all points south.

Burt asked, "Everyone is here now, why not have a meeting and bring this up."

They all made a face as if indicating, 'sure, and why not?'

Steven and Eddie were talking nearby and picked up on what they were discussing, Eddie said, "I never did understand why we had to hang around two days anyway. Go for it, tomorrow sounds good to me."

Steven added in his two cents, "If anyone was left alive besides us, they would certainly be at the White House, or at the Pentagon. I say we do it, do it soon."

As they broke up and headed towards the front of the lobby, Van Camp asked, "Who wants to explain our decision to the group?"

He was asking, trying to catch everyone off guard, anticipating that they would ask him to do it. Well, he was correct and no one said anything. Wanting to keep them on his side, he added, "Stay close to me guys. Add in comments at any time. There are bound to be a lot of questions."

Van Camp knew all the answers to any questions that these few people could throw at him. They were not as educated and talented as he was, but sharing the spot light would be a good thing, just on the small chance that the crowd might go hostile. Maybe, they were the only ones that wanted to leave Delaware.

Van Camp did not need to say anything to get everyone's attention, as their arrival got everyone looking his way. Even with Joe-Joe giving commanding concentration to the TV, Alice tapped him softly on the shoulder and pointed to the front of the lobby.

Joe-Joe, not quick on many things, but was quick this time, turned off the TV and DVD player, and faced them.

With the group's attention, Van Camp started, "A few of us were discussing our options."

Lisa did not like the tone of this meeting after just the first sentence, said, "What do you mean, 'our options?'"

Van Camp was not ready for questions so quickly, nor was he prepared for Lisa's bitching attitude. He responded, "Well, we are all in the same situation. As I said, we were just discussing our options. We have not made any decisions for anyone, as it stands now, we have all agreed to stay here for two days and then head south."

He looked at Lisa for additional questions or comments from her, there was none.

Van Camp continued, "We were thinking, why wait two days, why not just pack up, and head out tomorrow."

Waiting for questions, there were none, he continued, "We discussed, as before, to head south to Florida. It was suggested that on our way south, that we would stop at 1600 Pennsylvania Avenue, and then swing over to the Pentagon."

Still, no one had comments or questions. Eddie spoke up and said, "Those detours off I-95 would be well worth our time to check out. If anyone is still around, we assumed that they would be in one, if not both, of those two places."

Ben joined in. "Yeah, like he said, we will check out those places and reevaluate what we do next."

Even though that part, the reevaluation, was never discussed, the decisions makers acted as if they did, besides, to them, what he just added made perfect sense.

Alice spoke up with a question and a tear in her eyes. "Leaving tomorrow? Can't we stay a few more days?"

Van Camp, felt that he was most qualified for this question, said, "I'll take this one."

Then, looking as if he was speaking at a funeral, said, "You know, we have already looked north, south, east, and west and found no one. We believed that we can search everyday for weeks, and that we will end up with the same results. We need to look elsewhere."

"But family and friends," she questioned.

"I know, we all are missing family and friends," he responded sincerely.

Ben added, "That came up too, but we believe that it would be a good idea to search other places."

Burt joined in with, "Heading south tomorrow, in two days or two weeks, will not change what we have found in the last two days here."

The group up front nodded their approval, and the group that was sitting, as if on que, also agreed. No one really wanted to admit it, but it was clear that they should not stay where they are. At least, not stay there any longer than needed, and that the two days there, was plenty of time.

Alice, secretly agreed, but wanted to make sure, asked, "Will we have time to return home once more before we leave?"

"Oh yeah, we won't leave until tomorrow morning. There is plenty of time to return home and get back here today."

Nobody was against this decision. In fact, no one could recall why anyone had decided to wait two days before heading out to start with.

Burt brought up the following, "As far as supplies go, we can get what we need, when we need it."

Joe-Joe spoke up and asked Burt, "Easy for you, you have a new car."

Burt, not sure if he was angry with him, or that he wanted help in getting a new car of his own, answered, "That's right. If you want a new car, let's you and I head out after this meeting and get you something that you would like."

Joe-Joe had a smile as if someone just gave him a brand new car of his choice. "Cool man. Yeah, that will be cool. I want a BMW, a big one."

"Okay then, you and I can do that," answered Burt.

Jeff asked, "Do we all want to drive our own cars, or should we double up?"

No one had an answer, Billy Bob suggested, "It does not matter to us. My brother and I were in security, we could take up the lead some times, and at other times, we could take up the rear. As far as who rides in what car, he and I are together."

Jeff added, "I will hand out walkie-talkies to everyone so we can all stay in touch at the same time."

For a few minutes, the group talked between themselves to see whom, if any of them wanted to start a carpool. For the most part, everyone wanted his or her own car.

Ben added, "I believe that everyone here would like their own, new car. But remember, you can always get a new car when we get to Florida. No real reason for all of us to have a car driving to the same place."

Van Camp spoke up, "I will keep my car and get me a new one when we get to Florida. Does anyone else want a new car?"

No one else raised his or her hands. It appeared that getting a new car could wait until they all reached Florida. One would have thought that for a drive that far, that a new car would be nice, but the knowledge of driving a car that you are familiar with, was more important than having a new car right now. Too many things have already been taken away from them, to then add in the loss of the car that you have owned for years.

"I need gas," voiced Kitty.

Van Camp, keeping things under control, said, "We will all leave here tomorrow at the same time, and then we can fill all of our tanks before we hit I-95."

Burt added, "I have pumps and hoses. We can pump gas right from the tanks and bypass the gas pumps."

Everyone looked at him, as this was a good idea. He added, "Not sure if the pumps will work anyway and not sure if everyone can afford the trip for the pumps that will take credit cards."

The mechanics of the trip had been taken care of. They had directions and a way to communicate. Next, they must decide just when tomorrow to leave.

"Leave here at 9am tomorrow," asked Van Camp.

A few 'Okays' were said, and that made it so. Tomorrow, 9am, they leave Delaware.

Wanting to give this group a name, for his diary, Van Camp asked, "Do we have a name for our little group?"

A few people discussed names between themselves, but nothing stood out. Finally, "Bakers Dozen," was suggested by Joe-Joe.

Some repeated, "Bakers Dozen," and it stuck.

Van Camp did not like the name, he would have suggested something else. However, in time, he would change it to something that he liked. Something like, 'Van Camp's Dozen,' "The Van Camp Group,' or 'Group Van Camp,' his favorite.

Lisa threw in a monkey wrench to mess things up, she asked, "What if someone does not want to go?"

Another question that caught Van Camp off guard. Ben spoke up and answered, "Okay. We aren't telling anyone here what to do, just suggesting what most of us should do. If you want to stay here, then you stay."

Joe-Joe wanted to bring up the TV show, The Weakest Link. Why don't we just throw her fat ass off the show? Tell her, 'bye-bye.' He thought that they could have a Tribal Meeting and vote her off as they do on the show, Survivor.

Ben was going to give no more attention to what she asked, she was too damn big to take care of anyway. Just keeping her fed would require a full time person.

"Do you want to stay here," ask Van Camp.

"No, I don't want to be here all by myself."

Van Camp addressed the group, "Does anyone here want to stay? Does anyone here have a better idea? Or, does anyone here have anything to add?"

No one said a thing as everyone looked around the room at each other.

Ben, realizing that this was not prison, not the military, or a job where they had to follow directions, suggested, "Look. No body up here is telling anybody what to do. If you want to stick with us, great, if not, you can form your own group or head out on your own."

Lisa took this as an attack on her as an individual, responded by bitching with, "I was not talking about me. I want to stay with the group. No way, do I wish to be alone. I was just asking in the event that someone else might be thinking about it, but was afraid to ask."

This calmed Ben down a little, he asked again, "Anyone have other plans than leaving with us tomorrow?"

No one did, but there were more questions. "So we leave here tomorrow at 9am, get gas, and head to DC with Billy Bob in the lead."

The group looked at each other, and nodded approval to their plan. With that settled, Van Camp announced, "Okay then, with no more business to discuss, we will meet here tomorrow at 9am, packed and ready to go."

CHAPTER 25

THE LAST DAY IN TOWN

THE MEETING BROKE UP WITH some sadness. Sadness that they were leaving, apparently for good. They would be leaving their family, friends, co-workers, their homes, and jobs for places unknown. Additional sadness for a few of them because they were a part of a group of people that they had nothing in common with. Well, except for the Brown brothers.

Burt, Joe-Joe, and Ben met at the front door to the lobby and decided to leave in ten minutes to find Joe-Joe a BMW. When asked what kind of car Ben wanted, he said, "Not sure. I'll check it out and see what is on the lot. Don't think I will have any luck putting one on order."

This got some smiles from these guys.

Joe-Joe then spoke up and suggested, "I don't mind checking out the Hummers first. I might find something that I like there instead."

Burt said, "Okay, then we be off to the Hummer dealership on 13 near Wilmington. You guys are in luck. I know where the place is and I know where they keep the keys."

Alice approached Kitty, "Can I ride with you. I will share the driving, I just don't want to drive that far in a car by myself."

Kitty had hoped to drive with her, but decided not to ask now that Alice had asked first.

"Fine with me," Kitty answered with a warm smile. Without saying it, they both wished that Lisa would ride by herself or with one of the guys. She was just so big that you knew that it would be an issue with her getting into and out of any car. A truck with a low tailgate and ramp would be most appropriate.

Lisa walked right past them and did not say anything. Kitty and Alice looked at each other smiling, as they were both happy about the same thing. Lisa headed to her room, she needed a nap. Rose Marie wanted to ride with someone, just to share the driving, but decided that she would rather be alone. She could make friends and bond with these people later. She had the rest of her life to do so.

Van Camp made his way back to his room and added to his notes on today's meeting. He even went as far as to include his prediction of how the drive to DC would be.

Jeff spent time with his walkie-talkies. He made sure that each had a new set of good batteries, and that it was operational. Maps of Delaware and Maryland were set-aside for each driver. He did not know how many vehicles there would be in this convoy, but it could not be over fourteen. He prepared fourteen piles of identical items on the front desk. Each pile included a walkie-talkie, maps, flashlights, and a pad of paper with pen. He grabbed the paper and pens from behind the front desk. He just thought that this was a good idea.

Once his duties were completed, he found a comfortable seat in the lobby and tried to take a nap. He knew that tomorrow's drive would not be easy. Not that it would be hard to find, or hard to keep everyone in line, or even a long drive, but the unknowns that are unknown.

Some of the unknowns he considered would be, for example, parked vehicles in the middle of the road. Roads closed for whatever reason. If a toll road, could they get by the tollbooths? Were there trains that crossed the highway that now had them blocked? Were any of the draw bridges up? Were there crashes that blocked the roads? He knew that the absence of traffic does not mean that you can drive as fast as you want.

Not wanting to give this any more thought, he made his way to the lobby to watch a little TV.

Bob Billy noticed what Jeff had left on the front desk and went to investigate. He picked up a map and walked over to where Billy Bob was trying to take a nap.

"You want to decide how we are going to get there," he asked his brother.

"After my nap," was the response.

Understanding that his older brother was boss, he placed the map back on the front desk, and joined him for a nap in a chair, two down from where his brother was.

He was glad to be near his big brother and that made him feel safe. If his brother felt it was okay to take a nap right then, then he would follow his example.

Eddie and Steven were at the coffee cart and started to talk to each other. Steven asked, "Do you think that we should have some weapons?"

"Not a bad idea. We should find a gun shop nearby and fix ourselves up," was the reply.

"I don't have a problem with those two brothers taking the lead," Steven commented.

"Makes sense to me," Eddie responded. Then, wanting to make them seem more important than they were, he added, "Let the officers hang back a little and send the enlisted guys up to run point."

"Should we give them our binoculars," asked Steven.

"No. Unless we find another set at the gun store, we should keep ours."

A short pause, Eddie added, "If we find another set, we keep the best ones."

"Of course. Do you know of any gun stores around here," Steven inquired.

"Yeah, I remember passing one a few miles from here. When we head out, just turn south."

"I'll drive, you can ride shotgun," Steven instructed.

For these two military types, they were off to prepare for war.

Jerry did not know what to do with himself. He wanted to make one more trip home, just to make sure that no one was there, and to leave a note. Driving home was something that he was not very thrilled about doing. Seeing again an empty home was not cool, but he boosted his morale by thinking how he could pick up some personal items while he was there. He sadly realized that this might be his last time here.

He would make it a point to grab some pictures of his family members and a change of clothes. He needed socks and another pair of shoes.

A few hours later, early in the evening, those that had stayed made their way into the kitchen to fix themselves something to eat. Nothing elaborate, just sandwiches, a little salad, and a few of them heated up some soup. Then it was back to the lobby anticipating another meeting later that evening.

The trio were in the Hummer's dealership looking at only the ones in the showroom, about 6 with an open space where the yellow one once was.

Burt pretended as if he was a sales person. "Will this vehicle be for you or for your wife?"

Ben answered back with, "My girl friend. My wife already has one. Got to keep my girlfriend happy, don't you know?"

Joe-Joe, not quick to respond to this joke, simply said, "It will be for me."

"Okay then, pick one and I will go and fetch the key," Burt said with a smile. While he waited for them, he walked over to the doorway used to bring vehicles into and out of the showroom and blocked it open. It had closed itself after he left earlier.

"I want this one," shouted Joe-Joe with much excitement.

"Give me the last two numbers on the card hanging from the mirror," Burt instructed.

"727," was his response. It was more than Burt needed, but he would not say anything.

A moment later, Burt returned with the key and handed them to a most excited Joe-Joe.

"Take it for a ride, but don't be gone long," Burt said to Joe-Joe, as he jumped into the driver's seat and started it up.

"Will be back in a few minutes," he said, as he made a few, three-point turns, to make his way out of the . Out the door he goes, cutting across the medium on 13, heading south.

Ben yelled over, "14."

"14 it is," he answered, and headed to the room with the keys.

Burt returned quickly and handed the key to Ben who was already inside adjusting his seat and mirrors.

The motor was started and he squealed wheels out the door, doing the same as Joe-Joe. He ran across the lawn before crossing the medium, heading south on 13.

Burt went to the display case and picked up a bunch of brochures about the Hummer. Some of the accessories were complicated and it would be made easier to understand if they had a manual.

With a supply of brochures, he got back into his yellow Hummer and waited on their return. He just knew that they would be happy with what they already selected. Everything else in the lobby was equipped the same, except for the color.

Naturally, the ones on the showroom floor were loaded from leather seats to a GPS. All they needed now was some gas and CD's to play on the CD player along with a few DVD's to watch.

Lisa, having taken a nap and shower, headed to the kitchen to feed. Two sandwiches, two bags of chips, two large, non-diet sodas, and she was off to the lobby to rest from having eaten the two sandwiches, the two bags of chips, and from having to make two trips to the soda stand for sodas. If everyone left her alone, she could nap and not expend any energy bitching, about whatever.

Alice, instead of taking a break in the lobby, or going to her room, decided to take a ride back to her house one last time. She asked Kitty if she wanted to go a long, but she declined. Mentioned that she wanted to take a long, hot shower, and follow that with a power nap and then into a new makeup scheme.

Kitty did just that, she headed to her room and took a shower and nap.

Alice left the lobby and drove home. All the way there, she cried. This would be her last trip to her home and the last chance to have any closure about her children and grandchildren.

At her house, she decided to shower, change clothes, and pack a few things. Before long, she was headed back to the hotel. The only thing hard about the drive back, was driving and crying at the same time. Without incident, she made it back okay.

After she unpacked and repaired her makeup, she joined the others in the lobby.

CHAPTER 26

ONE MORE MEETING

I T WAS ABOUT 8PM AND almost everyone had returned to the lobby. For the most part, it was small talk about how their day had been and what they expected to see along the way to Washington. The group had almost completely accepted the situation that they were all in it together. It was still, very apparent that they had to get along.

If this were it for the rest of the world, as in no one else, then it would make a massive amount of sense, and mostly common sense, to learn how to interact with each other. It was not as if this was a job and at 5pm, that you could just head home and deal with this stuff tomorrow. This group, this new lifestyle, is 24/7.

For Joe-Joe, he was thinking that this was an episode of Survivors, Delaware Bay.

The last person to make it to the lobby was Van Camp. As he walked in, he made a quick count of everyone there and realized that he was the last one. This upset him because he wanted to know what, if anything, did he miss. He could not very well go around and ask everyone what was going on. The only thing that he could reasonably do, would be to ask Ben how things were going. Other than that, he would improvise.

Ben could not really answer him with any certainly, of what he had missed, as he had just gotten back himself. Ben wanted to talk more about his new Hummer, than to talk business with Dick.

Alice approached the two men and waited patiently until they had stopped talking and looked her way. Ben noticed that she had been crying and he was in no mood to hear her complain about this, or that, and especially on why she was crying, this time.

Van Camp noticed also that she had been crying and found this to be an excellent time to score points. He asked, "Are you okay Alice?"

"I'm okay, just a little upset still about my family. I know that I cannot do anything about it, but still, I wish I had closure."

Both men shook there heads showing understanding and compassion towards her. For Van Camp, his emotions were genuine, for Ben, he was just being nice, and being nice right now for him was a hard thing to do. He wanted to take anyone that wanted a ride in his new Hummer. He simply had something new and wanted to show it off. Usually when he had something new, he had stolen it and could not very well show it off.

She asked them, "Are we really leaving tomorrow?" She knew their answer before she even asked, she had hoped that just maybe, something had changed.

Ben really wanted to leave tomorrow so that everyone could see his new Hummer, and not to hang around here while this little lady could search for her family that no longer existed.

As Van Camp answered her question, Ben faded away like a snake in tall grass.

Van Camp was trying to decide whether to hug Alice or not. At most companies that he worked for, that was frowned upon, but here, there were no company rules to follow or violate. He thought for a quick second and decided that to give her a hug would be to his benefit, and just a side benefit to Alice.

As he gave her a hug, with the required three pats on the back, he clandestinely looked around to room to see who was watching. He was trying to judge everyone's impressions that he was giving to anyone that noticed his little show. From what he could tell, he scored high and he was most proud of himself.

After a self-pat, on his own back, he changed his attention from himself, back to Alice. He said, "We are all in the same boat. All of us here had lost everyone. We don't know how or why, but we do know that we are alive and that we have a plan."

He leaned back and looked into her tearful eyes, and added, "You will be okay. We will take care of each other." He was careful not to say that he would personally take care of her. He was not a detail person and did not want the day-to-day responsibility to take care of her. It was his destiny to care for everyone, in a managerial sort of way only.

Alice shook her head in agreement and walked away, not saying a word. She took a seat and wept quietly to herself. If Van Camp had been an honorable guy, he would have taken a seat next to her for a short period to ensure that she was okay. It was clear that Ben was not going to take the case on that one.

Kitty did notice and made her way over to sit beside her. This kindness only made it worse for Alice as she broke down into a loud wailing. Not only did this catch everyone's attention, but it also acted like a motion to call a meeting to order. Not exactly a requirement of Robert's Rule, but it worked.

For those that were not aware that she had simply broken down, thought that maybe she was hurt. Those that really cared, they gathered around as if their presence would improve the situation. The others, Ben, the Brown brothers, and Jerry, stayed away from the crown giving the impression, that they cared, but would give her a hug, a little later.

Well, not Ben. He felt that if she was to spend the time cleaning up behind him and cooking, that she would not have time to cry. With everyone there, and at a point where it was quiet, Van Camp saw the advantage to call a meeting to order. He announced,

"Now that everyone is here, we should have a little meeting."

Standing in front of the lobby, as this gave him a commanding position of authority over everyone, he was ready to set down some ground rules for tomorrow's drive. However, before he could start, Billy Bob and Ben were quickly beside him.

CHAPTER 27

TAKING THE LEAD

VAN CAMP WAS STANDING UP front with Billy Bob and Ben standing along side him. This gave the impression, if only to himself, that he was the manager in-charge of transportation, and that these two, were assistant managers.

For Billy Bob, they were equal and he had his little brother as his personal assistant-assistant manager.

In the view of Ben, these two were just temporary until he could con them out of their position, or to con others to believe that he was the one that was really in charge.

"It has been agreed upon that we head south to Florida. Has anyone changed their minds to stay here," questioned Van Camp.

No one said a thing. Wanting to keep things rolling and him the only one asking the question, he continued, "Let me just go around the room and ask each of you to speak out."

Ben added to stay as one of the leaders. "Like a Judge does to a jury when he wants to be certain that the jury, all voted the same way."

He looked at both Billy Bob and Van Camp as they both responded with a confirmatory head shake. For Van Camp, this was not the time to take a stand. For Billy Bob, he wanted to take a stand, but only if Van Camp had indicated that they should do so.

Going around the room, Van Camp asked Lisa first. "Yes. I am with you guys. No reason to stay here."

Alice and Kitty responded nodding yes before being asked.

Rose Marie was slow to respond, but knew that she had to agree and to follow the flow. With her cats gone, no job, not to mention any people or future left for her, she said, "I am with you."

The trio of self-made managers, looked over a Joe-Joe, who was only half-paying attention. Joe-Joe suddenly realized that they were looking at him, wanting an answer. He did not expect them to pick him next, he assumed they were going in the other direction and asking the ones sitting next to Kitty. He could only come up with, "What?"

"You with us," Ben asked, and deep inside, really wanted him to decline. No reason to take along a slacker anywhere with you. He would only take away from those that contributed.

"Yeah man," was his response.

"I am with my brother," announced Bob Billy, with Billy Bob giving him the love sign in appreciation.

Eddie and Steven spoke "Yes sir," as if they were given an order to acknowledge.

That left Jerry, Burt, and Jeff.

"Do we have enough supplies," asked Jeff.

Van Camp was quick to reply with, "Yes, anything else we need, we can pick up on our way down to Florida."

"I'm in," was his response.

Jerry said, "Me to."

The last member, Burt, who said, "Let's get rolling."

"Tomorrow morning," Billy Bob spoke up. He then looked over at the other two and asked, "9AM okay?"

Both were slow to respond, but all agreed that 9AM would be just fine.

"Okay then, to recap. We leave tomorrow morning at 9AM," announced Van Camp as if this was the last thing they needed to discuss.

Billy Bob quickly spoke up and said, "We should take care of a few fine points now and not wait until tomorrow morning."

Ben knew exactly what Billy Bob was trying to say. "Yes," he interjected, "We have radios to pass out and to decide who drives with whom."

Jeff spoke up and said, "Once we figure out how many cars we have, I will see that there are three radios in each one. Suggest that we all use channel 19."

Those who knew about radios shook their heads in agreement. The ones that had no idea what they were talking about, looked confused.

Jeff noticed that and wanting to help, said, "Anyone who needs help with them, I will be more than glad to show you how it's done. It's very simple, easy to use. Easier than a cell phone."

"Maps," asked Alice.

Burt added in with, "It's just us on the road. Following one another should be a no brainier."

"All the way to Florida," questioned Joe-Joe.

Billy Bob thought this to be a stupid question, he responded with,"How hard can it get. Get on Interstate 95 South, and don't get off until you are in Florida."

For the road-traveling people, this was funny. For Joe-Joe, he did not want to appear like an idiot, so he just smiled and will make it a point not to be the first, or the last car in the convoy.

"Is anyone going to be in charge," asked Alice.

Van Camp wanted in a most serious way to say, 'yes, that it would be him.' However, he decided against it.

Billy Bob held up on responding, but Ben said, "We don't really need anyone right now. Maybe later."

That seemed to satisfy everyone for the moment. Burt spoke up, and said, or suggested, "I have commercial license, along with a few others. I have been driving long and short halls for years. I am very familiar with I-95."

Everyone turned his way, as he added, "Not so much that I want to be in charge here, but I would like to take the lead for the convoy."

That pleased everyone and without any discussion, it was decided that Burt would be up front.

Billy Bob said to the group, "My brother and I will take up the rear. If we keep it reasonably tight, we will be able to see everyone, all the time. No one should be left behind."

Same as for Burt, no discussion, and they were elected to be the last car in the convoy.

Lisa wanted very much to bring up some questions about food, snacks, and drinks for the ride south. Instead, she mentioned this to Alice, anticipating that she would say something.

Lucky for Lisa, she did. "Food and drinks for the trip?"

Steven thought he would be a good one to answer that question. "Take what you need from the gift shop. If you need more, we can stop anywhere along the way. That should not be a problem."

Not a problem for you,' thought Lisa.

'Must be a problem for Lisa,' thought almost everyone there believing that she must be in a car by herself for two reasons. One, she needed the space for food, and two, no one wanted to be anywhere near her when her body cuts loose with body noise and body odors.

Van Camp wanted to end this meeting with something from him, instructions for example, said, "Tonight, or before we leave tomorrow morning, could everyone fill their tanks up. No need to start out having to make pit stops right away."

"We will make our first stop at the White House. Every car should make it there on one tank. We can fill up again there," suggested Burt.

Everyone seemed to agree.

Steven added, "The next stop after the White House will be the Pentagon. It's on our way and a logical place to check out."

Again, everyone agreed. No one believed that anybody would find anyone, but might find something of interest, and maybe just a little bit helpful to what had happened to everyone.

Without ending this meeting officially, as following Robert's Rule, everyone got up in ones and twos. Some headed to their rooms to look over what they wanted to pack.

A few mingled around to hold some small talk. Not sure if it was to have small talk, or that those who stayed behind, did not want to be left alone. There was still the fear of going to your room and returning to find that everyone here had disappeared also.

CHAPTER 28

LEAVING DELAWARE

ALICE WANTED TO GO BACK to her house and look for her family, but thought against it. No need to see an empty house, again. Once was more than enough. She was grateful that she did take the time to leave a note, just in case.

She made a trip to the gift shop for a few snacks to place in her purse. Then, to her room for a good cry and good nights rest. She does not like to drive long ways and was not looking forward to this trip, but realized that she had to stay with the group. Once more, she cried herself to sleep.

Before she went to her room, Kitty stopped by to see that Alice was okay, and saw that she was. Kitty then went back to her room to comb her hair a few hundred times and wash off her makeup. She wanted a fresh look for the drive south. She wanted to look nice for her visit to the White House, in the event that people were there, and if they were people there, then surly there would be cameras.

Rose Marie had already loaded up her car with the few things that she had taken from her house. She was pleased that she had a few CD's in her car to help pass the time for the trip. She would have gotten a new car for the drive, but wanted to enjoy a little longer, the cat smell in her car. In her mind, she would get something new in Florida, and with a little positive thinking, she could slowly start to forget about her cats.

Van Camp was now rethinking about his car. He initially thought to drive his car south, and then get a new one down there, but now, why wait. Why not get a new one now, and another new one later.

This was a good managerial decision. With the possibility of newer cars in the future, not possible, then why not get a new one every time that you can.

He wanted a luxury car, more luxurious than what he had. He felt that should anyone see this convoy, they would see the Hummers as workers, no one of authority. Anyone in a luxury car, well, they had to be the one in charge. If he truly had his way, he would get a limo and sit in the back reading the newspaper. Yet, he knew that no one would volunteer to drive him around in that fashion. Maybe, just maybe, in the future, when he was in control and a leader, he could swing that.

So off he goes, by himself to find a new car. He made it a point to let Ben and Billy Bob know his intentions. He was careful not to tell them what he was doing, but to allow them to think they were giving him permission to venture out on his own.

With that, Van Camp was going car shopping.

Ben, because he had the Black Hummer, was satisfied with his car. He headed out and filled his tank. In addition, he picked up a five-gallon gas can from Lowes and filled that up also. He did not want to run out of gas and bum a ride from anyone.

Ben, while getting gas, filled up his car with treats for the ride down. He placed a small cooler in the back seat with some sodas. He would ice it up before he left tomorrow.

I thought about getting a new car, but knew that if he ever got back with his parents, that they would want their car back. And, if he had a car that he did not pay for, then it must be returned.

The more he thought about this, the more he tried to talk himself into getting a new car, he only needed a reasonable reason. Then an idea hit him. Leave his parents car at the dealership, and he would lock it up and take the car keys with him. Even while he was in

Florida, his parents had a spare key and could get the car. Problem solved, as he would have a new car for the trip, and still maintain ownership over his parent's car.

Now, his only issue was to select a new vehicle. He was not sure if he wanted a Hummer, which was a reasonable choice, or, a sports car. Something to look hot in for the babes. However, there were no babes, so that idea sucked. Might as well get a Hummer, because it was the logical choice.

He knew where to go and he was off to pick up a new Hummer. He would; if possible, he would not select a red, yellow, or black one. Might as well stand out a little with his own color.

Bob Billy asked Billy Bob, "Should we be getting ourselves a new car?"

Billy Bob liked the car he had now, but knew he would like a newer one even better. "Sure. Are you going to get one?"

Caught a little off guard, he answered, "No, thought we would ride down together. Get me one once we get settled."

"Okay, what do you recommend," asked Billy Bob.

It was not that often that this oldest brother would ask his younger brother to make a decision. Bob Billy liked being asked, and gave this some serious thought.

"We should get a Hummer. Might as well look like Rambo."

Billy Bob, that was a good decision, not necessarily a good reason, but he would have chosen a Hummer also. If his younger brother had selected something else, he could and would easily,

change his mind.

Steven looked at Eddie; they both had the same idea. They would get themselves a Hummer for the same reasons. For them, the Hummer was nothing more than a military vehicle painted anything but green, and had leather seats with a radio and CD player.

Eddie says to Steven, "Want to take a ride to the Hummer Dealership and get ourselves some wheels?"

"One each," asked Steven.

Eddie, after giving this some thought, agreed. So, without telling anyone where they were going, they headed out and up to the dealership. Eddie drove and Steven rode shotgun, leaving his car behind.

Van Camp was the first to arrive at the Hummer's Dealership on Route 13. He really wanted a Cadillac CTS Coupe or Escalade, but thought that a Hummer would be better suited to drive hundreds of miles with unknown driving conditions. Once he was inside the showroom, he stood there momentarily, expecting to see two or three sales guys eagerly looking for his business. It did take a second or so for him to regain his thoughts that he was alone and would search for a new vehicle by himself. In the past, he would always tell the salesperson what he wanted and waited for them to bring the car off the lot to him. This time, he would only look at the ones on the sales room floor. He assumed that these were the top of the line, and were cleaned up for immediate delivery. Besides, he had no idea where the keys were kept. In the past, the ones on the showroom floor, well, the keys were always inside the vehicle.

A black one caught his eye, and it was close to the open doorway making it easy for him to drive it out and away. He got inside and started it up, as the keys were in the ignition.

He had no idea what type of things to look for in a Hummer. Luxury cars just had luxurious things to test. He had no idea that this Hummer allowed him to add or take air out of his tires while driving and he did not care. He only wanted something that he could go around or through obstacles for his trip south.

Figuring that this one was as good as the next one, he started to make his way out the door. He knew that he should fill the gas tank, but was pleased to find that it was already full. Before he was all the way out, Billy Bob and Bob Billy came in with Steven and Eddie close behind them. He was pleased that they all had the same idea as him, but was more pleased with himself that he was the first one there.

Van Camp wanted to stay and oversee what they were doing, but because he knew very little about the Hummer, and he did not want to risk losing the one he had, he smiled and said to them, "They got great deals here."

They returned his sarcasm with smiles. For Van Camp, he had a new Hummer, just like everyone else. In some ways, he must seem to be like them, and then he can control them under the assumption that he had 'walked in their shoes,' or 'driven in their vehicles.'

The Browns made their way to the last Hummer on the showroom floor. They were happy, but wanted those spinning wheels. Seeing that Steven and Eddie were there looking for a pair of Hummers, and noticed on their way in, that Joe-Joe was walking the lot, they settled for the one, in hand, rather than one on the lot. Then, why not? It had the keys inside, was cleaned up, had a full tank of gas, and nothing was in their way to drive out the door left open from earlier. For them, they squealed out the door leaving behind them smoke from their spinning wheels.

Steven and Eddie, seeing that the showroom floor was empty, headed out to the lot in front of the showroom. There, they met up with Joe-Joe.

Joe-Joe said, "Looks like we had the same idea."

Eddie answered with, "Yeah, but I wanted a cleaned-up one from the showroom, but everybody beat us to it."

Steven asked, "You guys know where they keep the keys?"

Joe-Joe had not considered this and could only shrug his shoulders. Eddie saved the day by saying, "They got to be in the showroom floor someplace. My guess is they are on some peg board or something."

"How do we tell which keys, go with which hummer," asked Joe-Joe Eddie, quick on his feet, said, "Let's look for the keys first, then we can figure it out."

Steven and Joe-Joe agreed that this had to be a good, workable plan. Together, the three of them headed to the showroom. Once inside, they started to look everyplace. Joe-Joe found a few on a desk and realized how their numbering system worked.

"I got two sets of keys," he proudly announced as he held them up.

Steven and Eddie each wanted to find the keys first, but it happened the way it did. A minute later, Eddie found some keys on a desk also, "I got some keys."

Steven asked, "How many?"

"I got two keys," answered Joe-Joe.

"Three for me," was the answer from Eddie.

"That's five keys we've found, not a bad start," added Joe-Joe.

With that, the three of them headed out together to find their new Hummers.

Before long, they each had a Hummer to their liking. Other than their color, they were similar inside. For the most part, pick your color and drive it away.

With their tanks not filled, the three of them raced to the nearest gas station and it looked as if NASCAR had opened the pits for anyone on the lead lap.

Before long, the parade of new Hummers arrived back at the hotel. No one parked in the spaces provided because it was just them, and they were too big to easily park within the painted lines. Those, with their first brand new car, wanted very much to show it off. Yet, with everyone with a brand new car at the same time, there was nothing to show off. They were left where they were, waiting for the drive south.

A few of the guys made a trip to the gift shop for what little remained for a light snack before they went to bed. With a long day tomorrow, might as well be rested.

CHAPTER 29

HEADING OUT

V AN CAMP WAS THE FIRST one to show up at the lobby. He was early and did not expect anyone else to be there yet, which was okay with him. His few things were packed and stowed in his new Hummer. By being ready, he could help anyone else earn a few brownie points.

Jeff was the next to arrive in the lobby, and with him were the radios. He looked at Van Camp and said, "I am going to leave these here, load up my car first, then come back and check out the radios."

"Can I help," asked Van Camp. He did not really want to help, but knew he had to ask.

"Yeah, you can start out by taking the radios out of their boxes, and installing the batteries," Jeff said, and without waiting for a response, headed back to his room to grab his things to pack in his car.

Wanting to make this a good thing for him, Van Camp took his time with the radios. This way, when the others arrived, they would see that he was doing something besides giving instructions.

Sure enough, everyone started to show up, early. Early, as if they were late, that they would be left behind. A few of them walked on by and loaded up their cars with their things. Some, Lisa for example, made it to the gift shop for a snack or two, or three.

When Rose Marie arrived in the lobby, she had nothing to say, and nothing to ask. For her, she was leaving her cats behind and heading south. She would simply get into her car and go with the flow.

Jeff came back and easily noticed how slow Van Camp was with his chores. He grabbed the ones that were ready and started to hand them out. He instructed, "Leave them on while we are driving. When you want to talk, press this, talk, then release."

Those instructions were easy enough, and he added, "Remember, when you talk, you cannot hear anyone else. In addition, you are talking to everyone at the same time. So don't talk unless you have something important to say."

By 7:30, everyone was in the lobby and ready to go. Each had a radio and a full tank of gas.

Van Camp announced with much authority, "We should line up our cars like we are in a funeral procession."

Most everyone thought that was somewhat funny, except for Alice. She knew that now, she was leaving and maybe never coming back. Life for her and her family were over.

At the last minute, Alice decided to drive her car to Florida. She tells Kitty, "Kitty, hope you don't mind, but I believe that I would rather drive myself."

Kitty looked disappointed, but did ask, "Why."

"It's not you, I am having a hard time after loosing my family, and then to turn around and loose my car," Alice answered.

"I understand, that's why I kept my car," responded Kitty. This conversation was ended with a, girl-to-girl, kind of hug, without the man to man, three pats on the back.

On his way out, Joe-Joe made it an effort to be in the middle of the group. It was decided earlier that Burt would take the lead, and the Brown brothers would take up the rear.

Burt, in the lead Hummer, was just outside his driver's side door. He had his arms raised to get everyone's attention. It worked, as everyone looked his way. He then let his right hand and arm swing around some as if he was about to start a drag race. To his approval, everyone started to rev their engines as if they, even in single file, were ready to drag race.

Van Camp thought this was stupid and a waste of gas, but decided that since he was the only one not thrilled with what Burt was doing, that he would just go along with the flow. He reluctantly revved his engine.

It was agreed to drive to Route 301, head to the Chesapeake Bay Bridge, past Annapolis, and follow Route 50 to Washington. So much for saying that it was as simple as, getting on I-95 and driving south.

CHAPTER 30

CHESAPEAKE BAY BRIDGE

Y OU WOULD HAVE THOUGHT THAT with everyone gone and with no traffic, that the roads would be cleared, and that, they could make good time. Not so, in most places, cars, like the ones they saw earlier, had pulled over to the side and left abandoned. Here on the open highway, some cars had pulled over, and some had not. They had not crashed into each other, but had stopped in the driving lanes.

Burt, being the professional driver he is, was very attentive. He was never caught off guard with the cars that were blocking his lane. He would use his turn signal and ease into another lane to pass. When there were cars that blocked all the lanes, he slowed down in plenty of time to drive on the shoulder, or even the medium, allowing those behind him to stay together and not to be driving all over the road.

This procedure worked fine until they reached the Chesapeake Bay Bridge. There were many cars stopped at the bridges' highest point and it was impossible to navigate past. Slowly, he brought the convoy to a stop in the center lane of the westbound span.

Burt then got out of his vehicle and indicated with a hand motion across his neck, that everyone should either cut off their heads, or cut their motors off. Everyone did the latter, except for Lisa. She thought it meant for her to stop eating. It was only after she swallowed her Snickers bar completely whole, that she turned off her engine.

Van Camp was quick to make his way up to Burt. In addition, he wanted to be at the center of whatever it was that had caused them to stop.

Most of them were slow to reach the front of the convoy because they were busy looking out and over the bridge. This was a nice view and well worth taking a minute or two, to check-it-out.

Van Camp knew right away the reason they had to stop when he caught up with Burt. It was easily surmised that it would require that two or three cars, along with one bus, a US. Naval Academy bus, needed to be moved.

The bus appeared to be the easiest to move, as it still had the motor running. Burt sprinted over to the bus, and without grinding the gears, or choking the engine, moved it a hundred or so feet forward and against the curb.

Steven and Eddie were the first ones to come up and stand next to Van Camp. They watched Burt move the bus and without saying a word, those two walked over to two cars that obviously needed to be moved. Naturally, Van Camp stayed in place in the event they needed direction.

Eddie was able to move his, as he must have found the keys.

Steven had an issue, because without the keys, he could not set the car in neutral, or turn the wheel.

Next to arrive at the scene, were the Brown brothers. Billy Bob picked up quickly the same scenario as the others. He tells his brother, Bob Billy, to give Steven a hand.

Bob Billy looked pleased that he had something of importance to do. With no need for instructions, he walked over to Steven's car and said, "Open the door."

Steven did so as suggested. He was about to get out of his car when Bob Billy said, "Stay put. Press down hard on the break pedal."

Just after Steven did as asked, Bob Billy grabbed the steering wheel, and yanked it hard towards him. In just a few yanks, the steering wheel had broken free. Not only that, he could move the transmission into neutral.

Because they were level, on the bridge, it required both of them to move the car forward. Once the car had a little momentum, Steven got out and left it to roll on its own.

It never did reach a lot of speed. When it crashed into another car, there was very little damage. But, it was important that the car was moved and where it ended up, that it would no longer be in their way, as only one car was blocking the convoy.

The six of them, Burt, Eddie, Steven, Van Camp, Billy Bob, and Bob Billy walked over to the last car blocking their way. It was a little Mazda Miata, convertible. They all looked at the car with the same thing in mind, except for Van Camp.

Burt said, "Let's do it."

Everyone had a smile on their face, again, expect for Van Camp. He, trying to talk down at their level, said, "What?"

Billy Bob said, without looking at him, "We are going to flip this bad boy. Maybe even flip it over the side."

"Burial at sea," jokingly added Steven.

Van Camp did not think this to be possible and was unwilling to help. It was obvious that he was not going to pitch in, when Steven said, "If you are not going to help us move it out of the way, then you must move out of our way."

Quickly, not wanting to be left out and to blend in as a team player, Van Camp said, "No no no. I can help. No need to let you guys have all the fun."

All five guys figured that he was full of bull, but knew that they probably could use the help.

With some grunts and groans, the back end of the car was picked up, and turned so that the front end was facing the guardrail.

Burt reached in, placed the car in neutral, and released the hand brake. A slight push and the car was up against the guardrail.

Like a bunch of kids getting ready for a ride at Disney World, they gleefully giggled between themselves. Except for Van Camp. On a call of, "One, Two, Three," by Van Camp, the car's back end was lifted up and the car was now standing on its nose. The group all got in together, side-by-side, and without too much difficulty, was able to topple the car over the guardrail.

With the drop as far as it was, all six boys, I meant men, were able to maneuver to the guardrail and watch it hit the water.

"That was cool," said Bob Billy. "Can we find another car?"

Billy Bob gave him a look, as if suggesting, 'Grow up little brother.'

Bob Billy got the hint and said nothing more. The subject was dropped as quickly as it came up.

The others showed up, just as the car was tipped over the side. The only one not there was Lisa. She had come up on a Little Miss Debbie delivery truck and thought she had died and gone to the great food buffet in the sky.

With some difficulty, but determination, she was able to open the back door and hauled her big butt inside. Lucky for her, that the truck had already made a few stops, as there was some room for her to look around.

Even with everything packed in brown cardboard boxes, with only black letters stenciled on the sides to identify its contents, she knew exactly what was in each box.

With little concern, or reason to be neat, she threw the boxes of what she did not want on the floor. The three boxes of her favorite items, well, they were stacked neatly near the door.

Alice looked around and noticed that Lisa was not in sight, everyone else was, just not Lisa. If she had not seen the car hit the water, she would have guessed that Lisa had fallen over the side by the size and sound of the splash. She was not thinking this to be funny, but knew that they both might have weight about the same.

She asked no one in particular, "Anyone see Lisa?"

The group looked around and nothing was said until Burt spoke up and answered, "With the way that Little Miss Debbie truck is bouncing around, she must be inside feeding."

This got some laughter from everyone, even Van Camp. Billy Bob then spoke up and said, "That's good stuff. I want me a few boxes."

He walked over to the truck with his little brother in tow. Bob Billy added, "I hope she saved us a box or two."

This time, the laughter was not as loud, but the group did see the humor in this.

Bob approached the back of the truck and looked at the three boxes that Lisa had stacked near the back. When she noticed what he was looking at, she immediately responded with,"They are mine. Back off."

This caught Billy Bob off guard. Not that his guard needed to be up, he just did not intend to move those boxes, much less take them.

Quickly, Lisa apologized for her uncalled for response. "Sorry. I like those and they were the only ones here. There is plenty for everyone."

Bob Billy said to his brother, "Man. She was about ready to kick your ass."

Billy Bob responded with, "I thought that. And you know, I believe that she could."

Wanting to stay on her good side, Billy Bob said, "If you want, I will take these to your car."

"Thank you. That would be nice."

Lisa did not really see his actions as being, all that nice, or polite, but rather that he might take one or two packages out for himself. Then, on the positive side, she could take three more boxes to her car and save herself a trip.

Bob Billy then said to his older brother, quietly so Lisa could not hear, "Kiss ass. You must want some of that."

"No way man, I'd need a map and a GPS to get around and find what I want. I would not mind if you took a shot at that."

"Give me an elephant gun, and I'd take a shot at it."

Both of them laughed and made it a point not to look back at Lisa in fear that she had heard them. It was better for them to walk away as if they said nothing.

Lisa did not hear them, but did notice that they were laughing as they walked away. Not only did she assume that they were laughing at and about her, but she was going to ignore them because people were always laughing at her behind her back.

Without missing a beat, she ram-shacked the delivery truck a little more until she found three more items that she could not do without. Quickly, as if someone was going to take them from her, she lumbered herself down off the truck, with her goodies, and took them back to her car.

On her way back, she passed the Brown brothers and thanked them.

With a simple, 'you are welcome,' from Billy Bob, all three of them kept moving and they did not stop for small talk.

After Lisa dropped off her treats, she inconspicuously opened the other boxes to see if anything was missing. She was already angry and had a plan on how she would respond to them for what they had stolen from her. With nothing missing, she was now mad because she could not enjoy jumping in their faces for steeling. Either way, she would have been mad at someone or something. Now, she was just plain mad at having not to be mad at someone or something. She was bitch-less.

Steven and Eddie, without realizing it, were thinking in military terms. As if by habit, with their binoculars, they first scanned north on the Chesapeake Bay, then south after crossing over to the south side guardrail.

Each time, they were looking at the boats that were in the water. The smaller one, privately owned, appeared to be empty and drifting with the current or tide.

The larger ones, mostly company owned oil tankers, were anchored, as if waiting to dock to unload at the oil refineries just north of Annapolis.

They were in the, 'same boat,' as the smaller crafts. No one was onboard them either, and only because they had their anchors out, were they not drifting with the current and tide.

Steven tells Eddie, "Damn man. Would have thought that someone would be out there."

Eddie answered, "Don't know. Just don't know what to think."

Steven turned his head and was now facing the bus that Burt had moved. He said to Eddie, "Why not load everyone up on the bus?"

Eddie responded with, "Not a bad idea. We could take turns driving, and make faster time. It will be our new home on wheels."

"I'd bet that she has a head onboard and we can cut down on our stops," added Steven.

As if thinking additional positive reasons to commandeer the bus, they came up with some reasons, not to take it over.

Eddie started out with, "If she breaks down, we are all stranded."

"Who would want to sit next to the fat lady," joked Steven. "No one will, because you can't. To keep the bus balanced, everyone must sit on the opposite side.

"There might be road obstacles that a bus can't maneuver around," added Steven to focus on serious matters.

"Diesel fuel. It might be hard to find," was an additional, against item from Eddie.

"You know, if we are going to get a bus, why not get a nice one instead of one built for the military, by the lowest bidder," joyfully kidded Steven.

With both men having been onboard military transportation buses, they knew all too well that creature comforts were not on the manifest. The vote for not taking the bus was an easy one.

Alice and Kitty were at the railing together and Kitty asked, "Do you think that anyone jumped off the bridge?"

"No way," responded Alice. "I think that what ever happened everyplace else, happened here also and probably at the same time."

Kitty, with a little thought, and after she ran her hands through her hair to keep it in place, said, "You're right. Here, there, anywhere, everyone just got up and left earth."

Rose Marie had made her way to the railing and was standing with everyone else. She had nothing to say, but only smiled at the other girls as they smiled back.

Rose Marie wanted very much to get close with the other ladies, but figured that maybe later, they would have some quality time to spend together. Then it dawned on her, what choice do I have? This was not like having a job and if it does not work out, just quit. This was not like having neighbors that you did not like, and then you could just move, or even friends, that you could always dump and pick up new ones. For now, and for the rest of her life, these other women would be it.

With no reason to hang around, one by one, everyone loaded themselves back into their cars and hummers. Within a few minutes, the convoy was again moving.

With the group now over the Chesapeake Bay Bridge, it was an easy ride on Route 50 into DC.

CHAPTER 31

THE WHITE HOUSE

THE CONVOY SLOWLY PULLED UP to the main entrance of the White House. Even with the gate opened and no one in the guard shack, the lead vehicle did not enter the White House grounds, but preceded a few car lengths past the gate and parked it up against the curb.

The others in the convoy did the same. It was as if the White House driveway was sacred ground and entrance was not done without displaying a degree of reverence. If not anything else, obtaining permission.

Without anyone saying a word, the group gathered at the fence and looked inside as if they were a group of tourist visiting for the first time.

For Eddie and Steven, this was the living quarters of their Commander in Chief.

Lisa could only think that the kitchen had to be well stocked and of all the rooms to visit, the kitchen was first on her list. No reason for her to take a tour of an empty building, on an empty stomach.

Van Camp did not like the fact that the President was not a Republican. He was more upset with the party affiliation of the President than the fact that he might be dead and the country is without leadership.

Then he thought, 'Maybe, just maybe, I could take that position. Besides, why not? It was vacant and someone needs to fill that slot.'

Rose Marie said to Kitty, Alice, and Lisa, "I want to take a peek into the First Lady's closet."

Alice smiled and responded, "I'd bet that she had some pretty things. She always looked so nice. Especially at the White House parties."

Lisa had no desire to respond. Even if she were to find something that she liked, no way would anything fit. Yet, she could always use a new purse.

Lisa, after changing her mind, said, "Let the men do the men stuff here, and we girls can visit the living quarters."

That idea placed a smile on the ladies faces. It did not occur to them that they would be trespassing or stealing. If no one was around to take ownership and it was not marked as, 'Keep out,' then what these treasure hunters found was theirs. Besides, this was the 'People's' House and these 'people' are there to check it out.

Ben knew that the White House had a ton of riches, but knew just as well, that nothing that he found really had any value. Not now, besides, there was no one a round to buy anything from him, but still, he wanted to, scope it out.

The Brown brothers could not care one-way or the other. The White House was empty of people just like the rest of the world. This was just one stop on their way to Florida.

Joe-Joe had seen every show about the White House on VHS, Bata, and DVD's, along with all the shows on the Discovery channel. Of everyone here, he knew his way around all the rooms inside. For him, a visit to the White House was no more than a class trip after studying about it first.

Jeff wanted to visit the Communications Room, if there really was one. He also believed that there was a War Room, and if so, he wanted to see that too. The only details he knew about the White House was what he saw in the movies.

Jerry was not impressed and was just as happy staying where was, and to take a nap. He knew that all the people in the world were gone and going inside looking at another empty place was a waste of time.

Burt on the other hand, he wanted to drive up the driveway to the place where, according to what he saw on the news, where the President would greet guest as they arrived in their limos.

He figured, why not, and walked back to his vehicle and started the engine. The passenger side window was lowered and he shouted, "Anyone needing a ride to the White House? Might as well go up and arrive in style."

No one responded right away. Those who wanted to go inside for a look, were ready, but still not sure that what they were doing was right. The ones who initially had no desire to go inside, were now rethinking it over. Almost as if realizing, 'Why not? We are here now and might as well take a look.'

Even with Burt sitting in his car, waiting for riders, everyone returned to their own vehicle. Once everyone was loaded, Burt took the lead with a U-turn and eased his way past the guard shack and onto the driveway.

He made his way up the driveway and stopped at the stairs. In the back of his mind, he wanted very much, to see Marine Guards standing by the doors, at attention in their dress uniforms.

Steven and Eddie also wanted to see Marine Guards standing by the doors, not at attention, but at the ready to block any, and all, uninvited guest with deadly force.

Van Camp noticed how empty it seemed. Even with the knowledge that no one on earth was left but them, he felt that of all the places in the world, that here, at the steps of the White House, that there should be something besides plenty of nothing. It did not take long before everyone was heading up the steps.

No one ran up the steps like schoolchildren on a school field trip, instead, with respect for this place, they quietly made their way up the steps and entered by twos into the first of many hallways. Initially, everyone felt as if they were in a museum at closing time. The only sounds were of their own footsteps and the rubbings of Lisa's thighs.

Van Camp announced, "Does everyone agree that we should meet back here, in say, thirty minutes?"

No one responded at first, but slowly, and not with loud voices, they all said things to the effect, 'Yeah, okay with me, see you in thirty.'

This pleased Van Camp in that he was able to suggest something that everyone could agree upon at the same time. Even with this being a small item, it was yet another example for those to remember him by.

With his duties out of the way, Van Camp made his way to the Oval Office. If anyone in this group was suited to sit behind that desk, it most certainly was him.

Finding the Oval Office was easy enough, and he quickly had a seat behind the desk. The only thing that would have made this moment most memorable was, if he had a crowd looking at him, or at least, someone to take his picture.

As if he was a child sitting at his father's desk, where he worked, he went through all the drawers to see what items the most powerful man in the free world would have. To his surprise, nothing there surprised him. The top, center drawer that normally kept pens and pencils, along with different sizes of paperclips, well, that was what was there. Along with a small note pad with his initials at the top.

It was this item, and nothing else that impressed him. It impressed him so much that this note pad was the only thing he placed in his pocket.

Just as he placed the note pad in his pocket, and before he could open another drawer, in walked Steven and Eddie.

Van Camp assumed that they did not see what he just placed in his pocket. He knew that it was okay to take it, even by their standards, but he did not want anyone that may report to him in the future to have this over his head.

His only response to them was, "I wish one of you guys had a camera."

Steven walked up to the desk, and asked Van Camp, "Can I have a seat?"

Van Camp was caught a little off guard as he thought he said sheet, as in a sheet from the pad of paper he palmed into his pocket, and not seat. Steven repeated, "Come on man, let me have a turn."

Eddie was quick to add in, "Yeah, I want to give it a shot, let me have a seat. Can't believe that we are in the Oval Office. I too, wish one of us had a camera."

Steven did not see the importance in the camera, and said, "Hope you have a Polaroid. Either one of you guys know how to develop film?"

Naturally, they did not and that only dampened their excitement of being here. Van Camp made a mental note about his remark and decided not to put him in charge of organizing any parties.

Ben strode in and he looked like a man on a mission. A mission to find items of value. Maybe not valuable right now, but possibly in the future.

Steven and Eddie easily picked up what Ben was up to, and they did not like it, they did not like it at all. Yet, there was nothing for them to do.

Ben made a beeline right to the President's desk and without saying a word, went into all the drawers. The only thing he found and snatched up, was a few pens. Nice pens, not the ones by BiC, but the nice Cross-pens.

With the pens now in his pocket, Ben made his way out of the Oval Office on his scavengers hunt. As he left, Steven and Eddie could only give him dirty looks.

For his thirty minutes, Van Camp spent them all here, in the Oval Office before heading back. He walked around looking at everything and sitting in every chair. He could only fathom the number of world leaders that had visited this room.

For Eddie and Steven, after they took turns sitting in the chair and going into all the drawers, they too, headed back.

Unlike Van Camp, they did not take any souvenirs. That little note made Van Camp uneasy. He was going to suggest to them as they were leaving that maybe they should take something, but decided against it.

Rose Marie, Kitty, Alice, and Lisa found the living quarters. As Kitty and Alice took time in the closet with Rose Marie looking into the dresser drawers, Lisa had to take a dump.

Kitty found a sweater that she liked, and took it. Alice was able to find a great pair of sandals that she could wear in Florida. To Rose Marie's surprise, the first lady also had one of those round roller things to get lint/cat hair off your clothes, and now,

that was hers.

Lisa wiped up, cleaned up, flushed twice, and quickly found her way to the closet. She looked around the closet until she found a purse that she wanted. She would have never paid for a purse like this one, but she had to take something.

She emptied what she had in her purse into her new one, and then made her way back to the bathroom to add a roll of toilet paper to her purse. Not the whole roll, just a sizable amount, for emergencies. This did end up being a whole roll, just without the cardboard centerpiece.

For the ladies, spending their thirty minutes in this one part of the White House, was not long enough, but they were okay with it. They knew that they had to move on. And it quickened their stay as the foul odor from the bathroom reached them. The ladies, without saying it, agreed that Lisa should have given them three courtesy flushes instead of waiting until the end with only two. Jeff did not find what he was looking for and after almost thirty minutes of searching, he headed back, trying not to get lost. Joe-Joe took the tour and not taking too much time in each room. Every time he visited a room that he was not familiar with, he made a mental note of its location and possible purpose. Then, the next time he watched the White House on a DVD or video, he would grade it based on the accuracy on what he remembered.

For Joe-Joe, this was a wonderful tour. Sadly wonderful, that he could appreciate what had happened to the world that allowed him to take this trip.

For the Brown brothers, this was equally a wonderful trip to experience. With them being in security, and this being one of the most secured buildings in the world, this was a trip of a lifetime.

Instead of looking at the artwork or even imagining the importance of this home, they counted security cameras. Guessing where they kept the weapons and ammo, was high on their things to look for They were surprised that not all of the doors they checked were locked. They spoke about this and concluded that if you made it inside, then you had permission to go where you wanted. And what areas were secured, well, they just had to have an armed guard guarding that door or room for sure.

Bob said to Bob Billy, "I would love to be on guard duty here."

Bob Billy answered, "If you were, could you tell anyone?"

With some thought, he answered, "Yeah, just the ones that I don't like, and then I can kill them."

This was funny to the both of them. Other than comments about camera locations and which room to visit next, little more was said until Bob Billy said, "Time to go back."

His brother nodded and they immediately turned around. Just a little over thirty minutes of allotted time had arrived, everyone was back outside looking at each other trying to figure out if anyone was missing.

Each wanted to show an effort to finding anyone left behind under the belief that, if they were missed, that they would be given equal time for their search and safe return and not forgotten. Other than what Van Camp had, the other only souvenirs were a sweater, sandals, and purse with a half roll of White House toilet paper.

With no fan fair, everyone loaded up and headed out towards the Pentagon.

CHAPTER 32

THE PENTAGON

DRIVING TO THE PENTAGON WAS easy in Washington without any traffic. The traffic lights were still working, but ignored if they were red. A few were out all together. Some vehicles were not pulled over to the side of the road. Mainly, because there were just too many of them, with so little available space to have pulled off to the side in an orderly fashion at the same time.

Scores of them were stopped, one behind the other at intersections, as if waiting for the light to change. It was then a simple task to go around them, as there was never any oncoming traffic. Their driving had to remain alert so as not to be taken by surprise by a stopped car or truck in the driving lane. The others that were riding shotgun looked all around as if expecting to see someone, anyone.

As they neared the Pentagon, most everyone was looking over at the Ronald Reagan International Airport, anticipating air traffic. Naturally, there was none.

The ride to the front of the Pentagon was very somber. Steven did not like the fact that this building was not under heavy guard. Not so much that it was empty, but it should be very well guarded.

Eddie had the same feelings.

For Billy Bob and Bob Billy, they knew that this must have taken an army of manpower to patrol the grounds, not to mention guarding the miles of hallways inside the building.

Just as they did at the White House, the lead vehicle pulled a little passed the main stairway allowing all of them to be parked at the steps.

Unlike the White House, not everyone felt it was important to go inside. Steven, Eddie, the Brown brothers, along with Burt, Jeff, and Joe-Joe, were the only ones that wanted to venture inside. Steven spoke to the group and said, "We should take our radios with us, and keep them on. It's a big place and no need to loose anyone."

Eddie added, "I don't believe that there is a real need to undertake a long tour. We should get in, check it out, and just leave."

No one seemed to disagree. For the most part, that was just common sense. If anybody were here, someone should have been stationed at the front door.

For those who remained outside, a few of them stepped out to stretch their legs. Lisa wanted to go inside to use the ladies room but had no desire to hike up the stairs and down any long hallways. She assumed that in a military building, that there would be no handicapped stalls for her to slip into and clog it up. Aside from the fear of the long walk, she was fearful that if she did find a restroom, that she would be stuck and no one would be able to find her. And if someone did find her, nobody would be able to get her out.

She stopped over and asked Alice, Rose Marie, and Kitty if they would walk inside with her. As most women did, if one had to go, the rest of them would join in for the ladies pilgrimage to the toilets.

As expected, the men inside found no one and nothing of importance. Only very long, very empty hallways.

The ladies had better luck, as the restrooms was close to the lobby where they came in. To the joy of Lisa, they had a handicapped stall that was wider than they usually were. For the first time in years, she was able to walk in forward, and then turn around, rather than having to back in.

Alice and Rose Marie did their thing with Kitty also adjusting her makeup and hair. Even without the thousands of military men that were normally stationed here, she wanted to look good, just in case.

For Rose Marie, out of habit, she looked at herself from all angles to see if she had any cat hair on her clothes. In a small way, she was disappointed that she did not. Reminding her that she had not seen her cats, or any cats today.

After three courtesy flushes, Lisa was done and ready to head back. Kitty, Rose Marie, and Alice gave each other a look after the second courtesy flush, with the three of them grateful she was able to go here and do her business, and not somewhere along the road. Without saying it, Kitty was thinking of just how big a tree would need to be for Lisa to hide behind to do her business. Well, she could always hide behind the Rockies, she joked silently to herself.

Rose Marie was thinking the same thing, only she thought that it would take one of those 200-year-old trees out on the west coast for her to hide her behind, behind.

It was not long before the guys had met back up at the lobby with grim faces. Not that they were surprised of not finding anyone, but they had some hope to find something, which was why they decided to stop here on their way south.

It was at this time that the ladies were headed back with Lisa's legs doing that rubbing thing. The men were immediately alerted to the sound, not remembering that it was Lisa, and not being able to see around the bend in the hallway, believed that they had struck it rich with someone, or something. Whatever, it had to be most important and that it needed an urgent response.

Without saying a word, they started to run in that direction. From where the ladies were, they could hear them running, but like the guys, they were unable to see around the corner.

This got them excited and they started to walk a little faster. The sound of Lisa's legs changing cadence, created more excitement with the guys.

Steven got on his radio and called to the ones outside, excitedly explaining what was going on. Kitty was doing the same, reporting their findings.

Neither the guys, nor the ladies had noticed what was truly going on. The ones outside, with their own excitement, quickly made it up the stairs to join in. Now, all the radios were squawking away with no one really listening, just talking, and talking, and talking.

Then, almost as this was rehearsed, they all arrived at the same time at the lobby door. Surprised, dirty, and confused looks were on everyone.

For the next few minutes, everyone had something to say and ask, but no one had any answers. It was soon, with much disappointment, they realized what had happen. Nothing had occurred, except that their hopes were raised a little. The ones not out of breath, headed back first with the tired ones taking up the rear. Not exactly, Lisa was not out of breath and was taking up the rear and trying her hardest not to allow her legs to rub loud enough to be heard.

With little fan fair, the convoy was again heading south. Nothing was said between anyone, as his or her temporary high had created a very deep low. It was a long quiet drive down I-95 with the Brown brothers in the lead this time.

CHAPTER 33

THE REST STOP

WITH A CONVOY THIS SIZE, it was apparent that they would be making more rest stops than they would if each had driven by them selves. In your own car, you knew how much gas you had and how long it will last.

Bob Billy tells his brother, "Why don't you pull into the next rest stop?"

"Yeah, okay," he answered.

With that, Bob Billy decided to use the radio to give everyone a heads up. "Breaker 19. Breaker 19," he spoke into the mike.

"Breaker 19! Who are you, Smokey and the Bandit," Billy Bob asked jokingly to his brother.

"I don't know what it means, but that is how it's done."

"Yeah, it's done that way in the movies," commented Billy Bob.

Before this conversation could go any further, "Go ahead Breaker 19."

"Good buddy, we are going to take a break at the next rest stop. Over," excitedly answered Bob Billy knowing that he, and whomever it was that answered him, justified how and what he said over the radio.

"10-4," was another response.

"That went over well," bragged Bob Billy, looking over at his brother wanting his approval.

"What do you say next," asked Billy Bob.

Not wanting to lose his moment of joy, Bob Billy answered, "Nothing more needs to be said. I said it all, 10-4 good buddy."

They both looked at each other and after a moment, laughed at their situation.

Burt, who was at the end of the convoy, slowed down a little, he wanted to make sure everyone pulled into the rest stop and that no one either did not get the message, or was not paying attention and missed everyone else pulling off the highway.

Burt chuckled to himself a little because he wondered how anyone could miss everyone else pulling off the road. Then, another chuckle because he knew that he had someone girls that were driving and everyone knows, that girls don't know how to follow.

The rest stop was just minutes away from where it was announced that they were going to stop. As Billy Brown pulled in, he courteously looked for a space that was close to the main building, and with room for everyone to park.

Bob Billy realized that he was looking for a parking space, said, "We don't need no parking space man. You can double park, you know."

Billy Bob did not want his little brother to have one up on him said, "I know that, just seeing if you were paying attention."

"Yeah, I be paying you attention. Attention that you be looking for a parking space that you doesn't be a needing."

Even if this sounded like mean talk between the two of them, it was not. They were brothers, and twins to boot, and the more they talked that way, the closer they got as brothers.

Burt was satisfied that everyone pulled off without anyone going astray. His job as the 'rear guard,' was performed to standards.

This first rest stop on I-95 was one of the larger ones, and importantly, it has electrical power, but still, no people. There were three or four gas stations, a Cracker Barrel, I-Hop, Burger King, KFC/Taco Bell combo, and a Subway. There was one thing unusual about this rest stop. Not so much that it had cars, trucks, and campers, without any people, but that there were not any McDonald's.

As you would expect, Lisa was the only one who noticed that. For any and all of the fast food joints, she knew the menus by heart. She always hated it when you were in line for a while, and when the person in front of you was finally asked, "What can I get for you today," or something like that, they would act as if this was their first time there and that they had to, now, read the menu. Left to right, and top to bottom, as they had to read the entire menu and then decide. They could not have read the menu while they were in line for the last twenty minutes, but no, they had to read it all and right then as if the menu items where not there before or that they would be changed soon.

For Van Camp, what he noticed was that there weren't any flies by the over flowing trashcans. Normally, bees and flies would be everywhere, along with some seagulls being drawn in by the stench of the trash.

Once everyone exited their vehicles and before they walked into the main building, Steven held up his hand for everyone to stop and listen. Even those that were never in the military and unaccustomed to this hand signal, kind of, sort of, knew what it meant. No one spoke up and asked why, as they stood there in silence, listening to what ever it was that Steven had heard.

Off in the distance, they heard a couple of 18-wheelers with their motors running. Not very loud, just at an idle and you could see some exhaust coming out of a few of them. It was easy to spot them as the few that were running, had those tall exhaust that were behind and higher than the cabs.

Before Van Camp could suggest anything, Billy Bob said, "My brother and I will check them bad boys out."

Everyone seemed please with that for a number of good reasons. One, they had to visit the restrooms first, or, that they just knew that there was nothing for them to see. It would just be a few empty trucks with their motors left running.

Sure enough, the Brown brothers found three empty trucks

parked side by side with their motors running. After turning off the motors, they headed towards the main building to make a restroom call for themselves.

Inside the lobby, near the racks of maps and tourist attractions pamphlets, was a wall of phones. Mostly, they were direct dials to hotels at the next exit. Two on the ends were for rental cars, but that made no sense, because if you were here, that you had gotten here by car, so why would anyone need a rental.

Alice, knowing full well, that no one would answer, tried them all anyway. She did get the expected, disappointing results, but she felt better that she at least given it a try.

Lisa said aloud for others to hear, "If you want cooked food, make sure it was wrapped well."

For most everyone there, they had assumed that vending machines would be on the menu today. For Kitty, it was a trip to the magazine counter for a copy of Glamour and Self.

Lisa walked right over and into Arby's restaurant and got in behind the counter. She started to tear into a few of the sandwiches that were under the heat lamps.

She knew that they had to be a few days old, but figured that if they did not smell bad, that they might be acceptable enough to eat.

Van Camp noticed what she was doing, but decided not to say anything. It was like taking a bone from a hungry dog and you did not need to be in management to understand and appreciate that.

Beside, if she ate one of them and got sick, then she deserved it. However, if she ate one and she seemed okay, then she could be the official food taster for the group. On top of that, if anyone knew anything about food, it had to be her.

A few of the guys that were standing near Van Camp, noticed that he was staring at something, and that caught their attention. Jerry, Eddie, Steven, Burt, Jeff, and Joe-Joe turned in his direction and everyone witnessed a professional food scavenger, scavenging for food. She was the human version of a, 'bottom feeder.' Steven and Eddie wanted to say something, but decided against it. It was enough watching her without saying anything. This could even be an episode on the TV documentary, Planet Earth, or Survival of the fittest and the biggest.

Each sandwich, about twenty of them, was carefully opened so not to have any cheese stick to the wrapper. Each sandwich was then carefully raised to her nose for the scent test. You would see the same enthusiasm and degree of detail of someone sniffing good wine before giving it the swish test. Only in this case, you would not catch her spitting anything out.

Every move she made was carefully orchestrated, as not to waste any steps. Each time she made a judgment call on a sandwich, she made a face and some noise. The size of her smile corresponded directly with the sounds she made. It was apparent that a good smelling sandwich, received a big smile and a positive sounding, 'hummm.'

Then from a good sandwich to a bad one, the smile decreased, and the 'humming,' got less audible.

Out of the twenty or so sandwiches, she found two that received her, 'I will eat you today award.' At the conclusion of her testing, those two sandwiches were gone in two bites each without anytime for chewing. It was a simple, insert into mouth, swallow, repeat.

There was a wide range of reactions from the guys. Steven and Eddie, having been in the military, did not see anything odd about this. For Jerry, Jeff, and Joe-Joe, this was most gross. Burt did not care one way or another, just as long as she did not prepare his meals in the future.

The Brown brothers watched with enjoyment, 'Food Testing 101.' Bob Billy was the first to say something "Did she save anything for us?"

Joe-Joe, who had not said very much up to this point, said, "If she did, you don't want it."

Alice walked over and said to the group, "I tried all those phones over there, and nothing."

No one seemed surprised that there were no answers, but everyone were surprised that she wasted the time to try, and that they were even more surprised that she wasted more time to tell them, as if they cared.

Ben had made his way to the gift shop and got in behind the counter and up to the lottery machine. He asked, "Anyone know last weeks winning Power Ball number?"

Kitty was at the magazine stand and said, "Yeah, I have it, wait a minute."

She placed down her Glamour magazine and picked up the local paper. On page two, she found the winning Power Ball numbers for Friday, last week.

"You ready," she asked Ben.

"Go ahead," he answered.

She called out the numbers and he keyed them in on the lottery machine. A moment later, he printed out a ticket. She asked, "What did you do?"

With a con-man smile, he answered, "I printed me a winning Power Ball ticket worth 25 million dollars. The machine was still taking orders from last week."

Kitty looked confused as Ben added, "Maybe I can't collect the 25 mill, but if the world comes back to life, I will be a rich man." In a small way, she wanted a winning lottery ticket also, but did not want anything to do with Ben. She still did not trust him and she did not want him to think that she did, or that they had anything in common. Or worse, that she wanted to start up a conversation with him.

Rose Marie overheard them talking as she was reading a Dog and Cat magazine and wanted a winning lottery ticket. She did not much care, or never did pick up that Ben was a con man, as she simply wanted a winning lottery ticket, not an affair.

Rose Marie asks Kitty, "What are the numbers for the other big lottery?"

Without even looking up, she rattled off the numbers as Ben key them in. A second later, Rose Marie had her winning lottery ticket and her copy of the Dog and Cat magazine.

In thirty minutes or so, bathroom stops were taken care of; mostly everyone snacked on snacks from vending machines, and with Burt suggestion, every one headed out to fill up with gas.

The pumps there were working just fine. As long as you were able to have the pump read and accept your credit card, you got gas.

Van Camp spoke up and explained how he failed to see the reason to top off so soon. Burt quickly corrected him, who said, "We are not sure if we can get gas at our next stop. Equally important, we are not sure where our next stop is."

Not wanting to be corrected, Van Camp agreed and added, "Good planning, I like it." He made it sound as if Burt's plan needed his approval. From Burt's point of view, he did not need, nor did he ask for, Dick's approval.

Everyone easily picked up that Van Camp was trying to out-due Burt, but Burt came back with, "I am glad that you agree. Any other suggestions before we head out?"

Van Camp did not hear his question, as he was already walking back to his car. Burt just held his arms out, half way up as if expecting a response. To the few of them that were nearby and paying attention, gave Burt a few points and a score of zero for Van Camp.

Burt was not looking for points, just going through the motions for the good of the group. He looked over at Billy Bob and Bob Billy and asked, "Maybe he should take the lead this time."

"Yeah man, he be good at that. Just drive south, don't you know."

Burt gave this some thought and asked the two of them, "Why I-95? Why not US-1?"

Bob and his brother Bob Billy, looked at him as if thinking, 'Now why would you want to do that?'

Jeff, the computer guy, overhearing this conversation, spoke up and said, "It might be a better way."

Billy Bob and Bob Billy, looked at him, again thinking, 'Now why would you want to do that?'

Burt turned to Jeff, and said, "Yeah, on I-95, all we see is highway. On 1, we will be passing a lot of places where there might be people."

"Why not just settle for any people we find down in Florida," asked Kitty, who had walked into their conversation. For her, she was in a hurry to get to where ever it was that they were going. It was too much for her to keep her hair and makeup in good appearance if they were to spend extra hours and hours driving the scenic route to Florida.

Van Camp noticed the group meeting and hurried back to see what it was that he was missing.

By now, everyone had gathered under the canopy of the gas station, pump 5, for this unplanned gathering of travelers.

It was at this point, that some were again having second thoughts about heading south, so far from where they were from. It's doesn't get too cold in South Carolina or Georgia.

Alice, Rose Marie, Joe-Joe, and Jerry, were all fine with staying the way things were before this trip, as in, going back to the hotel near where they lived. Steven, Eddie, Billy Bob, Bob Billy, Kitty, Jeff, Burt, Lisa, Van Camp, and Ben, wanted to take the trip. They had settled in with the fact that everyone was gone and that they clearly needed to head south for better weather.

After a few minutes of the, back and forth to return or to continue on to Florida, or anywhere closer, it was decided again, to head south, to Florida. Then, a little more time was spent on which route to take, I-95 or US-1, as I-95 won out. Kitty was the one who pushed the most, as she had no desire to keep her appearance cooped up in a car for longer than need be. She was starting to get, 'look at me,' withdrawals.

"If we are going to drive, them let's drive the quickest and shortest route," she made clear to everyone.

With all the decisions now made, full tanks of gas, it was time to leave and to stay on I-95. Then, they had to decide on who will take the lead.

With Ben having no desire to be the lead vehicle, and wanting Van Camp to do it, said, "Let Dick take the lead this time."

The Brown brothers quickly agreed. "My brother and I will take up the rear," announced Billy bob, with Bob Billy in agreement.

Everyone else seemed fine with those decisions. Van Camp felt pleased to be nominated to take the lead, but not pleased that he had to be in the very front. Nor was he happy that he was not the one suggesting that he take the lead. Driving first was difficult and not very relaxing. However, he did not want to turn it down.

Wanting to show that he was a leader, in traffic as well as other things, he said to the group, "Let's go. Fall in behind me please. Stay close and alert."

Before long, the convoy was traveling south again, with gas tanks filled, on Interstate 95, and not US-1, with Van Camp in the lead.

CHAPTER 34

THE CRACKER BARREL

AFTER A FEW HOURS, IT was time for another rest stop, because the Brown brothers noticed at the same time, a KFC sign for the next exit.

"You as hungry as me," asked Billy Bob to Bob Billy.

"But we ain't in the lead, it ain't our call," sadly explained Bob Billy, as he looked at his brother, as if he did not know their place in the convoy.

"Shit man, get on the CB. Tell boss man Dick that we want to take a break," Billy Bob said quickly.

With Bob Billy a little hesitant to make the request, Billy Bob grabbed the CB and said, "Break 19, break 19, break 19. What you say we take the next exit for a break."

No one responded right away. Billy Bob spoke again into the CB, "Next exit please."

A response came back from Van Camp. It did not say who he was, as his voice was easy to recognize. "10-4, come on up and take the lead."

Without consulting with his brother, Billy Bob hits the gas and passed everyone, quickly taking the lead in plenty of time to make the exit.

"Damn straight. Anytime I see me a KFC, my stomach be a crying for some legs, extra crispy, with macaroni and cheese."

"You and that dark meat. You need to upgrade to white meat," joked Billy Bob to his younger brother.

Bob Billy looked at him, and asked, "Do you want to know why I like the legs, and not breast?"

"Don't know and don't care, as long as I get my breast. Crispy, regular, mild or spicy, don't care."

"Well big brother, I be telling you now," joked Bob Billy.

"Tell me quick before we get there. Don't want you blabbing while I be trying to eat."

Catching his thoughts, he said, "When mom would bring home a bucket full from KFC, Churches, or Popeye's Chicken, I always had the leftovers."

"What you be talking about Lewis," jokes a question from Billy Bob. "You be gettin the leftovers?"

"You, you be liken the breast, mom be liken the thighs, which be leaving me with them legs and wings. Them wings, too much trouble to be a messing with, so I settled for the legs."

Billy Bob gave him a look of, 'I still don't be a caring as he signaled for a right turn off the highway. He asked, "You be telling me you be mistreated and under fed by our Mama?"

"No man, just that by the time I had my hands up to reach into the bucket, you and Mama had everything be gone but the wings and legs. Thought that I might as well enjoy what I had, the leftovers."

Billy Bob gave the appearance that he did not care or really believed his story, but he said, "Tell you what little brother, when we get to KFC, I be getting you a bucket of breast and thighs. No wings or legs and I will make them double crispy."

Not thanking him, but Bob Billy responded, "That be nice. It will be real nice if you were to only eat legs and wings this time."

"Don't be pressing your luck little brother. We can both chow out on breasts and thighs and we can throw that Lisa woman the legs."

That got a laugh from the two of them that quickly faded as they pulled up in front of the KFC, and saw that it was filled with smoke. Filled with smoke as if it had a fire or something recently. Billy Bob got out of his car and just looked in at the restaurant with disappointment. Lisa pulled up beside him and with her window rolled down, said, "Why not we just do the Cracker Barrel across the street?"

When Billy Bob looked over at her, she was pointing off a little ways to the Cracker Barrel Old Country Store that was not filled with smoke, and that there were only a few cars parked out front.

"That be cool," answered Billy Bob, as he got back into his car and led the convoy away from the smoking KFC.

The rest of the convoy followed as everyone easily picked up on why they bypassed the KFC. No one saw any fire inside, just plenty of lingering smoke.

At the Cracker Barrel, none of the cars attempted to pull into a parking space; they just lined up one behind another. One by one, everyone got out, made the normal stretching motions, and looked around. As with the rest of the world, nothing was happening.

Single file, they made their way into the Cracker Barrel. As they walked inside, it was of no consequences that the place was empty. It was just that in another time and place, it would have been packed full of people. Even the gift shops were usually packed at all hours of the day and night.

Lisa, feeling that she wanted to contribute to the group, and make a new start and not to bitch so much, decided to do a good thing, fix a meal for the group. She felt that everyone was always looking at the things she ate, as well as, how much she ate, and making fun of her, with negative attention. By cooking a meal for this small group, she would score points, and possibly, not bring as much negative attention to herself.

On a side note, while she was cooking, she could 'taste', enough taste samples, which should end up, equaling a full meal. Then she would only eat, a normal size, full meal, with the group. If her prediction were correct, they would be happy with a free meal, and only see her eat one meal, and that would be just as much as theirs was.

This idea was a 'Go,' and as Lisa walked into the restaurant last, she announced, "I will fix a treat for all of us."

That caught everyone's attention, and it was taken with immediate mixed emotions. The lazy ones, like Jerry, Jeff, and Joe-Joe, thought this to be a great idea. Eddie, Steven, and Ben, who were not lazy, liked the idea because eating chow in the military and while in prison, was always prepared by others.

Van Camp did not like that idea, because it was not his. However, he would be more than happily to feast on a free meal provided by someone else. As long as he was not involved with the cooking, or serving, or worse, cleaning up. Those three steps were just beneath him. Naturally, he would like not to do any of those steps and not have it noticed that he did not. However, he did make it a point to say to a few people that were around him, of how nice it was of her to step up and do something good for the group.

Kitty liked and disliked the idea. She liked Lisa's idea because she would not be placed in a position where she had to work or cook, as that would most surely mess up her hair and makeup. She disliked her idea because no way did she want to eat anything that Lisa cooked. Kitty believed that Lisa had gotten fat by eating whatever it was that she ate, and that she was going to fix the same kinds of foods for everyone. Just what this new world of theirs needed, a herd of people all built like Lisa, thought Kitty with a cringed face.

Alice was okay with it, as she did not want to make waves. It did cross her mind that if she did not help cook, then she would be needed to help clean up at the end. Then again, there was no reason to clean up as they were only going to eat here once, and then move on down the road.

Burt liked the idea, as he wanted just to eat. He did not want to spend any time cooking or cleaning, but would do his fair share to eat all that was prepared. No reason to waste anything and there was no telling when they could eat like this again.

Billy Bob and Bob Billy thought this to be a great idea as there was nothing more pleasing to them, but to see a fat girl with a big butt, cooking them something to eat. The two of them would had been much happier to sit in the kitchen just to watch her cook, but knew that if they did sit in the kitchen, that they might be called up to help out, and no way were they acceptable to having to help. As they agreed, it was a woman's way to cook, so don't get in her way. Especially, if she were way, way big.

Rose Marie liked the idea of someone cooking for her, or for anyone else, as far as that mattered. This gave her time to visit the gift shop for some little toys that she believed that her cats would enjoy. For her cool cats, not all of their toys came from the pet store. Some toy items were just pretty in color and that they easily rolled or made noise. Rose Marie knew that, even if she never saw her cats again, that there must be other cats in the world that survived. That was totally possible because here they were, alone, but they did survive and with luck, so could a dozen or so cats.

In the kitchen, Lisa was pleased to see that the grills were still turned on and an ample supply of eggs, bacon, sausage, ham, and scrapple were still available. She also found a big pot of grits cooking away, or it was more like simmering a little. After she pulled the crusted top aside, hot grits were ready to be served. Off to one side, was a large container of prepared pancake mix with smaller containers of blueberries, peaches, and other items to be placed in the pancake batter close by.

Lisa was most grateful that everything was available and appears to be okay to use. It had crossed her mind that after she had announced to everyone in the world that she would cook them a meal, that nothing would be easily accessible to prepare, thus creating a big let down to everyone with her as the center point.

Another part of her reasoning for cooking, was because she, sort of knew, that survivors of anything, always wanted to get rid of the weakest, or biggest link. Keeping everyone happy with her, would keep her around a little longer and not be voted out just yet. With a smile on her face, along with the ability to taste everything that she cooked, she started out preparing a normal meal for everybody in the whole world.

In the dining area, everyone sat in two tables close to each other. For the most part, it was a table of girls and a table of guys. Van Camp was hard at thinking on how he could use this time as a stepping-stone to his Kingship title of, Mr. President, Mr. Ruler, or just plain, The King.

Then it hit him as he heard everyone saying how good it was of Lisa to step up and cook them all something to eat. That she did not want any help and that she did it without being asked or having it as an assignment.

'Drinks,' thought Van Camp. I could get the drinks. Quickly, he stood up and said, "I'll take your drink order while Lisa is doing her part."

That pleased everyone as much as it pleased them that Lisa was cooking. Ben was quick to pick-up on this sly move by Van Camp, and he thought to himself, 'good move, what is it that I can do to help?'

As Van Camp made the rounds with drinks, mostly sodas, Ben was up, and without saying a word, had placed down silverware that was pre-wrapped in napkins in front of everyone. He only said one thing aloud when he placed a set of silverware at an empty seat at the table. "Here is a good spot for our cook."

There were no jokes this time about her size. Nothing was said that maybe she should have two chairs to better even out the weight and to give the chair, or chairs, a fighting chance to survive the weight load.

This little comment from Ben, got a smile from everyone, and it took the focus off Van Camp, where as Van Camp quickly surmised that he had been one-upped.

The Brown brothers were just as quick as Van Camp to pick-up on the little war between the two of them. Billy Bob knew that he and his brother would need to step up and get into the act. Billy Bob tells Bob Billy, "Follow my lead."

Bob Billy knew what his brother meant; he just did not know what he meant it to be.

Billy Bob, stood up quietly and said, "I will take a trip to the kitchen to see if I can help bring anything out for Lisa."

Quick on the uptake, Bob Billy said, "Let me give you a hand. People like to eat hot food while it be hot, don't you know."

Ben and Van Camp knew that they had just witnessed that they both were just, 'one upped,' by the brothers. They did not like it, but knew that the battle for Kingship, was fully underway.

In the kitchen, Lisa was a cooking queen with scramble eggs on one side of the flat grill with bacon, scrapple, ham, and sausages cooking away on the other side. She did not make pancakes for breakfast, because that would have been just too much for her to do, by herself.

Everything was about done at the same time just as Billy Bob and Bob Billy came in. Lisa looked at them, as she was most grateful that she had help with this part, the service. It did not take long for the plates to be filled with a ton of eggs, and a few slices of everything else, as it was easier to place a little of each on every plate rather than taking orders.

Quickly, the Brown brothers served everyone and then took their seats. Walking out of the kitchen, Lisa headed her way towards the tables, looking for the easiest route where she would not bang into tables and chairs. Just as she was about to sit down, Alice started clapping her approval. The clapping of hands by everyone else quickly followed that. For this moment in time in the entire world, Lisa was receiving a standing ovation.

The Kingship competitors had to join in, but did so making it a point not to clap too much, too little, or to be the first ones to stop. Kitty, expecting steak and or lobster, was disappointed that she was just served breakfast in the middle of the day. Without thinking, she said to Alice who was sitting next to her, "Breakfast?" Lisa did hear what Kitty had to say, and responded. "Sorry little thing, the grill was on and it was the breakfast items that was out for preparation."

Van Camp wanted to step in and ease the predicted friction, "Then we can assume that everyone disappeared around breakfast time."

Everyone else nodded his or her heads in agreement. At this point, Lisa was starting to get pissed a little. Everyone started to talk about what they thought happened to everyone else, instead of praising her about breakfast. She wanted very much to lash out and bitch at them for ignoring what she had done, what she had done for all of them.

Rose Marie was quick to notice the change in Lisa. She clearly knew that Lisa was no longer the focus and with the start of breakfast, she should have gotten more than just a little applause from the group.

"I say we count our blessing," piped in Rose Marie."Everyone is gone. They have been gone for a few days now. And right now, we are feasting on a very delightful breakfast provided by our very own private chef. In fact, she is now a world-renowned chef, the most respected chef in the world. We should be nice to her because this is not Hell's Kitchen."

Van Camp, the Brown brothers, and Ben would rather talk about the missing people, than giving Lisa any more attention than they were now sending her way.

Lisa was quick to relax and made a mental note that Rose Marie was on her side. She still wanted to bitch about something, but she would hold it in and maybe, just maybe, her bitchiness would fade away.

Before long, breakfast was over. The only thing outside of the norm, was that no one came by to take away your dishes when you finished.

Slowly, everyone got up and made the pilgrimage to the gift shop and or rest rooms. The first thing that Rose Marie noticed was the cat and dog, salt and pepper-shakers. These types of items always caught your eye right away, as you enter gift shops, but never did anyone buy them, except for Rose Marie. She got two sets with plans to trash the dog ones, keeping the cats.

The next items she noticed were the throw blankets hanging against the back wall. There were the typical ones with Elvis, a unicorn, and the face of Jesus along with the Confederate flag. What caught her eye was the one of; you guessed it, two cats playing with a toy.

Even with these cats not as pedigreed as hers, she felt a connection with them. They did not have an owner and she did not have any cats. With the two saltshakers and blanket, she headed to her car.

Ben made his typical run behind the counter and opened the cash register. Billy Bob was not pleased that Ben got there before he did. Yet, wanting to say something that would count against Ben, he asked, "What are you doing back there?"

Ben knew full well, what and why he was asked this question. As with most con men, Ben had a quick answer. "Just grabbing some change. You know, for sodas and snacks in vending machines later."

That was a great answer, assumed Ben, and yes, it was a great answer according to Billy Bob.

Everyone else made a quick run through the gift shop, not really doing any shopping. It was just a habit, that most people would do as they passed a gift shop, to go inside.

The only other one to pick up items was Lisa, as she bagged herself a supply of snack food.

The next stop was the gas station. It worked out that Rose Marie's credit card worked on one of the pumps. With everyone else either being lazy, or they just figured that they would all use the same pump, Rose Marie had a couple of hundred dollars charged to her account before all was said and done, and pumped. And, as a good steward of her money, she collected her receipt.

With stomachs and gas tanks filled, bladders emptied, it was off again on southbound Interstate 95, with Burt in the lead.

CHAPTER 35

SMOKE SIGNAL

A FTER ABOUT AN HOUR OF driving, dark smoke was billowing into the sky off in the distance. Not a lot of it, but enough to catch a driver's attention.

It appeared to be smoke from the burning of tires. Either someone was sending a smoke signal; there was civil unrest with tires burning in the middle of the road, or just a regular fire. It rose some two hundred feet or so, straight up. It was then picked up by the wind currents and directed southward. The smoke trail went southward until it was over the horizon, some ten miles, or so, from where they were. Normally, you would move on with life, as if you never saw the smoke trail.

Burt, now in the lead, pulled over slowly after he decided that he wanted a group decision as to whether they should check it out or not. It was too much to discuss to a dozen or more people on a CB, all sharing the same channel.

Using common sense, and acting on instinct, he pulled right up and stopped in front of a highway sign giving the distance in miles until their next exit or turn-off. Richmond Virginia was the next city with 25 miles to go.

He knew that someone would always ask, "Where are we?" Then

he would politely point them in the direction of the huge green and white road sign right above their heads.

Naturally, someone trying to be funny, would always ask, "Are we there yet?" That reply would only get a negative facial response of, "you be a dumb ass."

For those who did not notice the smoke initially, they did once they were out of their cars and on their way towards Burt to ask why they had stopped.

Billy Bob said jokingly to his brother Bob Billy, "Dumb ass white people."

"Why did you say that?" his brother questioned.

"Look around you man," he explained holding up his right arm, pointing all around where they were standing.

"There is no one on the roads but us, and Burt still had to pull over to the shoulder."

"Habit, a good habit, I guess," answered Bob Billy.

Van Camp was the first to approach Burt, and he asked, "Why did you stop?" He had notice the smoke, but did not think it was an issue worth stopping the convoy.

Pointing towards the smoke, Burt said, "That might be something, and it might not. A signal of sort, maybe. Thought it would be worth the trouble to check it out."

By now, everyone was standing together talking about the smoke. Not everybody wanted to go and see, mostly the women and Joe-Joe, as they gave the smoke no mind.

"It could be a signal," suggested Eddie, with Steven in agreement.

Lisa spoke up, and said, "I'm going back to my car to take a nap. When you guys get back, wake me when we are ready to resume our trip."

Ben said softly to Billy Bob and Bob Billy, "Tell her it's a cookout and she'll lead the way."

"Nah, let her go and let her enjoy her nap," suggested Billy Bob. Ben and Bob Billy looked at him expecting an explanation.

One came, "If it's really a cookout, they best have a full size pig just for her, or there won't enough to go around."

Everyone enjoyed Billy Bob's explanation as Ben added, "If you tell her there is food and she does not find any, she might eat one of us."

Laughter all around, but this only lasted for a few seconds as the seriousness of the situation of reality returned.

For a bunch of guys in a world void of people, they sure had a good time picking on one person. Well, she was big enough to be three people, but still, not very nice.

'Funny what they were saying, but not nice,' thought Van Camp. He wanted to laugh at what was said, however, that would not be very, 'managerial' of him.

Alice, Rose Marie, and Kitty agreed with Alice saying, "Why don't some of you boys go and check it out. We can wait right here until you get back."

Eddie said, "Not a good idea to split your forces in half."

Steven responded with, "We are not at war. No need to have everyone go off hunting down the smoke. We have radios and it can't be that far away."

Wanting to be in charge, Van Camp said, "Okay. Who wants to go and who wants to stay?"

Steven, Eddie, both the Browns, along with Jeff mentioned that they wanted to go.

Van Camp asked Burt, "You going?"

"Nah, I'll stay here. My eyes are strained from driving. It would be nice to close them for a little while," he answered.

Van Camp said, "Okay, let's go."

Wanting to allow someone to take the lead, not as in leadership, but as in to lead the way to the smoke, just in case there was some danger, he asked, "Who wants to lead the way?"

Billy Bob quickly announced, "My brother and I will take the lead this time."

Wanting not to miss this trip, Van Camp said, "Fine, I would like to take up the rear."

Everyone was happy. Those who wanted to go, could go, and those who wanted to stay, could stay. Van Camp like the way things turned out. It was orderly and everyone had his and her way. Now if they could find something interesting with this little excursion trip of theirs, that would make his day. At least, he would be one of the first to see what it was, and could return to fill in everyone that did not go, on the details.

It did not take long for everyone to return to his or her vehicle. Billy Bob had soon pulled out and headed down the highway, just a little ways before he slowed down, giving everyone a chance to catch up with him. Bob Billy was standing on his seat with his body sticking out of the moon roof. Once everyone had lined up properly, he did the typical hand wave, as if this was a wagon train heading west, indicating that it was time to go.

It was less than a mile to the exit where they pulled off. This was a basic cloverleaf interchange and taking the first exit headed them west, towards the smoke.

Billy Bob was not driving as fast as Burt was, and Bob Billy asked, "Why you driving so slow man?"

Pissed that he was asked, he answered, "I am not familiar with the area, and if this is a signal, there might be something else to spot before we get there."

Realizing that what he said was common since, Bob Billy said, "Sorry man. Got used to you always driving fast."

The smoke source was easy to spot, and it was what everyone expected, a bunch of tires burning. Not exactly, a pile of tires in the middle of the road burning to create a signal, but a pile of old tires behind a gas station that doubled as a place to buy used tires. Everyone got out and walked behind the gas station to get a better look at the fire. What they saw surprised them.

Eddie was the first to spot it, and said, pointing, "A plane crash. A little plane crashed right into the pile of tires."

He was right; the small private plane had apparently clipped the top of the gas station roof and broken in half. The engine had fallen into a pile of tires and got it burning. The rest of the plane had skidded across the parking lot. For the most part, it was still intact.

Eddie, with Steven right behind him, quickly walked over to the plane. There had to be someone inside. A crash like this one had to have killed anyone onboard and there should be a body, if not a body, then blood.

The plane was on its side, leaving only one way in, or out. It took both Eddie and Steven to open the door and this gave hope that someone would still be inside, a dead someone, but someone just the same. It took a few minutes until it cracked open. Then, all of them peered inside at the same time, as if no one wanted to be the second person to view this discovery.

Inside, there was blood, but no body. This quickly canceled out any excitement they were expecting should they have found a body. Ben was the first to say something.

He said, "Look at the blood."

They did, but did not see the importance.

Because no one said anything, Ben said, "See the way the blood puddles. If he got himself out, or he was pulled out, the blood would be somewhat smeared around. You see there, it just pooled, no blood trail."

Bob Billy, not sure what he was getting at, asked, "That tells you what?"

"The body vanished. Vanished, as it was never carried off," added his brother, Billy Bob. "Also, and most important, the pilot never got out on his own."

Everyone looked at him with the, 'tell me more Lieutenant Colombo,' expression.

"It took us a lot of effort to get in. So how did he get out," added Billy Bob?

"This is not good," suggested Van Camp.

Eddie joined in with, "So much for the theory that everyone boarded buses and that they were shipped away. Looks like everyone but us, simply vanished."

Ben said, "Beam us up Scottie," as he attempted a little joke. To these guys, this was a good discovery and tentatively,

answered a few questions. Not the answers they were looking for, as this only created more questions.

"Should we tell the others when we get back," asked Bob Billy.

"Might as well," suggested Ben. "No reason to keep this to ourselves."

Billy Bob looked at his brother indicating that he agreed with Ben. "Besides," Billy Bob spoke up and said, "They will be asking what we saw anyway."

No one moved, as they all kept looking inside the plane, if the longer they looked, that they would see something that would answer other questions. Or at the very least, create a few more questions. Either way, no one was in any hurry to move on.

Sadly, they moved away, one by one, and back into their vehicles for the short trip back. It was then that they headed north on I-95, only to turn around in the median, just a mile after they entered the interstate.

It was easy to spot where they would turn around, as this was the only place on the entire interstate from Maine to Florida where there were people.

The U-turn was easy at this location as there were no guardrails between the lanes. Not to mention that Hummers, nice and clean as they were, could easily manage the off road course.

Ben, wanting to take the lead, was first out of his vehicle and heading towards the center of the group."We found that a small private plane crashed and caused a fire to a bunch of old tires."

No one said anything, or even looked as if they wanted to ask any questions. Ben added, "Nothing else was there. We did find it odd that the pilot's body was not inside the airplane."

"Why was that odd," questioned Rose Marie.

Van Camp wanted to put in his two cents, added, before Ben could respond, "We had to break into the plane. It was clear to us that someone had to be still inside the plane."

Everyone was quiet, expecting more information from Van Camp. He answered with, "The body in the plane simply disappeared. There was blood, but no body."`

"Beam me up Scotty," joked Ben trying to get more mileage from this joke.

Not wanting Ben to say any more, Van Camp went on to surmise his opinion, "We got the impression that he just disappeared like everyone else. Don't think that people were somehow herded up and moved away."

Nothing was then said, it was all quiet. An eerie silence because standing in the middle of an interstate highway, you would expect to hear traffic speeding by.

"So what now," again questioned Rose Marie?

"Head south," responded in unison, Ben, Van Camp, and Billy Bob.

Ben looked over at Van Camp and asked, "You taking the lead this time?"

Without first thinking of an answer, Van Camp responded with, "Sure."

Ben was surprised of his quick response. He had wanted to see him 'hymn and haul,' a little.

Van Camp was also surprised of his quick answer, but figured that if he had,'hymn and hauled,' a little, that it would draw negative attention to him.

Without any more questions, or reasons to delay the drive south, all the vehicles were loaded up and onward they went with Van Camp in the lead.

The Brown brothers liked taking up the rear, so they just waved everyone on past them before they got in behind the last vehicle.

CHAPTER 36

SOUTH OF THE BORDER

V AN CAMP DID NOT LIKE being the lead vehicle again. The drive
was much more difficult than he had imagined. This was not a
simple drive on an interstate without any traffic, the difficulties came
with the occasional car, or truck stopped in the driving lane. Most of
the time, it was easy enough to signal a lane change and then, make
the move. Then sometimes, two cars were blocking both lanes and
it was easier to drive on the shoulder, as long as you do not stay on
the shoulder too long.

For the drive, it was sometimes speed of 75 mph or more, and
then it was down to a craw where there were a lot of abandon cars
and trucks.

Wanting to release the lead to someone else, Van Camp knew
that he could not simply pull over and ask, or suggest, that anyone
take his place. He wanted to make the next rest stop a place, to more
easily, bring up the suggestion. And while he was at it, he might as
well make that person happy with the new assignment and clearly
having it indicate that he, Van Camp, was a good leader. Someone
worthy to follow. It was at this point on I-95 that the, 'South of
the Border,' signs become more frequent. For anyone that has ever
been on I-95, signs for 'South of the Border,' appear to be about one

every mile for the three or four hundred miles before its exit. There was even a sign past that exit, 'Oops amigos, you missed the exit for South of the Border.' 'Fireworks, everyone likes fireworks,' Van Camp thought to himself. He could pull over, in 53 miles, and it was his belief that everyone would want to pull over there. By then, gas would be needed, a trip to the restrooms would also be in order, and he could somehow weasel out of the lead driver ownership. And, to add to their supplies, fireworks would be cool, assuming that they would have something to celebrate in the future.

The Brown brothers, they also noticed the signs for 'South of the Border.' Bob Billy says to Billy Bob, "What we need is some fireworks."

Billy Bob looked over at him, and said; "Now that be cool."

With both brothers in agreement, Billy Bob got on the CB and said, "Breaker 19, Breaker 19."

Burt came back with, "Go ahead breaker 19."

"Would like to make a pit stop at, 'South of the Border.'"

It was silent for a few seconds before Van Camp came back with, "10-4. Will pull over at 'South of the Border."

Nothing more was said over the airwaves, but it was apparent that the next rest stop would be, South of the Border, in a little more than 50 miles.

Burt, he thought it to be a great idea to pull over there. He had always stopped there anytime he was passing by. It was cool to stock up on fireworks, and this time, he would get more. Simply because the price was in his favor.

Lisa was all set for the stopover, as she could stock up on junk food. She knew this to be a major tourists stop and gift shops were always filled with rows and rows of chips, candy, and cakes. She might even be able to find a few boxes of Little Debbie's.

Kitty knew also that this was a tourist's stop, and that she would find an assortment of hand mirrors. She needed a few to keep in her car, if they were going to be making all these stops before they get to Florida.

For Eddie and Steven, fireworks were like kids toys. For either of them to blow something up, they wanted to measure the gunpowder by pounds, not ounces. They did not want to knock over a coke bottle; they wanted to knock over a jeep or tank. Yet, whatever, they would take a tour of the firework stores and pick out the powerful ones.

Ben, like the idea of taking a pit stop. He enjoyed the fact that he had time to plan a scam. Not that he needed to scam anyone out of anything, just yet, it was simply, that it was who he was and what he was. So now, if he had no one to swindle, he would stock up on some fireworks.

Rose Marie and Alice did not care much about fireworks. For Rose Marie, they drove her cats crazy and Alice thought fireworks not to be a good idea around children. If you wanted to see fireworks, she thought, take them to a fireworks display on the 4th of July.

Even with Jerry being as lazy as he was, and driving was a lazy thing to do, he was tired of being tired of driving. A break in less than an hour would be great. As far as fireworks, he was not impressed. He never like the idea that after you lit the fuse, you had to run away. He would much rather light the fuse and stay near by. No reason in his mind to do something, then run away from it.

Joe-Joe had never heard of, 'South of the Border,' and he was not sure if they had to go through Mexico to get to Florida. The more signs he saw with the Mexican sombrero as their logo, he was convinced that they would indeed be making a stop in Mexico.

Thinking more to himself than he normally did, he was going to ask those with him, and how they were going to pay in American money. All this thinking gave him a headache and he nodded off mentally about this problem of his.

Jeff, did not care one way or another. They needed to take a break, fill up on gas, and this place was as good as any.

Less than an hour later, Van Camp was pulling off the exit. He was now plotting on how to park his car, making it easy for someone else to park in front of him, taking his lead position.

This was done with little effort, as he pulled in front of the one restaurant that had the fewest cars in front of it. He parked with plenty of space between him and the sidewalk, leaving it open, to anyone that wanted a shorter walk to the restaurant.

Lisa was the one car that pulled up close to the sidewalk. She felt that if she had a choice to walk a sorter distance, then she would take it, especially if food was inside.

Alice and Kitty followed her example and they pulled in between Van Camp and Lisa.

With all those cars that could potentially take the lead, Van Camp was pleased, however, he did not think that to be a good job for a woman driver.

As with the other rest stops, everyone headed inside for the restrooms. Once that was completed, everyone congregated between the restrooms and the diner style restaurant.

No one was hungry at this time, after the last breakfast, and or lunch that was provided by Lisa. Other than Steven putting on a pot of coffee, and Lisa taking a trip to the gift shop, everyone else headed out to fill up on gas.

By the time Steven came out with fresh coffee, and with Lisa carrying a large bag filled with snacks, everyone but Van Camp had filled up with gas. All the vehicles had pulled a way a little from the pumps and then, turned off their engines.

For those who had filled up first, they had all wandered down to the closest fireworks shop where everything was, 'Buy one, get one free.' The shop next to it was, 'Everything Half-Off.'

Everyone understood the pricing, except for Joe-Joe. He even had trouble with deciding which burger was bigger, the McDonald's Double Quarter Pounder, or others half pounder. Even the Double, Quarter Pounder got him so confused that he would end up ordering the double hamburger and not understanding why they were so little. 'Wasn't a double burger a double burger,' he would always ask himself while eating the three little bites of a regular double burger.

Not wanting to embarrass himself, he would wonder through the store like everyone else, but would not buy anything.

Ben loved the fireworks store. What he really wanted was something that he could use as a flash/bang bomb. The sort of tool that police would use to confuse the bad guys, as they would rush in and over take them. Having been a participant of an arrest that was aided by a flash/bang bomb, he new more than most people how effective they were, and he wanted some. Alice had no desire to purchase any fireworks, but knew that there might be harmless sparklers on sale. Those she felt safe to use around her grandchildren.

For Rose Marie, no way and no how would she get anything that would alarm her cats. She might find something that could entertain them, not sure, what that would be, but thought she would look anyway. Besides, here she was in a Super Warehouse of fireworks and she might as well check it out. She never did find anything, but saw a number of items that she would most certainly get, if she did not have any cats.

Once she realized that she would never have cats again, she headed back to her car to cry.

Joe-Joe was close behind her, only he did not cry once he got back into his car, but scanned his radio hoping for some news. As expected, he found nothing, not even the stations that you were to tune to, in the event of an emergency.

Steven and Eddie teamed up because they were both at the smoke grenade section of the store. It must be something with military people that they always wanted to cover up stuff with smoke, before they would then blow it up.

They also picked up a couple of boxes of cherry bombs and other ammo, I meant, other similar fireworks.

Kitty only did the casual walk around. She really did not want to get anything, but liked to walk around anticipating that most people would look her way. With everyone, especially the guys, looking at fireworks, she left the building, saving her, 'walk around, look at me,' until a later time.

Lisa was walking past the Brown brothers and they easily heard the rubbing of her thighs. Billy Bob says to Bob Billy, "If her legs were to create a spark, even just once, we will be blown out of this world, along with half of, 'South of the Border.'

Before Bob Billy could stop laughing to respond, Lisa let go with another of her thunder farts. Well, you would have thought that the world was coming to an end, with the responses everyone gave her.

Billy Bob and Bob Billy turned her way expecting to see the mushroom cloud created by an atomic bomb going off in the desert. Ben did not initially know that it was she, as he thought that maybe someone had found the flash/bang bombs and set one off.

Everyone in the store had no desire to stay there any longer. Partly, they wanted to get back on the road before it got too dark, but mostly, to avoid inhaling anything that came out of Lisa's fat ass.

As if this was a Chinese fire drill, the store was emptied and everyone was back in his or her cars with motors running, the AC turned on, and the windows rolled up.

With the way they all started to pull away, it gave the appearance that all of them wanted to be the lead vehicle.

It ended up with Kitty as the lead car. She had pulled just far enough out, and up-wind, and that allowed everyone to get in behind her. The Brown brothers ended up as the second vehicle.

Burt, he timed it so that he would be the last car to get into line, as he liked being at the end of the convoy. With nothing else to be decided, with restroom visits out of the way, and with filled gas tanks, and a breath of fresh air, Kitty pulled away as the leader.

CHAPTER 37

ON THE ROAD, DAYDREAMING

THE CONVOY HAD BEEN DRIVING for a few hours now with Kitty doing a good job leading. She knew enough not to drive too fast and to be very aware of vehicles parked in the driving lanes. She had a good habit of signaling in plenty of time to allow those behind her to respond.

Even the Brown brothers were commenting to each other on how surprised they were to see a girl that was pretty, and drive half decent.

Even with a couple of hours behind them, it was too soon to pull over for gas and make a trip to the restrooms, but not soon enough for Lisa to suck down a few more packs of Little Debbie's cakes and pies, along with 2 liters of non-diet soda. Yet, it was just long enough time to cause boredom.

For those that had CD's, they had music to listen to, others, only static on their radios.

The weather was clear with no moving traffic or backups, and basically, there was nothing special about the drive. It was just very sad that the more they drove, the emptier the world looked. With Burt, at the rear of the convoy, he did not care who was leading, as long as they were doing a good job, and certainly, Kitty was. For him, driving was just that, driving. As long as he had a decent running vehicle, excellent road conditions, and a place to go, he was good. With no check-in time, or any type of verification by anyone on where he was or where he was going, life was cool.

As Ben drove, he daydreamed about what his next con should be. He did not like spending too much time between cons, as he was afraid that he would lose his edge over his victims. Well, he did not consider them as victims, just someone that was not as smart as he was. Beside, they always had a choice of being conned, or not being conned. It was not as if he held a gun up to their heads, he just had his hands in their pockets.

Yet, with only thirteen others to con, that made his selection of who, what, when, and for how much very limited. Limited that if he conned just one person, and they told just one person, soon everyone in the entire world would know, literately.

Therefore, his goal was now was to con someone, anyone and not get caught. Then again, anything that he wanted in the whole world, was now available, and that would require him not to con anyone, no one at all. He sighed to himself and thought, 'what a crappy world this turned out to be. A good con man, like me, has nothing to con anymore.'

It was not as if he had to turn his life around, and to find a legitimate job, there were just no jobs to be found, as Ben may soon find himself growing his own food and or raising his own hamburger meat. Okay, no hamburger. Not a good career move for such a skilled con man. Then again, if he did find something illegal to do, there was no one around to catch him, charge him, arrest him, put him on trial, and no place to lock him up, with no one available to guard him.

He would never find himself on trial waiting on the verdict from twelve jurors, as there were only thirteen people left in the whole world. Someone had to be the victim; you would need a witness or two. Let's not forget about a judge, and two sets of lawyers along with a court clerk and bailiff.

"Life sucks," said Ben to himself. Even with everyone else in the world gone, he was more concerned about himself. Again, he said, "Life sucks."

The more Rose Marie drove, the more she saw cats in the clouds. Most people saw other things, mostly Elvis and Jesus in the clouds. She was already making plans that after getting settled in Florida, where ever in Florida they would end up, that she would visit a toy store and stock up on stuff cats. She had a few little ones at the back window of her car, but not too many. Add to this, a trip to a mall to find cat photos, and cat nick knacks. She would avoid looking in the Spencer's Gifts shops, as anything related to cats there, were always negative. Drunken cats, dead cats, along with ugly cats are on T-shirts, mugs, and posters.

Rose Marie also had plans to visit a pet store for some cat food. Just in the event that cats would someday return.

Alice, the more she rode down the highway, the more she thought about her children. She would even cry for a few miles with sad memories before a few good ones would make her smile and laugh. She had settled down to the fact that she was alone. The other thirteen people were just that, a group of people. They were not family and would never be. Even if she wanted a boy friend or even a new husband, her pick'ens were going to be slim. Hell, she knew that her pick'ens were slim even when the world was filled with people. After you reached a certain age and weight, the only ones left are the ones that no one else wanted. She hated her life right now.

As Lisa drove, she would glance up at the clouds. There was nothing special about the clouds today, just that, with very little imagination, each cloud was a different dessert, Taste Cake or Pie or a dessert special from the Friendly's Kids, or Chuck E Cheese menu. After a few hours of this fascination, Lisa's hunger pains started up again. There was nothing physical with these pains, just the mental pains of not having her hands busy shoveling food into her mouth.

Her parents were always mean in reminding her how she learned to eat by herself before she learned to walk. Then, soon after she learned to walk, along with her added weight, she began to waddle at an early age. As long as she can remember, her legs have always rubbed from the knees up.

She did have the skills to drive and forge for food in her car while driving. With one knee raised up to hold the steering wheel straight, she successfully could find, and determine what the food item was in the back seat by the feel, size, and sound of the wrapper.

"Little Debbie's, coffee cake, 4.5 oz.," she said aloud with much pride that she was almost 100% positive that she was most correct. Then, without easing up on the gas, along with staying in her lane, she opened the Little Debbie's, coffee cake, 4.5 oz and with only a single purpose, to shove the whole cake into her mouth without dropping a single crumb.

She always liked putting as much into her mouth as she could at any one time. No need to waste trips from the wrapper to her mouth. It would take her longer to chew, but chewing food was something that she loved. She only swallowed because it would allow for more food to be shoved in, and then chewed and chewed. Other than having a lot of weight and unable to run, her chewing style was just another thing that she had in common with a cow. Now this is someone that could use a second stomach. After washing the coffee cake down with a warm 2-liter nondiet coke, she burped once and farted twice. With that out of the way, she felt very pleased with herself. Her feeling good about herself ended when she realized that soon, there would be no more Little Debbie's cakes and pies. In fact, there would be no more cakes and pies, of any kind at all in the whole world. This new world of hers was really going to suck. This sad news was only offset when she realized that she was now the fattest person in the world. Then again, on a good note, there were no more Weight Watchers meetings to attend and she could set her own goals. Life was good.

For Eddie and Steven, driving for hours and hours was no different from how it was serving in the military. If you were standing watch, that was for hours and hours with nothing to do except to wait to be relieved. For them, this drive was like reporting to a new duty station, just another adventure. Their orders were clear, make it to Florida, and set up a new life. With both men now officially out of the military, they had to find new lines of employment and a new place to live anyway. They both thought separately that military life had made them more competent to make it in the new world of theirs. At this point, they were not thinking one way or another if they were going to like, or dislike this new world, or their new duty station.

For Jerry, this was easy work, just drive. No need to make a decision on which way to go, because you just follow the car in front of you. No need to worry about getting lost, because there was a car behind you that will aid in keeping you with the group. There was no reason to consider when to stop or pull over; someone in the front of the group will make that decision. This was a monkey-see, monkey-do operation with no immediate need for change or improvements. Going with the flow was easy as this was the only flow to follow in the world.

Van Camp, driving by himself was just fine. This way, he could dream up all the ideas that he wanted to dish out later. He was able to talk aloud to himself, allowing reviewing which voice mannerism gave him more of a managerial, authoritative, sounding voice. Some of his ideas included who would be on watch, for how long, and what they should be watching for. Someone had to control the process of feeding everyone along with housing. Simple things like, going to the bathroom, showers, changing and the storing of clothes.

He thought that Lisa should be in charge of food; she apparently had the most experience in how to find food. Steven and Eddie, being they were x-military, had a good sense on guarding stuff. Well, maybe not like guarding for an enemy attack or wild animals, but, but looking out for whatever we might need guarding from. In addition, as supplies become short, food starts to run out, we might need a guard or two to keep things and supplies in order.

As for me, thought Van Camp, 'I can manage myself.' Life will get better for me as I have more responsibility.

Kitty was enjoying her drive as the leader, as it was nice to have all the men in the world following behind her. She just knew that each of them, even the ones she did not like, must have been thinking about her. For the women, they were thinking about her and how jealous they were. She would be nice to them, but would always try to stand a little taller.

For short periods, she would give thought as to what she would find in Florida. Not so much as to living conditions, finding food and water, but on how the high humidity and sun would affect her hair and makeup.

In her little mind, no matter how many women there were left in the world, she had to be the prettiest. On a negative side, with fewer women, then her competition would not be as great. For her, the world was what she wanted, to be the prettiest woman in the world, and not what she wanted, to be the only, prettiest woman in the world. For Kitty, competition was good because she always came out ahead, except for her last job, where a pretty man took her place.

For now, she would wait to see how much she really enjoyed the new world, without glamour, fashion, self-help, and makeup magazines.

Jeff, as he drove, figured out in his head the number of miles driven, the number of miles to go, and the number of gallons of gas that he would need to make the trip. He would then factor in the same calculations to the other vehicles in the convoy.

In his mind, he was creating computer code that he would later write into a computer program. Not sure what good it will do him or anyone else, but it kept his mind alert.

Once he realized that he was creating code that would never be needed, he focused on code that he thought would be necessary. He looked into the calculations on survival. What it would take to survive for his group of survivors.

He would need to figure out how much food and water they would need a day, and how much they should store. Living quarters would need to be mapped out for each person, or each group. Other items such as fuel for transportation and utilities that needed to be calculated out, and on how to store them, and how to use what they had wisely.

For now, Jeff believed that he was needed to help with the administration of things in the new world, not so much with the procurement of supplies. Certainly, not for him to do anything physical.

Joe-Joe was not thinking all that much. He never did anyway. Only that now, while driving, he had to concentrate longer than he did for anything normally. It took thought to remember to stay between the lines and not to follow too close or hang back too far. At least for him, once they are in Florida, other than staying with the flow of things, he believed that he would be okay. It would however, required him to find something else to occupy his time from watching TV. The only thing he could think of now was to watch grass grow and then decide when to cut it. Life for him, was most uncertain at best.

Billy Bob and Bob Billy were just taking in the view. With Billy Bob driving, he mainly kept an eye on Kitty as she led the way south. Along this stretch of Interstate 95, there were not very many abandon cars and trucks to maneuver past.

They did pass one police car, a South Carolina State Police, with the lights flashing, but, and as expected, no one was around. The way the police car and the car in front of it were situated, it appeared that the police had pulled that car over for speeding, or something similar.

Bob Billy would look out for a short period, then sit back and close his eyes. Then, when his brother noticed that he be trying to sleep, would ask him a question. He did that because he felt that he should remain awake and to keep him company while he was driving.

As long as they are together, life would be just fine. Except, to mention that they would need some type of entertainment, that is, entertainment dealing with women.

CHAPTER 38

SNACK TIME

K ITTY WANTED TO FIX HER hair and makeup, and needed to do so with both hands and a large mirror. Her appearance was just not getting the proper treatment needed while she was driving. She figured that she would give the CB radio a try, and suggest that they stop at the next rest area. Not wanting to give the real reason for her stop, thought, if asked, to say that she wanted snacks and stuff.

Lucky for Kitty, there was another rest stop coming up in a few miles. On the CB, she says, "Okay to pull over at the next rest stop?"

No one responded right away. She was not sure if anyone had heard her. Lisa did, and was glad that someone had suggested it. She was in a serious need for a trip to the bathroom.

At the same time, Burt, Ben, Billy Bob, and Van Camp, replied with, '10 4, roger, can do,' and 'okay,' at the same time. It was impossible that everybody knew what the responses were. However, for what Kitty understood, she believed that it was okay to stop. A mile before the rest stop exit, Kitty activated her turn signal and noticed that the car behind her had done the same. A mile later, they pulled off the interstate.

This rest stop was one of the smaller ones. There was just the one little building that housed the restrooms with a little area for the vending machines. On both sides were picnic tables and trashcans filled to overflowing without the normal flies and yellow jackets looking for food.

For no particular reason, the women and the men took their seats at opposite's ends of the picnic tables after making their pit stops and getting something to drink. Segregating themselves was for no apparent reason other than the restrooms were at opposite ends, and they simply took the nearest seat as they approached the tables.

Naturally, Lisa was at the vending machines looking at the rows and rows of junk food. Ben was standing beside her when she asked, "Do you have any change?"

Ben looked at her thinking, 'I don't have enough change on me to empty the entire machine for you, you fat cow.'

He only replied with, "Stand back please."

This was not the answer Lisa expected, a simple, 'No, sorry,' would have been just fine. Then, before she could respond, as she did backup a step, Ben kicked in the plexiglassd a huge hole to the rows and rows of junk food.

Lisa did not give the look of, 'thank you,' but the surprise look as if she just hit the jackpot on a slot machine. As she was thanking him, she had both hands inside with two items in each hand at the same time.

In some ways, this was typical for the two of them. Ben was breaking and entering and stealing, and Lisa was forging for food. If she had more hands, she would have gotten more than just four items at a time.

Ben looked at her, not in amazement, but as in, he expected this behavior, and asked, "All that just for you?"

Quickly, she answered with, "Of course not. I am getting a few things for us girls."

Ben reached in, grabbed a Snickers bar for himself, quietly walked over to the guys' side, and sat down.

Lisa, after grabbing all that she could hold, made her way to join the women. Not wanting to appear to them as a pig, she said, "With Ben's help, we hit the jackpot ladies."

If you were one to read a person's facial expressions, it was easy to see that Lisa was glad to offer to share, but hoped that no one would take anything.

The men got themselves into some small talk, and like most men, the subjects went between sex, hunting, sex, sports and sex. There were a few jokes and all of them were on sex or about sex. The women sat there in silence as each reminisced about their past and uncertain future. For them, sex was not top on their list.

For Kitty, it was more important in making it a point to, stay attractive. She knew that with her looks, that having sex had not been an issue, and should never ever, ever, be an issue.

The only thing that Alice focused on was her grandchildren.

Rose Marie, for her, reminiscing about her cats was sad, with happy memories.

Lisa wolfed down two candy bars, and was thinking about starting on her third.

As the guys talked, Van Camp as always, wanted to take the lead in the conversation, however, this time, he felt that it was important for him, just to listen. As a future person of authority over them all, he felt that there was no need for them to hear his points of view about sex, hunting, or sports. Especially sex. Van Camp remained outside of this little chat, as well as above it. However, he wanted very much to know each mans strengths and weaknesses as they related to sex, hunting, and or sports.

With this only a short stop, it was soon over and Kitty was back in the lead.

CHAPTER 39

OVERNIGHT ON I-95

KITTY WAS STARTING TO TIRE of all this driving, especially being in the lead. As much as she enjoyed it, she would not want to take the lead again. There were plenty of other drivers to share the driving, and she was pleased with herself that she had done her share, and thrilled that her, 'fair share,' was soon to be completed and to have her ticket punched.

Up ahead, she could clearly see about five or six signs for hotels and motels along with more signs for gas stations and fast food joints. In her view, as the lead vehicle, it was time to pull over, eat, fill up on gas, and spend a night in a hotel. No way did she expect them to drive all the way to Florida in one day. With Florida a very long state, she knew it would take another day just to drive from one end to the other, and they had already been driving a full day already.

Continuing with her good driving habits, she signaled early indicating that she would be exiting the next exit. In good military precision, each vehicle down the line did the same with their signaling.

Even with Burt being the last member of the convoy, he was aware in plenty of time that they would be getting off soon. His habit was always to use his signal and even with no one behind him, he knew that the person he was following now knew, that he knew, that they would be pulling off soon.

In general, everyone was pleased that Kitty had pulled off when and where she did. As the custom, the convoy pulled up to the first gas station and everyone started to top off their tanks.

Each time a credit card was used and the pump responded that their purchased would be approved, and that you could pump gas, a sigh of relief was felt by all. There was the hidden fear that someday, and that someday may be today, that the credit cards would no longer be accepted, or that there were no longer power to operate the pumps.

At this particular set of pumps, there was enough room for everyone to gas up at the same time. With the pumps pumping away, groups of twos and threes would gather and chitchat small talk, as they would stretch to release the kinks in their joints from driving all day. Well, not all day, but for a few continuous hours. Van Camp saw this as a perfect opportunity to start a meeting.

Then Billy Bob, along with Ben, was equally keenly perceptive that this was a good meeting opportunity, but who would call it first? And what for?

Burt, the only real driver here and knew best when it was time to take a break, spoke up and said to the group, "I believe now would be a good time to take a break from driving and check into a hotel for tonight."

Everyone but Van Camp, Billy Bob and Ben, responded with, "Good idea, sounds great."

The closest hotel near them was just across the lot from where they were, a Hampton Inn. Ben, wanting to take a lead in this, announced, "Hampton Inn."

He pointed towards the hotel and without waiting for anyone to say yea, or nay, he was back in his car heading that way, assuming that everyone would follow.

Van Camp was also going to suggest the Hampton Inn, but Ben was quicker to the draw than he was. To make up for this, he ordered, well not ordered, but strongly suggested that once everyone found a room, that they were to meet back up in the lobby.

Billy Bob, after realizing that he had been ignored for the first two commands by leadership, wanted to get in his two cents. "When you get a room, let me have your room numbers and your cell phone numbers again so I can make copies and pass them out."

Everyone seemed to, sheepishly follow these three commands from three different people. Nevertheless, all seemed to agree that someone, or many someone's, had stepped up and suggested what they should be doing next. No reason for them to hang around a gas station if they had somewhere to go with things to do.

With Burt already at the hotel, others quickly returned to their vehicles and followed his example. For them to get a room, it was nothing more than walking down the first floor hallway, past the front desk, entering the first available room. That part was easy as no one had a ton of luggage to drag around. Except for Lisa, she had her bags and bags of treats that she did not want to leave in her car in the event she wanted to eat them all tonight, while watching TV.

Right behind Burt, Rose Marie was the second person to arrive at the hotel. A little sadden by the lack of a gift shop and or, cat merchandise, she found the first available room on the right, just past the lobby.

With the bed not made and the bathroom without clean towels, she headed to the next room. For Rose Marie, she had the second room on the right, room 103.

She took her time freshening up before heading back to the lobby for another sad meeting. Sad meeting as they would only discuss how it's just us left in the world, we sill have to drive hundreds of miles, and we have no idea on what we will find. Then again, hearing the updates of the same old stuff, was better than being left out. For Rose Marie, it was good to be kept up to date with stuff.

Her only fear was that maybe, just maybe, when she did return to the lobby, that no one but her would be there. So, in a way, keeping up to date with stuff, gave her direction on what to do if she did find herself abandoned. Not wanting to be alone too long, she quickly finished up with her girl items and rushed back to the lobby.

Alice was behind Rose Marie and she took the room across the hall from her, room 102. For Alice, the room was made up and she had clean towels. Her first course of action was to make her phone calls. She did not want to use her cell because she wanted to save on the battery.

The hotel phone worked just fine, calls were routed quickly only to get again, lots of rings on some call, and answering machines on the others. For the answering machine calls, one had reached its limit on saving messages. Alice knew that all those messages were hers.

She did take a minute to take her cell phone from her purse; just on the slim chance that someone had left her a message. Nope, no messages.

Just like Rose Marie, Alice did not want to be alone also, so she hurried up with her bathroom duties and made her way back to the lobby.

Lisa headed straight for a room, once she noticed that there was no gift shop stocked with junk food. She walked right on past Alice and Rose Marie and took a room at the end of the hall. Because, at the end of the hallway, there would normally be a soda and snack vending machines next to the ice machine. She felt that if, or when, she needed a junk food fix, that the machines would be only a few steps away.

Before she headed back, Lisa had to rush through a few bags of chips and a Tasty Cake. Brush her teeth and then followed that with a number two. A number two in her room because she did not want to stink up the restroom near the lobby. Also, if she were to make a lot of noise, hopefully, no one would know it was her.

She ended up in the lobby after about thirty minutes with a full stomach and an empty butt.

Kitty was in such a hurry to find a room, that she walked right on past Alice and Rose Marie. However, getting around Lisa was no easy task. With this being an average size hallway, there was not enough room for anyone to pass Lisa without scraping the walls.

Not wanting to follow Lisa the entire length of the hallway, Kitty took the next room past Alice. It was then a mad dash to the mirrors in the bathroom. She was in need to see how well she held up, after all those hours of driving, and after having just gassed up her car.

For Kitty, good news, she still looks good. However, no matter how good she looks, it always required a little touch up to make minor improvements. Then, after a change of clothes, a second touch up of her makeup, it was a slow, stroll down to the lobby. She figured, the slower she walked down the hallway, that more people would see her, 'run-way' style of walking. The old one foot in front of the other, looking straight a head, without cracking a smile.

Naturally, once she arrived in the lobby, she expected every eye to look her way. She would then glance around the room, the way a politician would look around, as if he knew everyone, and wanted to make an individual eye contact, acknowledging that they were, the best of buddies.

This was followed by the, most correct way of sitting in a chair, by a lady. Not just a woman, but a lady. Even without a dress on, wearing slacks, her legs would never part, and her ankles would cross.

Lisa was the first one to see Kitty enter the room. Secretly she wanted to walk like Kitty, but knew that it was all but impossible. You can't have hourglass thighs rubbing the way they do and be able to put one foot in front of the other. In fact, she had not seen her feet while she was standing for years now.

The last time she was able to see her feet; she was standing in the shoe department at Walmart. Walmart always had those little floor mirrors at the end of the rows, where you would select shoes off the rack. As far as sitting down like Kitty, no way. Why even think about the impossible when you know in your head, and butt, that sitting down gracefully was not attainable. For her, sitting was no more than a controlled crash with the possibility of crushing a chair.

As Ben made his way down the hall, he watched as Kitty wanted to overtake Lisa. For Ben, he wanted some entertainment tonight and Kitty was far out in front. He wanted sex. Not the kind of sex to populate the world, but simple sex to make him happy. Not to necessary make his sex partner happy, as in the past, as long as they were paid, they were happy.

He was thinking that if Lisa was the last woman in the world left, that he would rather do without and die, than to see her without any clothes on. She was just too damn big.

After selecting a room, one close to Kitty and far from Lisa, Ben did a simple face and hands wash up. That was followed by the combing of his hair, before he returned to the lobby. He was the first one there and had easy pickings for a good seat. One close to the front, if and when he would be needed to say something to the group.

Burt knew the importance of taking a break from driving and wanted very much to take a nap, but decided just to select a room and freshen up. It did not take long, and he was back in the lobby, right behind Ben.

For whatever reason, Billy Bob headed up the stairs to select his room for tonight. Bob Billy, out of habit, followed right behind him.

"Where are you going," asked Bob Billy.

"Thought I would get a room with a better view than the parking lot."

That made no mind to Bob Billy, as he continued to follow his older brother up the stairs to the third floor. Bob Billy was curious if his brother would have gone even higher if this hotel had more floors.

Then it was a quick strolled to the first door on the right. One quick swipe with their passkey, and there they found two queen size beds. Good for them, as in, no way, would they sleep in the same bed, brothers or not, just no way.

Speaking of beds, Billy Bob wanted a woman. Anytime that he was in a hotel, it was to have sex with a female. He tells his brother, "We need a woman. We have a nice room and even if she was not a nice woman, that be okay."

Bob Billy had not thought about girls lately, it was enough to realize that they are survivors, said, "Where are we going to find girls man?"

"We have a few with us now, don't you know."

"No way man," responded Bob Billy quickly. "We don't have much of a selection. Don't you know?"

"I knows that we do have a selection, not much of a selection, but we do, don't I know."

Bob Billy thought for a minute. He came back with a half smile, "What about them? Are we apart of their selection?"

Billy Bob now thought for a minute. He responded, "For them, they might want children. For me, I only want sex. Good sex or bad sex, as long as I get me some sex."

Both brothers laughed, but only for a second or two. The seriousness of their dilemma was very much present. Billy Bob then realized that his sexual needs might not be available for him, ever again. For Bob Billy, his need for sex was only awakened when Billy Bob mentioned his sexual needs.

Billy Bob and Bob Billy then headed back to the lobby. Billy Bob spent his time thinking about having sex with Kitty and not with Lisa. Bob Billy daydreamed his time away with how miserable his brother will be in the future, if he goes without sex for a long period of time.

Then, as it did his brother, Bob Billy now realized that he might be spending the rest of his life without sex. Not so much about him, but on how his brother will be when he has withdrawals. By the time these two reached the lobby, they were sad, and it would not have taken much of anything to set them off right now.

Joe-Joe took his passkey and ran on past Alice and Kitty. It was not to select a room by beating out the girls, but to get in the room quickly. He needed to turn on the TV. He ran more than halfway down the hall before he opened a room and locked it behind him. He even pushed over the, double lock, to avoid anyone coming in, even with a key. What Joe-Joe needed now was some, 'alone time.' For Joe-Joe, he was having TV withdrawals, and to most folks, it was not fully understood. Some people love to eat, others love to drive, some just love to look at themselves, still others, would love to manage the world, and then there was Joe-Joe.

Joe-Joe loved to eat in front of the TV, he loved to surf the channels, watching himself watch TV, and he loved having the control of what he watched as he managed his TV viewing.

However, as expected, he disappointingly surfed the channels up and down, and found nothing new. He was not even able to order an, in-room movie, as that function was not working.

With nothing creative to do, no new shows to watch or record, it was a quick visit to the bathroom, followed by returning to the lobby.

Before Van Camp headed up to find a room, he looked around the front desk to try to determine which room, or rooms, were the best. Him, of all of the survivors, it was him that wanted a suite, simply because he deserved a good room, a suite or bigger. At least one that had a small hospitality room attached.

He thought it would be proper to hold any small meetings near his room. It showed status and good planning on his part. As meeting that took place in his room, a room of authority, and not in the lobby, would give him an edge, if only in appearance, of being in the lead of leaders under his control.

Because Van Camp had been in many hotels, he guessed a good guess of the locations of a few suites. With the top floor the same size as the other floors, with fewer rooms, he surmised that they were suites. Quickly, he headed up the stairs and without difficulty, found a suite. A nice suite with a small office and a meeting area. Not very big, but plenty big for his needs.

For Van Camp, this was a good stop over for tonight. After washing up, he devised a plot to call a meeting, to call it to take place in his room, and to whom he would invite. No need to invite everyone, just the ones that were in competition with him on being the leader, king, president, God, emperor, Indian chief, or prime minister of the new world. Or, should he invite everyone else. Might as well spend time trying to create a following as well as co-leaders. From his point of view, there were a few followers and it was up to him to fill in the void in their little lives that were lacking anyone to follow.

The trip down to the lobby for Van Camp was productive. He spent half the time patting himself on the back for having selected such a suitable room, and the second half planning for tonight's meeting. Overall, he felt and could justify his future position of leader, king, president, God, emperor, Indian chief, or prime minister of the new world.

Jeff, before heading to his room, stepped in behind the front desk and tried to see if he could get anything to pull up on the computer. From the other side of the counter, it appeared that Jeff was just a typing away and hitting sites after sites. In reality, he was just going back and forth between hitting the ENTER and ESC key.

Seeing that he was getting nowhere fast, and before he created a crowd to see what he was doing, Jeff simply stepped away and headed to find a room.

Steven, just plan tired of driving, made a quick trip to find a place to nap. It will be a quick wash up, and then to lie down. If they need him for anything, they can come and get him. The only plans that he was aware of, was sleep, get up, and drive south for hours and hours.

Eddie needed something cold to drink and a little something to snack on. It was a quick trip to the chow hall, or vending machine area. For chips, he just broke the plastic, for a cold drink, he settled for a cup of ice and water from the sink.

Jerry didn't really care one way or another, as his day was done and the only thing he was really missing, was unwanted attention from his parents. He had always thought that he could do without the two of them, but after only a few days, he missed them. Not necessary the, 'on his case,' parts, but the part where he always felt loved.

CHAPTER 40

SOCIAL TIME

ONE BY ONE, EVERYONE SLOWLY worked his or her way to the lobby. There was no set time, or anything said about a meeting, it was just that no one really liked being left alone for too long at a time.

It was not so much the fear of being taken away, but finding yourself completely alone. It was felt in general, that if and or when you disappear, you would be with everyone else. It might be Heaven or Hell or onboard a spaceship. At least this way, you would have your answer on what happened.

As you would expect, small groups started to form. Mostly, it was the women in one group, and the men ended up being in two groups, a black and a white one. Not the black and white groups like back in the 60's, but more inline with the present survival status. No one knew each other's income or educational levels, so it was not an upper or lower class group, just that blacks and whites had more in common with other blacks and whites.

Slowly, as the evening progressed, these groups broke up into smaller groups, and those smaller groups started to attract the other small groups. Then, by the end of the evening, about 9:30pm, there was no single group. Just small pockets of people where everyone was blending in and blending out. The black and white, and men and women's groups, had all but disappeared.

Naturally, some trended to stay off on their own, not getting too involved with anyone. Van Camp, of course, made it a point to belong to all the groups. Once he contributed to the group's conversation to make a point on something, just to make himself known, he would mosey along to the next group to contribute a point or two to their conversation.

He was not looking for followers at this time, just doing some recon on the people. He wanted, as before, to know all about everyone. Not so much their income or education levels, but their levels of being under his control someday.

Ben was on the same mission as Van Camp, to recon the people. Even if a con job was not in his best interest right now, he wanted to stay sharp and on top of his skill.

There wasn't much of anything being said any more, about what happened to everyone. They each knew that nobody had an answer. Just the same old theories over and over.

Nothing was said about the trip to Florida, as that was where they were going and that they were half way there.

People for the most part talked about what they did in their lives as far as their jobs, and where they went to school. Only a little bit was mentioned about family members left behind, As they all had the same story to tell.

As an FYI, Van Camp and Ben where sizing up on which ones would be workers, followers, leaders, and most importantly, their competitions.

Other than playing follow the leader, to Florida, and making group decisions, like, who is, or who should be in charge, never really came up.

To Ben and Van Camp, and some with Billy Bob, Steven, and Eddie, someday soon, there needs to be one person to take control. Maybe not control, as in, I am your leader, listen up or get out, but control, so that no one goes off on their own. Along with that, someone needs to find or grow food, supply water, and provide housing with working toilets.

None of those items seemed to be a big deal right now. Tonight was like a first date. You've seen each other around before at school, work, social events, and ET cetera. Now this was the time to get to know each other a little better if you want to go out with them again. Better yet, if you choose not to go out with them. With thirteen people to select from, it should not be very hard for normal people to find others that they are compatible.

Alice spoke up and asked the group, as she did not want to ask anyone in particular, what time are we leaving in the morning.

Of the self-appointed leaders, none of them spoke up. They were apparently caught off guard with Alice's un-solicited question.

Of all people, Lisa spoke up and said, "9AM."

Alice, not waiting for any yeas or nays, repeated, "9AM it is. Good night everyone."

With that, she was off to bed. Everyone else, taking her hint, started in ones and twos to head out. Nothing more was going to be accomplished tonight, other than not getting a, full nights sleep.

CHAPTER 41

OFF TO A GOOD START

THE NEXT MORNING, VAN CAMP wakes up earlier than usual. He had many unfinished concerns. It was just now troubling him that before everyone went to bed last night, there were no meetings. Nothing was discussed about their vehicles, food, clothing, and how much further they had to go. As if everyone was an old dairy cow, waiting to be told to head back to the barn for a good milking.

One little lady, Alice, without trying and only looking out for herself, had closed shop and sent everyone to their room.

With this thinking, Van Camp hurried to get dressed and out to the lobby. He wanted to be early and more importantly, be there before Alice. He knew that the Brown brothers would be late, but figured that Eddie and Steven would be early, along with Ben.

In the lobby, what he found was Eddie, Steven, and Ben enjoying some coffee in the lobby. It took Van Camp a second to gain composure so not to display his disappointment that he was not there first, fear that he had missed out, on their conversation, and worried sick that they had negative things to say about him. Then, before he could join in with them, Lisa, Alice, and Kitty came out of the lobby ladies room and they had a continuing conversation of their own. With Alice doing all the talking.

Van Camp did a little two-step as if he had no idea which way to go, and it was true. He did not know which way to go, should he join in with the guys, or the ladies.

Before he could make up his mind, he heard Billy Bob, and his brother Bob Billy, come in from the front parking lot. Billy Bob announced, "Nothing new outside."

Ben returned a comment, "Thanks guys."

Van Camp was not sure what that was all about, but before he could comprehend all that he had missed this morning, Bert came from the other lobby door from the side parking lot.

Bert says to Eddie, "Yeah man. Nothing out back."

Eddie answered, "Thank you, thank you, thank you."

At this point, Van Camp had to make a double effort not to show his emotions. It was clear that they gotten by this morning completely without him. They made decisions and carried them out without his direction, and or approval.

Trying to put a positive spin on this, he surmised that at least Joe-Joe, Jeff, and Jerry were still in bed. No way does Van Camp want to miss-out on everything, and worse, to be the last one to arrive.

That high note was chopped in half as Joe-Joe, Jeff, and Jerry came out of the kitchen with drinks on one cart, and a large pot of scramble eggs on another. Jerry had a hand full of dishes and silverware to pass out.

Jerry announced, "This is nothing like Lisa's meal the other day, but for the price, you are all winners."

Joe-Joe spoke up and explained, "Between us, we only knew how to scramble eggs, and we made plenty for everyone."

Alice spoke up, which again caught Van Camp off-guard, and said, "You guys are wonderful. We won't kick you out of Hell's Kitchen just yet."

Van Camp was now in the process of doing a second two-step, to his already started two-step. He was the last one here and had zero input to all those things accomplished this morning.

Adding to his embarrassment, Steven spoke up and said, loud

enough for everyone to hear, "Glad you could join us today Van Camp."

At this moment in time, in front of everyone, Van Camp had, just had to, to come up with a memorable statement that would both, evaluate him in status, and justify his tardiness. Well, he was not technically late, just the last one to come in. Like a bride is never late going down the aisle, just the last one to show up.

While his mind was racing at a mile a minute, it was not fast enough as everyone, everyone in the entire world, waited for his response.

Ben broke the silence, and asked, "Cat got your tongue?"

Rose Marie never did like that saying, but kept her feelings to herself. No need to have anyone to start up with cat jokes, and she had heard them all.

For a man of many words, he had none available right now. Van Camp simply shrugged his shoulder and announced, "I love scramble eggs."

As expected, most everyone took what he said in stride. From their points of view, he was no different than they were. Except for Ben and the two brothers, they had figured out his game plan, and that for today's game, he lost.

For Van Camp, it was only the first out, in the bottom of the ninth inning, and he was still in the lineup.

It was not long before all the scramble eggs were gone and the coffee was cold. Van Camp, wanting very much to promote himself, said, not suggested, well, almost commanded, "Time to head south?"

At first, no one paid him any attention. It was not until Alice stood up and answered, "I will be ready as soon as I make one more trip to the ladies room."

Then, it was after she got up, that others indicated that they were ready to head out and south. One by one, everyone started to move towards the parking lot, or to their rooms.

Just before Van Camp was going to ask the group, 'who wanted to take the lead today,' that question was already asked, and answered.

Bert said, "If no one wants to take the lead, I will be glad to do it again."

Everyone seemed pleased that Bert wanted the job.

"We will take up the rear," Billy Bob announced, and no one seemed to care.

It took about thirty minutes for everyone to line up, as Bert did a very visible head, and car count, before returning to his vehicle. Without much input from Van Camp, the group was again heading south on Interstate 95.

CHAPTER 42

A BAD DAY FOR DRIVING

AFTER A LITTLE BIT OF driving, Kitty looked into the rear view mirror and to her alarm, noticed bags under her eyes. Even with sound reasoning that bags under her eyes was okay for now, considering the lack of sleep, too much crying, not to forget about driving all those hours, that these bags would be expected. Everyone had bags under their eyes right now. Acceptable for everyone else, but not for Kitty. No one in her fashion magazines has bags under their eyes, only those in the trashy weekly magazines found in all supermarket checkout aisles.

Kitty knew that repairs were needed. Normally, a woman, who was driving, would wait until she got to where she was going, and before getting out of the car, would make the corrections.

With the skill of a blind person, she was able to reach into her purse and simply finger through until she found what she was looking for. While she was doing her purse search, her driving performance never wavered. She kept a steady constant speed, stayed in her lane, and didn't miss a single sign on the road. However, things were about to change for Kitty and the convoy. Kitty, using common sense, and having done this a million times, waited until she saw a long stretch of straight road, as there were no red light to cause her to stop for thirty or more seconds of driving.

Most of the drive, I-95 was a straight road between cities and waiting for a good stretch of straight road did not take long. With a little makeup brush in one hand, the little plastic container that held the face powder in the other, and her left knee doing the steering, she was set to do some face repair work.

Having a straight road, normally, for Kitty, was a good thing and not a big deal, yet, for this drive, there were sometimes cars and trucks abandoned and parked in the driving lanes, because not all cars and trucks were pulled over to the shoulder. And for Kitty, this was the case.

The lead car with Burt behind the wheel, made a slow, calculated lane change, which was done with plenty of time with the use of his turn signals. He was able to maintain speed and had no reason to step on the break. Maybe if Kitty had noticed the brake lights light up, that maybe that would have caught her attention. Instead, she missed the leader's lane change.

Then, out of the corner of her eye, she noticed two cars in front of her, one in the left lane and another in the right lane of this two-lane highway. The car in the left lane was Burt; he had made the change without her. The car in the right lane was just sitting there, sitting there as in parked right in her way.

Kitty's response was quick, but not a good one. She would have done better yanking to the left to get by ,and then move in behind Burt, but instead, she banked to the right and onto the shoulder. As unexpected as could be, there was another car parked on the shoulder. It was another quick turn to the right, sending her off the road.

Burt, who was always looking in his side mirrors out of habit, noticed Kitty's wild ride behind him. He knew better than to slam on his breaks, but quickly eased himself off to the shoulder, and naturally, after turning on his warning hazard lights.

Behind Kitty, were the Brown brothers. Bob Billy was driving and saw immediately what was going down. He yelped out a yell that woke up, and scared, his older brother, Billy Bob.

As with most people that are riding shotgun in a car, when they are awakened by the sounds of someone screaming, they look straight ahead as if expecting to see them about to crash into something head on. Instead, no head on traffic, but Kitty making her second hard right to miss the car parked on the shoulder.

Both men watch helplessly as Kitty then left the shoulder and skidded on the grass, before turning over about a dozen times.

Right now, Kitty was not really, clearly thinking straight. She had visions of her being killed in this wreck, but she was not worried about dying. She was concerned about her appearance. Even with her car swerving back and forth, and then rolling over and over, she made the time to look in the mirror to see if her hair stayed in place, and that her makeup was not smudged.

Her rollovers were very quick, as she was already driving about 75 miles per hour. It did not help that once off the shoulder and onto the grass, it sloped downward, at a sharp angle. If anything, the car seemed to be picking up speed, before she crashed, and bent around a tree.

Kitty had hit the tree so hard, that you got the impression that after wrapping around the tree, that the front and back bumper touched each other.

The rest of the convoy easily pulled off to the side. Only Steven, Eddie, and Van Camp rushed down to inspect the accident. Burt, he knew that with an impact that severe, that no way could she survive, and there was no need to rush down the hill just to see a dead person.

The others did get out of their vehicles and stood together at the top of the hill. Each of them was telling each other what they saw. There were some debates on how many times she rolled, how fast she was doing, and what may have caused her to crash in the first place. Hardly anything was mentioned about her condition.

With the way the car looked wrapped around the tree, even if she was alive, she had to be hurt badly, and there was nothing they could do without 911.

The military training of Steven and Eddie took hold as they arrived quickly and had a single focused of getting her out. Van Camp showed up and was grateful that Steven and Eddie had beaten him there. He wanted to be there to supervise, but not to do anything physical himself.

Burt was the last to arrive, and he said to Van Camp, "She's dead. No way to survive that terrible crash. No way."

Van Camp shook his head in agreement. He now focused on what to do next. Not on what it will be like to lose someone, or to see someone killed in an auto accident, but on how he can take a leadership role in this situation.

Eddie was the first to look inside and see the condition of Kitty. He never said anything, but moved aside to give Steven a chance to take a look.

After Steven had his look-see, he and Eddie walked over to Van Camp and Burt. Eddie said, "She's dead. It looks like she had every bone in her head crushed."

Steven added, "She hit so hard, that the steering wheel, even after it collapsed, still crushed her rib cage. The steering wheel actually went into the car seat, right through her."

Eddie, while shaking his head side to side, said, "If she would have lived, she would have died soon anyway."

At this point, no one knew just what to do. Burt asked, "Can we get her out?"

Eddie looked at him and asked, "Why man? She's dead. It ain't like we can take her to the hospital or morgue, or funeral home you know."

"I know that," was a quick, but not a mean response. "Should we bury her or something?"

Van Camp stepped in and said, "We can do that."

Steven, as somber as face as he could muster up, said, "She's all crushed up in there. We don't have the equipment to get her out."

Looking around for approval, he added, "It would be a nice and proper thing to do, but I believe that getting her out would be next to impossible.

Eddie spoke up and confirmed what Steven had said, "Yeah, he was right. She was crushed in her seat and our manual labor will not be enough to get her out. I say we leave her where she is."

All four of them seemed to agree, and disagree. They knew that getting her out to bury, would be the right thing to do, but knew that getting her out would be impossible. Let's just say a prayer and move on, was the general censuses of this small group. At the top of the hill, all was silent. It was easily noted that there was no mad rush to remove Kitty from her vehicle. That rather made it official that she had died and there was nothing heroic to do.

The few that did not make the trip down the hill, were looking for those that did, to fill them in with some of the details as they returned.

Bert spoke up to no one in particular, "Her death did tell us one thing."

Everyone stopped talking and gave him their undivided attention. This had better be good, thought most everybody.

Taking a deep breath before starting, Bert explained, "Sorry, but she is dead and her body is still here."

"What you be talking about," question Billy Bob.

"If all the people here on earth just died, from whatever or whoever, then their bodies would be all over the place. Here, Kitty passed away and we can see her."

Some grumbled a little, but Alice was a little selfishly happy, that they were not in the same car as they had initially planned. She spoke up and asked, "You are saying that people didn't just die here, but were taken away?"

"I don't know, really. I know as much as everybody here. But it does narrow down what may have happened."

Bob Billy spoke to his brother, so as not to be heard by others, "You think we should stay here, and see if she disappears?"

"No man, we should keep moving," came a somber answer. The brothers didn't think that anyone overheard their conversation, but everyone did. No one responded, but without anything else being said, the group, minus one, headed south.

CHAPTER 43

BACK ON THE ROAD, MINUS 1

ROSE MARIE HAD ALMOST GOTTEN over the lost of her cats, as she focused on what little she knew about Kitty. With the death of Kitty, that left her with Alice and Lisa. Not exactly the top three women in the world to start up a new civilization. Yet, Eve did it alone with Adam. Then with Adam, there was no one to compare him too.

She started to think more realistically about how and when she might die. Kitty had died quick and easy like, where as everyone here may end up slowly starving to death. For the first time ever, she was entertaining the thought of taking her own life. Not to get even with someone, not to make a statement, not because of some chemical imbalance, just that she had no desire to suffer a long, slow, and painful death.

She did assume that others might be thinking the same thing. For the guys, maybe not taking their own life, but, to cut down on the numbers of us that were left. To survive, it would be easier with fewer people around.

However, on the bright side, thought Rose Marie purposely changing the direction of her daydreaming, thinking that she should get herself a new car. A new car would take away any cat odors.

Leaving me with that new car smell and without a layer of cat hair on the seats. She would even lose that one cat toy under her seat that keeps rolling around with that little bell ringing every time she hits a bump in the road.

Her red Honda looked nice, naturally, any car would look nice after you keep wrecking it and having it re-painted. With the new front and rear bumpers, it looked like a new car from the outside. With the inside, a complete detail job along with new carpet, the car had an all-round look and smell of a new car. A new car with one hundred thousand miles on it.

Also, a new car would come with a trunk that would not always flood if you drove it in the rain. With a dry trunk and no miles on a car, that would make her happy. A dry trunk, no miles on a car, and no payments, that would make her really, really happy. Yet, she would still search for a cat air freshener to hang down from her mirror.

The tears for Kitty were replaced with a smile for a new car, and ended the thoughts of taking her life. A new car that will not require a down payment, monthly payments, proof of auto insurance or games with the sales people, and their managers, in getting the highest price for your trade-in and the lowest price for your new car.

With Joe-Joe, his life remained about the same. Because TV was so much a part of his life, he had seen tons of people die. With all the murders, suicides, accidental, and health related deaths, it was always over in a few minutes.

Most shows would go directly from the moment of death, to the graveside. Even the headstones came completed with the name, date of birth, and the date of death chiseled in completely, after just one commercial. In the time it takes to see two sets of TV commercials, everybody was back in their cars, driving down the highway.

Bert had seen many automobile tragedies that resulted in deaths. It was never a pretty sight and he could recall them all. He remembered their time and dates, where he was headed from and heading to. If he was carrying a load, he knew the details of his cargo.

However, this one was personal. He did not know Kitty, but

because they were in the same boat, she was going to be someone that will be missed.

The next time everyone gets together, Bert was planning to ask, that if he were to die in an auto accident, and if they could, bury him. Then he figured that he would just drop the subject and not bring it up. He made it a point not to think about death or dying, for him or anyone else in the group. That he would just drive, and drive carefully.

Just as Lisa finished licking the sugar off her fingers from her latest, high calories and low value treats, she was then able to think about Kitty. No reason, from her point of view, to mix pleasure dining, with anything else, but with pleasure dining.

With her fingers wiped clean to the bone, and cake still in her mouth, she was prepared to think about Kitty, just as soon as she swallowed.

With Kitty gone, she felt more attractive. Still, not as desirable to men as Rose Marie and old Alice. However, for now, she had the bronze. Third place may be last place, but she placed. Also, the average weight of all the women in the world had gone up. Another death or two, and she can reset the weight/height medical charts. Soon, 'Fat' will be where it's, 'At.'

Jeff, thinking in numbers, and not on the human side of the loss of Kitty, was just a calculating away. One less mouth to feed, one less person to house. One less person getting sick and needing attention. Beside, she looked like a high-maintenance girl anyway.

As far as re-populating the world, that thought never crossed his mind. He was not getting any sex before now anyway, so getting some now, or in the future was not something that he was concerned about, just yet.

It was not until just now, with the loss of Kitty, that sex had entered his head. It was painfully accepted that he was going to die a virgin. Probably, the only virgin in the entire world.

With that train of thought, running off the road into a bridge abutment would save him from being a virgin for the rest of his life, or worse, having sex with Lisa.

Ben was more angry than sad that Kitty died. He knew that he wanted to fool around with her. Now, he only had Rose Marie, Alice, and Monster Woman Lisa available. For Ben, re-populating the world was not high on his list of things to do.

Bob Billy asks, "So, you going to put a hit on that big girl, now that the skinny one is gone?"

After a snicker smile, he responded with, "No man. She is too big for me. You can have her."

A few minutes of silence go by, Bob Billy questioned, "How do you think we'll die? Think we'll both go at the same time?"

Billy Bob giving this some thought, answered with, "Yeah, if you be the one driving."Alice was sad today. Just as sad, as she was when it settled in, that her family was gone. Kitty was her only family until just a few minutes ago. She did not know if it was harder to know for sure that a loved one was dead, as in Kitty, or that someone may be dead, as in her family.

She still considered Lisa and Rose Marie family, more like cousins, and not as sisters. For the guys, they were uncles and nephews.

Alice was starting to allow in thoughts to end her life. To end it like Kitty did. Then again, there was always the hope that her family was alive and well, some place, somewhere. She felt too damn old to be in this situation. If there is a God, then where is he? Jerry, going over in his head about Kitty, recalled how his father had warned him about the results of wild and fast driving. How it could kill you, your friends, or some stranger with a family.

His dad had a few stories from his younger years where he lost friends in auto accidents. Accidents that were caused by the lack of common sense. Naturally, Jerry just knew that this would never happen to him or any of his friends, until just now.

The more he gave this some thought, the more he had respect for his dad. Even the things that his dad had told and warned him, that he didn't want to hear about, were for his own good. That his dad was a good dad, and hopefully, that he could pass on these same good qualities of parenting to his own children.

How sad it was that it took the death of Kitty for him to start to appreciate his father.

Van Camp knew most company policies regarding the death of employees on, and off the work site.

He was always happy when the death occurred while not working. Other than acknowledging that someone has died while at home, it was a lot less paper work than for those who died at work.

His biggest issue was that there were always people who never knew the deceased; felt it was our duty as a company to send everyone home. The lost man-hours always screwed up his projects. For the dead guy, he was done for the day. For his scheduling, he treated this as a long sick day.

For the death of Kitty, this may have caused everyone to start rethinking that the drive to Florida may not be all that good of an idea.

For the next meeting, it may be clouded with crying and crap. It may be hard to control things. Yet, as a light bulb went off in his head, "I can promote myself to counselor."

Let the ones that can't handle a simple death, lean on me. I'll be their rock, their helpmate. I can make this, a win-win. A win for me to score points, and a win for them, giving me as someone they could trust.

For the next hundred miles or so, Van Camp was the man, with a plan, and that gave him a smile on his face, with plenty of pride, and ego.

Eddie gets on the radio and transmits,"Sam, Tom, Eddie Victor, Eddie, Nat."

Steven replied with, "Go."

"Eddie, Frank, Irene, Victor, Eddie."

Steven, "F A B."

Of everyone listening in, Billy Bob was the only one that knew what was communicated. The message was for Steven, as he was to turn to channel 5 on the CB.

Half the group missed the transmission, so it was ignored, the other half heard, but did not know what to do about it.

Billy Bob tells his brother to turn on the other CB, to channel 5, but to leave the one that they already had on, alone.

Van Camp thought he knew what was said, but he did not. The only thing that he could do, was to watch all the cars in front, and behind him. To anticipate someone, or two someone's, to turn off, slow down, or speed up. The more nothing happened, the more he seemed to get upset. There was communication going on and he was unable to contribute, or at the very least, eavesdrop.

Steven, "Break channel 5, come back."

Eddie, "Just checking in. Trying to stay awake. Over."

Steven, "10-4."

Steven again, "Of all the ones to die, it had to be the hot one."

Eddie, "10-4. We could always share the big one."

Steven, "Negative. I say again, Negative."

Eddie, "Okay good buddy. Catch you on the flip side."

Steven, "Out."

By the time Bob Billy was able to turn to Channel 5, their conversation was over. Not sure if they missed anything, Billy Bob informs his brother, "At our next meeting, I will suggest that we all stay on the same channel."

CHAPTER 44

QUICK STOP

A S THE CONVOY APPROACHED A highway sign that indicated that a rest stop was 5 miles ahead, and that the next one was 80 miles more, everyone had the same thought to pull over now, and not 80 miles later. Except for Bert, as he wanted to keep going. 80 miles was only 80 more minutes down the road. They had just stopped a little while ago when Kitty crashed and died.

A few headlights blinked and Bert got the hint that they wanted to stop, and not try for another 80 miles. For the benefit of those behind him, he turned his signal on to acknowledge that he would make the next stop. Even with 5 miles to go, it was thoughtful that he kept his blinker on for the whole time.

As they pulled in, the gas station was the first thing they approached. It made sense to fill-up, then make a visit to the hospitality building to take a break.

Bert pulled all the way up to the last pump. Others pulled in behind him and there were enough pumps for everyone to fill-up at the same time.

For now, all the pumps were working and accepted credit and debit cards. Bert, out of habit, tallied the cars to see that everyone was accounted for. Billy Bob and Van Camp did the same thing. It was just another reminder that they were short one and that she was dead.

Other than those three guys counting cars, and everyone filling up, nothing was said. Everyone was at the rear of his or her vehicle, just pumping gas.

Van Camp wanted to be the first to make the suggestion, asked the group, "Are we going to go inside before we head out."

"Yes," quickly answered Lisa.

Everyone thought that the only reason that she would want to go inside, was to forge for any food left under the heat lamps. That was 50% true, as that was her intentions, with 25% of her wanting to look for any other foods, that were not under the heat lamps, and the remaining 25% for her, was to take a bathroom visit. Most people go to the restrooms to relieve themselves, however for Lisa, it was to make more room, and to take care of the, cupcake poops. If you have never experienced the cupcake poops, then try eating 24 at a time.

Even without Van Camp's suggestion, it was for the most part, assumed that they would take a trip inside. They all, after parking, walked in as a group as if they just arrived on a Greyhound Bus. The men headed towards the men's room. The women did the same, except they made the trip to the ladies room.

One by one, they started to come out and a few of them made it behind the food counters near the food court as others put a hit on the vending machines. As if this was his duty in life, Eddie was looking to make a fresh pot of coffee.

A few people were already seated when Van Camp came back, as he was prancing towards them, as if he needed everyone's attention as he joined the common people.

Van Camp was so consumed to have his shirt tucked in and his sports coat buttoned, with his hair combed, that he forgot to zip up.

Everyone noticed it, as it was obvious when you see an opened zipper on bark blue pants with your tidy whites flashing through. Burt was quick to say something to put him down. He announced, "Check out this guy. It appears that he had to count to eleven while he was in the bathroom.

It would have been over, and done with for Van Camp, as he quickly zipped up, but instead of the story dropping, every time someone made it to the seating area, the story was broadcast repeatedly.

Van Camp did not have a comeback on this current negative situation of his. Yet, what he did was to give those who laughed a score based on how much they enjoyed his misfortune.

Those with highest scores were also his competitors for leadership of the world. This was true, as Ben wanted as much of this bathroom humor to be associated with Van Camp.

Billy Bob tells Bob Billy, loud enough for everyone to hear, "There are better ways to count a bakers dozen."

"Bakers dozen," asked Bob Billy in confusion. He knew how many there were in dozen, but there are 13 people in this group. Billy Bob was proud of himself that he made a good cut on Van Camp, but embarrassed about his brother. It short, it took the joke off Van Camp and onto the two of them.

Billy Bob explained what a bakers dozen was, and Bob Billy, seeing the disappointment in his brother, quickly added a great comeback. "I know what a bakers dozen is. I was just counting that fat chick as three instead of one."

Everyone was happy. Van Camp was pleased that the joke was now on Lisa. The brothers' had redeemed themselves, everyone else got a good laugh. Well, not everyone.

Lisa was ticked. Even with her getting this kind of treatment her whole life, it just should be different now, with those that are here. They should be more than just friends, if not close friends, and then make it an effort not to be cruel.

Ben didn't really care much about her feelings. Not meaning to be mean, he just had to say it. He said this to no one in particular. "If we were to go to Canada, then she would weigh less." Everyone had understood the Canadian/American conversion and had gotten the joke. Bob Billy looked over at his brother for a little clarification. Billy Bob just shot him a look, suggesting, ask me this question later. Not in front of everyone.

This whole conversation was a bummer, and Kitty was not even discussed. After two or three minutes of total silence, as a group, they started to get up and mosey their way back to their cars. Before long, they were back on I-95, heading south.

CHAPTER 45

SECOND NIGHT ON I-95

THEY WERE ONLY COVERING ABOUT 400 miles a day and were getting ready to stop for the night. Rest stops were often and lengthy. However, they should reach Titusville sometime tomorrow afternoon. It would be nice, thought Bert, if they were to arrive while there was still daylight.

At one of the last exits in Georgia, there were about six or seven large hotels. With Bert in the lead, he took the exit and headed for the nearest gas station for everyone to fill up. With the tanks topped off, without issues, everyone seemed very pleased that they were still able to use their credit cards for gas.

With filled tanks, Bert headed towards the closest hotel, a Hyatt. Bert had never stayed at a Hyatt, as he could never afford the price, especially, with him never using the pool, tennis courts, weight room, etc., it was a waste of his money.

There was a huge overhang at the main lobby entrance and Bert pulled right under. Almost everyone was able to pull his or her vehicle under the roof at the same time. The Browns vehicle only stuck out a little, but that was okay with them.

Bert was the first to enter the lobby, and he was amazed. The lobby area alone, was bigger than most of the hotels and motels, that

Bert had stayed at before. Of course, those hotels/motels were only the smaller ones with a dozen or so rooms with an office. They were all located on secondary highways that were once primary roads back in the 50's & 60's.

It was old hat now, as everyone was in the groove on what to do when checking-in. One by one, they passed around the master key, and then found their rooms. Probably, in just less then thirty minutes or so, everybody ventured back to the lobby area.

Well, everybody except for Lisa. Just as everyone was casually checking to see if anyone was missing, you could hear Lisa scraping her legs together coming down the hall.

It appears to be the start of another meeting with everyone in attendance, however, according to Robert's Rule, this was not a meeting. Everyone just seemed fine in his or her little chosen groups. If anyone wanted a meeting to start, no one said anything. Joe-Joe got up and made his way over to the TV, that had a VCR/DVD player, to see if he could get it working. He knew he could get the TV running, but he really wanted the VCR/DVD to work. He was not looking forward to the Countrywide commercials or any messages that tells you to turn to the emergency channel, just to find it not working.

Joe-Joe had carried his backpack with him into the lobby. Not that this was a big deal, but everyone else had left their things back in their rooms.

As Joe-Joe took out a couple of DVD's from his backpack, he could feel that everyone was looking at him. He turned, faced the group, and said, "Since we are not having a meeting, I thought we could watch a little TV."

With most everyone wanting to see a show to gear down from the drive, it was apparent to Van Camp, the Brown brothers, and Ben, that this was not a good time to even suggest to have a meeting right then.

Yet, if you were paying attention, you could see the four of them making eye contact with each other, as if suggesting to the other, for them to say something.

Van Camp had enough business savvy not to say anything as there was never a good time to schedule a meeting where no one wanted to attend. He kept quiet as if he would enjoy a little TV with the workers.

For Billy Bob, not Bob Billy, he didn't have the business savvy, when not to schedule a meeting, or business savvy how to schedule one that no one wanted to attend. So he did nothing, he just sat back and waited to see what Van Camp or Ben would do. For Ben, he didn't care. A con man does not need any rules to schedule anything. He doesn't necessarily need business shrewdness, just con savvy. He only had one rule, schedule whatever, whenever, wherever, and however meeting you want. To be in control, you must control people's time. If you can control the what's, the when's, the where's, and the how's, you control the con. Ben stood up and spoke easy like, suggesting that after the TV break, that later on tonight, there should be a meeting of everyone. Just to regroup.

This was done so well, that both Van Camp and Billy Bob took note of how everyone sheeplessly responded with his request.

With a few seconds of dead silence, Ben suggested, "How about 8:30 or 9PM?"

For the most part, this was a, 'no brainier,' 8:30 it was. Ben thought it would be cool to let someone else agree to the time, that he himself had made available. Van Camp and Billy Bob had been caught off guard and vowed to themselves, not to let this happen again. Even if they had to team up, not to let someone of his character loose, and in control.

The two of them had no idea that he had been in prison, but had a bad feeling about him and assumed that he had.

Before Joe-Joe had it up and working, a trip for most everyone was made to the vending machine area. Ben busted open the snack machine, but had no luck forcing free drinks from the coffee/hot chocolate machine. For cold drinks, that was difficult for free bees. It took him one kick, followed by two hard kicks to crack the front panel of the cold drink machine. With that, you would simply reach inside for a soda, juice, or water.

Van Camp did ask Joe-Joe if he wanted a drink. Not that he wanted to be nice or that he cared, but to give the appearance that the two of them were working as a team.

When everything settled down, Joe-Joe had a series of Jeopardy shows to play. It wasn't the favorite of everyone there, but it was something to do until 8:30.

Watching Jeopardy, as statements were spoken by Alex, and as he waited the answer to be in the form of a question, Joe-Joe answered them correctly, each and every question. It certainty gave the impression that he was bright, very bright. It was not as if he got most of them correct, but he got them all right.

In the middle of the second show, it was no longer fun for anyone else to enjoy the show. No one else had a chance to shout their, in the form of a question, best guess. Joe-Joe had it all wrapped up.

Other than not being fun, it was not a negative situation towards Joe-Joe. With this group, in the backs of their minds, they wanted someone to be in charge. And that that someone, should be very, very intelligent. It appeared that Joe-Joe was well educated, more than Van Camp.

Tired of all the correct answers, only because he wasn't coming up with any, Van Camp spoke up and suggested, "I've seen this show. What else do you have?"

As if he was also board with Jeopardy, Joe-Joe, with a smile, said, "Hang on. I have a few, Wheel of Fortune." No one knew this, but Joe-Joe was not very bright, not very bright at all. He had seen those shows a million times and had simply memorized the questions.

Same thing with Wheel of Fortune. He would wait until just before the contestant made his or her, first guess. Joe-Joe would then, shout out the correct phrase. He would then make fun as the contestants struggled to complete the puzzle. This only reinforced how everyone thought of him as being a genius.

After watching only the first half of the Wheel of Fortune, everyone had had about enough of Joe-Joe. His genius status had dropped to an, irritation status. It was generally seen as exasperating for one person to have all the answers to everything.

Everyone started to talk in little groups, then before long, the only person watching the show, was Joe-Joe, and he did not care about what anyone thought about him, he only cared about what he was watching on TV. He was just fine watching the show by himself. As long as he could hear and see the show, they could talk as loud as they want. As long as they didn't continually walk between him and the TV, he did not care who was walking around. In addition, as long as he had the remote and could fast-forward the commercials, he was the happiest person in the world.

After two shows of The Wheel of Fortune, he found the second series of Survivor.

This show, never seen by Ben, Billy Brown, or Van Camp, had caught their interest. This was especially true as the survivors made alliances and voted.

Everyone else had seen the show and knowing the results, they continued talking between themselves. There was nothing for Joe-Joe to answer, so he just watched the show.

Ben and Van Camp were trying very hard to listen in on the show, and not to miss conversations going on around them.

Billy Bob was quietly explaining to Bob Billy why he was so interested in watching Survivor. He didn't have the time to listen to the show, listen in on the groups near by, and to explain the details about what was going on. Billy Bob just wanted Bob Billy to shut up and watch the show.

Bob Billy did eventually shut up once he noticed all the girls running around in their bathing suits/underwear.

So, for Ben, Billy Bob, and Van Camp, there was a new approach to, creating a following, or subjects, for themselves after picking out the way teams were formed, from the show. It was clear to Van Camp, that he must strike up an alliance, with Ben to work against Billy Bob, and for him to work up a second alliance, with Billy Bob, to go against Ben.

Billy Bob was not as sharp as Van Camp, he only thought about being friends to both, and assuming that it depends on which way it goes, having them as friends, was a good thing. He felt that if he was to be the leader, he could, and should, be able to expect loyalty from Ben and Van Camp. If one of them took charge, they would already be his friend, and he would keep the friendship with the other.

In Ben's case, he had picked up some ideas from the show, as a training manual, on how to influence people into teams. He could always make a good person do bad things. If anyone were to survive, it would certainly be him, along with those he handpicked. There was just enough time to view one more Survivors episode, and the season finale of, The Apprentice, with Donald Trump.

CHAPTER 46

ANOTHER MEETING

J OE-JOE REALIZED THAT IT WAS almost 8:30, and time for the meeting. He would rather watch TV, but knew that he needed to pay attention to the meeting, even if he was not going to contribute. Then, as if getting ready for a news conference, Van Camp, Ben, and Billy Bob made their way up to the little stage in the hotel lobby. No attempt was made to see if the microphones worked, they were just glad that the lights were still on. Before the meeting got started, a few in the group stepped out to make a trip to the rest rooms and to freshen up their drinks.

Everyone returned before 8:30. Being on time was easy, as everyone was already there. There were no people talking with you, holding you up, and naturally, there were no other meetings going on. No phone calls from home, or other employees to cause you, to be late. On top of all that, you wanted to make sure that no one else has disappeared and you did not miss anything.

For the three self-appointed temporary leaders, no one wanted to start the meeting. It was as if they had recalled their latest TV show, The Apprentice, and saw that being too aggressive was not always a good thing. Neither of them wanted to be fired before taking the job. However, after a long, slow minute, not one of the three had said anything.

Ben, not as tactful as the other two, and being a con, wanted to take control right away. He figured that he could not be fired from a job that he did not already have.

Van Camp, being cautious as he began to say something, figured that he could not be fired, because you cannot be fired from a job that was never posted.

Billy Bob was more than happy to say, "Okay let's get started." He then says to the group, "We lost Kitty today."

No one said anything, and oddly enough, it was not mentioned again. It was not even suggested that they observe a moment of silence.

You could only assume that the person you just met the other day, was now dead, and that you did not experience any personal loss. You were only thinking about staying alive as you recover from losing everyone else in the world.

Once it was realized that they should move onto the next item, whatever the next item would be, Bert spoke up and asked, "Anyone have any problems with their car or truck?"

Van Camp, seeing his opportunity to slip in, asked, "What kind of problems?"

Everyone turned to Bert as if he had the inside scoop on car issues. He answered, looking at Van Camp, "Nothing in particular. If something is due to break, or needs to be replaced, now that we are stopped, would be a good time for repairs."

The group thought this to be something of importance to bring up in a meeting. However, Billy Bob, wanting to jump in on this conversation, and to crack a joke, said, "Hell man. If my car breaks down, I'll just get me another one. A brand new one." This did receive a few expected chuckles from the group.

Bert, not wanting this to be a joking matter, responded, "Just a thought man. We can move onto something else."

All three of them on the stage, wanted quickly to move on, tried to speak at the same time. It would have not been an issue, if there were only one microphone for them to share, or a podium for the one speaking to stand behind. For the present set up, all three could talk at the same time. And they did, or tried.

Van Camp wanted to talk about the time to leave tomorrow. Ben wanted to know who wanted to go back, stay where they were, or to continue. And, if to continue on, is Titusville still acceptable.

Billy Bob wanted to know what Lisa was going to fix for breakfast tomorrow morning.

These three leader hopefuls, all stopped dead in their tracks, remembering the reasons Donald had fired some people along with why some were voted off Survivors Island. No one wanted to stand out in a negative way.

Van Camp had the most to offer in how to pleasantly interrupt and say what he wanted to say without even causing his opposition to respond with simple negative facial expressions that would be noticed by others.

Putting his question last, he asked Lisa, "Could you provide us with breakfast tomorrow morning."

Lisa was happy to be asked, answered, "What time and does anyone want to help?"

Rose Marie was not going to respond. She felt that if she did, it would set a precedent for the women to cook while the men folk sat around reading the newspaper and making decisions.

Alice felt the same way; in addition, she was tired of cooking all her life for her family. This time, she wanted to be waited on. Bob Billy tells Joe-Joe, "Damn man, if she can eat for three, why can't she cook like there are three."

Joe-Joe answered back, "Just how big is the kitchen. Can she even fit? How can she cook on the grill if she can't reach it?"

Both guys tried to keep their laughter down, but it was not easy. Billy Bob gave Bob Billy another one of his looks, hinting that he should stop whatever it was that he was doing.

Joe-Joe, feeling bad that he made the joke, volunteered. "I'll help you out. Not much of a cook, but I learn fast."

Bert, wanting to recover from the joke earlier, said, "Me too. As long as we don't have to cleanup."

Lisa responded to the two of them with a big smile. Not a pleasant smile, because she still had food between her teeth. Not just little pieces, but large enough to see from across the room.

"7:30 okay with you two," she asked.

Both guys smiled, without showing their teeth, and nodded yes.

"Okay then, we'll have breakfast, hot and ready at 8:30. Any later than that, it will be old and cold," announced Lisa, and for the first time in days, she had nothing to bitch about, but the day is still not over.

That pleased everyone, and Van Camp, wanting to capture the positive moment, asked before Billy Bob or Ben could butt in, "Is everyone still onboard to continue to Titusville?"

That was Ben's question and he did not like Van Camp asking for him, but showed no emotions that he was a little pissed.

No one responded, they only looked around anticipating that someone else would say something.

Wanting to jump in, Ben asked the question that Van Camp had asked, "Are we okay with leaving tomorrow, say, about 9:30?"

That seemed fine with everyone. The breakfast and departure times have been submitted and approved.

Joe-Joe raised his hand, indicating that he had a question. No one in particular acknowledged him, so he just spoke out. "Do you think it would be a good idea to venture out at night?"

With no one giving him an answer, but he did have everyone's attention, he added. "Maybe things are different at night."

Billy Bob answered, with his brother agreeing with a big snicker of a smile, "Like vampires."

Not everyone responded the same way. While half thought this to be a good joke and a waste of time, not to mention that it might be dangerous traveling around at night in an unfamiliar area. The other half, not necessary believing in vampires, thought it to be a good idea.

Billy Bob was now sorry that he had made a joke out of this as he noticed that not everyone thought this to be a funny, or even a bad idea.

Ben, wanting to make a comment for two reasons. One, to make himself a part of this debate, and two, to volunteer as one that will venture out, not too far, but far enough to satisfy everyone's curiosity, said, "I'll do it."

Bob Billy then volunteered him and his brother.

Van Camp, wanting to be a part of this, and not make the drive in the dark himself, came up with a managerial plan. "No need to have anyone head north, we just came that way. Same for the south, we'll cover that tomorrow on our way to Florida." Everyone nodded in agreement, because, that did make sense, and nobody else wanted to go out, now that east and west are covered.

"I will stay here, on the radio with Ben, Billy Bob, and Bob Billy," announced, as if he scheduled the entire event himself.

Joe-Joe asked Ben, "Can I ride shotgun with you?"

Ben answered, "Yes, no problem." Yet, Ben really wanted to be by himself. He didn't want some young kid riding around with him as he looked for things to steal. Well, not steal, just to place items of interest and value in his custody.

Then again, thought Ben, 'this could be someone that will be my 'boy,' my little Hop Sing, or Hey Boy. He could do things for me like, spy on others, run errands, and support anything I want to have done, or want to do.'

With a smile showing full acceptance to have him ride along, Ben tells Joe-Joe, "Ready to head out after we finish up here?"

Now that this little matter has been worked out, there seems to be nothing else to bring up, this meeting was soon adjourned.

Breakfast and a time to depart tomorrow have been established, and for the rest of the night, it was free time.

Not free time for Ben, Joe-Joe, Billy Bob, Bob Billy, and Van Camp. These guys wanted to get started on this little adventure so they could get back. They've been driving all day and not happy about driving any more tonight. They did volunteer, but not to do this all night.

Van Camp gathered everyone up in the same way that a general would muster his troops. "You guys need call signs?"

Bob Billy didn't know what a call sign was, but he knew he wanted one. Before he could ask, his brother said, "No need, it's just the three of us."

Ben shook his head in agreement and added, "Channel 19, right?"

Just then, Eddie was walking by. Overhearing their conversation, said, "If I might offer a suggestion?"

Not waiting for an answer, "I would suggest channel 9. 19 is good, a truckers channel, but 9 is the emergency channel."

Because he was in the military, it was generally believed that he was right about things involved with communications. They all agreed to set their CB's on channel 9.

After a quick radio check, Ben with Joe-Joe, Billy Bob, and Bob Billy, headed out to their cars. Van Camp was just as happy to stay in the lobby area. He did have enough common sense to sit himself down near a window to allow for the best reception possible. Jeff felt like watching a movie. He went over to Joe-Joe's backpack, and assumed correctly that there were other DVD's, movie DVD's, that he could select from. He was not in the mood for any game, or reality shows. Jeff just wanted a simple, non-complicated, movie to enjoy.

What he found was, The Towering Inferno with Steve McQueen. He was sure that this movie came out a little before his time; yet, it looked like something he would enjoy.

Lisa asked Jeff, "What did you find?"

"Towering Inferno with Steve McQueen."

Lisa was not asking because she cared, but the type of show would determine her next move. If this was a game TV show, then she knew that there would be breaks between shows. If a movie, then she was looking at stocking up on food and snacks that will last her 90 plus minutes, instead of the typical 30 minutes for a show. Once she settled down to feast and watch TV, it would just cause her to bitch about having to get up and restock.

It ended up with Jeff, Lisa, Eddie, and Steven, sitting around the lobby and watching Steve McQueen fight a fire in a large skyscraper. The rest of the survivors, went to their rooms.

Alice continued to place phone calls home. Even the sound of her children's voices in their voice mail recordings, placed a smile on her face. She had called so often, left so many messages, that their mailboxes were full, and no longer taking any new ones.

Alice thought that a full mailbox was just another piece of hope. If, in the future, the mailbox starts to again, take messages, that would indicate to her that someone had listen too, and then deleted them. Her hope was that this would happen someday. Hopefully, before she gets too far away.

CHAPTER 47

OUT AT NIGHT

B EN TELLS JOE-JOE, "I'LL DRIVE."
Joe-Joe was pleased that Ben wanted to drive, as he did not. He just didn't like the way Ben sort of made it an order, not as if they were teammates and you tell someone to, 'go long.' More like, 'I lost the ball, you go and find it.'

Whatever, they were going to be in the car for only an hour or so and that Joe-Joe thought that he might as well make the best of it.

Ben and Joe-Joe drove west. Well they believed it to be west; as they saw the Brown brothers drive to the main road, and turn right. Ben felt that making a right out of the parking lot, would be east, leaving them to turn left, or west.

"I was going to go that way," said Ben.

"Good thing we saw them. It would have been a waste of time to cover the same area twice. Not to mention, seeing them later and believing that we found other survivors."

"That would suck," answered Ben.

And, as with other recons, they found plenty of nothing. Same as up north, no people and no animals. It was even commented by Ben, that there should at least be bug hits on the windshield, especially at night.

After about thirty minutes of driving, Ben tells Joe-Joe to, "give Van Camp a call."

By this time, Joe-Joe just took it in stride that Ben always sounded as if he were barking orders. Orders from military people, he believed from his countless hours of TV war movies, always seemed as if they were, 'barked out.' It made orders, seem like orders, comply or die.

Van Camp responded to Joe-Joe's call, "Okay, we figured as much, but it was well worth the time and effort to make sure."

"Have you heard from the Brown brothers," asked Joe-Joe.

Before Van Camp could respond, Bob Billy aired over the radio with, "Browns here. Same with us. We passed through four or five small towns, four or five McDonald's and one shopping mall with a Walmart and did not see nothing."

Van Camp came back with, "Typical US of A. Small towns, plenty of McDonald's and a Walmart."

Joe-Joe, wanted to make a joke, said, "You should stop by Walmart and check to see if a greeter is on duty. They are always open 24/7 and there should be greeters at the door."

Well, no one thought that was funny, but it did make sense for them to re-think if they should scope out a Walmart or two. As everyone knows, Walmart has everything. It might even make sense, for other survivors to actually live at a Walmart.

Seeing the lull in communications, and with nothing to check out, Van Camp made a command decision, and said, "Head on back guys."

Ben and Billy Bob, at the same time, thought, 'who is he to be giving orders to me, out here on the road? While he sits back with a cup of coffee in the hotel lobby.'

Billy Bob took the radio from Bob Billy and said, "While we are already out here, maybe we'll just drive a few more miles before we turn back."

This was more of a statement than a question. Ben added, "I agree, Joe-Joe and I are going to check out the next town, then we will turn back."

For Bob Billy and Joe-Joe, they easily picked-up on the power struggle. Naturally, Bob Billy would agree with his brother, and Joe-Joe took it to be in his best interest to concur with Ben.

Van Camp decided to share the same opinion, but in reality, he was accepting their ideas, and he did so. "Great idea. Call when you decide to head back or find anything of interest."

Van Camp felt it was best that he went along with them, and not fight it. Mostly because they were out of sight, and they could easily communicate with each other without his knowledge, and he would not be able to pickup on facial expressions, or examine their body language. For whatever happens next, he would stay off the radio and remain in the lobby until their return. At least this way, others that are here will see that he is doing something for the good of everyone.

The movie, Towering Inferno with Steve McQueen, is a good movie, but not all that great. Just not good enough to watch it twice. Right now, it had everyone's total attention, as a few people, as in all movies with a rescue, had not followed directions, and had rushed the rescue helicopter, and caused it to crash. Jeff had seen this movie a number of times before, and he was only half-interested right now.

One of his goals in life, when watching a movie or TV show for the second or third time, was to find flaws or errors in the filming or story.

In car chases, he would look for previous skid marks in the road where that driving stunt had been rehearsed. Someone getting into a cab, cab number 727, and then getting out from cab number 554. He enjoyed catching the flaws when two people are having a conversation, and as the camera angle changes, one of the actors is now looking down, and before, he was looking to his right or left. Or that their hair was blown out of place, and then the next shot, it's now all brushed or combed.

For night shots in towns or cities, the streets were always wet. Then, there was this bridge in LA that was always in movies and commercials.

Lisa, believing that the end of the movie was near, was now in the, 'force feed' mode, for what snacks she had left over. She didn't want to leave any behind, nor did she want to finish it after the movie. Taking what's left back to her room was out of the question as she already had enough food and junk to carry to her room. And, with no desire to make two trips, she forced handfuls after handfuls in her face, being careful not do lose one crumb.

Others that were there were focused more on the movie and generally shouting out directions to the characters. The moans and groans from Lisa were ignored, as no one wanted to interrupt her during her feeding frenzy.

Jeff, bored with the movie, looked over at her and thought it would be easier to take a bone from a hungry dog, than to ask her to share some popcorn.

Unnoticed by everyone, Lisa got herself all choked up and was unable to breathe. She had sucked down a pound or two of cup cakes, and Little Debbie's, and all of that was now stuck in her throat. Her fat round face was now starting to turn blue.

Unable to make a sound, unable to even rise up out of her seat, and because she was so far back into the couch, she was unable to stamp her feet on the floor to attract attention, she knew that she was soon going to pass out, and possibly die.

A quick thought ran through her mind that made her angry enough to bitch out her final words, if she could speak. She was bitching to herself because she knew that the Heimlich maneuver was made for regular size people. Not for anyone that would require, 'Hands Across America,' to perform this task on her. On top of that, she knew that there were not enough people near by that could get her up and out of her seat anyway.

Poor fat Lisa was frozen in place and time. Her eyes and mouth were wide open, arms were sticking straight out, as if reaching for a ladder, and her fat little legs, nothing was going on there, they just stayed stuck together.

For the first time in her life, she wanted to let loose on a very loud fart, that would cause everyone to look her way and give aid. As with the rest of her body, nothing was moving.

It did not take long before she passed out. From her point of view, she had died. Once she saw the light go out, she knew she was dead.

Jeff looked her way again and noticed that she had stopped eating. Not so much that she was turning blue, and with her arms sticking straight out, only that her mouth was open and motionless. It was odd that her arms were not in continuous motion like a steam shovel. Digging her hand into her lap, rise out with a full load of treats, and then drop the load into her mouth. A mouth, much like baby birds, waiting to be fed.

Because Jeff was gazing longer than normal at her, Steven took a quick glance her way. Steven knew quickly that she was in a bad situation. He yelled, "She's choking! Got to get her up!" As expected, Eddie, x-military, got right up, and approached Lisa with Steven at his side. They both knew that they had to get her out of her seat, and faced down on the floor as soon as possible. Jeff was more concerned to place the movie on hold, than to give immediate attention to Lisa. And that may have been a good thing, because he did not get in Steven and Eddie's way.

With gentleness and strength, they were able to get Lisa to crash onto the floor. With her arms out the way they were, it was a, perfect four-point landing.

Van Camp did not see what had happened, but he thought that maybe a car fell off a jack. It was more of the vibrations off the floor, rather than the sounds of two human cranes, beaching a whale. Either way, it did catch his attention.

It was at this point that Steven realized that the Heimlich maneuver would not work in this situation. His next quick action was to start smacking her on her back. Not the best thing for someone that's choking, but the only option. However, before he could start smacking, he had to decide where. Her back was so big, he didn't want to waste time, energy, and her life by hitting the wrong spots. It also caught his attention that with layers and layers of fat back, his hits must be firm and decisive.

Eddie was thinking the exact same thing. He said, "You smack that half, and I'll take this half."

It only took a few hits between the two of them before Lisa started breathing again. With that, her arms went limp and she crashed again to the floor, creating another simulated earthquake that caught Van Camp's attention a second time.

Eddie, once it appeared that Lisa was going to be all right, said, "We could not let you go until after breakfast."

The two of them were just glad that saving her life did not require mouth-to-mouth, because if it did, she was going to die.

Still down, Lisa was more concerned about standing up, and not about breakfast for everyone. Standing up, from the ground, and not from a chair was something to her that was more important than a meal.

Once she was up and had spitted out some phlegm, she joked with, "Don't eat the popcorn here. Not good for you."

Jeff, having found, and pressed the pause button on the VCR, and missed the rescue, had never heard anyone complain about popcorn before. Either it was popped, or not.

Van Camp came over, and it struck him as odd that Steven and Eddie were all over Lisa. Of course, she had enough for the both of them at the same time, but not here in the lobby. Take it outside to the parking lot and be careful of the parked cars. Besides, if they were fighting over her, it had to be the loser that won her.

Wanting to put this behind her, Lisa sat back in her chair, and with a smile asked, "What happened at the end of the movie?" Let's not miss it on account of me."

Jeff, pleased with his actions during this emergency, proudly said, "I had placed it on pause. I'll just move it back a minute or two and get it restarted."

Everyone wanting to see the ending, had quietly sat back down, giving Jeff visual permission to restart the movie. This little incident with Lisa was just that, a little incident.

Van Camp, after piecing together what had happened, thought this to be and odd group. You would think that with the world void of all people, that for anyone that was left, that their safety, if not their life, would be in your best interest. This lady almost died, and a minute later, it was movie time.

'Maybe,' he thought, 'being the leader of this group may not be worth it.'

'Nah,' he answered himself. 'No matter who, I will always be the most qualified to be a leader, their leader, everybody's leader. If not then, one of them might be in charge, and no way could I allow that.'

Van Camp simply walked back to where he was with the CB's. Both teams should be reporting by now and he didn't want to give the impression that he had left his post, or worse, gone to bed.

Bob Billy, remembering the apparent friction between his brother and Van Camp, asked, "Should we call back now? We are heading back, right?"

"In a minute. Boss man can wait," answered Billy Bob.

"Okay man. Is there anything we need while we are out here? You know, beer, guns, beer, ammo, beer."

With a dangerous smile, Billy Bob responded, "You can never have too much beer and ammo or too many guns."

"If we pass a liquor store or gun shop between here and our place, can we stop?"

"Yeah, if we stop, we'll call Van Camp and tell him that we are heading back. If we don't fine one, we'll just call him from the parking lot."

Ben tells, or strongly suggested, depending on whom the teller is, and who is the tellie,'to give Van Camp a call and say that we are on our way back. On our way back with nothing to report.' Pleased to be turned around for the return trip, but disappointed that they found nothing, Joe-Joe called in.

Van Camp replied, "10-4. Are you twenty or so minutes out?"

Before Joe-Joe could ask Ben's opinion, Ben said, "25."

They were really twenty or so minutes away, but Ben wanted to make it a point not to agree with Van Camp, and he would drive just fast enough to have it take, 25 minutes.

After the movie, everyone but Van Camp headed to their rooms to call it a night. Van Camp was going to stay until both teams return. He wanted any news to be given to him before anyone else heard about it.

Ben and Billy Bob pulled in at about the same time, and parked close together. The four of them, before heading into the lobby, started up a conversation with the details on their, 'nights run.'

Van Camp noticed the car lights passing by the lobby doors leading to the parking lot. He assumed that was either Billy Bob and Bob Billy Brown, or Ben and Joe-Joe. He didn't want to run out to greet them, but felt it was more dignified to sit here and wait.

After waiting more time than he felt was necessary to park your car and then walk to the lobby, Van Camp got up and headed out. In the back of his mind, he was thinking it could very well be someone else. Another survivor possibly, even space people. UPO, Undefined People Objects.

To his alarm, he noticed that the four of them were wrapped up into a discussion ranging from who won last's year Super-Bowl and who would volunteer to satisfy Lisa. Nothing was said about the night's drive.

Unable to wait and find a polite way to stop, two on-going conversations at the same time, Van Camp belted out. "Did you guys hear about Lisa? She almost choked to death tonight.

Billy Bob asked, "Who did she try and eat?"

Three of the four found that to be extremely funny. Naturally, either Van Camp didn't get it or that he didn't want to show, that he got it.

Ben, wanting to continue with the jokes, said, "No, no. That's not it. She didn't have enough to eat and her throat collapsed in on itself. Like a black hole, you know."

For Joe-Joe and Bob Billy, they could have heard jokes all night long. They would have, if it weren't for Van Camp putting a halt on their entertainment.

"She's okay guys," Van Camp said, trying to let it be known that they were being disrespectful. "Find anything tonight?"

Ben was the first to respond. He reported, "Nope. Same as Delaware. I was even looking for bugs to splatter on my windshield."

Ben said this, and for the first time, he showed a little emotion.

It wasn't that everyone in the world was gone, but that he only had a very small number of people to con. Then on a good note, if he were caught, it would not result in jail time.

Billy Bob concluded this meeting in the parking lot with, "I think we are it. What can I tell you?"

Of the five guys there, not one of them had anything to add. Ben, as he stepped away, said, "Good night all. See you at breakfast."

Ben and Billy Bob, after driving an extra hour, were right behind him and going to bed.

Van Camp was pleased that he was going to sleep with everyone safe and sound, and that he had status reports that were current. He headed back inside.

Bob Billy and Joe-Joe, they weren't as tired, and they talked for about twenty minutes or so. Just talked about stuff, before they headed in.

Another day down with tomorrow, the end of their drive. Titusville Florida, USA. No one knew for sure, or even planned out what they were going to do once they get there. Do they all have single homes, close to each other? Maybe, an apartment house, or better yet, condominiums.

These general questions were on the minds of everyone just as they fell off to sleep.

Billy Bob says to his brother, just before lights out, "What do you think we should do about finding a place to live?"

Bob Billy was giving this some thought just as his brother asked him. "Apartments are cool. Everyone is close, but then it's just like the projects."

"Single home," he added. "Single homes require someone to cut the grass once a week. I don't want to cut no grass.

Billy Bob was impressed that his little brother had an opinion.

Generally, he did all the opinions for him.

Bob Billy spoke a little more, with, "Condos are like, like high class apartments with no grass to cut."

Shaking his head approving to himself what he just said, continued with, "Yeah, give me a condo. Top floor condo with a pool on the roof."

"The top floor," laughed his older brother.

"Yeah man. Like George Jefferson. I am moving on up. And if I am moving up, I might as well move to the top."

The Brown brothers soon fell asleep with smiles on their faces. With so much lost, with family and friends gone, at least now, they had some hope.

CHAPTER 48

BREAKFAST BY LISA

L ISA WAS UP EARLY AND grateful that she was alive. She had heard from many friends, doctors, and diet groups that her tonnage would cause her an early death. She knew that what she ate and how much she ate, was her problem, but never thought that the function of eating would do her in.

Instead of bitching to herself and starting out the day in a bad mood, she was going to be cool and try to chill out. She was going to spend a little more time today putting herself together. An extra few minutes to comb her hair, apply a little makeup, and something bright from her small, but double-extra-large wardrobe to cheer up her day.

This would have been a good start for a perfect day until she realized that she needed clean underwear. For most people, clean underwear was not that much of a problem. You washed them, and when you needed more or replacements; you simply went to almost any store, and grabbed a six-pack. However, for Lisa, hers did not come in six-packs, but three-packs and most often, as singles. On top of that, usually only Farmers Markets and Dollar stores carried her size. Running out of underwear was always a problem as it was usually a supply and demand issue. She just demanded too much of a supply of cotton to create drawers, covering that much area.

Above the neck, looked good with the improvements completed, but from the neck down, dirty undies covered a large area. With all else that she was thinking about, her cheerful day had taken a turn, a turn for the worse, or in a bitch-able direction. She suddenly realized that she had to cook breakfast for everyone. Alone in the hot kitchen, with hot grease splashing up, to splatter all over her combed hair, fresh makeup, and her non-grease repellent, brightly colored outfit, was a real bitch.

In a small way, she was sorry to be alive, or at the very least, not to be alive with so many people around. If fewer people had survived, she would not need to cook a meal for a dozen folks. Her cheerful meaner had returned to the old, mean, nasty, bitchy person that she was.

For anyone to complain about his or her breakfast today, well, it just might be his or her last breakfast. Lisa would strangle them, then wrap them up in her dirty underwear, and throw them away. After that thought, Lisa did a mental re-organization of her attitude. She recalled that yesterday could have been her last day on earth, and that her cooking breakfast for a few people, could in no way, be all that bad. At least not worth bitching about.

Before she could change her mind, she quickly headed out and on down to the kitchen with a good and positive outlook. It was not that good or that positive, that the group would enjoy a five star breakfast, but for sure, good enough to outdo IHOP.

Once in the kitchen, she searched out for anything usable for breakfast. This was not that bizarre of a task, as she would eat anything for breakfast. Anything that just might not be good enough, or acceptable, for everybody else in the world.

Finding food was easy for her. She could smell food. She could even smell eggs. Yes, rotten eggs are easy to smell, but eggs kept refrigerated are not. She went right to the supply of eggs, butter, and bacon. She was not able to pick-up any scent for onions or cheese. She did for the tomatoes, but the stench told her that they were rotten.

Having all that she needed, with the grills working, she sets a goal to have everything ready at 8:30, even with no one to help.

Then again, no one else was really needed because there would be no cleanup. Yet, she could use a little help setting the table and serving the food. Whatever, she would do her best and making it a point not to volunteer in the future. If asked, she would say, 'No,' and then add, 'because it would be polite to share responsibilities of preparing meals with others.'

Eddie was up and walking on down the hall towards the kitchen. What he needed was a pot of coffee to start out his day. His mind, not at 100% just yet until he had a cup of coffee, was thinking about what type of place he wanted when they arrive in Titusville sometime later that day.

Coming out of his room as he walked by, Steven says, "Morning. It's good to see that someone else is up and awake at 07 early."

He was answered back with, "Morning. Going for coffee?"

"The only way to start the day off," joked Steven.

As the two strolled down the hallway, they got on the subject of where and how they will live. Mostly on where, as in, hotel, single home, or apartment.

Rose Marie and Alice had shared a room for the night. Rose Marie had had about enough with Alice making all those phone calls home over and over and over. Alice was tired on hearing about Rose Marie's cats, over and over and over.

Without saying anything to each other about living arrangements in Florida, they pretty much knew that they would not be sharing a place together.

Not saying much more than, 'good morning,' the ladies washed up and dressed. They were even thinking separately that when they sat down for breakfast, that they would make it a priority not to sit next to, or across from each other. Neither one wanted to hear anymore about the others kids or cats.

In addition, they were each trying to take their time getting ready and not to be the first one to make it for breakfast, fearing that they would be stuck helping out. So in one way, each wanted to hurry up and leave the other behind, at the same time, slow down to be the one, left behind.

Ben was starting to, re-enjoy, waking up in a comfortable bed, that was not attached to a jailhouse cell wall with a fellow inmate below him in the lower bunk. Great pleasures from not hearing the sounds associated with hundreds of men guarded by dozens of guards. Steel doors were not slamming open or slamming shut. When anyone talked, they always had to talk in their outside voice, not their inside voices. It was never quiet, even in the middle of the night. It also felt good to wake up on his own, and not timed by others.

Then, there would be breakfast with a few people, and a few of them were women. A bad breakfast right now, was better than a good breakfast, while locked-up. Lisa could serve burnt, cold food, with cold coffee and warm milk, and Ben would be one happy con man.

Yet, not happy enough, to arrive early to help Lisa out.

Bob Billy finished his shower, and while drying off, asked his brother, who was still in bed, "What kind of place are you going to move into?"

Billy Bob returned a look of confusion. Not so much that he was confused from just waking up, but that his little brother asked a question suggesting that they would not be living in the same place. It had never crossed his mind that they would ever split up. Billy Bob, in some ways, wanted his little brother around to carry out some minor duties. Duties such as cutting the grass, if they had a lawn. He would be needed to take out the trash and keep the house clean, for example. Do dishes, vacuum, and clean toilets. No way would Billy Bob do tasks that his brother, because he was younger, should perform.

Bob Billy, was not the brightest, only because his brother kept him thinking that way, knew enough that he wanted to live on his own. If he were going to cut grass, do dishes, take out the trash, vacuum, and clean toilets, it would be his grass, his dishes, his carpet, his trash, and most importantly, his toilet. If anything were different between these two, his aim was better, much better. Bob Billy, seeing the delayed response, asked, "You know, when we get to Florida."

Billy Bob, fully awake, sitting up in bed, came back with, "You mean like my place, not ours?"

"Yeah. We can each have our own place. We can be neighbors."

"Never gave it any thought. Figured that we'd always be together," answered Billy Bob, with his thoughts more into how to keep his place clean on his own.

"We be together my brother, just not 24/7. That's all," responded Bob Billy, not wanting to get into much detail just then. Details, like who will clean what for whom.

Billy Bob, not happy with the way this was turning out, decided to set the subject aside for right now. He needed more time to consume a new direction that his brother wanted to take. A direction that he himself, did not approve of, said, "No problem bro, we'll see what kind of places are available for us when we get down there."

Bob Billy agreed with a head shake, but inside, he knew that anything they wanted would be available. It was not as if they had to buy or lease a place. He picked up that his brother may not like the idea of the two of them splitting up. Well, that was just tough, he would need to get over it.

Van Camp was up and wanted to look good for the day. He wanted to look good for breakfast and for their arrival in Titusville. He believed that it was always easier for people to follow someone that dressed well. Today, everyone would be deciding where to live. If he was going to provide direction, or suggestions, he should look the part of someone that should be listened to.

One issue he needed to focus on was his pants and shirt. They were clean, but could really use some ironing. Ironing for most people, was nothing complicated, but for Van Camp, he had never ironed before.

The simple task to set up the ironing board, from his point of view, needed an engineer. Or, someone below him in authority, that he could command, or tell, to execute this important assignment.

After a few minutes of spending time looking for directions on the ironing board, Van Camp had it up. Not all the way up, just half way. Low enough that he would iron his shirt and pants while on his knees.

More time was wasted after he realized that the iron should be plugged in, and turned on for it to heat up. Once it was heated, he realized that it needed water. The iron was unplugged, and taken to the bathroom sink for water. Van Camp plugged it in again, but forgot to turn it on.

He waited for the water-filled iron to get hot, and after a few minutes of more wasted time, he remembered to turn on the iron. Half way into ironing his shirt, it occurred to him why the Chinese were well known for their laundry work. Especially ironing. They were short enough that they could iron without kneeling.

Even with all the handicaps, Van Camp successfully completed his ironing, and with pride, headed to breakfast.

Everybody else, Jeff, Burt, Jerry, and Joe-Joe, had mingled together and were heading down also. Normally, for a group of guys heading towards a free breakfast, there would be a race to see who would be the first one to take a seat, and place his order. With Lisa the only one known to be in the kitchen, arriving first, might set up one of them to volunteer and help. These guys wanted to be served, not servers. This was not discussed between them, but they secretly wanted Alice and Rose Marie in the kitchen with Lisa.

Lisa was cooking away, placing dozens of scrambled eggs in a large bowl. Along with the eggs and bread, there was a huge stack of bacon, cooked well done. Taking a short breather, she grabbed the platter of bread and butter and headed to the dining room. As she walked in, those that were talking, stopped, and everyone smiled in anticipation of a five star breakfast.

Lisa noticed that the table was not set and decided that she was not going to worry about that. She announced, "I will be right back with eggs and bacon."

Van Camp picked up quickly that he could pass out the silverware. Not so much in being a nice guy, but as he placed a set down, he would, or should, receive a, 'thank you,' from everyone.

Billy Bob tells his brother, "Find us some plates will you." With the idea of living on his own still fresh in his mind, Bob Billy did not care too much for the order he just received. It would have been nice to be asked. Whatever, he would do it, with the good thought that starting tonight, that his brother would be getting his own plate.

For the first time feeling some independence, and a little cocky, Bob Billy asked his brother, "A plate just for you? Or should I find plates for everyone?"

Twice today, his brother had spoken for himself. Billy Bob was realizing that things were changing. He did not like the idea that this was happening in front of everyone, but wanted to defuse it for now. "Sorry. I meant to ask you brother. I'll help you and we'll find plates for every one."

Lisa returned with the eggs and bacon and placed them in the middle of everyone, which was easy because they were all sitting at the same, long table.

Steven, Ben, and Eddie were quite please with breakfast. For x-military and x-cons, this was a good breakfast. For the others, they wanted a little more. Some slice tomatoes and fresh Danish. By the time Lisa took a seat at one end of the table, silverware and plates had been delivered. Assuming that this was all that she made, Billy Bob and his brother, made it a point to take all that they wanted. All that they wanted, if they were to have seconds. These two pigs were afraid that there might not be enough to go around twice and felt that they deserved seconds.

Because Lisa had eaten as she cooked, she was just going to sit back and watch everyone eat. And, to accept the 'thank yous,' and praises. In addition, wearing makeup and having her hair combed, she wanted to give the impression that she may be fat, but not a fat slob. However, for her not to eat with food in front of her, required that she bite her tong. Really, to bite her tong.

During this, 'five star' meal by some, and a, 'one star' meal by others, no one really said a word. If was as if they all knew that hot meals like this one, would soon be a thing in the past. Eating a hot meal, made them feel good. And thinking about their future, made them feel sad.

Lisa was a little pissed that not everyone thanked her for breakfast. She didn't expect a standing ovation, but some just nodded approval as others thanked her. Whatever, she would still bitch about it. Even if everyone thanked her individually, she would bitch about the ones that thanked her, the least. It was hard enough not to eat, and just as hard for her not to bitch.

With a limited menu, or no menu, and without a waitress to warm up your coffee, breakfast did not take that long before everyone started to put down their forks, and wipe their lips. Bob Billy, was quick to notice this and asked the group, "Are we still set to head out soon?"

This open announcement caught him off guard, as he had never spoken out, like that before. Billy Bob was especially surprised over this. In a matter of a few days in this new world, Bob Billy looked as if he wanted to be more active and independent. More active and independent, away from his older brother, but not too far removed.

No one answered him right away. He was not being ignored; it was just that no one had an answer. It was always assumed that they would head out after breakfast.

Billy Bob wanted to team-up with his teammate, said, "I'm with you my man. Let's push in our chairs and hit the road."

"I don't want to hit it too hard," joked Jerry.

For a moment, everyone was a little loose. They knew that they would be headed out shortly, and that was a good thing. Yet, they knew that their journey would be over soon, only to start a new life, a new life in every way known.

Van Camp, not wanting amateur Bob Billy and Jerry to add or say anything else, chimed in and asked the group, "Thirty minutes okay with everyone?"

Everyone seemed to agree as they left the table and headed back to their rooms to pickup what little belongings they had. Lisa, then made a quick stop back in the kitchen. Not to clean up or see that everything was turned off, she was looking for snacks, snacks that she could take in the car with her. She also delayed her exit from the dining room anticipating additional encouraging and appreciative words about her breakfast. None came.

CHAPTER 49

ANOTHER ONE BITES THE DUST

J ERRY WAS SO THRILLED TO see the, 'Welcome to Florida,' sign as the convoy of survivors crossed over from Georgia into Florida.

In his excitement, and for a stupid reason, he turned back to check out the backside of the sign. Because it was located in the center medium, he had assumed that the sign would have, either 'You are leaving Florida, or Welcome to Georgia,' painted on the backside.

It didn't, as most people would think, and before Jerry could turn back around, he had strayed too far to the left and now had all four wheels on the shoulder. With inexperience, he had cut it too hard back to the right, causing him to flip repeatedly. In the blink of an eye, and without wearing his seat belt, he was thrown out.

Burt was following right behind Jerry, and he was very much surprised that anyone could flip a Hummer, and not initially concerned that there was a car crash, going down right in from of him. Burt, did however, know enough not to slam on his breaks with the others behind him. He easily maneuvered around the, still rolling over and over Hummer, and pulled safely on to the center medium.

Just as he was coming to a stop, he witnessed Jerry falling underneath, and crushed. Even after crushing Jerry, the Hummer rolled four or five more times. Before Burt exited his vehicle, he knew that Jerry was dead. Even if he were not dead, he would not live long.

There were no 9 1 1s, to call for medical and police help, but Alice tried anyway. Mostly out of habit. After four rings, Alice hung up. Maybe she thought that things might be different in Florida.

It seemed like such a waste that two people were killed on a simple drive down an interstate, in daylight, good weather, and with no traffic. Burt made it across the road and stood over Jerry's crushed body. It was so badly crushed, that there was no reason to check for a pulse. Even someone with an un-trained eye, could see that this was a dead person.

Ben came over and stood beside Burt. After looking at the body of Jerry, he looked back at everyone else, that mostly; were still in their vehicles. It had happened so fast, that they were still trying to sort out in their own heads, what had just happened. Both Burt and Ben knew that there was nothing else to do. As odd as it may seem, they were ready to move on.

The others that were still in their cars, without saying anything, were also ready to, hit the road, but safely, as they wanted to continue on, without any delay, because something as simple as a burial, or even a few words over the deceased, seemed to them to be a waste of time.

Lisa, was thinking that now, it was one less person to feed. Steven and Eddie, it was one less person to guard, and sadly, one less person to stand guard duty. Alice did not know Jerry all that well, and would not miss him. Van Camp saw this as one less person to rule over, and or, one less person to compete with, for leadership.

Ben had one less person to con, and for the others, this was no more than a bump in the road. The goal for the group was to make it to Titusville, this afternoon, well before nightfall. If they were going to have a meeting, they could do that later. It would be too difficult to hold a meeting near a squashed dead body, on the side of the road, only hours away from where they were going.

Burt, convinced that he was the best driver, as he was a professional, took it upon himself and suggested that he take the lead for the rest of the trip. In some ways, no one else wanted to be the lead vehicle.

There was nothing fancy about this restart. Burt headed his car to the front of the pack and waited until everyone fell in line behind him. He noticed that Van Camp, took up the slot, at the rear, with the Brown brothers in the middle of the pack. Ben had pulled in right behind him.

Burt was not sure if having Ben behind him was such a good idea. He felt that he could not trust him, and it would not surprised him if he would hit him, with the 'pit maneuver,' to throw him off the road. That would put Ben in a closer race to be in charge, and cut down on the competition with the ladies. Ben had to set those thoughts on hold, as driving became more intensive. For the remaining drive, everyone was on his and her toes.

Lisa hasn't seen her toes in years, but she knew enough to stay on top of them. With two people already dead from, avoidable accidents, no one wanted the same fate, even if an accident was unavoidable.

Keeping safe distances between each other while driving was one way of staying alert. More time was focused on the car in front of them, and more often, they would look in their mirrors to make sure that the one behind them, was not too close, or too far away. For most of the drive, up to now, the leading car was more often in the left, or fast lane. Now with Burt up front, it's the center of the road. Along with those precautions, they are driving about 10 miles an hours slower.

There was still the occasional road hazard, cars in the road and at some highway exits; cars were backed up and onto the highway. Thankfully, there were no raised drawbridges for them to cross, or stopped trains, blocking the road.

CHAPTER 50

NEXT STOP, TITUSVILLE, FL

L ISA WAS ENJOYING HERSELF RIGHT now. She had a full stomach; plenty of snacks within arms reach on the front seat beside her, and a smoothing CD playing, by the late, Lou Rawls.

The fact that she labeled Lou Rawls, as the Late, Lou Rawls, caused her to chuckle a little. Everybody else in the world, except for those in this caravan to Titusville, could be called, Late.

This little chuckle turned into a smile that allowed her to see in the rear view mirror, that she had snack food and eggs, stuck between her teeth. With most people, squishing your tongue around your teeth a little, would clear it away. For the tough ones, a toothpick did the trick. However, for Lisa, usually there were layers of food stuck between her teeth and that was almost always picked away using a fork. Not a plastic one, as they were never strong enough and always broke.

With no forks available, she tried using her fingernails. This was difficult as she had short ones. Having long fingernails made it difficult sometimes when shoving chips and pretzels in her face. The way she shoveled food in, you'd think that she was saving up for an entire winter with just one feeding.

The seat belt kept her in place, making her unable to move her face closer to the mirror. The seat belt was, all out of slack, as it took every inch to cover over, her double, triple size boobs.

Her only option was to scoot her head that way, and naturally, that would put her off-center for driving. With the amount of food in her teeth, it would have made sense to pull over and park her car. This was not going to be an easy, quick task. There was more food stuck in her teeth than some people eat for a meal.

The next sound that she heard, louder than the Late, Lou Rawls CD, was the warning strips that are found on the shoulder of the road. Quickly, she mentally responded, but physically, she was slow to move. Being slow to move was a good thing, because she was able to ease back into the center lane, and not shoot across the highway as Jerry did.

Those in front missed the excitement. The ones behind her, had flash backs of those that had crashed and died.

Lisa didn't slow down; she maneuvered back in line and resumed as if nothing happened. Her heart was pounding away and the food in her teeth, was something that she had forgotten about. When she did remember, she decided to keep her mouth shut until they came to a stop, a complete stop.

She returned to her old ways and started verbally bitching at herself. Not so much that she was almost killed, not that she had food stuck in her teeth, not that she needed and industrial size scale to weigh herself, but that if she was killed, that she would be left on the side of the road to rot. Left to rot because she had food in her teeth. What a rotten way and reason to die.

Van Camp was paying attention as Lisa left the road. His heart skipped a beat, not because she could have been hurt or killed, but that there would be one less person that he could rule.

The Brown brothers, instead of being concerned in a positive way, made a joke about it. Billy Bob says, "Damn, you'd think that by now, that she could drive and eat at the same time."

"She was probably eating with both hands and driving with her legs," added Bob Billy.

"No way man," interjected Billy Bob. "She had to be driving

with her stomach. One swallow, the car veers right. Two swallows, and the car veers too the left. Just chewing, the car goes straight."

These guys were more pleased with themselves on their jokes, than on the good fortune that she did not crash.

After a few miles, Lisa calmed down some. It came to her attention, that she was alive and well. If food were to run out, that she would have a day or two of meals stuck in her teeth to keep her going.

She felt like that battery bunny, the Energizer. That she would keep going and going, long after everyone else had starved. But to get there, she would need to maintain her, eating and eating. Apparently, not a difficult task, as long as food is available. Not necessarily hot, cold, or fresh food, just available food.

Billy Bob, now that he was finished joking about Lisa, asked his brother, "So, you want to live on your own?"

Catching his breath from laughing, Bob Billy answered, "Not necessarily alone, alone. But my own place."

"Okay," agreed Billy Bob.

Responding, Bob Billy explained, "Yeah. My own place, my own stuff, and my own mess."

Bob Billy did not mean to add in the,'mess' part. It just slipped.

Billy Bob taking offense, asked, "Are you saying that I am messy? You be as messy as I am. I just may be a little more of a slob." "No. Only that what ever I clean up, it will be my mess. If I do dishes, I only need to wash one fork, one plate, and one glass, at a time."

Billy Bob thought this over, and in some ways, he thought that this could be a good idea. Yes, he would need to start and clean his own mess, if he wanted too. And yes, any show on TV that he wanted to watch, he could see them without having to compromise on watching other shows that he had little or no interest.

"That be fine with me my brother. Just hope that we not be too far apart," Billy Bob said in a most sincere way.

Bob Billy was happy. He was not sure how his brother would be with this. "No man, we be close. Even neighbors."

Both smiled, as if they had each, out-scored the other. In the action of knocking knuckles and high-fives with each other, they almost drove off the road.

It looked more serious than it was, with all the dust and stones kicking up from the right hand shoulder. Billy Bob was back on the road and under control, in a matter of a few feet.

Bob Billy had a quick thought, that the first time he was going to be on his own, that he would be in a grave.

With Billy Bob back to normal driving, he suggested, "The next time we do the high-five, we stop the car first."

"You got that right," responded Bob Billy. "You want me to drive awhile?"

"Nah, I got it."

Alice almost slammed on the breaks when she saw the brothers heading off the road. Her only reaction was to snap the car a little to the left, and then right. Before she could react or do anything else, they were back on the road and up to speed.

She had pictures on the dashboard that fell onto the passenger side floor and seat. She loved those pictures, but decided to leave them be, until they were stopped and parked. She had seen about enough of cars running off the road for one day.

For Rose Marie, Ben, Burt, Eddie, Joe-Joe, Jeff, and Steven, they were just driving. Every time someone went off the road, they would ease up on the gas a little and leave another car length between them.

Cautious driving was at a premium. And to mention, their exit off Interstate 95 to Titusville, was coming up soon. Burt, who was in the lead, knew it was up to him to give proper warning when they were to turn off. No way did he want to miss the exit. How could he justify being a professional driver, if he could not drive some place without getting lost. Granted, he had never been to Titusville, but reading a map and following posted signs, was not rocket science. He would be just too embarrassed to have everyone make a U-turn and double back.

CHAPTER 51

TITUSVILLE, FL

AFTER TAKING THE TURN OFF I-95, Bert drove a little slower than the posted speed limit. It could also have just seemed that way after traveling at the higher speeds for the last couple of hours. Yet, Bert was really driving slowly, and it was because he wanted to scout the area. Hoping that there still might be others.

Titusville was just a few miles off the interstate, so it did not take long to see the sign, Welcome to Titusville.

Bert pulled into the first large parking lot on his right. It was a mall that had Macy's and a Sears as the main stores. As he pulled in, he was already at a very empty part of the lot. He then slowed down to a craw, giving everyone the hint that he was stopping. This time, the cars did not stop, one behind the other. With so much room, everyone, more or less, pulled up beside each other as if this was going to be the start of a drag race.

They were there, Titusville. Now what?

Van Camp, seeing an opportunity to call a meeting to order, raced to the center of the group, which ended up being at the front of Bert's car.

However, he was not as fast as Ben and Billy Bob. Ben and Billy Bob seemed all fresh and in control, and here was Van Camp, not in control, out of breath and sweating. At least Van Camp had enough wisdom to know when he had been beaten to the punch, and he would just stand with them, letting them do all the talking until he had calmed down some, stopped sweating, and to catch his breath.

This was a big high for everyone, getting there almost with everyone safe and sound. Also, a big downer, as in, what do we do now, and, we did not all make it.

Billy Bob, speaking from the point of view of someone in security, said, "We should find ourselves a hotel for now."

Bob Billy looked confused because he wanted a place of his own. Even if this was a hotel room, he wanted a place not with his brother. There had to be a million homes that he could pick from, not the same hotel.

Billy Bob, catching a look at his brother, was quick to add, "I know that we all want our own place, but for now, let us all stay together until we have a better lay of the land."

Ben thought this to be a good idea, and added, "I agree."

The group appeared to be okay with this, only because it seemed like the next logical step. Most of the guys were thrilled, because Lisa would be close by to cook up another meal. The ladies were happy, as they were not sure if it was soon enough for them to be on their own. And, that Lisa would be close by to cook one last meal for the group.

Van Camp, after saying nothing up to this point, wanted to say something, anything, but could not come up with anything of value. He just didn't want to blurt out that he agreed, or disagreed. He knew that he had to add in his two cents.

"How about that hotel over there," Van Camp finally said, as he pointed towards the Marriott Suites, caddy corner to where they were.

As if they were a school of fish, all turning the same way at the same time, looked off to see what Van Camp was pointing too.

No one responded one way or the other, only that they all looked over and slowly nodded in agreement. With nothing else to bring up, everyone moved back into his or her vehicle for the drive across the street.

Van Camp, after a quick glance at his watch, suggested to those that could hear him, "Want to meet back up in the lobby, say around 6:30?"

Those that heard him, for the most part, shook their shoulders suggesting that, that was just fine with them. The ones that thought they heard him, turned to others, and asked, "What did he say?"

"Dick said something about 6:30," returned a few comments. As it stood, 6:30 would be the next meeting time. 6:30 came with everyone showing up. When Van Camp did a head count, he had forgotten about the two that had lost their lives on the drive down. He counted three times before he realized his error. Well, not an error, he was just rounding up.

Ben had also forgotten to include the two road-kills for his first count. Billy Bob, his counting reminded him that this was just two less people that would need his protection.

The three contenders for the head spot, neither wanted to start out first. The only decisions now were on where you wanted to live. Items like food and water were not on the tops of anyone's to-do-list, not just yet.

What Ben really wanted to do, was to talk about what each person should do, for the common good of the group. Naturally, he wanted to do the least and control the most. Like in prison, a few were telling many when to get up, eat, play, and go to bed, and now, where to live.

Billy Bob wanted to bring up housing. Wanted to know what everyone was planning to look for, when and where. He knew that you had little control if everyone were to move far apart. At the very least, keep his little brother close.

Van Camp, wanted to bring something up for, and hopefully, where everyone would agree.

Could they use a judge right now? A leader would be a grand item to bring up. Someone must be in charge, and that someone, should be him. He is the 'J' in Judge, the 'L' in Leadership, the 'K' in King, and the 'C' in Cool.

With some wise, constructive personal critique for the present time and place, he decided to hold off on seeking any position that would put him in charge of a group of people that might not be in the mind frame to be under control by anyone just right now.

Burt spoke up, and asked, "Does anyone have anything they would like to bring up?"

No one had anything that they wanted to discuss just then. Yet, Steven did, and he said to the group, "Should we venture out and look at some of the surrounding area?"

The group was slow to respond. Yes, this was a good idea, and yes, they should, but no, no one wanted to volunteer for the drive around after having already completed hundreds of miles in the last few days

Eddie quickly responded that he agreed with Steven. Both men decided that they would volunteer to drive east and west for a short time before returning to the hotel.

Burt, feeling that he was the one hosting this meeting, said, "Other than getting a good nights' sleep, tomorrow looking for a place to live, is there anything else, we should bring up?"

It was now Van Camp's time to speak, or announce, "Should we use this hotel as our base?"

Before he could entertain answers or suggestions, Billy Bob added in, "That makes a lot of sense."

Alice surprisingly spoke up and said, "We should keep a white board or bulletin board here in the lobby for information.

After a pause, she added, "It worked well for me when I had to get messages to different members of my family."

Van Camp shook his head in agreement, thinking that he should have mentioned that before.

Ben, wanting to keep an evil eye on everyone, said, "Yeah. And when you get an address, add it to the board."

For all the things in the world, that they should now focus on right here and now, a white board should be low on the list.

Everyone seemed as if they had had about enough of meetings, making decisions, and driving for now. They were where they wanted to be, and it was time to, 'take five.'

Slowly, the meeting that everyone wanted to attend was now a meeting that everyone wanted to leave early. Knowing that when they woke up in the morning, they were not in store for a days ride.

To make a long story short, Steven drove west and Eddie drove east. Steven drove almost an hour and as expected, saw more of the same, nothing out of place. Just places without people.

Eddie had the luxury to end up on the coast and he enjoyed a view of the ocean. As elsewhere, no one. No one and no signs as to what may have happened. As he drove south along side the shoreline, he noticed a large number of private boats. Some of which were well suited to be your first home and your vacation home, all rolled into one. Except for the fact that he could not swim, it would be nice to live on a boat.

After giving this some thought, he figured that that he could have both, a nice home and a nice boat. His only decision now was if he should have the house next to his boat, or a house a short distance away. If he had to drive back and forth, then he would need a nice car.

Both guys headed back on or about the same time. Steven's ride was quicker, as it was mostly straight, wide roads. Eddie, being near the water, had only curvy, narrow roads.

They returned to the lobby without smiles and with the expected, disappointing news. A few had stayed up waiting on their return, hoping with any news about anything. With nothing new, they headed off and called it a night. Steven and Eddie were tired and disappointed and welcomed a good night's sleep.

The Brown brothers, Ben, Van Camp, and Burt were the only ones that stayed in the lobby after hours, so to speak. Each of these five guys did not want to be the first to head out, and to leave four behind. It was equally considered by everyone, that any meeting of three or more would be a meeting to take control. It was just too much of an unknown of what they would miss, that they would stay up all night, not to miss anything that was said, or worse, agreed upon by a few.

For now, it was just small talk as fatigue kept anyone from starting up, or joining in, on complicated issues. With the fatigue, yawning was making the rounds. If was definitely a power struggle between the top five Alpha Dogs of the world.

Bob Billy was the first to start giving hints to call it a night. Mostly, he directed his hints towards his brother, which was unappreciated.

For Ben, it was well past, 'lights out.' He was ready to call it quits for the night, but not to be the first one.

Van Camp was ready for bed when Steven and Eddie returned. Now, he waited for anyone to drop a hint about going to bed, so he could, according to Roberts Rule, second it.

Burt, the weakest of the five, took the hint from Bob Billy, and after a yawn of his own, mentioned that it was time to turn in. Van Camp was quick to agree with Bob Billy looking pleased that this day was over.

As hoped by Van Camp, Bob Billy, and Burt, Ben and Billy Bob surrender to the request. It was now a rush to bed, as it had been a long day for all. They knew that tomorrow would be a special day, and they wanted to be one of the first to return to the lobby, rested.

CHAPTER 52

MARRIOTT, TITUSVILLE, FL

ONE PERSON AT A TIME started to show up in the lobby with coffee, soda, or juice in hand. Lisa did not volunteer to fix breakfast this time, and because no one else stepped up, there was no breakfast. Only items taken from a broken into, vending machine and the broken into, gift shop were available today.

Jeff had pulled over a folding table near the lobby. After a closer look at what he was doing, it pleased everyone. No, it was not breakfast, but a dozen portable new GPSs. He was setting them up using the hotel's location as base. He named this location, Marriott.

As he was asked what he was doing, he would explain that as we all fanned out looking for a place to live, that we should have, 'bread crumbs' to find our way back here.

The ones that were unfamiliar in the art of updating a GPS, asked if he would, plug in everyone's home address as they become available. Jeff seemed very pleased with himself as now, everyone wanted to be his friend.

Burt wished that he had that idea first, and asked Jeff if he could use some help. Van Camp, overhearing this, also asked to get involved.

Jeff told Van Camp that he had plenty of help, now that Burt was working with him.

Billy Bob and Bob Billy were not familiar with the setting up of GPSs, and contributed with compliments for his creative idea.

Ben was happy that Jeff did not need any more help, as he did not have much use for a GPS in prison. He thanked Burt for, not only, coming up with the idea, but to pick up enough GPSs for everyone.

Wanting to get into something for the group, and get the credit, and take the focus off of Burt, Van Camp walked over to the main door and pickup a number of real estate brochures for apartments, and houses for sale, and for rent in the area.

By the time Lisa, the last person to show up, had a seat in the lobby, everyone that wanted a GPS, had one along with the brochures from Van Camp.

Joe-Joe thought this whole approach was like the first day of school. The only thing missing was name tags on everyone's desk. This latest gathering was different from any of the meetings that they had before. Everyone there was a complete stranger to each other a few days ago, and now, they are all new friends, and the only, friends that they would have in the world.

Today will be a, 'new start,' or a, 'new end.' The beginning of the, 'new start,' 'end of the start of the new end,' the 'start of the start,' or the, 'end of the end'. Or, it could be the, 'new end start,' 'new end start end,' whatever.

With GPSs all around for everyone, and no longer the need for the responsibility to do any more, lead driving, life was good. Burt, without considering the price of a home, he could pick one that he liked. Naturally, he needed three or more garages with a shaded driveway to work on his cars. Not to forget that he no longer needed a driver's license for anything he wanted to drive. For Ben, no more prison time, no matter what he does. That made him happy in one way, but sad in that now the excitement of doing a scam, without the possibility and penalty of being caught, was gone.

The more he considered this, the sadder he became. If he was to work out a scam, he only had a few people to choose from in this new world. Add to this, what ever he needed from now on, was simply free for his taking.

The desire for wealth, in money or things, had no value now. No matter what he had or wanted, was now available to him at no cost. Yet, he could always use a fellow con artist to be his partner, or competitor. He sat there calmly in his thoughts, waiting for anyone but him, to start up this little gathering.

The Brown brothers were there, but when Billy Bob took his seat, his brother did not sit down beside him, even with an open chair on either side. Bob Billy figured that he might as well start now by being his own man. However, he did take a seat that was not to far from his brother, and he made sure that he was facing him. Just small simple steps for now, this separation process might take some time.

Billy Bob only slightly noticed what his brother did, but gave it no more thought as they were sitting, face to face. Billy Bob thought this to be a good idea because they could bounce facial expressions off each other easier this way, rather than sitting side by side. He saw his little brother as not someone that wanted to shed himself from him, but used good sense by sitting where he did. Naturally, his good thinking came as a direct result of the On-The-Job training for everyday life, which he was always dishing out.

So the two of them, sat there separately, scanning the Real Estate pamphlets that Van Camp passed around moments before. Alice enjoyed a comfortable spot in one of the love seats. Her eyes were red from crying last night and this morning. Her right index finger was one phone call, short of a blister. Without a 'redial' button on the hotel phone, she had to dial '9' to get an outside line, then '1' for long distance, followed by seven more numbers. She had her cell phone, but wanted to keep that as an, 'open line.'

As she searched the Real Estate pamphlets, her interest are for a home that had five or more bedrooms. Assuming that her family was still alive, and that they would want to move down here to Florida.

While she rubbed some lotion on her fingers and hand, mostly on the one finger, she vowed to herself that the first thing she does in her new place, was to set up speed-dial on all the phones. Her phone message was not going to be a simple, you have dialed this number, but to leave a message, in her own voice, that she was alive and to please, please leave a message.

Rose Marie sipped her coffee and looked for cat hair on her clothes. It occurred to her that she had gained some free time every day, after realizing just how much time she did spend on cat hair removal. There was the time spent after she was dressed in the morning, and the time at work. At work, she did this routine a couple of times a day, that she had to set aside time for this activity. It was so much time that it crossed her mind to add this to her time card.

Joe-Joe sat there, just looking all around. He was not going to start up a conversation, take the lead or volunteer for anything. He was here because there was no place else to go, or no place else to be. He knew that somebody would always step-up and he would not step-on them, as he would step-out of their way.

Lisa paged through the Real Estate pamphlets provided by Van Camp. Giving this a lot of concentration, she wanted something simple, and all on one floor. If she could find a house level to the ground, that would make her day. She had no desire to go up or down steps, or have an incline up to her home. Just not having to walk up hills or stairs, will calm her down a little everyday.

In addition to looking for a place to live, she kept an eye out for restaurants and donut shops. She would place them in her GPS for those daily time outs, with food. No good reason to spend time and effort looking for a meal. Besides, the GPS does have a direct hit to FOOD.

If she didn't find exactly what she wanted, her next option was to drive further south towards South America. Panama to be exact. She did not have a particular city or town in mind, just that she was in Panama.

Steven and Eddie had a seat next to each other. Every time they were seated, they were less and less sitting at attention, seated more like a civilian. Neither one of them wanted to speak up and start this meeting. There was no need for them to be in-charge or to take charge. Anyway, after today, they will have their own, private, home, without rules and regulations. If they did not make their beds in the morning, then it was not made.

Soon, they will start having meals instead of chow. They will have chores to do instead of having, The Duty. Setting your own time when to go to bed, when to get up. And, it can be changed as often as they wanted. They won't be giving or taking instructions or orders. Life will be good.

It was noted by everyone that they were two people short, Kitty and Jerry. Nobody apparently wanted to bring up this subject, as they already had a full day ahead of them. No reason to start out on a sad note.

Van Camp knew it was time to get something started. Nothing was planned at this time, only that everyone had shown up. It was general knowledge that today would be House Hunting Day and really, none of the adults here needed instructions. Maybe Joe-Joe could use a little direction, or at the very least, ride with someone. Van Camp stood up and waited for everyone to stop talking and to focus their eyes his way. The quiet ones, Alice, Burt, Rose Marie, and Lisa, looked his way. But the rest of them, had no desire to hear anything he had to say. There was no meeting scheduled at this time, nor was there a reason for one. People could just be sitting together for no particular reason.

The Brown brothers gave each other a look, indicating that neither one of them wanted to look Van Camp's way. Ben noticed this and walked over to sit next to Billy Bob.

Ben, Billy Bob and Bob Billy leaned closer to each other, as if they wanted to huddle, into a conversation and leave Van Camp out. Not only leaving him out, but to ignore him.

Van Camp was keen on this and looked for an easy way out. He must look good, say something important and do both, ignore them, and not ignore them. Van Camp looked over at Jeff and started to direct his comments towards him.

Jeff, did not like the idea of being singled out, but was polite anyway. Van Camp spoke to him, in a voice so to be heard by everyone. "Does everybody have what they need for today?"

Ben, not liking what Van Camp was trying to start, said, "What do you think we need?"

The Brown brothers were quick to look Van Camp's way and express that they too, had no idea what they needed."

Burt, feeling lucky, chimed in and added, "We're set. We have maps, GPS to get back, and good weather."

Van Camp, realizing that his term as today's leader, had expired. "Just wanted to be helpful," he finally submitted.

Steven and Eddie got up, as they were going to be the first ones out. Moments later, everyone slowly moseyed their way to either their cars, or back to their room. In any event, Van Camp was alone with no one to lead. After brushing himself off literally, he led his own way back to his room.

CHAPTER 53

NEW HOMES, ALL AROUND

ROSE MARIE DROVE EAST. EAST because she knew that she would eventually find the ocean. Once she finds the shoreline, she would decide then, if she would drive north or south. If after she drove fifteen or twenty minutes, north or south, and did not find the waterfront house that she wanted, she would turn around and search in the opposite direction.

She had more of a dream, than income, to live in a huge mansion; right on the water, and now, her dream could come true. She wanted something on high ground, knowing that someday, there would be a flood. Also, something strong to handle the bad winds and rainstorms, normal for this part of the country.

Rose Marie came to a dead end, right at the ocean. She didn't turn right or left, just parked there for a little while. It was more fun to think about finding the house of your dream, than to hunt around for one, alone, in an unfamiliar area.

On a good note, she did not worry about neighbors. No one would be up late at night playing loud music, looking into her windows, or complaining about her having too many cats.

On a sad note, no neighbors or cats. It was difficult for her to be both happy and sad and to have no one to express her feelings to, or at the very least, having a cat give her that, 'blaa blaa blaa' stare that really means, 'I love you. Pet me and give me a treat. I don't know anything about your problems. Give me a treat, rub my back, and give me a treat.'

Before she started to cry, Rose Marie turned left and drove north. Having been driving south for a couple of days, north seemed like a change. It only took a few minutes before she was driving by many large homes, all within her budget. The task now was to select a few that looked nice from the outside.

One did catch her eye, as it really stood out from the rest, possibly because it seemed new. After a quick U-turn, without first checking for on-coming traffic, she drove right up the driveway. Inside, it was love at first sight. That was made easy, as this was a model home. Furnished to the 'T' with the best of the best of everything. The only thing that she did not like, was that one of her four garages was a realtors sales office. Yet, with three empty and available garages, this little eyesore could be tolerated. Tolerated even more with the asking price of 6.5 million dollars, not counting the furniture.

Other than finding food, linen, and girl things, she was ready for immediate occupancy. With no one, or cats, to share her new home with, life was okay for now. Not good, and not real bad, just that life would be lonely in a lovely, 6.5 million dollar home. Lisa only drove a few blocks from the hotel. With plenty of strip malls in this area, she found a number of Donkin' Donut shops along with a good assortment of fast food, and diners. She understood that food would someday soon, be in short supply, that maybe it would not be as terrifying short with a large number of food places nearby. Food places, such as McDonald's, Arby's, TGIF, etc. were all up and down this strip of four-lane highway. This seemed like a decent part of town. Medium size homes near everything. Everything as there was even a Curves, in one of the strip malls, right next to a pizza shop and a Subway.

Lisa found a ranch style house with a, For Sale sign in the front lawn. This was a very attractive little street, well maintained with the houses only a few years old. Even the cars that were on the street and driveways, were nice cars. Nothing special, just that there were no older cars that showed much needed repairs, or that they had much needed repairs, repaired. No one had a coat hanger for a radio antenna, red and yellow tapes replacing broken tail and break lights, and all the quarter panels, and car door paint jobs matched the rest of the car She did not see any 'Fear' this, or 'Fear' that decals on the back car windows.

Lisa was spending more time looking at everything around the house, and not much time, looking at her new home. When this did kick in, she parked and made her way to the front door. Everything was going just fine until she found that the front door was locked.

With this, she started to bitch. She bitched about the door being locked, the sun was too hot, she needed gas for her car, and she had to go to the bathroom.

Thinking, and hoping, that the back door was unlocked, she bitched her way around back. Even with the back door unlocked, she still bitched about the sun being too hot.

Once inside, and after a quick pit stop, Lisa found this to be most satisfactory. Most satisfactory, because it had plenty of cabinet space in the kitchen. If she were going to horde food, she would need a place to horde it.

She felt that she would grab a bite to eat, and take a nap, after her long search for a place to live.

Steven was not in the mood to shop for housing. His hotel room was just fine and the pool was open and not crowded or full of kids. What food he wanted for now was in the kitchen, gift shop, and in vending machines on every floor.

Once everyone returned, he would figure out who had the best deal. Best deal as in location, location, location. He would pick a place that had, at one time, a high population. With the world as empty as it is, no reason to live in an area with nothing but trees.

Alice was not much for going out on her own. This trip to Florida was the biggest thing she had ever done alone. She did not want to venture out too far from the hotel, in fear that she would not find her way back. Even with the GPS, she was still fearful.

Added to that, when her family drives down, directions would be easy. Interstate 95 South, turn off at Titusville, look for hotel on left.

From the parking lot of the hotel, she could see some homes close by. Knowing that all the homes would be empty, she would simply drive down the first street of homes and pick one. As time went on, she could always move.

Once Alice found a nice street, she parked in the middle of the block. What she had in mind was to pick two homes, one to live in every day, and the second, hopefully next door, to entertain company. Simply keep the spare home nice and clean, but lived in, and then trash her first home. She was just plain tired of housework.

Luck was in her favor as she did find two houses together, that does fit her needs exactly. She would always have a clean kitchen, family room, and bedroom, 24/7.

Van Camp wanted a big house, not a big home, just a big building that was bigger than anyone else, and the biggest house on the block. A big house only for the reason that a big man, with a big position at his work, and in his community, should live in a big house. Only common working people whose positions and work titles, are held by more than a few people at a work place.

For example, you don't have more than one bank president for any one bank, but there will be a couple of vice-presidents. Even bank managers, you have one for every bank and a ton of tellers. This means, no bank manager lived in a big house, and certainly not a bank teller. A bank president would have the biggest house, with vice presidents living in a big house, but not as big as his was going to be.

Bank managers have 'okay' size houses, and bank tellers, well, the higher the income of the spouse, then the closer in size to a bank manager there house would be.

Van Camp loved having the work force population, placed in their place at work, and at their home. He was not concerned with race, color, religion, or even sexual preference, only gross income as a passage to the proper class, first class, his class.

In addition, you can't move into his class if you are a lottery winner, or have been awarded a large sum from a settlement.

So for Van Camp, searching for a house was somewhat easy. Just look for a neighborhood with big houses, and then find the biggest of the big. Finding a good neighborhood was a little harder. Generally, there would be a sign displaying the community by name on the main road. The nicer the sign, the better the odds were that he would find something in his assumed elevated, and exaggerated element.

Billy Bob and Bob Billy traveled out together. First stop, liquor store for some cold beers. Bob Billy suggested getting the beer, simply because there were no cops around so you could have open containers in your vehicle. Additionally, their long drive was over, and it was a hot Florida afternoon.

With some Classic Soul Town music on their CD, favorite hits from Don Cornelius, and his Soul Train TV show, these two brothers were two happy brother, brothers. They had their drinking and driving at full swing, the only thing missing was dancing. Singing loud and moving with the music in their seats would do for now.

Neither one wanted a single home, they were more accustomed to apartment style living, and for them, moving into a condo would be more to their liking. Apartment style living was only a verbal upgrade from public housing. The same as town homes, as they are really row homes. Duplexes were really just two end row homes that were attached.

In one way, Bob Billy wanted to live close to his brother, but not with him. If they were to find a condo that they both liked, he wanted to be in a nearby building, and not something in the same building, and certainty not on the same floor.

For now, the beer was cold, music was loud, and house hunting was easy when you did not need a deposit, a credit check, references, or a lease to sign. The closer they were to the ocean, the nicer the condominiums seemed to be. They spoke about wanting to be on the top floor, with an ocean view. Neither one of them likes the water, but having an ocean view gave a little more value to their place.

Billy Bob threw his empty beer can out the car window and that irritated Bob Billy. He says to Billy Bob, "What'ya doing man?"

"Ain't no big deal bro. Don't no body care now."

"I care man. This be my neighborhood. We ain't back in Delaware. There be no one around to clean up your mess"

"What'ya mean, my mess?"

Bob Billy, didn't really mean for it to come out that way. Yes, he was tired of cleaning up behind him, and that was one of the reasons why he wanted his own place. "You know man, our mess. Now there be no body to collect trash, sweep the streets, you know."

Billy Bob did calm down and agreed with what his brother had said, not realizing that it was a put down. "You be right," answered Billy Bob, as he made a U-turn to retrieve the beer can from the middle of the road.

This reversal of attitude placed a smile on Bob Billy's face. Maybe after he lives alone for a little time, he will appreciate even more that he needs to clean up behind himself thought Bob Billy. Finding the beer can was easy with nothing else on the roads.

As Billy Bob stepped from his car, he was quick to notice a large condo off in the direction of the ocean, as they would have missed it from inside the car.

Billy Bob pointed, asked Bob Billy to step out, and then asked for his opinion.

Bob Billy got out and was pleased that he did. This appeared to be no ordinary condo. It was probably 15 or more stories tall and looked as if there was a pool, cabana, tennis, and basketball court on the roof. A basketball court with fencing, the kind of fencing you would find on jailhouse roofs and inner city parks.

After Billy Bob tossed the beer can in the back seat, they were off to explore their new find. It only took a minute or two before they were in the front driveway, a huge driveway surrounded with palm trees, benches, and statues.

It was quite a mixture of items. Missing was a play ground for kids, but there were benches for old people to sit, and statues for young hippy types. This had all the appearances of a Vegas hotel.

Ben headed out, but in the back of his mind, he was not ready to live on his own just yet. He was thinking that it might be a good idea just to hang around the hotel for a few days to see how everyone else does.

His search was more in the order of what there was in this part of town. Banks were no longer important to him. Mostly, he looked for liquor stores, gun shops, and places to pick up food

After about an hour, he headed back.

Burt, sort of wanted to look for a new place to live, but he did not really want to put in the time. It made common sense to him to wait until others were all moved in and stable. He would just head back to his room, to try and find something on the TV. With luck, he could find a movie to rent, for free.

Joe-Joe was not going to look for a home, just a house with power, plenty of power. If he could, living in a Radio Shack, Best Buy, Home Depot, or even a mall, would be just fine. Heading towards the parking lot exit, he stopped and started to put some thought as to which way he should go. After a few minutes, he decided to head towards the mall that they initially stopped after exiting I-95.

After a few minutes of driving, Joe-Joe started to daydream on how it might be a good idea to live in a Sears. Normally he suspected, Sears were always located in a mall, and malls had everything. He figured that Sears had a furniture department where he could set up house. All he had to do was to rearrange some furniture around, and he could make himself quite comfortable. Dishes and kitchen appliances would be new and plentiful.

He could find the biggest TV; in fact, he could find many big TV's. High Def, Low Def, any kind of Def. Along with that, there would be a large assortment of video, music, and MP3 players with a supply of batteries.

For power, there are always power generators with emergency lighting, and tools in the hardware department. He could move all the clothing of his size to one place and never do laundry.

There was always a DVD store in a mall with more movies, or

TV shows that he could see in a lifetime. CD's of all varieties are in rows and rows and they are there for his pickings.

Hopefully, there would be a food court with some foods still available and safe to eat. A good book store would be a plus along with a toy store for games. A real plus would be a Bose store and an Apple computer outlet.

Eddie was out and about, and was driving and driving around. He was not in the mood to find a place, just not right now. He had no idea what he really wanted, even worse, he had no idea of what he did not want for a new home.

After a stop at a 7/11 for a soda and chips, he headed back.

Jeff, all brains and no smarts, had no thought what he wanted as far as a home goes. He would have been happy just staying at work in his little cubicle and write computer code all day.

Because everyone else seemed to be looking for a place, he thought that he might as well give it a try. His work was more important to him than a place to live, which was why he didn't really want to even venture out for a look-see.

He did however, drive for a few hours, a few hours of driving and not looking. So, hotel living just might do the trick for him. Not being sure just where he was or how far he had driven, he GPS'ed his way back.

Van Camp was getting tired of looking for a home. It was not that it took a long time or much effort, but the time was spent looking at homes and not telling the realtor how important he was. Knowing that you are wonderful is okay, but it's a lot better if you can tell someone.

It was late in the day, and Rose Marie had explored every room three or four times. It was time to head back, after writing down her new home address, and updating the GPS in her car. She would make a few stops to pick up some linen, food, general household cleaning items, and a few girl things. She had no desire to spend the night alone just yet and, her hotel room was okay for now.

Waking up from her nap, Lisa grabbed something else to eat. A Lean Cuisine, still frozen in the freezer, was microwaved. She had nothing to bitch about right then, as she was rested and full. Yet, she started to bitch about whether to return to the hotel, or just stay where she was. Bitching about staying there lost to bitching about going back.

After a healthy trip to the bathroom, Lisa headed back to the hotel.

Steven was in the lobby as everyone started to return. Not all at one time, but just enough to take away the boredom of being alone most of the day.

Ben was one of the first to return, with Alice a close second. She made her way to the front desk to use the house phone. This phone had a redial button and she would kill some time trying to find any family member that were still alive.

Van Camp returned to the lobby, and was surprised that many people were still out looking for homes. He was pleased not to arrive too late and miss out, on any conversations, but he did want to at least, make an entrance. An entrance, where everyone would be biting at the bit to have him fill them in on his search. Only then to say that,'he had a few in mind,' and that he wanted to hear about the searches of everyone else, and follow that with his managerial opinion of their choices.

Rose Marie, after being very satisfied with her new home, returned to the hotel, all the while, making it a point to remember how she would give directions to her home, should anyone ask. GPS or not, she liked being able to explain where she lives.

For the brothers, it was a quick elevator ride to the top floor. They had to bust in a few doors that were locked to gain entrance. Not being able to re-lock them in the future, well, that was not an issue with no one around to break in. However, Bob Billy wanted to lock his door to keep his brother from just coming in, unannounced.

They spent time looking together, but then they were checking out the rooms on their own. With all the doors opened, it was easy to walk in and out leisurely.

It happened that they each like the end rooms. For Bob Billy, it was good that there were a few rooms between them, and it was as far apart as they could be on the same floor, as he wanted a little privacy. Billy Bob, he like having the end room as it was next to the stairs, as he knew that some day, the elevator will stop working.

The new homes for these two, were almost alike. Both have a nice balcony, looking out at the ocean, with a good side view, Billy Bob facing north, and Bob Billy with a southern view.

Other than moving out the previous owners personal items, they were ready to move in.

Joe-Joe pulled up to the mall, at the Sears entrance. He noticed that if he wanted to drive his car inside, it would be rather easy because there were no doors. He only had to pull up on the curb and drive on in.

In the mall, he drove around looking at all the stores. Not as fast as the Blues Brothers did in the movie, Blues Brothers, but fast enough that his wheels squealed at every turn. After his little joy ride, he parked in front of the Sears, and next to a water fountain.

Joe-Joe made a beeline right to the furniture department and found that there were only two beds available, and that was just fine. He then moved over a few end tables, with lamps, into a corner of the furniture department and set up his bedroom. His next move was to the TV/electronic department for a TV. Most of the TV's were on with nothing playing. That was no surprise to Joe-Joe, as he already had made up his mind on what movies he was going to view, and review. He knew that he had a life time of DVD's to watch, only he was sadden that there would be no new releases for the rest of his life.

Eddie, with a soda and bag of chips, decided to drive around a little more. Figuring that as long as he was out, he should give it a second shot in finding a place. The more he drove, the more disappointed he seemed with the choices.

Setting his GPS to direct him back to the hotel was the only thing he seemed to have accomplice today.

On his return trip, Jeff, was trying to think up a good story as to why he did not find a place. He was just going to make up the places he stopped and hoped that no one would ask him where it was.

CHAPTER 54

TOGETHER AGAIN

B Y THE EVENING, EVERYONE HAD returned to base, The Marriott, mostly because no one really wanted to spend the night alone, not just yet. A few had a new home all staked out, and a few had a couple of houses in mind. For Eddie, Steven, and Ben, they struck out and would try again the next day. It was helpful as they heard what the others have found.

With these three guys, having lived on military bases, or in prison for the last couple of years, it was very possible that they were not sure what they wanted. Only that they knew for sure that they would have a place of their own, without a roommate. Well, without a roommate for now.

Burt, after he was able to watch a few movies, headed down to the lobby to see how everyone made out with their searches.

Jeff headed into the lobby and figured that if he didn't start up a conversation with anyone, that he would not have a need to make up a story about his bad luck in finding a place to live.

Around 7 PM, everyone had started to gather in the lobby. Those that had a place to live, bragged about it. The ones not yet with a place of their own, explained either why they didn't go out looking, or why they had fallen short in finding a place.

The conversations started to move towards what to do next. Getting to Florida, almost safe and sound, had been completed. For the most part, those who really wanted a place to live on their own, had found a place. Tonight, it appeared that everyone wanted to stay in the hotel, not exactly ready to move out and live alone, as there is always the fear that they will end up by themselves.

Joe-Joe, making a brave move, asked the group, no one in particular, if they wanted to see a movie or two.

What he got was a look of, 'what, movie, you want to watch a movie?'

Van Camp spoke up and said, "We don't really need to watch a movie now, not tonight."

Ben, along with Billy Bob, did not like the idea of Van Camp speaking for the group. Not only that, they each believed that there was no need for anything else, but a movie. There was no reason for a meeting, which was what they thought Van Camp wanted to start.

Ben, not having the pleasure of watching movies or TV for the last few years, thought it might be a good idea, and said, "What were you thinking of watching?"

Billy Bob did not say anything, but gave the facial expression that he also wanted to watch a little TV. He had had about enough of these meeting, now that they are here in Florida and having found a place to live.

Apparently, everyone except Van Camp felt like watching a movie, and if they had to have a meeting, then have one in the morning. This day had been a long day for some, and just boring for others.

Bob Billy, picking up that a power struggle was up and running, spoke up and suggested, without asking his brother first, said, "If we need to place anyone in charge, lets use the TV for help."

Van Camp, Ben, and Billy Bob looked at each other, then back at Bob Billy.

Bob Billy, who wanted to start and be his own, independent person without standing in the shadow of his older brother, suddenly he realized that he had arrived. He took a deep breath and said, "We can watch American Idol and vote on who is best. Then, we can check out the Apprentice, and if we don't like someone, we can Fire them."

On a roll, that surprised him and his brother, Bob Billy continued, "We can watch Survivors, and vote someone in charge."

Rose Marie jumped in with her two cents, "Like the show, Weakest Link, we can use the audience for help."

Burt, wanting to get onboard with this, suggested, "Sopranos. If we don't like whoever is in charge, we can have them whacked." As always, everyone but Van Camp thought this to be funny.

Billy Bob added in, "We can watch Gilligan's Island and make a radio out of a coconut."

Lisa wanted to watch a show from the Food Channel, but knew it was best for her to keep that to herself.

Steven, remembering older shows from the past, before he entered the military, suggested, "MacGyver, he could always get out of any situation."

"Why not let's watch a movie where people disappear?" Everyone looked over Eddie, expecting him to give a movie title, since he brought this up.

"Like The Body Snatchers?" questioned Bob Billy.

Billy Bob looked at his brother, correcting him with, "No man, that be a movies where people get replaced."

Eddie asked Joe-Joe, "In your collection, to you have, I Am Legend? The one with Will Smith?"

"I would like so see any of the Planet of the Apes movies," happily suggested Eddie, until he thought that to be a bad choice considering their current predicament.

Joe-Joe, having his complete inventory of all his shows in his head, responded quickly with, "No, but I do have, Dawn of the Dead."

Alice had not heard of either of these two movies. She was more into G and PG movies, such as, Snow White, Cinderella, and Bambi, for her children. With her grandchildren, the older ones, it was Old Yeller, Shaggy Dog, and Black Beauty.

For her, and her middle aged grandchildren, they enjoyed 101

Dalmatians, Winnie the Pooh, and the Lion King. Recently, with the youngest, it's Shrek, Alvin and The Chipmunks, and Wall-E.

Alice, as old as she was, had never seen any movie greater than a PG-13. So, if it was up to her to make a suggestion, it had to be a family show, and with this group, she kept her choices to herself. Joe-Joe, without waiting for anyone to suggest what to see next, placed in the next DVD. Of all the movies to watch, this time at night, after a long day, the documentary of the Biography, of Betty Boop. The Queen of cartoons was not well appreciated. This was a very boring movie for anyone over the age of 20, or younger than 60. All this did, was to create small conversations between a few, while they completely ignored the show. Others did their best to stay awake.

No one complained about the movie, and no one got up and left. For the same reason that everyone was staying here tonight, nobody wanted to be alone. Bad movie or not, at least they are with people.

CHAPTER 55

THE LAST GATHERING?

THIS LITTLE GATHERING STARTED TO wind down, as if they were cars running out of gas, and coming to a halt. One by one, they started to fade away. It was not noticed by anyone, as everyone started to either lower their heads down, or that they raised their heads up, then leaned back. In a manner of a few minutes, it was lights out for everyone in the world.

Van Camp, as he was dozing off, gave some thought on his current life's status. Not so much that everyone in the world had disappeared, or that his previous top positions in the work place no longer exist, or even that all of his previous coworkers, family, and friends were gone, but that he was going to miss his bed at home very much. He would also miss out on getting up in the morning and putting on a nice suit and his shined dress shoes.

Oh well, he concluded. Maybe tomorrow things will improve. Rose Marie, before passing out, gave her stuff cats a little hug. Not physically, but mentally. Coming to grips again that her cats were no longer going to be a part of her life, she slowly, softly,

cried in her sleep.

She did have a little trouble staying asleep, as every time she heard a noise, she was prepared to yell at her cats to stop whatever it was that they were doing in the middle of the night.

Lisa, with a full stomach, had fallen into a twilight trance. The kind of laziness that takes over your body after a heavy, Thanksgiving dinner, while watching a boring football game on TV.

With all of her Little Debbie's gone, and no other treats available, passing out would take her mind off eating. At least until she wakes up.

Without warning, it was one good burp, followed by a solid fart, that woke her, if only for a second.

Jerry heard Lisa, and he was just too tired to pay her any attention. He just thought that it would be polite of her, if she would just, at the very least, excuse herself following the burp. He did not expect her to apologize about the fart, because he assumed that she did not want anyone to know that it was she, but everybody did.

Giving this a little more thought, Jerry believed it to be better, if not polite, for her to warn people first. Not just letting one lose, and then give the apology. Give everyone a chance to run for cover, or under cover. Yell something like, 'fire in the hole,' 'fore,' or 'gas gas gas.'

He had never heard an elephant fart before, but if one did, it would sound something like Lisa. After that little humorous note to himself, he kept his head down and fell asleep.

Alice fell asleep while looking at the pictures of her family.

Joe-Joe, Ben, Steven, Billy Bob, Bob Billy, and Eddie had fallen asleep while sitting up, with Steven and Eddie at attention.

They all heard those familiar sounds from Lisa, but for the guys, this was not a big deal. At times, the guys wished that they could, 'out-fart' her, as farting was something that guys generally took much pride.

Steven thought that her fowl smell would keep away any mosquitoes, or wild animals, if there were any left on earth. He also thought that this to be the poison gas that killed everybody. She was the, 'Big Bang' that killed all the dinosaurs, and not the, 'Big Bang' that got the earth started.

CHAPTER 56

IN THE BEGINNING, DAY 1

Van Camp was the first to wake up and realized very quickly, even before he made his first move, that something was different, very different.

He could tell without even looking at what he was wearing, that it was not what he had on earlier. He knew that he was now wearing his jacket and tie, his interview suit, along with his favorite pair of dress shoes that were a size too big. He felt that this gave him an edge with the ladies.

He picked up that he was sitting in a chair with his head lying on the desk, not sitting in the hotel lobby. Slowly he raised his head, wiped the sleep out of his eyes and the slobber from his lips, and then opened his eyes in amazement. He was not in Florida, but back in Middletown, Delaware, at R.E.A. International.

R.E.A. International interview room, to be more precise.

He glanced around the room and was able to see, and count, that every one of the original interviewees, were there with him, and that all of them had their heads down on their desks. His first thoughts were that they were all enjoying a Power Nap.

Out of habit, he straightened his tie and cleared his voice before he looked around the room again. This time, he noticed that everyone was wearing what he or she had worn for the interview. Without much thought, believing this to be a dream, he placed his head back down on the desk, attempting to fall back to sleep, and hopefully into a different dream.

Rose Marie woke up lonely. Lonely as there were no cats in her face competing for attention. She raised her head off the desk and looked around. She was thinking, 'where are my cats,''this is not my bedroom,' and questioning, 'where are my cats?'

After shaking the cobwebs and cat litter out of her head, she continue to think and question, 'I am not in my lazy boy chair in the family room, where are my cats, and nor was I on my couch in my family room, and where are my cats.'

These thought were more prevalent to her than the normal questions of,'Where am I? What is going on here? Am I dreaming?'

Realizing that she was dressed, out of habit, she reached into her pocket to have cat treats handy for when her cats did show up for their treats, some affection, treats, acknowledgment, treats, a little praise, and a treat. As reality slowly came into clarity for Rose Marie, she sat up, looked around a little more, and realized that she was totally confused, as if she had sniffed too much catnip.

Lisa was the next person to wake up. Not because she had enough sleep, not that Van Camp had made any noise, or that her body clock said, 'get up,' but because her stomach growled loudly in hunger and that was followed by a large fart. If that had happened to a smaller person, it would have knocked them out of their seat. Not necessarily a small person, but anyone of normal size.

Realizing right away that something was different. Not in the same manner as what Van Camp and Rose Marie picked up, but by the sound of her fart. In bed, the sound would have been muffled a little because of the mattress, sheets and blankets. In her chair, the sounds just ripped away. If there were any cars near by, it probably would have set off their alarms or raised a few garage doors.

She made it a point to lie still. As if she did not just passed enough gas to fill the Hindenburg, in the event anyone was near by. After a few seconds, she had to raise her head and look around, just to see if anyone was looking at her. And if so, she would look at them as if asking, 'was that you?'

To her amazement, she was back at R.E.A. International as if she and the others had never left.

Kitty heard the sound created by Lisa and thought that they were at war. Not sure who they were at war with, but there was definitely an explosion. Then it came back to her that she might still be in the process of crashing her vehicle off the highway.

She understood that explosions and car crashes had smells, and that the smells that she smelled now, just had to be sulfur, gunpowder, gasoline, oil, and or charcoal. She had no idea what sulfur, gunpowder, or charcoal really smelled like, but knew the smell of gasoline and oil. Because she did not notice any of these smells, she assumed this to be mustard gas, and soon would need a gas mask.

With tears in her eyes, she raised her head off the desk and looked around. Not only was she surprised that there was no war going on around her, but also that she was back at R.E.A. International. With this realization, she was convinced that she had been given a type of laughing gas, as this was very funny. So funny, it brought tears to her eyes, so to speak.

Trying to ignore the smell and believing this to be a dream, she laid her head back down on the desk, being careful not to mess up her hair. She was a little upset that she had cried some, as this would mess up her makeup.

Then again, she was alive and not crashing and rolling down a hill in her car. These thoughts only caused her to think about falling back to sleep and dealing with this later, if there was a later. Jerry heard the noise and was just too lazy to look up. He was still very sleepy and saw no need to wake up just yet. The fact that he was sitting in a chair was not that important to him, he figured that he would simply look into the matter when he got around to it, another time.

Alice raised her head and looked around and what she saw did not make her happy, confused, or sad. It was just another reason to cry about how much she missed her family members. She believed this to be a dream, or more precisely, a nightmare. Like Jerry, she saw no reason to getup just yet and laid her head back down.

Burt heard the noise and was confused. He guessed that it was Lisa doing the 'Lisa thing.' It was easy not to let it bother him, he would pay it no mind, but he thought that she should have more self-control of herself. Next time, she should take it outside. Burt, still tired, kept his head down.

Jeff and Joe-Joe raised their heads at about the same time and gave each other the same look, the look of confusion. Between those two, all seemed normal even with their bewilderment. With nothing more than a nod between them, they laid their heads back down. Not so much that they believed this to be a dream, but each one of them felt a little drugged and laying their heads back down was in some degree, mandatory and appreciated.

The others, Ben, Billy Bob, Bob Billy, and Eddie did the same as Jeff, Burt, and Joe-Joe. They raised their heads, looked around, and laid their heads back down again.

Steven jerked his head up, instantly wide-awake, and alert along with being confused, was not normal for him. He was a little baffled this time because he was back at R.E.A. International. He quickly stood up to take stock of where he was. Before he could say anything, he noticed Sandy.

CHAPTER 57

WAKE UP

"WILL EVERYONE WAKE UP, PLEASE," commanded Sandy. Steven and Eddie were the first to sit up, and they sat up, straight and tall. Even with their eyes not fully opened or cleared, out of military discipline, they were up and at the ready, seated at attention.

Van Camp, the Brown brothers, and Ben came in at a close second. The others sat up slowly, and soon, everyone was up and looking around. Sandy was standing in front of the room very patiently waiting for everyone to look her way.

After a minute of everyone looking around at each other, along with a few quick questions being asked between them, with a few questions directed towards Sandy, the group soon quieted down and gave her their attention.

"I know you all have a number of questions to ask, and I will do my very best to answer them for you," she explained, looking around at all of them.

Van Camp was the first to ask, "What's going on?"

"If you would please, hold your questions for now. What I have to say will answer all of your questions that you might have. And believe me, you will all have the same questions."

"My family," blurted out Alice.

"They are all fine, but please, let me explain," instructed Sandy, with her hands up indicating that everyone should settle down and relax.

Lisa, well, she was more concerned with trying not to fart again, as she knew one was building up inside her and coming soon, very soon. Her other 'first priority,' was when could they get something to eat. Could they order in?

Sandy lowered her hands and started, "As you can see, everyone is back at R.E.A. International. In reality, you never really left. You have always been here, right here in this room."

Even with instructions to hold all questions, as all of them would be answered, a few questions did pop up. Ben rudely asked, "Lady, what are you talking about?"

Alice again with, "What about my family?"

Sandy, now looking as if she was ready to drop her cool, again raised her hands indicating that everyone should shut up, and listen.

Van Camp picked up that she might lose control and offered to help. He said to the group, "Let her explain. No need to waste time with asking questions that she will eventually answer."

Steven wanted to add in his point, "Let the lady talk. We all have the same questions and I want to hear the answers."

Sandy looked at Van Camp and Steven and greeted them with a slight smile, indicating that she appreciated the help.

She continued, "You are all under the belief that you were here seven days ago." A short pause for effect. "In reality, you have only been here for about seven hours."

That created a response from Billy Bob, he said, "What you been smoking lady?"

As odd a question as this may seem to be, to her, and everyone else in the room, that was a serious question.

Ben said aloud to himself, "Now that is the way to serve prison time."

After he said that, he wished that he had not.

This created some murmuring between everyone that Sandy had to again, take control.

"My new Hummer," asked Burt.

"In your dreams," laughed Billy Bob, with those who had caught on to what had happened. For Joe-Joe, he wanted special attention for his answer, but none came.

"This can take all day if I am continually interrupted. Or, we can wrap this up soon and you can all go home."

This did bring order to the group. Even with them being informed that it has only been seven hours, their feelings were that seven, seven long days had passed. And, until proven otherwise, in an orderly fashion or not, they wanted to go home. They were all mentally tired, if not physically worn out.

Without another attempt to cut her short, she tried to move things along. "You have all been here, at R.E.A. International as part of an experiment."

This did not go over well, and that maybe using the word, 'experiment,' was not a good choice as this created some additional murmuring, but not as much as before, and it soon ceased. "Thank you," Sandy said. She continued with, "An experiment where you all were sent into a deep sleep. Completely harmless." She looked around at the group, not so much to see if they were paying attention, but to see if any side effects were evident and that everyone was still awake.

"Once everyone was asleep, we were able to monitor your dreams. Not only to monitor them as individuals, but to allow your dreams to interact with other dreams in this room."

"Did you make a video of this," asked Joe-Joe.

Some in the room thought that he was joking, but others realized that he had a valid point. Was this something like a reality show? Will it be on TV?

"To some degree, yes, but please, let me continue," she appealed to them.

The group was again silent. She added, "Everyone fell asleep seven hours ago."

"How did we fall asleep," questioned Ben. He did not like the idea that anyone had control over him and that he, was the one that was taken advantage of.

Looking a little ticked, she said, "That was my next piece of information."

Ben bowed to her request, only to allow her to finish. Then by him allowing her to continue, he somewhat, had control.

"A harmless gas was released into the room," she answered and looked around the room, indicating with her facial expression, that she challenges anyone to ask another question until she finished.

"We monitored your dreams as individuals, in a non-invasive way. With our newest network technology, we were able to assemble all of your dreams, as one big dream. Weaving all of the dreams together."

Confusion was heavy on everyone's face, except for Van Camp. Even if he were confused, he would not show it. He could manage people as well as manage what people think about him. Most of the time.

"With this correlation process, we were able to then unite each of you into each others' dream to the extent that you were all in the same, single dream."

A short pause to allow this to settle in. "The times that you were off on your own, away from the group, that was your personal dream. Then, you were dreaming as individuals. When you interacted with someone, anyone, or everyone in the group, then your dreams were connected."

Taking a quick breath, Sandy continued, "We had no idea on the directions that your dream, or dreams, would take. Only that you were all linked with this room as a starting point, a place that you all had in common."

No one had anything to say or ask, which was just fine with Sandy. She added, "We were able to follow the story line, as if watching a movie. This dream for everyone here, was most real."

Sandy looked around again to see who was the most confused, and it was Joe-Joe. She focused on him, and added, "Most people dream many different dreams a night, but here, we kept everyone linked to a single, united dream."

The group sat still, and no one had a thing to say or ask. Breaking the silence, Burt spoke up, and asked, "No interview, no job, and no pay?"

Even with this question being out of sequence of what she wanted to cover, she answered it anyway. "No, no, and yes."

Not the answer that he and the others wanted. Then, before a second question, or follow-up question could be asked, Sandy added, "I was going to tell you this at the end, but will answer it now."

The group was quiet and waited, "You will each be given a check for seven thousand dollars for today's activities. A gift from R.E.A. International for your time here today."

So much for asking additional unappreciated questions at this time as the group seemed very pleased with what was just said. She continued, "This check is non taxable and will not be reported to the IRS."

Van Camp knew that what she said was legal. It was less than ten thousand dollars, as anything more than that, had to be reported. Van Camp, was about to speak up and suggest, 'Why not pay us nine thousand,' but opt hold it for now.

He was glad that he did not say anything, but was pleased that Ben did. Ben asked, "Why not nine thousand? That is also an amount that you are not required to notify the IRS."

Sandy had gotten that question before, apparently, as she was not taken by surprise. She responded with, "Nine thousand it is, but you must agree not to let what happened here today, leave this room."

Billy Bob added in, "No problem with me. I can keep the secret here in this room as long as I can take the check to the bank."

This got a little laughter from the group and a knuckle knocking from his brother, Bob Billy.

"Why," asked Burt.

She looked at him and as soon as the room was again under her control, she continued. "Why. We wanted to see how people from all sorts of lifestyles would interact, resolve common problems, and in general, get along or not get along. Stay as a group, or stray on your own."

"Seven days," questioned Kitty. Normally she would not have said anything, but seven days seemed like a long time for an experiment.

The question was understood by Sandy. She answered, "Usually, it equates to that one day of your dream time, will equal about one hour of real time."

Everyone understood that, not so much as the mechanics of what happened, but that the answer seemed plausible. She continued, "Sometimes, the dreams go nowhere and is over in just under an hour or so. Then sometimes, the dreams will move into a couple of hours, like yours. We never let it get past seven or eight hours."

"Why," asked Van Camp. He just had to know as that had to have been a managerial decision.

"We wanted to keep the time you spend here to be a day or less."

Everyone seemed to see the logic in that, and everyone was apparently grateful that they were not here for the perceived seven days, and that everyone in the world was gone.

No additional questions came up at this time from the group, except one from Billy Bob, as he wanted not to lose sight of the money. He asked, "Nine thousand dollars, right?"

"Yes, on your way out, you will each be given a check for nine thousand dollars. But, and I repeat, but, you must sign a confidentiality form promising that you will say nothing to anyone outside of this room. We cannot obtain reasonable and reliable results from anyone that knows about this experiment."

For now, everyone was agreeing with whatever she said, at least until the check was in their hands and was cleared by the bank.

Ben's mind was racing on how he could con a check or two out of someone's hand, and into his. He felt that right now, it would not be wise and he did not want to risk the danger of his check being taken away or canceled, if he was caught, and he would settle for what he had. There was always later.

"What did you learn," asked Van Camp.

"Too soon to tell. These seven hours have provided us with months of information to analyze."

"Will we be able to see the results," he asked.

"Not really. The information is ours and you have been paid. Nine thousand dollars to be exact."

Not like being conned, Ben asked, "Is it fair that our minds have been violated?"

Not liking the tone of his question, and having gotten this response before, she had a canned answer. "You are most welcome not to take your check, or payment. Take us to court and maybe in ten years or so, you will get an answer for, or against,

R.E.A. International. Either way, for or against, you will not get the nine thousand."

Jeff finally spoke up and said, "Nine thousand dollars for seven hours work. Hell man, that's one thousand, two hundred and eighty-five dollars an hour. Twenty one dollars a minute and we did not break into a sweat."

After a few chuckles from the group and a number of,'I agree, give me the money,' the issue seemed closed.

Burt asked, "Has anyone ever gotten hurt? And, if a crime was committed, are there charges?"

Strange question thought Sandy, but worth answering. "No to both of your questions. It was only a dream. Regardless of how real it may have seemed, it was only a dream. A dream shared by thirteen others."

Alice was most excited that her children were safe.

Kitty could now afford a large double, triple whatever, from Starbucks.

Joe-Joe could pay his electric bill and price out a decent generator.

Jeff, he would keep his present job, but for his next vacation, it would be a nice one.

Burt still could not afford the car of his dream, but he could rent it for a weekend.

Lisa could now pay someone to diet for her.

Eddie had no idea on what he should do, he knew that he still had to find a job, but now he could take his time.

Same with Steven, he could afford a few extra weeks off before starting a new career.

Van Camp, well, he really did not need the money as much as the others did. Yet, in no way did that mean that he would not take it, and most definitely, he would not give it away or say anything that would cause him to forfeit it.

Ben now had some start-up money for a good scam.

The Brown brothers, for them, it was back to Wilmington and for the next two or three months, they would throw money away as if they could dream up a way to get some more.

Jerry, now that he was awake, he would put the money aside as if he had a day job. Only to take out a little each Friday to fake out his parents that he had a paycheck coming in. When the money runs out, he would explain that he was laid off.

Rose Marie was happy about the money, but that came in second with her cats coming in first. She would spend the next week or so at home with her cats. This she believed would make her feel a little better after spending a few days thinking they were dead.

The first thing she would use the money on was to change her spare bedroom into a cat room. Well, not really a spare bedroom, but her junk room. She could decide whether to throw it away, put it away, or give it away her, 'space hogging junk.' At least now, she could afford for someone to throw it away, put it away, or give it away for her.

For her cat room, everything, including the walls, would be carpeted. There would be polls, little cubicles, ladders, hanging things, and that would entertain cats forever.

Sandy added one last comment. "You can cash your check at any Middletown National Bank. On your way out, there is a branch southbound and another one northbound on Route 896." She made a phone call on her cell phone and the only thing anyone could pick up was, "We are done here. They are on their way out. Nine thousand dollars each."

CHAPTER 58

THE INTERVIEW IS OVER

ONE BY ONE, THEY LEFT the room. They were very happy in one way, in that, they each had a check in their hands for nine thousand dollars for only a day's work. Happy that this money was not taxable, and that it would not throw them over the allowable income limit for the year in collecting their unemployment. Yet, sad that they did not have a job, and in a small way, not very thrilled that R.E.A. International, had taken advantage of them. Nevertheless, Sandy did say to them, 'you have been paid,' indicating that not many jobs paid nine thousand dollars for a day's work, where you could sleep all day.

Outside, they passed others coming in and it was generally assumed that they were the evening interviewees, interviewing for the late shift. Late shift hopefuls that were in for a treat.

The Brown brothers talked between themselves, not about saying anything to anyone, but on how and what they would spend their nine thousand dollars, or the eighteen thousand dollars between the two of them. With this amount of money, they could party, party, and party, for many weekends to come.

Add to this, their money from 'The Cold Spot.' Maybe this time, they could each afford a good-looking women and not to share an ugly one. This amount of money that will never ever, enter a savings account, and they might as well spend it with flair.

Rose Marie, did not notice anyone coming in because she did not care. She only wanted to get home, after she made a bank run.

Her job hunting could start this time, next week, and she would be more selective on what ads she responded too.

With this money, she daydreamed about the next time one of her cats got ill, that she would respond more quickly taking them to the vet.

Before Kitty stopped to pick up her check, she made a pit stop in the women's room for a touch up. Even with nine thousand dollars to her name, she still had to look good. Only now, she could spend a little money to have her makeup applied by a professional. Not to look all that much better, just to pickup on a few tips so she could continue, and always look better.

Alice could only think about her grandchildren, and the money she had for them. Her thoughts about her children had changed a little. She figured that for years, that they had gotten a lot of her time to help them make more money as they had freedom to hold down full-time jobs. Other than a quick, 'thank you,' and, 'we'll see you tomorrow,' they had no money to share, not even a pay raise or bonus.

For those reasons, and more, she had some money and was not willing to share it with them. She was going to spend it all and will try and die broke, except for a little money set aside for her grandchildren. There were no plans to leave her children with anything.

Lisa was trying to decide what to eat first, and how much. Not in dollars, how much, but in volume. With this money, along with her health insurance that she would have when she found employment, surgery was her next option.

Better to be laid up for a few days because of massive weight loss due to surgery, than to spend months and months trying to lose it.

It crossed her mind that she could eat and eat for a few months, gain a lot of weight, then repeat the surgery. She had the money, and why not?

For the remaining guys, Steven, Eddie, Joe-Joe, Jeff, Bert,

and Jerry, they only want to leave without any delay. They had no additional questions to ask or statements to listen too.

Ben was calculating in his head how he could swindle a little extra money while he was here. Not so much for a second interview go-round, but anyone wanting to invest their nine thousand dollars.

All he would need was a plan to take advantage of those new interviewees going in now, as they were leaving. He wanted their checks. He would cash them right away and believed that R.E.A. International would rather take the loss, than to notify the police.

For now, his scam-plan was to plan a scam.

CONCLUDING NARRATIVE

E VERYONE, EXCEPT VAN CAMP, WAS in a hurry to leave. Some hurried out to cash their checks right away, others to hurry home and reunite with family and friends, being happy to see them, but not telling them why.

As the last one out, Van Camp, at the lobby door, stopped for a moment to let a few people in. It was, as he believed, to be the next group to be interviewed.

Van Camp wanted to say something to those arriving and was willing to loose his nine thousand dollars. He would not though, as that would not be very, managerial of him. Not that the nine thousand was not very important to him, but in the lightly hood, that he would be called back for a real job interview. Naturally, that would be based on R.E.A. International recognizing and appreciating his managerial skills and ability to keep company secrets, secret. And, according to him, his management skills were, are, and will always be impeccable.

Van Camp lingered by the door and looked over each one as they arrived. He counted fourteen interviewees. He figured them to be the new group and not employees by the way they were filing into the building.

He believed that employees would just park their cars and head in, not looking around as if they were lost, displaying that they had a place to be and knew where it was. This new group, after they entered the building, looked all around as if they were lost and wanted someone to say, 'may I help you?'

Two of them were young school kids, probably in high school. By the way they were dressed, these two girls were in Catholic school.

Next, were an old couple, apparently a man and his wife of, 100 years. He was pulling behind him an oxygen bottle and she was pushing ahead of her one of those walkers on wheels with a hand brake.

Walking, or prancing, through the parking lot was a, a, well, he must be gay. One of those gay guys that had the walk of a flamboyant gay. He was not, evidently, ashamed, or trying to hide his preference. Even from the head up, he had a smile that foretasted, 'look at me, I am gay in more ways than one.'

His outfit, Van Camp noticed, was pretty and sweet. He had never seen pink pants on a man before. And odd as this may appear to him, it looked appropriate. This young man was the total package of gayness.

Behind him, and making comments between themselves about the gay guy, were two young men that looked like gang members.

These two looked the part as if they were filming a rap video or doing a drug commercial, or even filming the TV show, COPS. Naturally, their pants were too low, their hats were too crooked, their shirts too big, their jewelry, too much, their tattoos, too many, grabbing themselves, too often, and their language, too foul.

In some ways, Van Camp would have enjoyed that group instead of the one that he was in initially. He felt that way until he picked up on the guy that was walking in close behind the gang bangers. This guy was tall, handsome, in a nice three-piece suit, and had the walk of good breeding. An obvious Ivy Leaguer, upper management type of a guy. One that would, by appearance only, would overtake him at any board meeting with just a smile and a twinkle of his eye.

Next to arrive, was someone in a military uniform. He was not sure of his military service, that his uniform was not something that he easily recognized. Navy, Army, and the Marines were uniforms that were not difficult to spot in a crowd. He could only assume that this might be an Air Force or Coast Guard guy. Maybe a reservist in the Salvation Army.

Behind him, were two Mexicans. They were short, had black untrimmed hair showing from under their ball caps. Tanned skin with their shirttails not tucked in. Well, maybe not tanned skin, but a little darker than normal and that made his assumption plausible that they were Mexicans.

Almost side by side with the Mexicans, was a redneck dude. He was wearing the redneck uniform of the day, flannel shirt, not tucked in with missing buttons, the top three. The few buttons that were remaining, were being pulled to their breaking point by his belly that stuck out so far that he had to lean back to avoid falling over. Frayed jeans, not store brought frayed, but well-worn frayed jeans. Untied hunting boots, and some old ball cap with a fish on the front and the Confederate flag on the back. Above the flag, was, 'You have your X,' and below the flag, was written, 'I have mine.'

He was unshaven and it seemed all but impossible that he would have a girl friend, must less a legal wife. This was most definitely a person that did not look in the mirror before he left his trailer.

His truck was easy to spot in the parking lot. None of his four tires matched, gun rack inside the cab on the back window, faded duck decals on the truck doors, extra large side mirrors to aid in pulling a trailer, naturally a trailer for his fishing boat. He had spent more money on his shocks, springs and struts than most people would spend on an entire car.

Van Camp thought that with the age of his truck, that it had to be paid for, but the shocks, springs, and struts, were the outstanding balance on his, Walmart credit card.

Taking up the rear, came a lady that looked six months pregnant. If not pregnant, then she needs to join Weight Watchers and not to assume Lisa's role.

With no one else in sight, Van Camp made his way to his car. Happy that he was headed home, and sad, that he was not participating in the second interview group, assuming that he was in the first group. He would never know.

Overall, Van Camp thought it odd that everyone simply got up and left. He was surprised that after days being together, thinking that you were the only people left in the world, that you would have connected and bonded with everyone, at least with one person, for life. Here, once you have your check, in your hand, the bonding was over. As if it's everyday, that you end up being a survivor with thirteen other people. Oh well. His last thoughts for today, were that he wished the new group, good luck. They would need it.